ALLISON
BRENNAN

MAKE
THEM

Revenge is priceless.

PAY

ST. MARTIN'S
PAPERBACKS

U.S. $7.99
CAN. $10.99

Don't miss these other titles in this series
from *New York Times* bestselling author

Allison Brennan

THE LOST GIRLS

COMPULSION

NOTORIOUS

SILENCED

STALKED

STOLEN

COLD SNAP

DEAD HEAT

BEST LAID PLANS

NO GOOD DEED

From St. Martin's Paperbacks

ISBN 978-1-250-10526-4

50799

Praise for these other novels by *New York Times* bestselling author Allison Brennan

"If you haven't been reading Brennan's truly exceptional Lucy Kincaid/Sean Rogan series, then you have been missing out. . . . In this mind-blowing installment, Brennan also gives readers a fascinating look into the mind-set of her epic villains. A chilling thrill-fest from beginning to end."
—*RT Book Reviews* (4½ stars, Top Pick!)
on *No Good Deed*

"Longtime bestselling author Allison Brennan reaches new heights in *Poisonous*, and this smart, sophisticated entry in the Maxine Revere series raises her to the level of Lisa Gardner and Harlan Coben." —*Providence Journal*

"A fast-paced, suspenseful read with interesting characters and sinister twists that keep you turning the pages for more."
—Karin Slaughter, *New York Times* bestselling author of *Pretty Girls* on *Poisonous*

"Allison Brennan's *Poisonous* has it all. . . . A twisty and compelling read."
—Lisa Unger, *New York Times* bestselling author of *Crazy Love You*

"Don't miss Max Revere's roller-coaster new thriller. Talk about grit and courage, Max never gives up."
—Catherine Coulter on *Compulsion*

"Packs in the thrills as investigative reporter Max confronts new murders and old family secrets in a suspense novel guaranteed to keep you up late at night!"
—Lisa Gardner on *Notorious*

Also by Allison Brennan

MAKE
THEM
PAY

Allison Brennan

St. Martin's Paperbacks

This is a work of fiction. All of the characters, organizations, and events portrayed in this novel are either products of the author's imagination or are used fictitiously.

MAKE THEM PAY

Copyright © 2017 by Allison Brennan.
Excerpt from *Shattered* copyright © 2017 by Allison Brennan.

For information address St. Martin's Press, 175 Fifth Avenue, New York, NY 10010.

ISBN: 978-1-250-10526-4

Our books may be purchased in bulk for promotional, educational, or business use. Please contact your local bookseller or the Macmillan Corporate and Premium Sales Department at 1-800-221-7945, ext. 5442, or by e-mail at MacmillanSpecialMarkets@macmillan.com.

Printed in the United States of America

St. Martin's Paperbacks edition / March 2017

St. Martin's Paperbacks are published by St. Martin's Press, 175 Fifth Avenue, New York, NY 10010.

10 9 8 7 6 5 4 3 2 1

I dedicate the twelfth Lucy Kincaid/Sean Rogan book to you—my readers.

ACKNOWLEDGMENTS

My readers have been asking for Liam and Eden Rogan's story for a long time, and if it wasn't for these requests, I doubt I would have written this book. I didn't really know who Liam and Eden were—why they lived in Europe, why they never visited, why Kane cut them out of RCK. It wasn't until I started writing *The Lost Girls* that I had an idea about why the family had split . . . but it didn't fully develop until I read a (mostly) disproven theory about a possible treasure at or near the Alamo. Everything clicked and *Make Them Pay* was born.

Thanking Deborah Coonts has become a regular occurrence for me, because she has continually helped me understand flying and small aircraft. I make a lot of stuff up, but I want it to not only make sense but be plausible. If I messed anything up—and I'm sure I did!—it was solely my fault. Ditto for the medical details—my cousin Dee Gifford helped once again, but mistakes are on me. Thank you both!

As always, special thanks to my agent, Dan Conaway, who keeps me (mostly) sane, and my editor, Kelley Ragland, who sees the diamond in the rough draft and helps me make the story shine. I appreciate the entire Minotaur/ St. Martin's team—I consider myself to be blessed to be on your list!

I can never forget my family. This time, my husband Dan really helped me with researching the Alamo by finding me articles about every theory, even those disproven, of missing treasures during that time. I didn't use even a fraction of what he dug up, but it all helped make the story plausible. And thanks to my kids, who are finally learning to cook for themselves . . . because someone has to do it when Mom is on deadline! I love you all.

PROLOGUE

Seventeen Years Ago

Liam Rogan didn't want to cry. Dammit, he was *nineteen* years old, he wasn't going to cry because his damn *feelings* were hurt.

"Hey," his twin sister, Eden, said.

"I didn't invite you in."

"Ouch."

She shut the door behind her and sat on the edge of his bed. They hadn't lived here at home in a year and a half. Last summer they'd stayed in Europe and worked at a museum. Their parents had *promised* to visit, but work got in the way. *Always.* And still nothing had changed. Their parents were obsessed with their work, their older brothers were both in the military—though Kane was starting something else now—and nothing had changed. Not really.

"I know how you feel, Liam. But it's not that bad. Mom and Dad just . . . I don't know, they love what they do. *Love* it. And they love us. They just don't know how to show it because they get so focused on their inventions."

"They love some of us more than others."

"That's not fair."

"Isn't it?" Liam walked over to his closet and pulled out

his heavy winter coat. He hated carrying anything onto the plane, but it was snowing in London.

"I know—"

"You don't know. You're a girl."

"Double ouch."

"Can't you take anything seriously?" Eden the light-hearted, Eden the angel. She was the only girl—well, had been since Molly died of a drug overdose—and could do no wrong.

"Liam, I take you seriously. I've always been here for you. *Always*. But you have this competition with Kane and Duke and sometimes I think even Sean. He's a little kid."

"Boy genius," Liam muttered. "And fourteen isn't little."

"I like him. He's fun."

Liam rubbed his eyes, feeling like a kid himself. "Look, I like him, too, but— Oh, I don't know. Just everything is Kane this, Kane that, oh look, Kane has this great new business."

"Kane followed in Dad's footsteps—he joined the Marines, became a war hero, and now is starting his own protection business."

"With JT, Dad's other favorite."

"Now you're really being ridiculous."

"Hardly. JT spent more time here than his own house throughout high school, and Mom and Dad brought him with us on every family vacation."

Maybe *that* wasn't fair. Kane's best friend had a difficult life, and Liam didn't lack compassion. It just seemed that sometimes his parents took care of the wounded in the world, ignoring those right in front of them.

But he couldn't stop now. "Duke was the perfect son, obedient, always doing the right thing, went to college, is serving his two years in the Army, being so *damn perfect* and noble and self-righteous. If we were Catholic, he would have become a priest. I can practically see the halo over his head."

"Liam—"

"And then there's Sean. *I* was always the smart one, Edie—but Sean did everything sooner, faster, better."

"Oh, stop it."

Being jealous—envious—of his own brothers was petty, but the feelings had been percolating for years. And then when he and Eden went to college in Europe it was like they didn't even exist anymore.

"What's really bothering you, Liam?"

He shrugged.

Eden got up and hugged her brother. "No matter what, Liam, you have me. Two peas in a pod, remember?"

"Until you find some guy and get married."

She laughed. "Not anytime soon. Do you think I'd let anyone get between us? You're my twin. We think the same, we have fun together, there hasn't been a time in our entire lives that you weren't there for me when I needed you. I can't say the same for anyone else in the family. Whoever I fall in love with has to love you, too."

"You could marry Dante."

She hit him. Hard.

"Ouch! That's going to bruise."

"You could marry Gabriella."

"Gross. She's like my sister."

"Exactly. Ditto for Dante. It's just . . . yuck. Besides, we turned nineteen last month, don't marry me off *now*."

There was a knock on the door. Liam said, "Come in."

Their dad, Paul Rogan, stood in the doorway. "Do you have a minute, Liam?"

Eden gave their dad a hug. "I gotta finish packing. Dante and Gabriella are going to be here in an hour, then it's back to England."

Her dad grinned. "England? Don't you mean you're spending the weekend in New York?"

"What? Really?" Eden laughed and winked. "You weren't supposed to know about that, Daddy."

He tugged her hair. "There's not much I don't know."

He was looking at Liam when he spoke. Eden raised her eyebrow and Liam waved her off. She blew him a kiss, then closed the door.

Liam stuffed a book in his carry-on. "Are you mad that we're going to see a Broadway show?"

"Sit."

"I have to finish packing."

"You're packed." Paul sat on Liam's desk chair. The room was functional, not personalized. Everything he valued he had taken with him to England. Liam didn't value a lot.

Liam sat on his bed. "What?"

"You mother told me I'm a fool. She's right."

"Mom would never call you a fool."

"True. She called me an ass." He tried to smile, failed. "Liam, I'm not good at expressing myself."

"It's fine."

"No, it's not fine. You are my son. Sheila and I never expected to have a large family. Even Molly was a surprise."

He tried to keep his voice light, but the sorrow crept in. Molly was the oldest of the six Rogan children and had died of a drug overdose ten years ago, when she was twenty. It had devastated all of the Rogans.

"Sheila and I get so wrapped up in our work that we often don't see what's right in front of us. I want to tell you that we'll change, that we'll be better, more attentive parents . . . but that would be a lie. Because I get so preoccupied in my work, I don't think I've conveyed to you, your sister, your brothers . . . we love all of you. We are so proud of you. There's not a week that goes by that I'm not bragging about you to someone."

"I know you love us. You're brilliant and the world needs you. You and Mom have invented some of the coolest things." Liam truly believed that. He kept up-to-date with his parents' work because he was interested. "I just wish, I don't know, I could have been involved. Like Sean."

"Sean?"

"You always talk to him about your gadgets. Those night-vision goggles? You and Sean stayed up all night working through the bugs on them."

"I guess, but—"

"And Kane came over the other day and you talked about how great it'll be to have a family business, that Duke is going to run the IT unit when he gets out of the Army. What about me?"

"You?"

"If Sean works with you and Mom, and Duke works with Kane, where does that leave me?" Dammit, he sounded pathetic and needy. "What if I want to invent things with you?"

"Do you?"

Liam shook his head. "But I have ideas."

"Liam—you have the best of Sheila and me."

Liam shrugged. He didn't want to be placated.

"Kane is all military, strategy, tactician. Duke is the organizer, a leader. Sean is just fucking brilliant, sometimes he scares me. There's nothing he can't fix, and he's what? Fifteen?"

"Fourteen," Liam corrected.

Paul looked confused for a minute, then nodded. "Right. But you and Eden are the visionaries. You see all the possibilities. Your mom and I see what can be, and we invent *gadgets,* as you say, to fill a need. We love it. But if we had a solid lead on the Alamo Treasure, we'd drop everything to find it. The history alone . . . No one believes it exists, thinking that it's just a myth. But we *know* it's there."

Liam had of course heard about the treasure from his dad and Uncle Carlo. What would now be tens of millions of dollars of gold and silver, lost in Mexico en route to Jim Bowie and Davy Crockett at the Alamo while the fort was under siege by General Santa Anna. Liam's parents had searched for other treasures over the years—they always had stories to tell about what they found and didn't find—but the invention business took over.

Liam loved history, but mostly he loved adventure. He wanted to find a treasure that other people valued; he would donate it to a museum and be recognized by historians and explorers. He wanted the same kind of stories his parents had, about the risks and rewards of searching for pieces of history. His father had often told him that the hunt for treasure was a timeless romance that attracted true believers with heart and soul.

"So?" Liam said. He was cautiously optimistic. Did his dad want him to go on a hunt with them? "What does the treasure have to do with anything?"

"Because we're close," Paul said. "And do you think Kane would be interested in searching for something that may or may not be in a specific location? Treasure hunting takes love, patience, perseverance. Or practical, frugal Duke spending money looking for gold? Or Sean, who would say, 'Why search for buried treasure when I can make my own money?' He doesn't grasp the value of history, not like you and Eden."

Liam had never heard Sean say that, but it sounded like him. Sean had been designing video games since he was ten and sold one last year. The money was in his college fund. Now he was working on another.

"I want you and Eden to join me on the expedition.

When we put together the funding, I want you there with me."

Liam didn't know what to say, but his excitement grew.

"We're close, Liam. Very close. Your mom is frustrated with me because I've been a bit obsessed ever since Sean decoded a section of the journal—a journal we've had for years but couldn't figure how it connected to the region. I know how to fund the expedition, it's just going to take some finesse. And we're just waiting on one more piece to the puzzle—Father Gregorio's map."

Liam's heart skipped a beat. "Uncle Carlo found it?"

"He knows where it is. He can get it, but it'll take a little time. Carlo and I talked about this. When we find all the pieces, and put together the financing, we're giving everything to you and Dante and your sisters. If this takes longer than we think it will, you and Dante need to take over the search. I have the utmost confidence that you'll find it. You have the heart, you have the knowledge, and most important, you have the spirit. I'm sure your sister and others will join you in the quest, but in the end, it's going to be because of you, Liam, that the world will finally have this lost piece of history."

A treasure hunt.

It wasn't about the gold and jewels or even the history or adventure. Yes, all that was important, but most important? His father had faith in him—faith he didn't have in anyone else. He believed that Liam could find a treasure that few people believed in and those who did could never find. Because none of those expeditions had the Romero journal, a journal that had been in Dante's family since their ancestors helped Father Gregorio hide the gold and silver.

"When?" Liam asked, almost unable to speak.

"It's going to take a few years. But the gold has been

buried for two centuries, it's not going anywhere. Go back to college, enjoy yourself, learn everything you can about the history of Mexico, Texas, and their relationship to Spain. Remember that what I love about you isn't the same as what I love about Kane, which isn't the same as what I love about Sean. I love you because you are the most like me. If I were twenty years younger, I would go with you. But by the time we put this all together, I'll be in my sixties. I'm happy to live vicariously through you."

"I—I don't know what to say. I won't let you down." His voice cracked.

"Liam!" Dante Romero's voice shouted from downstairs. "Get your ass down here, we're going to miss our flight!"

Liam zipped up his suitcase. His dad came over and hugged him tightly. "Thank you for keeping my dream alive," Paul said.

"It's my dream, too."

When Paul and Sheila Rogan died in a plane crash six months later, Paul's dream became Liam's obsession.

CHAPTER ONE

Friday Night, Present Day

Kane Rogan had been a Marine and a mercenary and had devoted his life to Rogan-Caruso-Kincaid Protective Services. He was ruthless when necessary but preferred clandestine operations to violent encounters. He wasn't a soft man, but he wasn't cruel.

Still, he had a deep-seated anger for those who hurt innocent people. And a violent rage against those who bought and sold human beings like property.

If Kane had known that the FBI had that bastard Angelo Zapelli in custody, then let him go, Kane would have taken him out before he crossed the border. Kane didn't care about any rights Zapelli claimed to have or a supposed illegal search and seizure—which resulted in saving dozens of lives. He didn't care that Zapelli was a Mexican citizen or that he had been detained without probable cause or any of that other legal bullshit that separated Kane from some of his closest friends.

Angelo Zapelli had sold his pregnant girlfriend and her sister into the sex trade, where they suffered at the hands of brutal men and women all for sick thrills and profit. Zapelli didn't deserve to live; he didn't deserve to breathe the same air as the women he betrayed.

For the two weeks Kane Rogan watched him, Zapelli clearly felt no remorse for his actions. But it wasn't until Zapelli started talking up a young and obviously underage girl that Kane knew the bastard hadn't changed. That he would once again sell girls into the sex trade or abuse them himself.

Neither of which was acceptable.

Which was why Angelo Zapelli now sat tied to a wooden chair in the middle of a decrepit barn outside Monterrey, Mexico. His face bled—from his mouth and a cut across his cheek and a gash on his forehead that would scar if Kane didn't kill him. A tooth that must have already been loose lay in a ring of bloody saliva on the ground in front of Zapelli. Kane hadn't tortured him, not yet, but Zapelli had put up a fight and Kane enjoyed taking him to the ground. Kane planned on killing him and he wouldn't bring his team or his family into it.

Not this action. Not this time.

Zapelli tried to put up a tough front, but he was soft. Strong and powerful around young women he could manipulate, use, and bully, he was weak inside, with clean hands and manicured nails. At first he fought, but now he cried. He'd lost his rage because he wanted to live.

Zapelli knew exactly who Kane Rogan was and what he could do.

"I swear," Zapelli pleaded, "I didn't do anything!"

Kane remained silent. He sat on a chair in front of Zapelli, gun in hand. Silence drew confessions from the weak better than torture.

Kane rubbed his jaw. Zapelli had gotten in one left cross, but that was it. Sore, a little bruised, but the punch hadn't even broken his skin. Kane stared at Zapelli. Sweat dripped down his face, mingling with the drying blood. He pontificated, lied, begged. Then lost it.

"Fuck you!" Zapelli screamed. "If I die, everyone in

your fucking family will die. You think I don't know who you are? Do you think I don't know that fed is almost your fucking sister-in-law? Do you think she's unreachable?"

Kane kicked the chair over. Zapelli fell hard on his back, unable to brace himself against the hard-packed dirt. He was stunned silent.

"You won't do anything because you'll be dead," Kane said calmly.

His family had been threatened before; they knew the risks. Kane had read Lucy into the program, she'd made many of her own enemies, but she was cautious and she had Sean. A low-level prick like Angelo Zapelli wouldn't be able to get to her.

But it wasn't Zapelli that Kane wanted.

Kane had spent the last few weeks putting together the key players in the human-trafficking organization that Zapelli fed. The Flores cartel who ran it had been mostly wiped out; their accountant was turning state's evidence and all but two of the family members confirmed dead. Kane had someone on the inside making sure the youngest Flores brother didn't start up the operation again.

But Kane understood this business well enough to know that there were others who would fill the gaps. Kane may have cut off the head, but those who had answered to the Flores cartel would be taking over, and Kane wanted to make it clear that there would be no more black-market babies. The sex trade was bad enough, but to use these women as breeders, sell their babies, put them back into the business . . . it was worse than cruel. It was evil.

Kane would not tolerate it.

He rose, walked behind Zapelli where he still lay on the ground, and pulled up his chair. When he was sitting up again, Kane resecured his restraints, then returned to his own seat. He had all day. Hell, he'd stay here all week and watch Zapelli die of dehydration.

"What the fuck do you want?" Zapelli sobbed.

"Your contacts."

"They'll kill me!"

Kane just stared at him.

Sweat dripped into his eyes and he blinked, in full panic.

Yes, asshole, you should be very scared.

Zapelli continued to beg, swear, argue, threaten, plead . . . he tried every tactic and Kane sat there.

Kane wanted to kill him. He'd planned to kill him.

But he'd promised he wouldn't.

He never made promises like that, and it bothered him on more than one level. Not only because it tied his hands in an operation but also because Siobhan Walsh had figured out his plan without him so much as saying a word.

Since when had the infuriating, sexy, too-smart-for-her-own-good redhead been able to read his mind?

"I know what you're going to do, and I won't stop you," Siobhan said the night he left.

Kane stared at her. "You know nothing."

"I want to kill him, too. Marisol wants to kill him. But remember what you told her, just two days ago? You can't come back from murder."

"He wouldn't be the first man I killed." He'd said it to scare her, but Siobhan didn't scare easy.

"You need information, you'll get it from him. But he's not worth another piece of your soul." She stepped toward him. He didn't move. He didn't dare move.

Siobhan whispered, "I still love you, Kane." She kissed him. He stood rigid, willing himself not to respond to her. She stepped back and smiled, just a little turn of her lips, and he itched to take her to bed, right then, show her that he wasn't the man she thought he was. That he took what he wanted and he had wanted her for years.

But Siobhan wasn't a one-night stand. She wasn't a

woman he could screw, then walk away from. She was a woman who demanded lovemaking, not mere sex. She knew it, and still she pushed him. "I will love you no matter what you do in Monterrey. But you're better than Zapelli. You're better than all of them. I'm not letting you disappear on me again. I will hunt you down and make you realize that you are the man I see, not the man you think you are."

And then she walked away. Siobhan walked out of his bunk and left him shaking with a hard-on.

He didn't want to love anyone; love was dangerous.

He especially didn't want to love Siobhan Walsh.

It looked like he had no choice in the matter, because as soon as she walked away he craved her even more.

It didn't take long for Angelo Zapelli to break, and Kane Rogan didn't have to say another word.

"Fuck you." But there was no venom, no fight. He was resigned.

"Names."

Zapelli gave up three names, and after continued questioning Kane was fairly certain those were the only players Zapelli knew. Kane had heard of two of them. One he was certain was dead, the other in hiding after he'd found out Kane was looking for him. And the third . . . a new player? Or was it an alias?

Kane would find out. He stood.

Zapelli started to cry. "I don't want to die. Please."

Had the women he sold as sex slaves cried and pleaded for their lives? Zapelli hadn't cared about them, and Kane cared less about the whiny, sniveling bastard in front of him. Angelo Zapelli was a waste of oxygen.

But Kane had made a promise. Even though he didn't explicitly say he wouldn't kill Zapelli, Siobhan had walked away believing he had.

He should shoot Zapelli now to prove to Siobhan that he was unworthy of her and her love.

But Kane was tired. Tired of the violence and the heartache and the misery that he'd been fighting for well over twenty years.

"Is Jasmine alive? Is she rebuilding Dom's network?" Kane knew that Jasmine was alive. He wanted to see what Zapelli knew.

"I don't know! I swear, I don't. I . . . I think so, but I haven't seen her, I swear! I'm out of the business. I only work for my dad now. I swear."

He was blubbering, but Kane didn't believe him— Zappelli wasn't out of the business. Maybe this beating would change him, but Kane wasn't holding his breath.

"If you want to live, tell me one thing."

"Anything. Anything."

"Who bought your son?"

Zapelli's mouth opened and closed and no sound came out until a gut-wrenching sob emerged. "No. They'll know it was me."

Kane raised his gun.

"New York! That's all I know, someone in New York, a business tycoon who has four daughters and wanted a son. He's powerful and has money. My son will have everything, everything! Why do you care? He's not yours! Marisol can't give him shit, she's nothing!"

Kane pistol-whipped Zapelli and he fell over again. Kane holstered his gun and took out his knife.

It took all his willpower not to slit the bastard's throat.

Instead, Kane cut the binds at his wrists, leaned down, and said, "I will kill you if you ever threaten my people again."

He rose and walked away. It might take the sobbing asshole a few hours to get out of his leg restraints, but Kane lived up to his promise. He didn't kill him.

In fact, Kane lived up to both promises. He'd promised Marisol that he would find her son, and now he had a lead.

Time to call in the cavalry.

And time to go home.

Home.

He hadn't thought of having a home for years. He'd enlisted in the Marines when he was eighteen, but he'd always thought of the house where he grew up as *home* until his parents died. Since then, he'd had home bases and camps and occasionally a long-term apartment in some border city.

But that all changed when he reconnected with his brother Sean, and then Sean and Lucy moved to San Antonio. Sean wanted him to live in the apartment he was building over the garage; Kane said no. Too close to civilization, to people. He needed his space. It was probably the only luxury he truly needed.

Yet Kane felt that Sean and Lucy's house was more of a home than anyplace he'd had in nearly twenty years. Lately, he'd been using Jack Kincaid's place near Hidalgo. Last month, when Jack came to help get him out of a jam, Jack told him the house was as good as his.

"I signed the property over to RCK. It's as much yours as mine now."

The Hidalgo property was perfect for Kane—a lot of space, a great location, and secure. But home wasn't just a piece of land. More and more Kane had been thinking of slowing down. Being more selective in the jobs he took. Spending more time with his family.

Home wasn't a place, it was the people, and for the first time in a long time Kane looked forward to seeing his family, taking time off, and spending more than a fair amount of time with a certain Irish redhead he hadn't been able to get out of his head for months.

Months? Try years, Rogan.

Thirty minutes later, Kane drove the borrowed Jeep to the remote, unmanned airfield where he'd landed his plane. He called one of the few people he trusted outside of RCK.

"Rick, it's Kane. I have information about Marisol de la Rosa's son."

CHAPTER TWO

Lucy Kincaid heard her fiancé, Sean, slip out of bed at four Monday morning. She groaned, stretched like a cat, and sat up.

He walked over and kissed her. "Go back to sleep."

"I can't."

"I didn't mean to wake you up."

"You didn't."

She hadn't slept well as it was, and neither had Sean. On Saturday he'd received an email from his son, Jesse, and immediately knew something was wrong, but it was against the rules of witness protection for Sean to contact Jesse outside of the marshals' office. Then yesterday Jesse's handler in the US Marshals Service called because of the email—Jesse had violated the terms of the program by contacting Sean. Sean convinced Jesse's handler to let him talk to Jesse, and they agreed that a face-to-face meeting might help the twelve-year-old understand the gravity of the situation.

If Jesse left witness protection, he would have a target on his back. And it pained Sean that he couldn't protect his own son.

Sean sat next to Lucy on the edge of the bed and took

her hand. He played with her fingers out of nerves more than anything. "What do I tell him, Luce?"

"The truth," she said. "He's just like you, Sean. He's a smart kid. Honesty is the only way to convince him to do what's right."

Lucy had met Jesse briefly before he and his family went into witness protection. It had been bittersweet—Sean had to say good-bye. He'd found his son and lost him in a matter of days, and now, only a month later, Sean was still having a difficult time accepting the situation. And, evidently, so was Jesse.

"I wish it didn't have to be like this." Sean was on edge, emotional, and in pain.

Lucy turned over his hand, kissed it. "Jesse knows this isn't your call, Sean, but it's for his safety. Just think how you would feel if you were in the same situation."

"Helpless."

"Yes, but also angry and betrayed and scared. He loves you."

"He doesn't even know me."

"That doesn't mean anything, and you know it. You saved his life. He wants to get to know his father, and right now it can't happen." Didn't Sean see what she saw? "He's been emailing you—against the rules—because he's trying to see how far he can go. He doesn't understand that the rules—at least, these rules—can't be broken. That it's too dangerous."

"I don't know how to fix this."

"You'll find a way." She kissed him. "You don't have a lot of time."

"I hate traveling commercial, and they're making me fly all over the damn country. I don't even know where he is."

Lucy didn't have to explain to Sean why the marshals were setting such protocols. They both knew it was to keep the Spade family safe.

Sean pulled Lucy into a tight hug. "I love you, Lucy. I'll be back tomorrow."

She smiled, trying to show a brave front for Sean. He didn't need her worries and anxiety when he was so stressed himself. "It's going to work out."

He nodded, kissed her. "Twelve days."

Her heart skipped a beat. They'd discussed eloping, considering everything that was going on in their lives. They'd even gone so far as to discuss the prospect with Father Mateo—the priest who would be marrying them at St. Catherine's. He talked them out of it.

"You've earned this wedding. What you both have been through these last two years, you deserve this one day of joy and love in front of God, family, and friends. And Lucy," Mateo added, *"your mother scares me. She calls me twice a week about details, and if she can't watch you get married she'll probably haunt me for the rest of my life."*

The wedding would be small and intimate, but those Lucy and Sean cared about the most—friends and family— would be there. Whatever life threw at them, they weren't running away or hiding. Together they were stronger.

"Twelve days," she whispered.

She walked Sean to the garage, kissed him good-bye, and watched through the kitchen window as he drove off in his black Mustang.

Once he was out of sight, Lucy started a pot of coffee, then went back upstairs to take a long, hot shower. She figured she'd go into FBI headquarters early this morning. She wanted to locate as many of the black-market babies as she could—sold in the human trafficking ring she'd helped stop last month—before she left on her honeymoon.

But after her shower, she got caught up in reading the news while eating a bagel and drinking coffee and suddenly she didn't have as much time as she thought.

"Shoot." Lucy rushed back upstairs to finish getting

ready. Sean texted her that the first of his short flights was done, but he was turning off his phone and removing the battery per orders of the marshals. Truth was, he'd been told to not bring a cell phone at all and this process was a compromise.

She sent him an emoji kiss.

I love you.

They'd had a recent setback in their relationship, and for a short time Lucy wasn't even certain they would survive. But instead of the events tearing them apart, they found a way to not only stay together but also love stronger. For nearly two years, Sean had been her rock of support. She'd leaned on him, he'd carried her when the weight of her life threatened to bury her. Now she was strong enough to be Sean's support when he needed it the most. Two years ago, she would have failed. Now, because of Sean, she could be the rock he needed.

Lucy had just strapped on her gun when the doorbell rang. She pressed the security screen in the bedroom to see who was on the front porch so early. Sean was more than a little security conscious, especially after he helped the FBI catch a money launderer last month. As soon as anyone crossed onto the property the system alerted him and Lucy. It took Sean a week to adjust the sensors so every squirrel that scampered up a tree didn't set them off.

An attractive, impeccably dressed woman with long sunstreaked dark-blond hair swept into a loose bun stood waiting. She carried a large shoulder bag and a small suitcase. She looked familiar, but Lucy couldn't remember meeting her. It didn't help that she wore large sunglasses. A neighbor?

While the visitor didn't look suspicious or dangerous, after the past month Lucy had become edgy. It didn't help that Sean was nervous; he rarely showed any stress, but this last month had been even more difficult for him.

Lucy pressed the intercom speaker. "Who is it?"

"Hello? I'm Eden. Eden Rogan. Sean's sister."

Eden Rogan? Lucy stared again at the screen. She had only seen photos of Eden and her twin brother, Liam, most of them more than a decade old. It could easily be her.

"I'll be right down," Lucy said. She grabbed her blazer and slipped it on as she walked down the stairs. She disengaged the alarm and unlocked the door.

Eden smiled and pushed her large dark glasses up to the top of her head. Immediately Lucy saw the resemblance—the dark-blue eyes that Eden shared with both Sean and Kane stood out the most. But there were other little things, like her smile and her strong jawline, tempered by her femininity, and the way she tilted her head, just a bit, as she assessed Lucy, that were very Rogan-esque. "So you're the girl who tamed the wild beast."

Lucy said, "Come in. We didn't know you were coming."

"My baby brother is getting *married*? Of course I couldn't stay away!"

The wedding was still two weeks off—well, twelve days as Sean reminded her this morning. When they were going over the guest list this weekend, they'd taken Liam and Eden off—they hadn't responded yes or no. Lucy had suggested that Sean call them—he said no.

"I haven't seen either of them in years. Something bad went down between Liam and Kane. I used to want to know what happened . . . Now? I don't care. Especially since they couldn't even RSVP. I'm staying out of it."

"I'm glad you're here," Lucy heard herself saying, though she wasn't sure she was happy. With everything that Sean had been dealt this last month, he didn't need surprise guests.

Eden walked in and looked around the large foyer with a half smile that was so much like Sean it was a bit unnerving. She turned and assessed Lucy. Eden's face appeared open, but her eyes were cool. Calculating.

Lucy needed to stop being so suspicious.

"So, you're Lucy."

Then Eden walked across the wide, open hall and stepped down into the living room. She surveyed the high ceilings, the furnishings, the multiple French doors that opened to the pool. "This place is fabulous. I never imagined that Sean would settle down, but well, stranger things have happened." She put her suitcase down on the floor and dropped her shoulder bag. "It's *Kincaid,* right?" Eden smiled and shook her head almost in disbelief. "Is that how you met? Because of your . . . brother, right? New partner at Rogan-Caruso."

Lucy wouldn't exactly say *new.* Jack had joined Rogan-Caruso Protective Services six years ago and they'd changed the name to Rogan-Caruso-Kincaid. Patrick had joined two years later.

"Not so new," she said.

"Time really flies, doesn't it? I haven't been back to the States in *years.* No reason to, until now."

"Do you have a place to stay?"

"Not yet—I wasn't sure I could get away, so I planned this sort of last minute. I came here straight from the airport. I've been traveling nonstop for the last eighteen hours. Milan to Heathrow and then just *waiting.* Wishing I'd been as smart as Sean and got my pilot's license. And then I was stuck in Customs at JFK for hours. I'm not a good traveler. I hate flying."

Eighteen hours of traveling and she couldn't send Sean a message that she was on her way? Lucy wasn't buying it, not completely.

That's when Lucy saw it, the tension under Eden's perfect makeup. She was a stunning woman—beautiful, really. But there were fine lines around her eyes, which were a little too bright. Either fatigue or fear or both. Lucy had a little sympathy for her, considering the transatlantic flight. Two years ago she wouldn't have thought twice about inviting her to stay. But now she hesitated.

"Where *is* Sean?" Eden asked. "He's never been one for sleeping in."

"He had to leave early. A case he's working on."

And just like that, the tension eased. It was subtle, and if Lucy weren't so focused on Eden she would have missed it. Was Eden relieved Sean wasn't here? Had she thought there would be a confrontation?

"Well, I'll be around for a while. I'll catch him when he gets back," Eden said. "Would you mind if I stayed here with you this morning? I need to find a hotel for the next two weeks. And truly, I *really* want to get to know you. I *hate* that Sean and I have been out of touch, but weddings are new beginnings."

"Stay with us," Lucy said. It just came out, and it was probably a bad idea. "At least for a day or two. My sister and her family won't be here until Sunday, we have plenty of room."

Lucy hoped Sean wouldn't be upset at her spontaneous invitation. But Eden was his sister. He hadn't seen her in years, and when he was nostalgic he talked about the time when he was young, before Liam and Eden went to Europe, where they'd lived since college. When Sean sent them wedding invitations he'd said they wouldn't come, but he wanted to reach out anyway . . . maybe this was Eden's way of trying to fix their relationship.

Yet, spontaneously flying halfway across the world and dropping by unannounced? Something was up.

Lucy wanted to talk to Sean about this, but he'd turned off his phone. He wouldn't turn it back on until after he left Jesse. Maybe not until he arrived back in San Antonio. She'd send him a message that he'd get as soon as he turned on his phone so he wouldn't be blindsided when he got home.

"Are you sure?" Eden asked. "Call Sean, please, make sure it's okay with him. It *has* been a long time. But he sent the invite, and I thought . . ." Her voice trailed off and she looked nervous.

"He's traveling, I won't be able to reach him until tonight. Let me show you around." Lucy gave Eden a quick tour of the downstairs—the living room, dining room, kitchen, family room. She skipped the other rooms—like Sean's office—and led Eden down the hall to the guest rooms. There were two on the main floor, each with its own bathroom. Next week, Carina and her family would have one and Lucy's brother Dillon and his wife would have the other. Upstairs was another guest suite, and Sean had partially finished the large space above the garage. It wasn't fancy but had a working bathroom. Lucy wished she could put Eden there because then she could secure the house— the garage apartment was on its own security system with its own entrance. The pool house was Kane's when he visited—he liked being separate from the house with his own space—and he'd been coming and going a lot over the last month. It was one of the reasons Sean started renovating the garage apartment—he wanted to offer Kane a permanent place. But for the wedding they needed it for family.

Just two days ago, Sean had treated her to breakfast in bed and announced, *"This is the lull before the storm. We'll be overrun with Kincaids and Rogans in a week. Enjoy the peace."*

Lucy had the distinct impression that Eden was the beginning of a hurricane.

"This place is *amazing*," Eden said. "I love it. Thank you *so* much, Lucy. I won't be a bother. I'll be out of your hair tomorrow."

Lucy showed Eden the security panel. Eden frowned. "Is something wrong?"

"Wrong?" Lucy asked.

"Sean has always loved his toys, but this system is . . . rather advanced. Overkill."

"We've both worked cases that have made us cautious," Lucy said carefully. "I work for the FBI."

"Oh, I know," Eden said with an almost dismissive wave of her hand. "Surprised, though, since Sean has never particularly liked authority. I suppose true love knows no bounds."

Though Eden's tone bordered on snide, Lucy decided to leave the comment alone. She didn't know Eden, and she didn't know much about her relationship with the Rogan family, other than there'd been a falling-out and Liam and Eden had left RCK when it was still Rogan-Caruso Protective Services. "Is Liam also coming to the wedding?"

"I doubt it," she said. "I really tried, but . . . well, some things can't be fixed."

Why did Lucy think Eden was lying? Why would she? Eden probably spoke the truth, but there was more to the story. Still, this visit was odd, especially with Sean out of town. She couldn't possibly have known—Sean didn't even know he was leaving until last night. Eden would have already been on a flight by the time Sean got the approval from the marshals to visit Jesse.

Lucy was now *really* late to work. She said, "I have to go. I'll try to get off early and take you to dinner. I'm not a very good cook."

"I would really *love* getting to know you better." Eden smiled and hugged her lightly. "Thank you for letting me stay. I promise, I'll be gone by tomorrow. There are several nice hotels in the area, and a resort I've heard *fabulous* things about. I'll find something."

"You don't have to leave so soon. Wait until Sean gets home so you two can catch up."

"We'll play it by ear."

Lucy grabbed the rest of her things and hesitated in the kitchen. Maybe she should take the day off. Except . . . she had no time to take. She'd already taken so much time off this year that she didn't even have vacation for her honeymoon. She'd told Sean they'd have to postpone, but then her fellow agents on the Violent Crimes Squad had each given up one of their vacation days to her as a wedding present so she could have a honeymoon. She'd almost cried when they'd taken her out to lunch and told her. She hadn't made the best first impression on her team. She got along with some of them, and others were wary. She didn't blame them. Trouble followed her and, unfortunately, touched everyone else. But all of them had given her time.

Eden stepped into the kitchen and said, "I'm just going to take a shower and sleep. I really am exhausted."

"Give me your phone number and I'll call you later, see if you need anything." Lucy wrote down her cell phone number on a notepad.

"Great." Eden rattled off her number for Lucy. "It's a US number. I have both—comes in handy when traveling."

Odd, considering how she said she hadn't been in the States in years.

Lucy left after showing Eden once again how to set and reset the alarm and reminding her to keep it engaged even when she was inside.

From her car, Lucy sent Sean an email asking him to call her when he had an opportunity. She didn't want him to worry, so added:

Nothing serious, just have some information for you.

Then she called FBI headquarters to tell them she was running late. As she drove, she was still apprehensive, so she called Sean's oldest brother, Kane. He didn't answer, which was par for the course. She left him a message to call her: "It's not urgent, just call when you get a chance."

Put it out of your head.

She had a full day ahead of her, and worrying about Sean's sister wasn't going to help.

But she really hoped Kane called her back soon.

CHAPTER THREE

Lucy walked into FBI headquarters even later than she'd thought she would. She stepped into the main conference room for the staff briefing they had every Monday morning and leaned against the back wall because there were no more chairs. Temporary Supervisory Special Agent of Violent Crimes Noah Armstrong glanced over at her and frowned, then went back to listening to the SSA of Cyberterrorism give his report.

Ryan Quiroz was also standing and he maneuvered over to her. "I got the evil eye, too, for being five minutes late. I had the boys this weekend," he whispered. "Drove them to school in Austin this morning, traffic sucked coming back."

Twenty minutes later Noah stood to give the report for Lucy's squad. Violent Crimes and Major Offenders was the smallest unit in most FBI regional offices. After 9/11, the FBI had changed priorities, allocating more staff and resources to counterterrorism, cyberterrorism, and white-collar crime. VCMO had been cut drastically, in some offices by more than 75 percent.

Lucy was already familiar with the cases that the team was working on. Noah went through them quickly, including her own case tracking babies who'd been sold on the black market. Last month she, Noah, and Nate Dunning, another agent on her squad, had uncovered a black-market baby ring. They had the best white-collar crimes agent helping crack the financial records of the organization, but it was slow going. Of seventy-two confirmed babies sold, they'd identified fewer than half. Some people were pleased with the results. Lucy was not one of those people. Forty-one babies and toddlers were still unaccounted for.

Noah ended with a surprise announcement. "You may not have had a chance to read your email this morning. ASAC Durant and I are conducting interviews this afternoon and tomorrow for anyone who would like a lateral move over to the VCMO Squad. We have two positions to fill, and because we already have two rookies on our squad, we aren't eligible for a new agent from the current graduating class at Quantico. We've put the notice out to other field offices for agents who have already completed their two rookie years to apply, but we want to look in-house first because you all know the area, the people, our staff. Violent Crimes is a demanding but rewarding squad to work for."

Two *positions?* Lucy knew that Barry wasn't returning after what happened to him in June. He'd nearly died and was still going through intense physical therapy, but who else was leaving?

Someone from the cyberterrorism squad asked, "When is SSA Casilla returning? Isn't his paternity leave up?"

"I don't have information on that," Noah said.

From her seat at the head of the table, Abigail Durant said, "I spoke with Juan last week. He asked for two more weeks and paperwork for a sabbatical. As you know, his wife is still ill, and Juan wants to make sure she's one hundred percent before he returns. As SSA Armstrong indicated, the VCMO Squad has demanding cases, and because of our mandated structure we find ourselves frequently short-staffed. Noah and I are looking for agents who have advanced training in criminal psychology and forensics and the passion to work on the squad. If we pick someone in office, they'll be sent for an intensive two-week VCMO program at Quantico to help bring them up to speed. That starts in November."

There were a few rumblings, and then Lucy noticed that Elizabeth Cook, an older agent on her squad, wasn't in the room.

Lucy glanced at Ryan, but he shrugged, not knowing what was going on any more than she did. "Armstrong is your buddy, I assumed you'd know."

She and Noah were friends and had been working closely on the black-market baby case, but he didn't talk personnel issues with her. He took his job as squad leader seriously.

If Juan wasn't returning, did that mean that Noah was staying indefinitely? She wouldn't mind—she loved working with him; they had a natural rapport and she trusted him explicitly. But she'd also heard rumblings—from her own squad, who thought Noah was a hard-ass and didn't like that he and Lucy had a history, to other agents who were intimidated because Noah answered to FBI national headquarters, not their own regional office. And then there was the not-so-small situation where Noah brought in the ASAC from Sacramento to take over the white-collar crime investigation that had stemmed from the black-market baby case. It ruffled more feathers than either he or Lucy had thought. Noah seemed to take the adversity in stride, didn't back down, and did his job. But he hadn't made a lot of friends.

After the meeting, Noah approached Ryan and Lucy. "My office."

They followed him. He closed the door. "If you were here on time, you would have been here when I told the squad before the staff meeting that Elizabeth Cook is being granted early retirement. There were questions, many that I couldn't answer because of personnel issues, but to summarize, we need every member of this squad to be capable of working any case we have. We only have eight sworn agents, the SSA, and an analyst, and we're not going to get more."

"I thought," Ryan said, "that she was going to move over to administration or white-collar."

"I don't have a comment on that," Noah said, "but we need two agents. We also need an SSA, because I'm leaving at the end of the month, provided we have someone in place. I've fulfilled my obligations to AD Stockton, we've ensured that this office is squeaky clean, and everyone here has cleared enhanced security checks. The difficult part is that Rick wants someone with experience and most SSAs don't want to move laterally into another SSA position. It's generally squad members who want the promotion, so it's a bit of a sensitive issue. This is a young squad, both in age and in years of service. You, Ryan, were a cop—but you've only been in the FBI for five years. Emilio is the oldest on the squad now that Cook is gone, but he's been on the squad for only three years. Lucy, you and Nate are still rookies."

"You don't want to stay?" Lucy asked.

He almost smiled. "Other than you, most people don't trust me. And that's fine—I didn't come here to win friends."

Ryan opened his mouth, then closed it.

"Go ahead, Ryan. Tell me what you think."

"I'm used to hard-asses," Ryan said. "You're not the hardest I've worked for. But people like to stir the shit, and consider you the interloper. Makes you easy pickings."

Noah laughed, then said, "Now, I know you both called in that you were going to be late, but don't make it a habit. Especially you, Lucy. I don't have to tell you that you'll always be under the microscope. And everyone knows we're friends, so that makes it awkward for me."

Lucy knew everything Noah said was true, but hearing it didn't help.

Ryan snorted. "Lucy puts in more hours than anyone else—except maybe you, Armstrong. Everyone else can go pound sand."

"Noah's right—and I'm sorry," Lucy said. "I had a surprise wedding guest show up at my doorstep this morning, and Sean isn't home."

"Wedding guest two weeks early? I'd have told them to hit the road." Ryan froze. "Unless it was your mother. Your mother came early?"

"No—no." Lucy almost laughed at the thought that her mother would go anywhere without calling multiple times to confirm plans. "Sean's sister, who lives in Europe. Showed up with a suitcase. I've never met her before, didn't think she was coming because she didn't respond to the invitation. But I'm putting Eden out of my head for the next eight hours. I have a lead on one of the black-market babies. I want to follow up on it this morning." She glanced at Noah. He was looking at her, but it was clear his thoughts were a million miles away. "Noah?"

"Ryan, are you done with assisting the SAPD on the officer-involved shooting?"

"Yeah, just have to write the reports."

"Go with Lucy this morning, do the reports tonight. I have a call, so excuse me."

They walked out of Noah's office. "That was odd," Lucy said.

"What? He's a workhorse and has no life. I suspect you would be, too, if you didn't have fun boy Sean at home."

She walked back to her desk and watched Noah leave his office, say something to Zach, the squad analyst, and walk out.

Definitely odd.

CHAPTER FOUR

Eden paced the guest room and realized that her initial excitement that Sean was out of town—and that Lucy had left her alone in his house—was tempered by the fact that he had the best security she'd seen outside of a museum. What she'd thought would be an easy job had turned south real quick.

Why was she surprised? Her baby brother was brilliant; he always had been. When Sean was six he'd taken apart Daddy's jeep. He couldn't put it back together . . . but Eden would never forget her father's face when he came out and saw Sean sorting engine pieces. Sean had no idea how the engine worked—but he knew that it "sounded funny" and thought if he took it apart he could figure out why.

He may not have been able to put the engine back together at the age of six, but he certainly could do it now—and then some. Eden had kept tabs on Sean, and not only because she loved him. He should have been hers, but Duke and Kane put their collective foot down on *that*.

Damn them.

Eden had wanted to come home after their parents were killed, to help take care of Sean, but *no*. Duke was going to be Sean's guardian. He'd asked her to come and *help*, and she knew exactly what *helping* Duke would have meant. She'd be taking orders from him, because dear old Duke would make all the rules. Where would Eden have been then? No *way* was she taking orders from her regal, don't-burn-bridges, perfect brother. *Hell* no.

Not that Kane's dictates would have been much different. Only he burned many bridges and was far, far from perfect.

Eden couldn't help but think about why Sean needed so much security. Though she had been cut out of the family loop years ago, she still had many friends in the States and kept tabs on everyone, especially Sean. He'd split from RCK a year ago—not a surprise to her. The only surprise was that it had taken so long for him to get out from under Duke's dictatorial thumb. And *of course* she knew about Lucy Kincaid. Not as much as she would have liked, but Lucy's big brother Jack was close to Kane, and therein lay the problem: Her oldest brother was a damn *psychic* where his family was concerned. Which was rather ironic, since he had shunned everything that was Rogan years ago to become a fucking *saint* of the downtrodden in Mexico. Didn't he realize that for every innocent he saved a hundred more were slaughtered? Talk about tilting at fucking windmills.

She had to calm down. She didn't know why seeing Lucy Kincaid made her all angry and bothered. She hadn't seen her baby brother in *years* and it wasn't Lucy's fault. Not directly.

"Focus, Eden," she told herself. "You have a job to do. Do it."

Unfortunately, Sean's fortress appeared impenetrable, even with inside access. She'd hoped to slip in, slip out, without Sean being the wiser—at least that was Plan A. Her brother Liam had other plans but deferred to her because her plan was smarter and safer for all of them.

If she couldn't do it her way, they'd have to do it his way. She worried about the fallout—but the job still had to be done. Even if Sean wasn't privy to Kane's deception, he'd put himself firmly in Kane's camp. Even if he wasn't entrenched, there was the not-so-little matter of his choosing a Kincaid as his best man. And he was marrying a Kincaid. What happened to family loyalty?

There was no way she could search Sean's house without him finding out. He had cameras everywhere except in the bedrooms, it appeared—and for all she knew, there were cameras she couldn't see. Still, he would know after the fact, though she had never thought he wouldn't *eventually* figure it out.

Would Sean even keep the bonds here?

Oh yes, he would. His house was Fort Knox Junior. He'd have a safe, in either his office or bedroom. It would be digital, with a fail-safe. Maybe with some sort of biometric scan. And if there were cameras in the halls, there would definitely be cameras in his office.

Eden was good at breaking into systems—but nowhere near as good as Sean. Her talents were more on the manipulation end of the equation—convincing someone to give her access. Playing a part: a girlfriend, an employee, a patron. Even playing herself—a sister. Stealing a card key to give her access and returning it with her mark being completely unaware of her deception. Hacking into the security system and overriding a locked door was not exactly in her skill set. Simple systems? No problem. She could pick a lock faster than her twin and old-fashioned safes with a tumbler were her specialty. But the high-end computer security systems went beyond her abilities.

Which was why, dammit, Sean should have been with her and Liam all these years.

Sean wasn't a soldier, he was an artist. He wouldn't need all this security if he were part of her team. Was that what this was? Kane's enemies were now hunting Sean? Or was this a Kincaid problem? Fifty-fifty. She damn well knew that Jack Kincaid had nearly as many enemies as Kane. And Sean was loyal, sometimes to a fault. If his girlfriend was in danger, he'd pull out all the stops.

Lucy is not his girlfriend. She's his fiancée.

Why did that bug her? Because she didn't know the girl? Or because she was a Kincaid?

Both, she decided. Definitely both.

"What have you been up to, little brother?" she muttered. "What mess has Kane created for you to clean up?"

She opened her suitcase and considered unpacking but wasn't positive that Sean wouldn't kick her out as soon as he came home. So she took the shower she'd told Lucy she wanted—that wasn't a lie—and considered her options. Ideally, she'd like to get Lucy to help her without Lucy knowing she was betraying Sean.

By the time Eden got out of the shower, she had decided that researching Lucy Kincaid was the first step. She knew the basics, but she needed more information. Information was king in her business.

Why had Sean picked Lucy's brother Patrick to be his best man?

Something else to look into. She didn't know much about Patrick Kincaid, only that he, too, had joined Rogan-Caruso and had his name on the door. For a time, Patrick and Sean had been running RCK East in Washington, DC, until Sean moved to San Antonio with his girlfriend.

Rogan-Caruso-Kincaid.

How could she forget?

Eden slipped on her robe and was reapplying her makeup when her phone rang.

"Hello, dear brother."

"You didn't check in. I was worried."

"I'm still assessing the situation."

"Did he kick you out?"

"He's not here."

"What happened?"

"No need to panic, Liam," she said. "His girlfriend let me in, invited me to stay. I took a shower and am in the process of assessing the security. Sean's safe may be beyond my skills."

"Shit!"

"Language, darling brother."

"We need those bonds. My source says Jack Kincaid is going to collect them after the wedding. If they go back into the RCK safe, we'll never get them. It's now or never, and never isn't an option."

He didn't have to explain the stakes or his reasons for this quest to her. "I'll send you a picture of the safe and you can bring in the right person."

"It's Sean's security we're talking about."

"Do you have another idea?"

He was silent. "You know what to do."

"Threats aren't going to work. We need to finesse this."

"Send me the photo, let me think. I'm still a few hours away."

Eden had flown commercial—on a fake passport—but Liam had a stop to make in Guadalajara first.

"I need you here, Liam."

"I'm on my way—I'm not going to let you face Sean alone."

"If we have to face him. Maybe I can convince Lucy to cooperate."

"You can't trust a Kincaid—not after Kane kicked us out and brought them into the business."

"I'm good at getting people to help me and they are never the wiser."

"That you are, Sis. Be careful."

"You too." She hung up. Liam was more than her twin brother, he was her best friend. He had her back. But when it came to Kane, Liam could be blind in his anger. Kane had hurt Liam every way except physically, and getting these bonds was only one small victory.

Eden hated that her family had been torn apart, but she didn't see any way to put it back together. The Rogans had never been close. Their parents had jet-setted all over the world working on this or that invention. There was no doubt they loved each other, but their kids were almost an afterthought. Molly had been in charge from a young age . . . was that why she turned to drugs? To cope with parents who were fun and interesting when they were there but worked all the time? After Molly's overdose, their parents had crashed and burned—they were stunned. Blind, perhaps, because they hadn't seen how far down the rabbit hole Molly had gone.

They came home. Started a new business, and, ironically, things got better. They were present. Engaged, for a while. Except then Kane went off to the Marines and shortly after Duke went to the Army and their parents took little Sean the genius everywhere with them . . . leaving teenagers Liam and Eden to take care of themselves, for the most part.

It wasn't all bad. It was more like they didn't have parents, but a much older brother and sister who fed them and clothed them and gave them a roof and came by more often than not.

So what happened? When her parents were killed and Sean nearly died with them, what had happened that the family further divided? The deaths of Paul and Sheila Rogan should have united the five remaining Rogan kids but didn't. They continued on in much the same way. If they could have truly joined together in everything, six years ago would never have happened. Kane would never have banished them, cutting them out of their heritage.

Eden pushed all thoughts of her past aside. The past had to stay buried. She walked down the hall to Sean's office and quickly found the safe behind a beach painting. Hardly hidden from prying eyes. Immediately she knew hacking it was well beyond her skill set, so she took several photos and sent them to Liam.

Everything was dependent on the bonds being in Sean's safe. Would he really keep all that money here? She leaned to *yes*. Their source said Sean had the bonds. Therefore, they were here, in the safe. No way would he leave $6 million in bearer bonds sitting around on the coffee table or stuffed in his mattress.

What if he had given them to the FBI?

No—*that* certainly would never happen. Too many questions, and RCK didn't want those kinds of questions. For all their noble intentions and all their claimed legitimacy, they were the same organization they'd been before they kicked her and Liam out.

And neither she nor Liam had ever killed anyone. Unlike *other* Rogans.

The hypocrisy of her brothers made her ill. She could do this because *they* were the traitors. *They* had betrayed Rogan-Caruso long before the damn *K* had been added to their name.

Eden took out her laptop and sat at Sean's desk. She wasn't even going to try to break into his computer yet . . . that would come, but she'd wait for Liam. She ran a search on Lucy Kincaid to see what she could learn that would help her figure out what to do. Liam's plan was the last option . . . she truly didn't know how Sean would react, and Eden prided herself on her ability to decipher human behavior.

There wasn't much about Lucy Kincaid on the public

record, and Eden couldn't access FBI files. She had a friend who might be able to help . . . but Eden had to tread very carefully there. If Sean was really in love, he wouldn't be happy if Eden ran a deep background check on his girlfriend.

A few things popped out, however . . . Lucy had been kidnapped when she was eighteen. There weren't many public details about that event, but now Eden began to wonder if Rogan-Caruso had been involved in her rescue. No . . . Eden would have known, that was eight years ago, before Eden and Liam were cut out of the business.

She knew almost everything about Jack Kincaid, and Lucy was the youngest in the family, born two years before their father had settled in San Diego with a permanent post at the Army base there. Eden knew the Kincaids were a large family. She wrote out the who, what, and where of all the other siblings. Patrick was particularly interesting. Coma for two years? Sean's best man? What was his story? That might be an angle Eden could work.

But the big problem was that Lucy came from a long line of law-and-order types. Lucy herself had a degree in criminal justice and a masters in criminal psychology. She'd know a con when she saw one, wouldn't she? Yet, she'd let Eden stay here.

A beep chimed through the house. Eden quickly shut down her computer, her heart racing. Maybe Sean wasn't out of town. Maybe Lucy had called him and he had come back immediately. That would change everything. Or maybe it was the alarm system and Eden had a rival for the bonds.

But no one else knew why the bonds were important. No one knew why Liam and Eden had to retrieve them.

She ran down the hall to the security panel and pressed the VIEW button. A whole series of controls popped up, including a small camera showing the exterior of the house.

A man was walking up the front stoop. How did she zoom in? She couldn't see anything at this angle. *Dammit, Sean, why are you so paranoid?*

Calm down.

She remembered exactly what Lucy had told her about the security—she just needed to focus. Hit the CAMERA button, then select the angle.

Front door.

As soon as the image came into view, the bell rang.

No. No fucking way.

Her mouth went dry as she stared at Noah Armstrong. He had changed—for the better. He'd always been handsome, the classic good-looking Greek god with the perfect hair and lightly chiseled features and strong jaw, all in a package of self-confidence and control that Eden had loved to make him lose. He was everything she shouldn't want— he'd been the most loyal damn soldier in the US Air Force. Duty. Truth, justice, American way–type nobility.

But now . . . there was something else. A maturity that had only been hinted at way back then. Had it really been six years? Six years, four months . . .

Why was he *here*? That didn't make sense. How did he know Sean?

Not Sean . . . *Lucy.* Noah had left the Air Force and joined the FBI. Lucy was in the FBI. What were the chances that they worked together? Eden thought he worked out of the DC office. What had changed? Because here he was, on Sean's doorstep, and he knew she was here, and Lucy was the only one who could have told him.

Noah pounded on the door. Faintly she heard, "I know you're here, Eden. Open the door."

She pressed the INTERCOM button. "Go away."

He turned to the camera. His face wasn't distorted like it would have been in most security systems—her heart skipped a beat. She didn't think she was breathing.

Grow up, Eden! You're not a lovestruck teenager.

"Open the door, Eden."

Damn. Damn, damn, dammit!

She disengaged the alarm and opened the door, all the while trying to figure out how to get rid of Noah before all hell broke loose.

Before Liam showed up.

CHAPTER FIVE

Noah Armstrong didn't know what he'd do if Eden didn't open the door, but he wasn't going to walk away. During the drive here, he'd convinced himself that he didn't care, that he had no desire for her, that all he wanted was to find out what the conniving bitch was up to and if it would hurt Lucy.

Nothing Eden Rogan did could be good. Why now? Less than two weeks before Sean and Lucy's wedding? There was no love lost between Noah and Sean, but Sean made Lucy happy and that was the most important thing to Noah. And, he grudgingly admitted, for all Sean's faults, he was honorable. He had a strong moral center that Noah admired. Sean's center might be a bit over the line that Noah was comfortable with, but when he did the wrong thing . . . which was more often than Noah liked . . . it was always for the right reasons.

Sean would also do anything for his family, which included Eden. If Eden was here, there was nothing legal about it. If she dragged Sean into one of her schemes, it could damage Lucy's career. Noah couldn't let that happen. No one, not even Sean, knew Eden Rogan like he did.

The door opened. And there she was, as if the last six years had disappeared. Just as beautiful. Just as alluring. Just as manipulative. She hadn't changed.

"Noah."

Her voice was a whisper, as if she couldn't catch her breath. How much of her reaction was a lie?

He slammed the door shut behind him and she took a step back.

He'd had six years to forget her, and he never had. He'd also had six years to remember how she had betrayed him. He'd loved her once, and getting over her had been so hard, even with everything she'd done. Yet right here, right now, all those old feelings he thought were gone forever rushed back and he felt that jolt in his gut that told him he still had unresolved issues with this siren.

She stood in front of him in a silky ivory robe, her long dark-blond hair darker, still damp from a shower. She had applied her makeup with a light hand; he'd always found her the sexiest when she wasn't all dolled up. Eden was almost exposed.

Almost.

She had never been truly honest with anyone in her life.

"Why are you here?" he said through clenched teeth.

She found her sea legs and smiled. "Me? In my brother's house before his wedding?" She laughed lightly, that fake little laugh that Noah knew signaled she was thinking up lies faster than a speeding bullet. "You're the last person I expected to see, Noah. Here. In San Antonio. Of all the cities in all the—"

"Don't." He stepped forward and was pleased that she stepped backward. She *should* be scared. He had half a mind to arrest her on general principles. "Tell me the truth. Now, Eden."

"How did you know I was here?" She snapped her

fingers. "You're an FBI agent. Sean's girlfriend is an FBI agent. Wow. Small world, isn't it?"

"You destroy everything you touch. If you're here to interfere with the wedding—"

"You and Sean are friends? *Really.* Now *that* surprises me from Mr. Law and Order. I *know* Sean. He'll never walk the straight and narrow. Makes you wonder if his little girlfriend is squeaky clean."

Eden walked down the hall and into the kitchen as if she owned the place. He followed. He wasn't letting her change the subject. She started going through the cabinets.

"What are you and your brother up to?"

"Liam isn't here. As I'm sure you know, since you're *so close* to Sean and Lucy, he isn't welcome. Though we *both* received a wedding invitation." She pulled out a coffee mug and poured coffee. The light was off. If Lucy had made it when she got up this morning, it would be very cold by now.

Eden was nervous.

"Perhaps Sean is extending the olive branch. Perhaps we could do the same thing." She poured cream and sugar into her mug and sipped. Grimaced. "Who likes this foul drink?"

"I can't imagine it's a coincidence that you're here while Sean is out of town."

"Unlucky, I guess." She poured the coffee down the drain and sighed dramatically. "No tea. Really, my brother needs to go to the store. He doesn't even *like* coffee." It was an act. It was always an act.

"Stop changing the subject, Eden."

"What do you want, Noah? Why are *you* here?"

What did he say to that? He didn't know why he'd come. When Lucy had commented that Eden was here, all he could think about was *her.* Why she was in San Antonio.

What she looked like now. How she smelled. How she felt beneath him.

How she'd said *I love you,* then twenty-four hours later lied to him and made a very bad decision. Had Noah been as honorable as he'd believed, he would have hunted her down and arrested her.

But he hadn't. He didn't have proof of her crimes—not tangible evidence. And he'd been unknowingly complicit in her theft. It made him feel dirty and criminal and he hated that feeling. So he resigned his commission in the Air Force and joined the FBI, where he would never have to investigate international crime and possibly—likely—find himself face-to-face with Eden Rogan again.

She'd lied then to distract him; she would say anything now.

"Sean and Lucy are my friends," he said as calmly as he could, "and they're getting married. They've been through hell over these last few months, and there is no way I'm going to let you screw with them."

She actually looked *hurt.* "I wouldn't do that to my brother."

"You would do it to anyone if there was a payday at the end."

"Bastard." She tried to slap him, but he grabbed her wrist.

He stared at her. Those dark-blue eyes didn't waver. She could stare at God Himself and lie without a qualm. Her bottom lip quivered. He reminded himself that everything about Eden Rogan was an act. She could be anything—anyone—she wanted. She was the master manipulator, an Academy Award–winning actress.

He hated himself for wanting her. He hated himself for having loved her, for still having feelings that came all too clear now, long after he had put her in the past. It had never been a good love. It was twisted, because that's what Eden did, she twisted everything right and good.

He dropped her wrist, tried to turn away, but Eden stepped forward, grabbed his face, and kissed him. He froze. He didn't want to give in to her seduction, but the kiss reminded him of a time, years ago, when he'd thought he could save her from her twin brother, from herself. In the back of his mind he remembered that she was here for a reason, that she often used sex as a distraction. And he'd let her. Even when he suspected she was up to something, he'd let her take him to bed because he wanted her. She had convinced him that she loved him. He had believed her because he loved her.

Or was it lust? He'd asked himself that question over and over for years.

He came to the conclusion that he'd loved who he wanted Eden to be, not who she was, and he couldn't expect her to change.

Yet those old, complex feelings churned up memories of what had been, and the hope he'd had that he could save her from herself.

"Noah," she whispered against his lips.

He kissed her back, hard, pushing her against the wall. Her arms went around his neck and she pressed against him. There was nothing between them except his clothes and the thin silk robe she wore. A moan escaped her throat, fueling his lust. He wanted her, but it was a memory of the past, not real. With Eden, nothing was real.

It took every ounce of self-control to push himself off her. He took several steps back.

Eden's face was flushed, her breasts rose and fell rapidly, as if she was as turned on as he was. Her robe had fallen open and she stood there revealing her nudity without any false modesty.

"Noah, no matter what happened between us, *this* was always good. *This* was always real."

"Nothing about you is real."

Her jaw clenched. "Don't."

"Leave."

"This isn't your house."

"I will find out why you're here."

"I'm here for my brother's wedding. That's it."

"Bullshit. I'd bet Kane might know why you're in Texas."

Her stunned confusion wasn't an act. She didn't even have a comment.

"How about if we call him?" Noah suggested, enjoying her panic. She recovered quickly and laughed.

"You think you know my family? If you did, you'd arrest Kane the minute you saw him. Don't bluff me, darling."

"Maybe it's you, Eden, who don't know your family." He stepped forward. "A lot has changed over the last six years, sweetheart. I want you out of Lucy's house before she gets home from work."

Eden glared at him. He'd hit a nerve. *Good.*

But he had to get away from her before he did something he'd regret—like taking Eden to bed. She was still the most beautiful, most frustrating, sexiest woman he had ever known. If she'd used her brains for anything other than her brother's schemes, she would have been the woman of his dreams. Beautiful and smart. But she was a criminal, and Noah couldn't let himself get sucked back into her web.

"I've always loved you, Noah," Eden whispered.

He stared at her. He wanted to believe her, but that old adage *fool me once* came back. He'd loved her once. But looking at Eden standing in front of him now, six years after she had lied to him, he realized for the first time that he really, truly did not love her. And he never could.

"You don't know the meaning of the word."

Noah walked out.

He slid behind the wheel of his car and drove off but pulled over at a nearby park. He needed to cool off. Memories of the past collided with trying to figure out what Eden was up to.

He hadn't planned on being in San Antonio more than two months. But his two months had turned into four months, and if ASAC Durant had her way it would be permanent. But Noah couldn't stay. There were many reasons, including the fact that what he'd said to Lucy and Ryan earlier was true. He'd already made enemies during his stint as temporary head of the Violent Crimes Squad. But the main reason, if he was to be honest with himself, was because of Lucy.

It had been nearly two years ago that he'd met Lucy—a murder suspect when her rapist was found dead only miles from her house after he was paroled. Noah had been attracted to Lucy—the first time he had truly been interested in a woman since Eden. He'd dated on and off, but Eden had ruined him in so many ways, including creating this suspicion he had of all women: that they were all hiding something from him. Lucy had changed that. She had a complex history but she was honest, a trait he'd found lacking in too many of the women he dated.

Yet Lucy fell in love with Sean. For too long, Noah stood back and waited for the relationship to fall apart. It wasn't a secret—at least to Sean—that Noah didn't think Sean was good for Lucy. Noah thought he was a better man. But Noah recognized that his feelings toward Sean stemmed directly from his rage toward Sean's brother Liam, who was the driving force behind most of Eden's illegal activity.

Last month, Noah almost ruined his friendship with Lucy, but she either hadn't noticed or completely forgot that he'd kissed her. Or, more likely, she had convinced herself that it was a friendship kiss, a comforting kiss, after what they'd gone through. Was she blind or was Noah?

It was in that moment that Noah realized he couldn't stay in San Antonio. While he accepted that Lucy loved Sean and they were in fact getting married, he knew he had feelings deep down that he could never act on.

The truth was, Noah had a piss-poor history with women. They were either incapable of being honest, like Eden, or they were taken, like Lucy. He wanted to go back to DC and figure out what to do with his career. Because right now being Rick Stockton's Golden Boy might seem like a great job on the outside, but it meant no settling down, no stability, few friendships. And no long-term relationships.

Noah shook his head, trying to clear his thoughts, and considered calling FBI Assistant Director Rick Stockton to ask him what he knew about Eden Rogan. Rick was tight with Kane Rogan, but Noah had no proof that Eden was up to anything.

She definitely feared Kane. Most people did, but there was something more between Kane and Eden and Liam. Last year, when Noah and Sean worked undercover together, Sean had alluded to a falling-out between Kane and the twins, but Sean didn't know the details and Noah hadn't pushed.

Noah had only recently met Kane and had no contact information. He didn't want it getting back to Lucy, not before he had answers. Maybe Lucy already knew Eden was a criminal, but if she didn't know, Noah certainly didn't want to be the one to dump it on her. Not until he had more information.

Finally having decided on a direction, he pulled away from the park and called Siobhan Walsh. Siobhan was a photojournalist temporarily living in the area while helping the nine surviving women of the black-market baby operation find permanent housing and jobs and working through the process of helping the noncitizens obtain citizenship. They'd been granted temporary visas—they'd been brought to the country illegally and against their will as part of the sex trade, but all wanted to stay until their stolen babies were located. Those who were US citizens had no friends or family in the area. Noah suspected most of them didn't have homes to return to. It was a heartbreaking situation and Noah had to admire Siobhan for taking on such a responsibility. She was publishing a series of articles about the tragedy that was both optimistic and full of sorrow. And helpful—the first article had given them a lead on one of the infants two weeks ago. Noah hoped the most recent would do the same.

"Hello," Siobhan answered.

"Siobhan, it's Noah Armstrong."

"Good news, I hope?"

"Lucy is following up on a lead this morning. I don't have a report yet."

She paused. "I know, I'm here with her. The PIO cleared it."

Noah knew that. He'd just forgotten she was doing the ride-along today. Of all days.

She added, "Did you need something?"

What could he say? He couldn't talk to her with Lucy there. "I had a minute, and wanted to tell you I read your article in the *Times* over the weekend. It was truly a stunning piece."

"Thank you, I appreciate that. And thank you so much for putting me in contact with someone in the FBI who could actually go on record."

"Not always easy in a bureaucracy," he said, and almost smiled. "Let me know if you need anything else. Are you staying in San Antonio for a few days?"

"Just tonight. I'll drive back to Laredo tomorrow afternoon. Sean's out of town, so Lucy and I thought we'd have a girls' night."

Somehow, that made Noah feel better—Lucy wouldn't be alone with Eden. Siobhan had known the Rogans for a long time and might already know that Eden was bad news.

Noah said good-bye. Who did he contact now?

Of course. Nate.

As soon as Noah arrived back at FBI headquarters, he tracked down Agent Nate Dunning. No one else was in the squad room, so he said, "I need to reach Kane."

"You don't have his number?"

"No, and I don't want to ask Lucy right now. It's a confidential matter and I need his specific knowledge." Noah hoped that sounded both vague and professional.

"No problem, but you know he can be hard to reach." Nate wrote a number from memory on his notepad and handed it to him. "Do you need me for something?"

Noah knew exactly what he meant. "Be reachable."

Nate nodded. "I'm working that underage prostitution case with SAPD, making calls and following up on missing persons reports. I can step away at any time."

"Thanks."

Noah went to his office and closed his door. He used his personal cell phone to call Kane.

Voice mail picked up immediately. "Rogan. Leave a number."

"Kane, it's Noah Armstrong. I need to talk to you about your sister ASAP." He left his number and hung up.

He sat at his desk and considered his options. He had a lot of clout in the FBI, but he still worked for Rick Stockton and Rick was very close to Kane Rogan. Would Noah even get good information out of either of them? He didn't know—and because he didn't know, that worried him. He needed someone whom he could trust explicitly, who would understand the situation without him having to go into detail. There was one person who fit the bill, though he hesitated calling her because it would put her in a difficult position.

But he called anyway.

"Hey, if it isn't the traitor," Kate Donovan said in lieu of *hello*.

"Traitor?"

"You were only supposed to be in San Antonio for two months. It's been four."

"If all goes well, I'll be back in DC early November." Kate was an instructor at Quantico specializing in cyber-crime and had consulted on several of Noah's cases. She was sharp, loyal, and bent the rules when necessary. Noah wasn't a big rule breaker—ten years in the Air Force as an officer had made him appreciate rules—but sometimes Kate's way was better.

It also helped that Kate was not only Noah's friend but also Lucy's sister-in-law. She would do anything to protect Lucy, even keep a secret or break some rules if Noah could convince her that it was important.

"I need a favor, and it has to stay completely confidential and off the record."

Kate became serious. "What's wrong?"

"I need a deep background check with no flags raised, focusing on the last six years."

"Who?"

"Eden Rogan."

Dead silence.

"I know it's asking a lot."

"I can't do what you want."

Noah swore under his breath. "I understand. Sean's almost family but I wouldn't ask if it wasn't important."

"No, literally—the no flags raised part. RCK keeps extremely close tabs on any background checks on their people. They will know. I might be able to cover my tracks, but they will definitely know *someone* is snooping. . . . I can dig around in the FBI. On the QT, at least find out if there's anything criminal on her. Now tell me why."

Noah didn't want to tell anyone about his history with Eden, but he was asking Kate for a major favor and he trusted her. "Do you remember when we first met that I had some reservations about including Sean in my investigation?"

Kate laughed. "*Some* reservations? You hated his guts. For quite some time."

"I never told Sean until he and I were working undercover together in New York. Years ago, when I was in the Air Force, I had a run-in with his brother Liam. Sean assumed that Liam was the reason I didn't like him—and that was part of it. What I didn't tell Sean then was that I had had a relationship with Eden." Why was this so hard to talk about? "I learned the hard way that Liam and Eden are thieves. And before you defend them—because I know RCK is hired to retrieve stolen property around the world—that's not what they were doing when I was involved. I've put together information over the years that RCK essentially disowned Liam and Eden, but Eden is here in San Antonio and if I know anything I know she's planning something illegal."

"Do Sean and Lucy know?"

"Lucy said Sean is out of town on a case and Eden showed up at her house today unannounced. I called Kane, but truthfully, I don't know him, he doesn't know me, and I can't trust that he'll give me the information I need."

"What information? Why are you doing this?"

"Because if Eden is here nothing good is going to come from it. Eden is a master manipulator. I don't know what she wants or why she's here and why *now*. That information is critical—and then I can talk to Lucy."

"I'll find everything I can and try not to raise flags, but that I can't promise."

"I'll take the heat."

"Hey—Noah—you're not in this alone. Okay?"

"Okay." He hung up.

Yeah, he was. He was in this alone, and if he didn't figure out what Eden was up to Sean and Lucy would pay for it.

Of that he was certain.

CHAPTER SIX

Of the seventy-two infants who'd been born to the women held captive for two years, the FBI and local police across the country had located nearly half. The accountant who'd turned state's evidence against the criminal enterprise had good records, but even he hadn't known where all the babies ended up. The money moved through multiple shell corporations both in and outside of the United States. The basic medical records the corrupt nurse maintained helped with age, gender, and birthmarks, but the little DNA evidence they had was incomplete.

During Lucy and Noah's investigation last month, they'd found a trail of dead and missing women and illegal adoptions. By the time they finally closed the case, they'd rescued only nine women. Many who'd delivered babies had been sent back into the sex trade; finding them would be next to impossible. Seven had been killed in the days leading up to the raid as the criminals realized the FBI was closing in on their operation. There was nothing Lucy or Noah could have done to stop the murders—other than let the organization get away with imprisoning young women for the sole purpose of breeding children who were then sold to the highest bidders. One infant and his mother had been rescued during the initial takedown of the Flores cartel and reunited with family in the States. The FBI and psychiatrists were working with the young woman to glean any information that might help in tracking the remaining infants, but she either didn't know anything or was too scared to talk.

The easy recoveries were of those who had been adopted by American parents. During the interviews that Lucy had been part of, they claimed not to know that the adoptions were illegal. They assumed the outrageous fees were standard. She didn't buy it. She *wanted* to, but there was no way that many people were so naïve. And even if they didn't know, their attorneys should have. Not unexpectedly, one attorney had handled most of the adoptions— and he was nowhere to be found.

The individual jurisdictions and courts were working with Child Protective Services to determine what was in the best interest of the children. Lucy wanted the parents prosecuted if the FBI could prove they knew full well how the infants had been conceived, born, and sold. Some of them would be. But some seemed to be ignorant of the plight of the women. And because most of the mothers were dead or had been "disappeared" back into the sex trade, the option was leaving the child with a family who had participated in the black market or putting the child into the system to be raised by foster care on the off chance they would be adopted. Neither option was satisfactory.

There were two babies Lucy was most desperate to find. The first was Marisol de la Rosa's firstborn, a boy who would now be two years old. They were hampered because the records were incomplete. He was one of the first to be illegally adopted. But they had one solid lead—an anonymous tip to the FBI gave them information that Marisol's son had been bought by a wealthy man in New York City who had four daughters. The New York FBI office was working that angle.

The other baby she wanted to trace had been cut out of his dying mother's womb during Lucy's investigation. He would have needed medical attention. The ME determined that the mother, who had died of pre-eclampsia during an emergency C-section performed outside of a hospital, had been approximately seven months pregnant at the time. The infant would have been between three and four pounds and in need of neonatal care.

He was exactly four weeks old today. Had he survived his ordeal? Where had they taken him? The FBI had sent notices to all local police, hospitals and clinics about the case and regularly followed up. They had DNA from the deceased mother and Lucy could get a court order for DNA of any infant who fit John Doe's description.

Siobhan hung up her cell phone and said, "That was Noah. He wanted to tell me he liked my article. Isn't that nice?"

"He's a good guy," Lucy said, though she thought it was odd that he would call Siobhan when he knew he'd see her that afternoon.

"Do you think this lead is solid?" Siobhan asked them. They were driving to Austin to meet a pediatrician who had contacted them about one of his patients, who Lucy was hoping and praying was Baby John, as Lucy thought of him.

"It's the only lead we've had about Baby John," Lucy said. "I talked to the pediatrician yesterday. He wouldn't give me any real information over the phone, but he seemed genuinely worried about his patient and willing to meet with us once he sees our credentials. Medical records are practically sacrosanct, but if a child is in danger we have some leeway. And Noah can get a warrant quickly— we have the AUSA on board with us, considering the circumstances."

"We'll talk to the doc first," Ryan added. "He wouldn't

have called in if he didn't think he had something. If we have any hint that the infant is Baby John, we'll get a warrant for DNA."

"You're at thirty-one recoveries now, correct?" Siobhan said, looking through her notes.

"Yes," Lucy said.

"But there were thirteen babies born to the nine surviving women, and none of them have been found."

"*Yet*," Ryan said. "We'll find them. We're not the only FBI office working the case. We have a forty percent recovery rate in a month. I'd say that's pretty good."

Maybe it was, but Lucy hadn't been sleeping well. She was so worried about the babies, about the surviving women, about Sean and his newfound son, Jesse. Sean was in pain, and Lucy couldn't fix it. Sean couldn't even have a real relationship with his son. Carson Spade was in witness protection and had taken his wife and stepson with him.

Lucy had suggested they postpone the wedding. Or elope. Something small and quiet without the big party.

"You're the only light in my life, Lucy. I'm not canceling or postponing or changing anything. If I could marry you right this minute I would."

The ironic thing was that Sean had always been *her* light, *her* anchor. When she was living in the darkness, he had brought her out. Always. She would do everything in her power to help him through this impossible situation with Jesse and the Spade family. Maybe it wasn't the best time to get married, but Sean was her life.

She'd realized over the last few weeks that Sean, the epitome of self-confidence, was insecure about their relationship. She didn't know why, exactly, but if being married gave him peace they would get married as planned.

She loved him. It was as simple as that.

"How are your boys?" Lucy asked Ryan.

"Good. Growing. I miss them." He frowned. "I was thinking about applying to transfer to the Austin Resident Agency—it would be a lateral move, but I'd be closer to the boys. But with Juan still out and maybe not coming back, and your buddy Noah leaving, and a new SSA coming in and filling two new agent spots, I don't think I'd get approved."

"Maybe it's the best time to ask," Lucy said. "I don't want to see you leave—I really like working with you. But these are your kids. You may not be living in the house, but they need you around."

"I know. San Antonio isn't too far," he said. "I'll think about it."

"But if you were living in Austin, you could see them more often, right?"

"Depends. Probably."

Lucy would miss Ryan—he'd been the first to really reach out to her and accept her into the squad. Nate too, but Ryan reminded Lucy of her brother Connor—all cop, a bit of a temper, a little rough around the edges. With Ryan, you always knew exactly what he was thinking and why. That kind of blunt honesty could be hard for some partners, but Lucy went out of her way to work with Ryan because there were no games, no secrets, no doubts.

He turned into the medical complex where pediatrician Carl Calvert had his practice along with two other doctors. "Take the lead, Luce, you know more about this case than I do." He turned to Siobhan. "Stay put. The doctor may not like a reporter in the interview."

She smiled. "I get it. I have plenty of work to do." She glanced around. "I'll sit on that bench over there, in the shade. Don't forget me."

Ryan and Lucy walked into the waiting room and Lucy identified them both to the nurse. Though the office seemed full, they didn't have to wait long before the nurse escorted them to Dr. Calvert's office. Calvert was in his sixties, short and trim, with a quiet manner.

"We know you're busy, Doctor, so we'll get right to the point," Ryan said after introducing himself and Lucy and showing identification. "You contacted the FBI after you read the article in the *Times* and said you may have information about one of the black-market babies we're looking for."

He nodded. "One of my new patients is a four-week-old male who was both adopted and born prematurely. I've seen him four times, the first shortly after his birth. He had serious breathing issues and I wanted to hospitalize him, but the mother refused. She was willing to do what it took to stabilize him, and within forty-eight hours he turned around."

"Can a mother refuse medical care if it puts her child at risk?" Lucy asked.

"Yes—and no. It's a gray area, and hospitalization was a precaution more than anything. I had his birth records, but because it was a closed adoption, I had no information about the birth mother."

"You still have his birth records? What hospital?"

He hesitated. "Agent Kincaid, this is a gray area for me. Medical privacy laws are such that I would be subject to fines and possibly lose my license if I reveal private medical information about one of my patients. However, because the child may be at risk, I wanted to meet with you. I can provide complete medical records if you have a warrant, and in fact have already prepared them for you."

"Excuse me," Ryan said, and stepped out of the office.

"He's going to call our boss. We can expedite the warrant now that we have more information," Lucy said.

"Good."

"You really think this child is in danger."

"No—I mean, I don't think he's in danger from his

adoptive parents. The mother is older, had been trying to conceive for more than ten years. I believe she is a good and attentive mother. I met the father once, at the second appointment, and he too seemed very concerned about his son's health and welfare. However, there are some . . . areas of concern. I've already contacted the hospital where the child was born to speak to the doctors on staff and to confirm the information I have in the files, and am waiting to hear back. I hesitate to say this, but I was surprised that they released him so quickly. The hospital is out of state, which isn't unusual in adoptions. According to the records, he was released in forty-eight hours. He wouldn't have been cleared to fly at that point—most airlines won't allow infants under the age of two weeks to travel commercially. But the parents are wealthy, they could have chartered a plane. I saw him seventy-two hours after his birth, wanted to hospitalize him as a precaution, but he was doing remarkably better two days later. He seems healthy for a preemie."

The doctor certainly looked conflicted. "I don't know exactly what inspired me to call," he continued. "I really hope I'm wrong. There was a reason I asked you to meet me at eleven this morning. The mother has an appointment."

Lucy looked at her watch. "It's eleven fifteen."

"She hasn't shown."

They were running. Lucy was certain of it. The so-called adoptive parents had seen the *Times* article and recognized that their illegally adopted child fit the description of the baby torn from Eloisa's womb.

"Dr. Calvert, your instincts told you that there's something suspicious about this family, otherwise you wouldn't have called," Lucy said. "The baby we are looking for was cut out of his dying mother's womb, then sold on the black market. The adoptive parents are accessories to murder.

All I need is the DNA of the infant and then I can expedite DNA tests. This is a priority for the FBI, and for me personally."

"I want to help, but the rules are there to protect everyone." He glanced at his clock.

"Did she call to cancel?"

He shook his head.

Ryan stepped in. "A warrant is being printed right now, but will you take an electronic copy until we get it here?"

"Yes," Calvert said without hesitation.

Ryan showed Calvert the warrant on his phone. "The original will be here within the hour. Our Austin field office will deliver it personally."

Calvert unlocked his desk drawer and took out a file. "Here's a complete copy of Joshua Morrison's medical file. Please let me know what happens, and if you need anything else."

"Thank you, doctor." Lucy took the file. Her hand was shaking. This child was Baby John. She was certain of it.

Tom and Danielle Morrison lived in an upscale gated neighborhood ten minutes from the medical center. Lucy reviewed the records quickly and called Zach Charles, the squad analyst, to follow up on Dr. Calvert's concern that the hospital birth records might have been falsified.

Someone had cared for Baby John after he was born. According to the hospital in California, the baby was born on Tuesday morning, four weeks ago—a full day *after* the baby was actually cut from his mother's womb. The records said his birth mother had delivered at thirty-five weeks. *Possible,* Lucy supposed, but the coroner believed that the baby was at thirty-one to thirty-three weeks gestation based on the mother's autopsy.

According to the records, they discharged the infant to the legal adoptive parents, Tom and Danielle Morrison, forty-eight hours later. They named the baby Joshua Thomas Morrison. Baby John—*Joshua*—weighed four pounds, one ounce when born and four pounds, three ounces when discharged. On his last appointment with Dr. Calvert, he weighed five pounds, twelve ounces—having gained approximately half a pound a week. That would put him just over six pounds now if he kept the same growth pattern.

"It's him, isn't it?" Siobhan said from the backseat.

"You can't put any of this in your article," Lucy said. "You need to get it cleared by headquarters."

"I know—the PIO lectured me and made me sign a gazillion confidentiality and liability agreements before he agreed to let me ride along with you for a few days. But . . . you seem confident."

"It's him," Lucy said. "And I think they bolted."

"So fast? Did the doctor tip them off?"

Ryan said, "Most likely, they read your article."

Ryan pulled up to the security gate outside the Morrisons' community and rolled down his window. He showed his badge and identification to the guard. The guard wrote down the information and Ryan's license plate number and then let them in.

The Morrisons' house was on a bluff with a view. It was stately and a bit too ostentatious for Lucy's taste, but the neighborhood was clean, with established trees and meandering walking trails.

"Million-dollar homes," Ryan said. "Not all of Austin is like this, but this development began about fifteen years ago and built out quickly before the housing crash. Maintained the values, for the most part."

Ryan turned into a circular drive and parked in front of steps leading to a narrow porch and towering main entry.

"Stay," Ryan told Siobhan before he and Lucy got out of the car. Lucy noticed that Siobhan had her camera out.

She'd already been forbidden from showing any agents in her photos, as a condition of the FBI cooperation with her series of articles, unless she had explicit permission, so Lucy wasn't worried about the exposure.

They glanced around, saw no one out except a gardener working on the house across the street.

"Quiet," Lucy said.

She rang the bell. Ryan stood next to her at an angle, watching her back and the street. They'd both been in difficult positions, and even in nice neighborhoods desperate people might stage an ambush. She didn't particularly like being paranoid on the job, but taking precautions wasn't paranoia, she figured, any more than Sean's recent upgrade in security was paranoia.

No one came to the door. They rang again. Silence. No dog barking, no sound of footsteps.

Ryan walked around to the garage. He returned a minute later and said, "There's a sporty Mercedes in the garage which is registered to Thomas Morrison, but the SUV registered to Danielle Morrison is missing."

"We should talk to the neighbors."

"You do that. I'll call Morrison's employer."

While Ryan was on the phone, Lucy crossed the street and spoke to the gardener. He didn't speak English, so Lucy switched over to Spanish. She knew several languages but was most comfortable with Spanish because she'd learned it simultaneously with English while growing up. "Do you know the Morrisons?"

He nodded. "*Sí*, senorita. I care for their yard on Thursdays."

"Did they cancel this week?"

He looked confused. "No. But they may have left a message. I started at six this morning."

"Did you see either of them today?"

He shook his head again. "The señor works, the señorita

has a new baby. I've seen her walking with stroller, but not today."

"Do you know if any of the neighbors are home?"

He pointed to the house two over from the Morrisons'. "I also work for them, the Guiterrezes. They referred my business to the Morrisons when they moved here. They're good people, always remember my family at Christmas. Been here since they built the house. Miz Guiterrez might be able to help you."

"Thank you."

Lucy waited for Ryan to meet her back at the car. "Morrison works for a law firm," he said with a scowl. "They won't tell me shit over the phone. Took a message. I left one, too. Let him know the fucking FBI is looking for his ass."

Lucy filled Ryan in on what the gardener had said, then they walked over to the corner house. The yard was a little more to Lucy's liking, tastefully decorated, a bit cluttered, and not as sterile as the Morrisons'. She rang the bell. Immediately a large dog barked and she heard a distant, "Spartacus! Quiet!"

The dog barked once more, then whined on the other side of the door.

"Back!" they heard, then the door opened. A woman was holding a huge black Lab by the collar. "He doesn't bite," she said, "but he might lick you to death."

The Lab wagged his tail so hard Lucy was surprised it didn't fly off.

They showed their IDs and Lucy said, "We need to talk to the Morrisons, but they aren't home and Mr. Morrison isn't at work."

Mrs. Guiterrez's face fell. "Oh, God, is something wrong?"

"We don't know yet, which is why we need to speak with them," Ryan said.

"May we come in? We have a few questions, and I would hate for your dog to escape," Lucy added.

Mrs. Guiterrez hesitated, then nodded and opened the door. "I'll just put him in the backyard. Have a seat in the living room."

She motioned to a room that didn't look used. Down the hall, Lucy could see a well-used family room with multiple gaming systems and *Dora the Explorer* playing on the television. That's when she noticed a little girl with dark curly pigtails pop up around the corner. She couldn't be more than four.

"Hi," the girl said.

"Hello," Lucy said. "What's your name?"

"Melissa. What's your name?"

"Lucy."

"We had a dog named Lucy and she died and then we got Spartacus."

Lucy didn't quite know what to say to that.

"Missy Sue," her mom returned, "you didn't finish picking up your puzzle. Remember what I said?" She raised an eyebrow.

"But we have company."

"All the more reason to clean up your mess."

The little girl sighed and walked back down the hall.

"Sorry about that. I don't have a lot of time. I have errands to run, then pick up my other two kids from school. Then it's gymnastics for Missy and soccer practice for the boys."

"We won't keep you long," Lucy said. They sat down in the living room. Mrs. Guiterrez sat stiffly. Worried. Suspicious? Did she know anything?

"Do you know the Morrisons well?" Lucy asked.

"Yes, ever since they moved in a couple years ago. The other family who lived there—Shelley was my best friend. Her husband was transferred to North Carolina, bless his heart. Better job, benefits, but Shelley was irreplaceable. Her youngest and my oldest are thirteen, they've been best friends since they were born. In fact—" She stopped herself. "Anyway, Tom and Danielle bought their house. We became friendly."

"But not like Shelley," Lucy prompted.

"You know how it is."

She did but needed to get Mrs. Guiterrez focused. "When was the last time you saw the Morrisons?"

"Saturday. Teddy had a soccer game in the neighborhood, so she walked over with the baby."

"Her baby?"

"Yes, precious little boy. Joshua was premature, has some health issues, but is doing very well."

"What do you know about their adoption?"

Now she was worried. "Is that what this is about? Does the birth mother want the baby back? It was a closed adoption. The birth mother isn't supposed to know where he is. And it's not right that they can just come in and claim the baby months after he's born. Poor Danielle."

"Poor Danielle?"

"She tried for years to conceive. Had multiple miscarriages. Adopted once, and the mother changed her mind. I don't think that's right. I mean I understand as a mother, but once you make the decision you shouldn't get to change your mind. That was right after they moved here, and Danielle was heartbroken." She looked firm. "You can't let that happen. Not again. Danielle is a wonderful mother, better than a teenager."

"Is that who she told you the mother was?"

Hesitation. "Nooo, but last time it was a sixteen-year-old who changed her mind, so I assumed."

Ryan asked, "Do you know if the Morrisons are on vacation? If they had something planned?"

Mrs. Guiterrez was starting to look uncertain. She

glanced from Ryan to Lucy and frowned. "I'd like to know why you're asking all these questions."

"Did you see anyone in the family yesterday?" Ryan asked. "Were you home?"

She said precisely, "We left for church at nine, then went to my in-laws' for lunch. We didn't get home until after three. I didn't see them, but that doesn't mean anything."

"What did Danielle Morrison or her husband tell you about the adoption?"

"Just that Joshua was premature. They brought him home on a Wednesday evening, I remember that. That would be almost a month ago."

Lucy gave Mrs. Guiterrez her business card. Ryan did the same. "If you see either of the Morrisons, please call us immediately."

She took the cards but didn't say anything. Lucy wasn't certain she would call. Or she would, but she would tell the Morrisons about it. If they hadn't left town, they would certainly leave if they knew the FBI was looking for them.

Considering that Ryan had already informed Morrison's employer that the FBI wanted to talk to him, Lucy exchanged glances with her partner, who nodded, and she said, "The baby they call Joshua may have been sold on the black market."

Mrs. Guiterrez paled. "No." Her voice was a whisper.

"We need to talk to them. If either of them calls you, let me know. If they come home, let me know. It's imperative. Do not confront them—desperate people do desperate things."

Lucy and Ryan walked back to their car.

"They really did run away, didn't they?" Siobhan said. "It's my fault."

"It's not your fault, Siobhan," Lucy said. "We would never have had the lead in the first place without your article—there would have been no reason for Dr. Calvert to contact us."

"But *they* read it, too. They knew I was writing about their son." Siobhan blinked back tears. "Do you think . . . did they know? That Eloisa suffered for *months?* That she was *murdered* for her baby because they didn't take her to a hospital to save her life?"

"We'll find them," Ryan said. "They'll be punished to the fullest extent of the law if they were party to Eloisa's murder."

"They have money. Contacts. And what if . . . what if they hurt Joshua? To protect themselves?"

"Listen to me," Lucy said firmly. "They might have enough money to hide for a time, but they bolted fast. They may not have had a solid escape plan. We have Joshua's medical records and will spread an alert far and wide—Dr. Calvert has baby footprints, blood type, and one more very important fact: Joshua has a distinctive birthmark on his shoulder."

"But they could h-hurt—"

"Their neighbor said that Danielle Morrison suffered multiple miscarriages and one adoption where the birth mother changed her mind. I don't think she would hurt Joshua. She has wanted her own baby for far too long." Lucy turned to Ryan. "Let's get back and follow up with Zach, the hospital, and Calvert, and get out an alert."

"I've already had their passports flagged and Noah is working on a warrant for financials."

"You're fast."

Ryan grinned. "Just good, Kincaid."

CHAPTER SEVEN

Noah Armstrong had been the last person Eden expected—
or wanted—to see.

The last time she'd seen Noah, he'd called her a thief
and she'd slapped him. *Thief* was common. She didn't steal
items in order to get rich the easy way; she reconnected
personal belongings with their legitimate owners. She
and Liam had been hired by governments, royalty, the rich
and, yes—on occasion—criminals.

They did far more than acquire stolen merchandise.
Valuable work that, while not always legal, was always
justifiable.

Unfortunately, a little misstep had created a big problem with the rest of the family. Either Sean didn't know
or he hadn't told his girlfriend. *Fiancée*, Eden reminded
herself. The Kincaids. The same Kincaids as the two
brothers who'd picked up the slack after Kane iced her
and Liam out of the business. Their heritage—their inheritance.

And left her and Liam in a serious jam.

Then the name change, rubbing salt in the wounds.
Liam had once wondered if it was more Jack Kincaid's
handiwork in ousting them—maybe behind the scenes, so

he could get a piece of the pie. It all came down at about the same time. Six years ago. Right when Jack Kincaid joined Rogan-Caruso

Rogan-Caruso-*Kincaid*.

And shortly thereafter, they were axed.

And then to learn that Sean was marrying one of *them*. *Really*.

Eden didn't want to steal from her baby brother, but desperate times and all that.

Eden walked through Sean's house. It was a nice place. He had a game room—of course. He'd always loved video games. A pool. Multiple bedrooms. Double-sized lot. Older house. Nice furnishings . . . a little too modern for her taste, but not overly contemporary. Everything appeared to have been picked for comfort, and Eden could have enjoyed her stay.

If she didn't have a job to do.

Her phone rang. Liam.

"Hello, dear brother," she answered.

"I'm here. Everything still good?"

"Yes." She glanced at her watch. "We have several hours before Lucy gets back. I'll let you in."

She hung up and looked at the security panel by the front door. As soon as Liam approached, she opened the door. "You're late. I was worried."

He grinned. "You know better than to worry about me, Sis." He closed the door behind him. "It's not like I can just cross the border, thanks to Kane."

"What did Dante say?"

"We're set. We just need the bonds. I borrowed Dante's plane, so we can get out easily. Two days and we'll have everything. *Everything*. We are so close, Eden."

He looked around and whistled. "I cannot *believe* Sean has settled down. You met her?"

"Yeah. She's pretty, but kind of cold. A fed."

"A *Kincaid*." He grimaced. Liam was 100 percent positive that Jack Kincaid had something to do with Liam and Eden being booted from the family business. Eden was only about 60 percent certain. But Liam did everything to extremes. He loved and hated with passion. "Sean should have been with us, Sis."

"Duke and Kane would never have allowed it."

"Sean always did what Sean wanted. He left the business, something I never thought he'd do." He shook his head. "I should have approached him then."

"I told you that was a bad idea."

"Because of his fed girlfriend."

"That, and because I heard through my friends in New York that he'd been working undercover for the FBI."

"I don't believe it."

"It's true—and it makes sense, when you think about it. Sean had a lot of baggage . . . doesn't look like he's carrying it anymore."

"Hmm. Well," Liam said, "Sean always did whatever would please Duke. I heard through the grapevine that he's going back. He was out only a year."

"Maybe he never really left."

"He left," Liam said. "I have my sources, too, Sis. But it doesn't matter—he picked his side, end of story. Where are we with the safe?"

"I don't even want to touch it. It's state of the art. I couldn't even get into Sean's computer. I've put out some feelers to anyone who knows about the safe and how we might be able to get around it."

Liam feigned surprise. "I'm stunned. You can get into any safe."

"Sean's security is better than most. There's a biometric scan on the safe."

"Prints? Optical?"

"Prints. And before you ask, yes, I tried to lift prints from his bedroom, and it didn't work."

"We'll have to bypass. How much time before his girl-friend gets home?"

"I can find out. Tell her I'm planning to make her dinner or something."

Liam laughed. "Now *that's* funny."

"Shut up."

He kissed her cheek. "I can't wait until this is over. We're so close, Eden."

"We have a little teeny problem."

He stared at her, eyes narrowed. "That tone, Eden. What problem?"

"Noah Armstrong is here."

Liam blinked. "Here? In San Antonio? And you didn't *lead* with that information?"

"I called my contact in DC, he's been here nearly four months."

"Hmm. Small world."

"It's serious, Liam!"

"What happened?" Liam demanded, turning from casual *small world* to dangerous in a heartbeat. "Does he know you're here?"

"Yes. He threatened me with some such nonsense as if I were here to interfere with Sean and Lucy's wedding."

"Is he still in love with you?"

"No.

Liam raised an eyebrow. "Are you still in love with him?"

She turned and walked away from her brother. Liam in-furiated her sometimes. He never understood that lying to Noah had been the hardest thing she'd ever done in her life. She had wanted to be *better* with him. She *did* love him.

But when she had to make a choice—between her

brother and their borderline lives, and the man she loved—she chose her brother. And she'd do it again. Liam had been the only person in her entire life who had never let her down. She'd thought that Noah might be the one person who could accept her, because she knew he loved her. But in the end, he didn't understand. And every other man Eden had dated since Noah was weak and stupid in comparison.

"The one who got away, Eden. You are always the one who walks. You're only hung up on him because he called a spade a spade and left."

"Screw you."

"It's true, sweetheart. But six years is long enough to pine after a moderately attractive, arrogant ass."

"You're impossible. You never understood about Noah and me."

He shook his head. "That's where you're wrong. I know you cared, and I wanted you to be happy. I love you, Sis, but this treasure is everything we've been working toward for nearly twenty years. It's our legacy."

"I know."

It was Liam's legacy. It had been Liam their father had gifted the information about the treasure to; it had been Liam's obsession that had been stoked from the beginning. But Eden loved her brother and his dreams had become her dreams.

"What surprises me," Liam said, "was that Noah showed up here. I can't believe that he and Sean are friends."

"Both he and Lucy are feds." Eden sat on the couch. "I've had all morning to dig around—quietly. I know, for example, that Sean is most likely returning from whatever he's doing tonight or early in the morning—there's no hotel room reserved under any of his credit cards. I couldn't find any airline records, but his car is gone—he has a black Mustang in his name and it's not in the garage. Also, Noah was Lucy's training agent before she went to Quantico. Which would explain why Sean went undercover with the FBI, if that's in fact what he did, last year. I couldn't get much about his service record, but guess who he reports to?"

"Rick Stockton."

She slapped her brother's arm and he laughed. "And you didn't tell me?"

"It didn't seem important until now."

"Dammit, Liam!" This was typical of her brother. He kept everything close to the vest. But it always pissed her off when he kept things from *her*. She was his twin sister, and he sometimes treated everything like a game. "What if Noah goes to Rick? Kane will show up, and everything will be ruined. *Everything*."

"There's no reason for Noah to call his boss and tell him about you. I don't know exactly what Noah's relationship is with Sean and his girlfriend, but Kane isn't the type of character Noah would trust. You know that, probably more than anyone."

Liam was right. Still, the unknown bothered Eden. The reason she and Liam were so successful at their job was because of information. Information was king. Lack of information was suicide.

"This relationship Sean has with Kincaid is serious," Eden said.

"I'd think so. They're getting married."

"I mean, I think it's the real deal. Sean has had multiple job offers since he left RCK, but they would all take him away from here. I talked to a couple of people, and they said he didn't want to be away from home. What does that tell you?"

"She's good in bed?"

"Dammit, this isn't about sex."

"It's always about sex with Sean."

"I think not this time."

Liam shrugged. "I don't see what you're getting at."

"My gut tells me that if Sean is as head over heels for this girl as I think he is, he gave her full security access."

"Really." He thought for maybe ten seconds, then shook his head. "You think she'd just open the safe for us? What do we do, explain to her that Kane stole the bonds before we could steal them from the jackass who stole them from Brazilian royalty? And do we tell her the truth about why we need them in the first place? If Kane knew how valuable those bonds really were, he wouldn't have locked them in the RCK vault for the last six years."

Which was the final straw. They hadn't even known Kane had the bonds until recently. Kane's betrayal had forced Liam and Eden to work for some nasty people, putting them under the thumb of a vicious criminal for the last six years.

The bonds would free them and lead them to the treasure. A win-win.

"We'll have to find a way to make her open the safe," Eden said.

"I have some ideas," Liam said, thinking.

"But it has to be soon. Noah could still be a problem. We need to get Lucy here before tonight." Eden hoped Noah hadn't already talked to her.

Liam's eyes glazed as they often did when he was assessing a complicated situation. "Okay—we do more research on this safe. If we can't open it in"—he looked at his watch—"two hours, we use Lucy. As soon as she gets home, I'll tranquilize her. She won't expect it. Use her prints to open the safe, grab the bonds, leave before Sean gets home."

"Sean will know that we stole the bonds."

"But not why, and if we get out fast they'll have no idea

where we are. They would expect us to go back to Europe, not to Mexico. They have no idea the real value of bonds."

"Kane will retaliate."

"Let him!" Liam said with sudden anger. "He betrayed us, disowned us, left us at the mercy of Rogan-Caruso enemies. Brought in others to replace us. He's not our brother anymore." He hesitated, then said, "I'll leave a note for Sean, tell him exactly what Kane did. Let Kane justify his actions. It'll also buy us time. If I can get Sean to doubt Kane, they'll bicker amongst themselves while we retrieve the treasure and change the world."

Eden relaxed, just a bit. She liked having a plan, even if it was precarious. "Okay," she said, "I'll figure out how to get Lucy home early, you work on the safe."

CHAPTER EIGHT

A pair of US Marshals greeted Sean Rogan at the gate when he landed at the Denver airport. They weren't happy. Neither was Sean. They'd failed and now the family they were protecting would be moved someplace else.

It wasn't even their fault that they'd failed—they had to keep a kid who was half Rogan from breaking strict rules, and that was a challenge Sean wouldn't wish on anyone.

Sean had spent eight hours flying to three different airports on the off chance that one of the many people who wanted Carson Spade dead knew that Sean's son, Jesse, had contacted Sean against witness protection protocols. He was tired and not a little bit crabby at the hoops he was required to jump through. The marshal in charge of the Denver field office felt, after talking to Jesse, that bringing in Sean would help the transition for the preteen.

"But this is it, Mr. Rogan," Marshal Tom Otis said. *"Jesse needs to understand the dangers to him and his family if he breaks protocol as he did contacting you. There will be no second chance. If he violates the rules again, the family is out of witness protection."*

They would end up dead. It wasn't just Carson Spade— the lawyer and accountant for a drug cartel—who was turning state's evidence. Jesse himself had seen and heard things that would get him killed even though he was a twelve-year-old kid. In some ways, Jesse was in greater danger because he was also Sean's son. There were people in the criminal underworld who would find killing Jesse just payback for the Rogan family's efforts to thwart the cartels.

The marshals and Sean drove from the airport to a small, unmarked office in a federal building. It was a satellite office with minimal staff and office equipment, but the security was state of the art.

The marshals searched Sean and he went through X-ray in the lobby, then was taken to a floor that was accessible only with a card key. The marshals had yet to say more than a sentence apiece, but Sean was okay with that, too.

Tom Otis greeted Sean at the door.

"We need to talk," he said, and ushered Sean into a small, sparsely furnished private office. The unmarked suite had three similar offices, and a conference room with a wall of glass. A receptionist sat in the lobby area, and the two marshals who had escorted Sean talked to her while Tom closed the door behind Sean and motioned for him to sit.

Sean complied. This wasn't Otis's primary office—it had a computer, desk, American flag, and wall of bookshelves with legal books and policy manuals and not much else. There were no windows.

"Jesse wants out of witness protection," Otis said. "I told him you were coming to talk to him, and he indicated he wants to leave with you. I need to know your intentions."

"I didn't put that idea in his head," Sean said. "He knows this program is the only way to be safe."

"But you and your brother are some kind of superheroes to the kid. He thinks no one can touch you."

"My brother is trained Special Forces—"

"I know who your brother is. It's you, Mr. Rogan. Sean. I didn't know until this weekend that Jesse didn't know you were his father."

"I didn't know he was my son."

"You can see the problem we have."

"I'll talk to him."

"You don't see it."

"I get it, Otis. Jesse needs to be in the program. I'm not arguing with it. It was my fucking idea—I don't like it, but it's the only way to guarantee his safety."

"Sit." Otis motioned toward the visitor's chair.

Sean didn't want to sit—felt too much like he was being disciplined by the principal. Or his brother Duke. But he sat.

"Jesse is twelve years old and just found his real father. I read the report, and I read between the lines. I talked to Jesse. A whole load of shit happened down in Mexico that didn't make it into any official reports. You're a hero to the kid. He wants to live with you."

"He won't be safe."

"He doesn't believe that."

"I'll convince him."

"Sean," Otis said quietly, "I don't see you walking away."

"I don't understand."

"Last month you said you understood that you had to cut all ties with Jesse in order to keep him and his mother safe. But I don't think you have even processed what that means."

Sean knew exactly what it meant. He wasn't happy about it, but there was nothing he could do. They were working on allowing Sean one visit a year at a location to be determined by the US Marshals, but that wasn't even set in stone yet. The Flores cartel would hunt down Jesse and his family unless they truly disappeared—new names, new city, new future. Carson Spade would be testifying multiple times as the federal government built their cases and went after the criminal organizations one by one. The legal system was certainly not fast, especially when dealing with international criminals. Because many of those Spade was testifying against were still fugitives, the Spades would never be safe. Not until the last member of the cartel was in prison or dead.

Kane was working on it.

"What do you want me to say? Madison will never allow Jesse to live with me permanently. She won't stay in witness protection if that meant she'd never see her son again. She's his mother. Jesse is angry now, but if he turns his back on his mother he'll never forgive himself. And if something happens to her because . . . Well, I'm not going to let that happen."

Otis was silent for a minute. "I'm in negotiations with the Department of Justice to grant you visitation with Jesse. It's a complicated process, and it's expensive. We're working to amend the witness protection agreement to include annual visitation at neutral locations. Normally the family would pay for it, but considering that the Spades' assets are frozen and they are living on the stipend provided by the program, that cost would fall on you."

"Not a problem."

He didn't want to get his hopes up. But any relationship with his son was better than nothing.

"A marshal will be assigned to you in San Antonio. He'll mediate between whichever office takes over this case—I don't know where the Spades will be sent at this point. And if I did, I wouldn't tell you—or Jesse, because I don't trust the kid not to spill the beans. I have a feeling he wants to be kicked out of the program, and if he screws up again he will be."

"I will do everything I can to make Jesse understand. I appreciate this. More than you know."

"You'll have to be read into the program. We'll draw up the documents."

"You'll also need to read my fiancée into the program. FBI Agent Lucy Kincaid. We're getting married next week."

"That shouldn't be a problem—she's already a federal agent, would have gone through extensive background checks. But I have to run it up the ladder, she'll have to be cleared just like you."

Sean nodded. "Thank you, marshal. For everything."

"Don't thank me yet. You have a difficult job—convincing that boy that he has to stick to the straight and narrow isn't going to be easy."

If Jesse was anything like Sean, it was going to be next to impossible. But Sean didn't tell the marshal that.

Thirty minutes later, Otis brought Jesse into the small, generic office. Jesse looked surprised and pleased. "You came."

Sean walked over to his son and hugged him. When Jesse's arms wrapped around his back and squeezed, Sean had to fight his emotions. There was nothing he wanted more than to bring Jesse home to live with him. He *could* make it work. He was trained in security. He would change his system. Teach Jesse how to defend himself . . .

But how would Jesse go to school? A private school? Bodyguards? How could he defend himself against a sniper? And Madison would be part of the package, she wouldn't let Sean simply raise his son without her in the picture. How could Sean protect both of them? He couldn't very well move Madison into his house. He could hardly even look at her without feeling a deep-seated rage that she'd not only married a money launderer but also never told Sean she was pregnant with his child.

The only way Jesse would have a remotely normal life was if he had a new identity, a life that involved school and friends and sports. Where he wasn't the stepson of a criminal. Where he wasn't testifying against some of the most dangerous drug lords in the Northern Hemisphere.

"We need to talk," Sean said, his voice cracking.

He glanced at Otis, who nodded and left them alone.

Sean walked Jesse over to the couch. They sat. "You look good, kid."

Jesse didn't smile. "You're not taking me with you, are you?"

Sean shook his head. "Marshal Otis asked me to talk to you."

"I'm not changing my mind. I don't want to stay in the program. I don't want to have a new name and live in some strange city. I don't want to even *talk* to Carson. I hate him. I hate him for what he did, for how he used my mom, for how he used me. I can't believe you want me to live with him!"

Jesse jumped up and paced. Sean didn't tell him to sit down; Sean would have done the same thing. He would have said the same thing. He may not have raised Jesse, but this kid was a Rogan.

"If you leave, you will be targeted," Sean said.

"But that's what you do, right? You and Kane, you protect people. I would be safe with you."

"I can't protect you twenty-four/seven. These people Carson used to work for have resources. They will blow up a car, a house, hire a sniper. They could plant a bomb in your school and kill hundreds of kids just to get to one—*you*."

Jesse stared at him. Sean didn't know if the kid believed him.

"And your mother wouldn't let you leave on your own.

She would leave, too, and that would put her in danger. You and your mother, while Carson sits in witness protection safe and sound."

"I don't care!"

"Yes, you do. Look—I get it. I'm not happy about this arrangement, but it's the best thing for you and your mother right now."

"Why do you even care about her? She lied to you! She lied to *me*. For my entire life. Now *I'm* the one being punished."

"You're not being punished." But Sean understood exactly why he would think that.

"You don't get it." He frowned. "Do you—do you not want me around? Because you're getting married and all that?"

Sean stood and walked over to Jesse. He put both hands on his shoulders. "If there was any way to keep you with me and safe, I would do it. But legally, I have no rights. And morally, I cannot allow you to put yourself in danger."

"It's not fair." Tears welled in his eyes. "It's not fair!"

"No. It's definitely not fair."

Jesse wiped away tears. The kid didn't want to cry, but sometimes you couldn't stop them.

"Look at me," Sean said quietly.

Momentarily Jesse tilted his head up. Sean stared into dark-blue eyes exactly like his own. *Rogan blue*, his mother had called them.

"I'm working with the marshals to come up with a visitation plan. They know I'm your biological father. They know I want to be part of your life. They also know how to do their job. To keep you safe, you have to take a new identity. You have to move to a new city, start a new life. But we'll be able to see each other. I don't know where or when, but we'll have regular visits."

Jesse looked confused. "When the marshals first told

us what would happen they said we couldn't talk to anyone in our old life. No one."

"That's true. It's not a common situation, but it can happen. Otis is a good guy. He's putting together a plan, and I'm going to make sure that in the documents I am legally recognized as your father. That will give me more rights. Then once or twice a year we'll both fly to a place the marshals have picked and we'll have time together. Really get to know each other."

"It's not the same."

"I know."

Jesse said, "I can't forgive my mother. I'm trying. You told me I need to forgive her, but I *can't*."

"You will."

"Don't tell me what I will do! I won't forgive her. I'm so . . . so mad at her."

Sean put his arm around Jesse's shoulders and walked him back to the couch. "Jesse, you and I are a lot alike. Kane said the Rogan genes are strong in you—for better and worse." What could he say that would help? What could he say that would help in the long term? "My parents were killed in a plane crash when I was fourteen. I was in the plane with them." Sean didn't like talking to anyone about what happened all those years ago. How he had buried his mother; how he had tried to save his father and instead watched him slowly and painfully die of internal injuries. Why was he spared? He'd waited days for rescue. "I was so angry with everyone. With my parents. With myself. My whole family. And I was smart, too smart for school, so I got into a lot of trouble. When a truly smart kid is seriously angry at the world, nothing good can come from it. It took me a long time to figure out how to channel that anger."

Sometimes it got the better of him, but he'd learned self-control. He'd had to. "But my anger only hurt me. I put myself in danger, I got myself into trouble. If you let the anger control you, you will hurt others. Your mother. Carson. Yourself. And if the cartel finds you, *they will win*. They will get away with all their crimes—drug running, human trafficking, murder, extortion. All those women who were killed for their babies . . . all because they were no longer useful to the organization. All the drugs brought into the country, slowly killing people. The violence. The murder. The fear these people instill in everyone that crosses their path. If you let the anger take over, *they win*."

"Carson said that another group will just take over. He said it's all just stupid, that the cops are tilting at windmills. I don't really know what that means, but it's not a good thing."

"It's fucked, Jesse. It's truly a fucked system. I'm not going to lie to you—hell, I will *never* lie to you, okay? Life is unfair. These people are evil. Law enforcement has their hands full, but they aren't tilting at windmills. Not all the time. Sometimes, they win. Sometimes, they save innocent people like those women who were used as sex slaves. My family, we're not cops, we don't have to play by the same rules, and we've made it our mission to hunt down and destroy the worst of them. People like the Flores cartel."

"Then why don't they go after you? Why are you safer than me?"

"I'm not testifying against them. I don't have firsthand knowledge of what they've done and who they've killed. I don't control their purse strings—their money, their livelihood. My life isn't safe—but I'm only in danger when I go into their territory. I'm not in passive danger—meaning, they're not going to go after me without cause."

His face fell. "I don't understand."

Sean didn't know how else to explain it. "They will only target me when I screw with one of their operations. And when I go into their territory, I know it and take precautions."

Jesse shrugged. What could Sean say?

"Jess—"

"You risked your life for me. You didn't even know me. But you went to Mexico and rescued me."

"You're my son."

"But you didn't know me."

"You are my *son*," Sean said firmly. "I will do anything to make sure you're safe. And I believe that witness protection is the only way to ensure you survive this."

Jesse bit his lip.

"Your mother loves you, Jess."

"Does she? I don't know anymore."

"She does," Sean said forcefully. "Do you think it was easy for her to be nineteen and pregnant? Did you know that I was expelled from Stanford?"

"She told me you were expelled, but I don't know why."

She hadn't told Jesse why? It figured. But Sean didn't let his frustration show. "I hacked into the university system and exposed one of my professors as a pedophile."

"And they expelled you for that?"

"They expelled me because I remotely took over a joint demonstration between the FBI and the university about cybercrime security, simultaneously exposing my professor and highlighting the flaws in their security system in a very public way."

Jesse's eyes widened and he grinned. Sean grinned, too, though he shouldn't have. "In hindsight," Sean continued, "I should have exposed him in a less dramatic way. That act cost me a lot—my brother sent me to MIT, I have a sealed juvie record, I created an enemy who nearly killed me years later, and . . . and most important . . . that act cost me you." Sean made sure Jesse was listening; there was no doubt that the kid was hanging on to his every word. "If I hadn't done it, Madison would have told me she was pregnant. I would have been part of your life." He hoped. He wasn't positive she would have included him, not after knowing what she'd done since Jesse's birth, or who her father was, or how she was dishonest with Jesse about Sean from the beginning. But he needed Jesse to understand.

"Would you have married her?"

Sean opened his mouth, closed it. "I don't know. I started college early, I was two weeks shy of my eighteenth birthday when I was expelled. I was wild. If we had gotten married, I don't know if it would have lasted. But without a doubt, I would have been in your life. That I guarantee. You don't have the name, but know in your heart: You are a Rogan. That means something. It means you're smart. You have good instincts. You can do anything you set your mind to. Which is why I know that you'll make this work. You'll find a way to forgive your mother, you'll find a way to live with this fucked situation. And I will be in your life from now on."

Jesse's bottom lip quivered, but he nodded. "Why can't I call you? A secure phone? Or an email?"

"Because security is only as secure as its weakest link. Anytime you bring in technology, there is an added risk. We'll find a way to communicate, but it might be the old-fashioned way."

Jesse wrinkled his brow. "What way?"

"Letters."

"Like, with a pencil?"

"Exactly. I'll talk to Otis about it. There will probably be rules about what we can talk about, even in letters. The marshals will most likely read them."

"Stupid rules."

"Normally, you wouldn't get an argument from me. I never liked rules. But some rules are there to protect you."

"And what happens when I'm eighteen? Can I do whatever I want?"

"That was already in the program—you can walk away when you're eighteen. But that means no marshal protection. If your mother stays in the program, you won't be able to see her again."

"But it'll be *my* choice, *my* decision."

Sean nodded. It suddenly all clicked. For the last month Jesse had had no say in anything that had happened to him. Carson had taken him to Mexico for his own selfish reasons; Jesse was put into witness protection because that was the only way to protect his family, but he had no part in making that decision. Even further back, Jesse had had no say in whether he got to know his biological father, because Madison had lied to him about Sean. Jesse felt manipulated, a pawn with no rights. He didn't think anyone cared about his feelings.

"When you're eighteen, you will legally be able to make your own decision. Go to college. Do whatever you want."

"I want to work for RCK. I want to do what you and Kane do."

"If that's what you want, I will support. But don't go into the business unless it's what you *really* want. This isn't the easiest life out there." He then asked, "Before all this happened, what did you think you wanted to do with your life?"

He shrugged. "Design video games. I heard that some people get paid to beta test games, and that would be fun."

"It *is* fun," Sean agreed.

"You did it?"

"I designed a game, sold the rights, made a small fortune. I've been hired to work through glitches in gaming systems."

"That's totally bitchin'."

"Anything else?"

"My grandfather said I would make a good lawyer."

"You'd want to be a lawyer?"

"No. Unless I was a prosecutor like your friend Matt. He's really cool."

"Matt is definitely cool. He was a Navy SEAL way back when."

"I could enlist. Kane was in the Marines, right?"

"Go to college first."

He shrugged. "Weren't you in the military?"

"No. I wouldn't have survived. I have some issues with authority." Sean grinned at him again. "But if you want, go the college route, become an officer. I definitely did better in college than I would the military."

"Was Kane an officer?"

"No, he enlisted right out of high school. But Kane wanted to be a Marine his entire life. My dad was a Marine. It was in their blood. Not as much in mine."

"I wish I knew about my other family. You, Kane, my other grandparents."

"I wish you could have met them. My parents were inventors. They created some of the neatest toys for the military—security, safety gear, one of the first computerized night-vision googles. Just know one thing: Whatever you want to do, you will do it. Of that I'm certain. Just give yourself these few years to grow up and figure out what you want."

He tilted his chin up defiantly. "I'm leaving the program when I'm eighteen."

"That will be your choice. But I need to know—to trust you—that you'll stick with it for the next five and a half years. I just got you into my life, Jesse—I don't want to lose you. I don't want you dead. Okay?"

Jesse took a deep breath. "Okay." He then hugged Sean tightly. "I love you, Dad."

CHAPTER NINE

Kane Rogan was beginning to lose his edge.

It wasn't just the injuries he'd sustained in May when he lost a kidney and nearly died. He could survive with one kidney, and he hadn't slacked on his physical therapy and training.

He continued hammering at the house that would one day belong to Marisol and her sister and their babies. The Honeycutt family had found the injured Marisol hiding in their barn and ever since had helped her and the other girls. The Honeycutts were good people, the salt-of-the-earth type that Kane respected. Kane was helping them convert an old bunkhouse into an inhabitable residence. He liked having something to do with his hands. But his brain wouldn't shut off.

It was Siobhan Walsh who was distracting him. The sexy, compassionate, infuriating Irish redhead who would not leave him alone. When she wasn't around, he dreamed of her. When she was around, she looked at him like a siren and he wanted to take her to bed. Worse, she was staying in Texas working on locating the infants sold on the black market, so he couldn't very well tell her to leave. He'd been doing everything in his power to help, not just because it was the right thing to do but also because the sooner they located every one of those seventy-two babies, the sooner Siobhan could go back to her former life and get out of his world.

He didn't know how much longer he could resist her.

"I love you."

Why had she said that? She couldn't possibly love him. She just thought she did. He'd saved her gorgeous ass and she equated that with something else, something more, something that wasn't there. But he wasn't going to ruin her life by bringing her into his. And though he was tired sometimes, he wasn't going to give up his job. He would die on the job. He'd always planned on it. He was surprised it hadn't already happened.

He should have killed Angelo Zapelli.

Ever since he left Zapelli alive in the barn three days ago, Kane had had the distinct feeling he'd made a mistake. He'd allowed his emotions—in this case, his unwanted feelings for Siobhan Walsh—to impact a tactical decision. Zapelli was a weak, sniveling bastard, but when he cleaned himself up he'd forget Kane had nearly killed him. The threat he'd made against Lucy deeply bothered Kane.

He'd have to talk to Lucy and his brother about it. He also contacted his friend FBI Assistant Director Rick Stockton to confirm that Zapelli was on the Do Not Fly list.

But getting into the States from Mexico was a piece of cake for criminals. He didn't need to fly. Rick assured Kane that if Zapelli was spotted in the States he'd be arrested on sight—a minor consolation.

Kane put in several hours of labor—alone, just the way he liked it—and wondered where Siobhan was. He didn't want to ask. He kicked back under a tree when he needed a reprieve from the mid-afternoon heat. He drank a quart of icy water and closed his eyes.

Admit it, you just want to see her.

Sure, he wanted to see her. He wanted to find out how she was doing with her articles and interviews, about the charity she had started to help the former sex trafficking victims get back on their feet, ask her how long she was going to stay in Texas. Because he was thinking he should return to Hidalgo until she left. Every time he saw her he got all twisted up inside and made stupid decisions.

Like *not* killing Angelo Zapelli.

Kane was still beat from his trip to Monterrey. He wasn't getting younger, and the hard life he'd led for twenty-some years was catching up to him. At least, that's what he attributed to falling asleep. He only knew he'd fallen asleep because of his erotic dream about Siobhan. An odd noise woke him instantly.

He didn't know immediately what the sound was, but he always trusted his instincts. He was immediately awake, hand on his gun, and listened as he surveyed the area. The half-finished bunkhouse. The tools to the side. He couldn't see the Honeycutts' place from here; it was about half a mile down the road.

"Mr. Kane?"

Marisol.

He rose from his spot and said, "Over here." She stepped into view. Her eyes darted right then left. "What's wrong?"

She stared at him with large hazel eyes and handed him a piece of paper. Her hand was shaking.

He opened it.

I know where you live.
A

"I—I thought . . ." Marisol didn't finish her sentence. Kane knew exactly what she'd thought—that Kane had killed Zapelli.

"Where did you get this?"

"At the house."

"Here?"

She shook her head. "The group house, in town. This morning, it was in the mailbox."

"I'll call in some people, have them sit on the place for a couple days."

He should have killed him.

"Where's Siobhan?" Kane asked.

"San Antonio, staying with Miz Lucy. She is, um, she said riding along? I don't know what that means."

"Good." If Siobhan was with Lucy, she'd be safe. Kane would make sure she stayed there for a couple extra days, until he could track down Angelo and do what he should have done in the first place.

This was the last time he was ever letting his emotions interfere with his job.

"Um, this isn't his writing," Marisol said. "But he wanted it sent to me, yes?"

Kane nodded. "He wants to scare you. I'll talk to George Honeycutt, Villines, make sure they're aware."

Assistant Sheriff Adam Villines was the Honeycutts' son-in-law and had been involved in the rescue of the women. He was as good a cop as Kane had met, one of the few he trusted. Villines would put his deputies on the house for as long as necessary.

Marisol said, "Thank you."

"How is Ana?" Marisol's younger sister was pregnant with twins. She'd been seriously injured during the rescue and gone into premature labor, which the hospital managed to stop. Her leg had been crushed and she would never walk without a limp, but she had survived a horrific ordeal.

"Bed rest. The doctors want her to rest one more week, to make it safer for the babies. But they're thirty-five weeks, and both three pounds, the doctor says. They would survive. We just want them bigger, healthier, for their lungs."

"You and Ana are strong, your babies will be just like you. And Elizabeth?"

Marisol beamed, thinking about her infant daughter, but tears were in her eyes. "A miracle. A miracle. Miz Honeycutt is watching her. What would I have done without them?"

"You would have survived. You're a survivor, Marisol. Never forget that."

He waited until Marisol left, then called Siobhan.

"Hello," she said.

His heart pounded. He didn't want these feelings for Siobhan. He didn't want to worry about her. "I should have killed him. He sent a note to Marisol at the group home."

Siobhan was silent. Damn, why did he have to be so gruff?

"Kane—"

"Stay with Lucy. Just a couple extra days in San Antonio, until I get this mess straightened out."

"Don't order me around like I'm one of your soldiers."

"It wasn't an order."

"Sure sounded like one."

"Don't start with me, Siobhan. I need to take precautions here, set up additional security, until I know if the threat was just Zapelli blowing smoke or if he has some muscle. If I have to worry about you, I can't do my job."

"You never have to worry about me, Kane. I told you that."

"I worry."

"You're impossible."

"So are you, sweetheart." He hung up before he said something he regretted.

He called Ranger, one of his most trusted men, filled

him in on the situation, and Ranger said he would take care of things, including verifying that Angelo Zapelli was still in Monterrey. Kane had a feeling the threat was hollow, but he couldn't count on it.

Kane showered in the bunkhouse—there was running water, though no hot-water heater yet. The lukewarm well water sufficed. He wrapped a towel around his waist and noticed the message symbol on his cell phone. He glanced through the calls. Most of them could be taken care of later, but one number had a DC area code he didn't recognize. He listened to the message.

I need to talk to you about your sister ASAP.

Kane's blood froze. His sister? What was his sister up to and why would a fed be calling about her?

Kane almost called Rick Stockton first—Noah Armstrong worked directly for him—but he needed more information about what Eden was doing.

He'd met Noah briefly last month when they turned over Carson Spade to the authorities, and learned he was friends with Lucy. If Kane's soon-to-be sister-in-law trusted Noah like Rick did, he couldn't be a bad guy, but Kane didn't trust easily.

Noah answered immediately. "Armstrong."

"Kane Rogan."

"Thank you for returning my call. I wouldn't have bothered you except that Sean is out of town and I wasn't able to reach him."

"You mentioned my sister."

"This is awkward for me—but I didn't know who else to call. Eden is in San Antonio. She showed up at Lucy's house this morning—after Sean left for his business trip, or whatever he's doing. She wasn't expected but talked herself into the house and is staying overnight."

A rush of emotions rolled over Kane. Anger. Fear. Confusion. Suspicion. Foreign emotions, because he usually controlled his feelings so extremely well. It took him a moment to put his thoughts together.

Noah spoke again. "When Sean and I worked together last year I told him I had butted heads with Liam. That's true. But . . . I have a history with Eden. I know they are both thieves. I'm aware that you cut them out of RCK, and I haven't spoken to her in over six years. But I'm going to tell you this—and I'm sure you know this is the truth—if Eden is here, so is Liam. And there is no way they are in San Antonio simply for Sean's wedding. They're up to something, and I swear, I will bring down the wrath of the entire Department of Justice on them."

Noah was right—Liam and Eden always had ulterior motives. But why Sean? And why now?

Kane froze. How did Liam find out about the bonds? "I know why they're here."

"Is it a problem?"

Damn straight it was a problem, especially if Sean was out of town. Eden was the queen of manipulation. Kane would have to give Lucy a quick and dirty lesson in all things Eden and Liam, and that would not be a fun conversation.

"Rogan—I need to know what's going on."

Kane had to secure the group home first—Zapelli had made a direct threat, and Kane couldn't leave those girls unprotected. Ranger was two hours out—Villines was closer, but Kane would have to touch base with him, ensure he understood the danger.

"Dammit, talk to me, Rogan! Are you still there?"

"Yes. I'm in Laredo and I'll be there as soon as I can, but I have a situation I have to take care of first. I need you to get Eden out of the house."

"But you know why they're here."

"Sean has something they want."

"Oh, that's rich."

"Excuse me?"

"A leopard doesn't change his spots."

"I'll be blunt with you, because I know you have issues with Sean. Sean doesn't know the value of what he has. I had him secure six million dollars in bearer bonds that we used as bait when we rescued Jesse last month. There was no easy way to return them to RCK at the time. Jack is going to retrieve them after the wedding. Liam wants them."

"How the hell does he know Sean has them?"

"I don't know." That was a lie. There was only one way that Liam could have learned that Sean had those bonds, and Kane was going to plug that leak personally. But first things first. "Under no circumstances can Eden and Liam get those bonds. I'm not going to explain anything more, because I don't know you. Rick trusts you, but that only goes so far with me. Get to Sean's house and don't leave Lucy alone with Eden."

"I thought you said she wouldn't hurt her."

"I said she wasn't violent. But they'll do anything, short of murder, to get those bonds."

"I want a better explanation, Kane."

"I don't have time right now—"

"I need information. Lucy is in Austin following up on the black-market baby case with Agent Quiroz. I assume you've already run background on all my agents."

"Of course," Kane said. "If Lucy's in Austin, she'll be busy. Get over to her house and keep your eyes on Eden. Do *not* let her out of your sight. Trust no one."

"Really, Kane—"

"I mean it. We have a leak at RCK. The only people I trust right now other than Lucy are Sean, JT, and Rick. Rick trusts you, so you're on the short list. I'll get JT to clear everyone else until we figure out who the mole is, but until I know how Liam and Eden found out that Sean had those bonds no one is to know anything that I don't want them to know." He paused. "If you need local backup, call in Dunning."

"Do not tell me who I can and cannot call."

"Dunning is a trained soldier. Armstrong, I don't have time for this bullshit. Sit on Eden until I get there." He hung up. He hoped Rick was right, that Armstrong was solid, because Kane was beginning not to like him very much.

Kane next tried Sean's number. Direct to voice mail.

"Sean, it's Kane. Eden is at your house, Lucy does not know what she's up against. Get home as soon as you can. They want the bonds. Under no circumstances can they have them."

He slammed shut his phone. He needed to get Sean a hot phone, one he always picked up, because these messages were getting tiresome. When Kane called, it was always critical.

But Lucy was always dependable. If she couldn't talk, she'd simply say so. He called her.

Her cell phone rang five times, then her voice mail picked up.

Lucy always answered her phone. He'd come to depend on it.

"It's Kane. Call me back."

He pocketed his phone. Wait—he'd just spoken to Siobhan thirty minutes ago. He dialed her number.

Voice mail.

Either she was still angry with him or something was wrong.

Shit, shit, shit!

He called JT on his hotline. That's what JT called it— he, Rick, and Kane all had a special phone. No matter what, they answered. No one else had the numbers. They rarely used it.

"What's wrong?" JT asked.

"Eden is at Sean's. Sean is AWOL. Don't know where he is or what he's doing. I can't reach Lucy."

"Get up there."

"I'm working on it. I need to know how much to trust Armstrong."

"Rick trusts him."

"That doesn't tell me shit."

"He's law-and-order but has been known to bend rules."

"Bend."

"Yes."

"Okay. I have to secure Laredo before I can go to San Antonio."

"You didn't bury him."

"I should have."

"You did the right thing."

"It sure as hell won't be the right thing if anyone dies because he lived."

"How?"

Kane knew exactly what JT was thinking, and it wasn't about Zapelli.

"Dante Romero."

"Aw shit, Kane! I thought he wanted Liam dead."

"That's what he wanted us to believe. But Dante didn't know that Sean had the bonds. He just knew that *we* had them. RCK."

JT didn't say a word. He didn't have to. He knew exactly what Kane meant.

Someone in RCK headquarters was working for Dante, and by extension—if Kane was right that Dante and Liam's split was all a setup—someone at RCK was working for Liam. Someone they trusted had betrayed them.

"I'm on it," JT said, his voice low and angry. "Stop them."

CHAPTER TEN

Jasmine Flores picked up the ringing cell phone, ready to throw it against the wall. Her entire world was crashing down, she was losing control, and people *still* wanted things from her.

Calm down. You're in charge of the family now. It's what you always wanted.

She didn't want it because three of her four brothers were dead. She wanted it because she had *earned* it.

She supposed that survival had, in a way, earned her the spot as head of family.

She answered, "Yes."

"Jasmine?"

"Who's this?"

"Thomas Morrison. We have a big fucking problem, and you need to fix it."

Morrison . . . Morrison. Well, shit. What the hell does he want?

"Not my problem," she said.

"The fucking newspaper! The fucking *New York Times* has been running articles about your fucked operation. They're looking for the babies. They came knocking at my door!"

"What did you tell them?" she hissed. Though it didn't matter—she'd been paid, she was in hiding in Mexico, and the feds already knew she'd been involved.

Proving it, however, was an entirely different matter, and almost everyone who knew anything about her was dead.

Yet now she had a loose end named Thomas Morrison.

"Nothing! I saw the writing on the wall and took Danielle and the baby to Cancún Sunday night. But I can't run forever."

"Not my problem," she repeated.

"It *is* your fucking problem."

She almost hung up. Except . . . Thomas Morrison was a lawyer. He was a smart guy, for the most part. Not on the same level as Carson Spade, but he could learn.

"I have a proposal."

"I'm listening."

"You need new identities. Clean, airtight. A safe house. I need a new lawyer. Someone who can build up my business, retrieve my money, clean it. I get you what you need, you work for me."

He didn't say anything.

"The offer expires in ten seconds. I already have two other accountants I'm looking at, and I'd rather have an accountant over a lawyer," she lied smoothly. After Carson Spade turned state's evidence, no one wanted to work with her, not until things settled down. But she couldn't wait a year or more. She'd go broke, keeping Dominick's operation running without the ability to launder her own money.

Silence.

"Five seconds.

"What do I have to do?"

"Come to me and I'll explain everything. Bring Danielle and the baby. They'll be safer." Hardly. But she needed leverage.

"Fine."

He wasn't happy, but Jasmine's job wasn't to keep her staff happy. "I'm sending a pilot. Meet at the private airport ten minutes southwest of Cancún in exactly three hours. Don't be late, or my offer is void."

She hung up. One problem fixed, now she just had to figure out what to do with Angelo Zapelli. Whether she could use him or should have him killed.

She watched as her youngest half brother swam in the pool with Gabriella Romero. Okay, she had two problems. Jose swore up and down that Gabriella had saved his life during the RCK raid last month. And try as she might, Jasmine hadn't found a recent connection between Gabriella and her enemies. Dante Romero was known to play all sides, and Jasmine wasn't confident that he hadn't set up the raid in the first place. He'd brokered the deal but swore—to her face—that his only involvement was when Sean Rogan came to him asking him to arrange trading the bonds for his brother. He'd had no idea that Jesse Spade was Sean Rogan's son—no one did. That latter part was true. The news had shocked everyone who learned about Jesse's parentage.

If Jasmine could get to the kid, she'd kill him just on general principles, though he'd gone into witness protection with his no-good stepfather. *Traitor.*

She rubbed her eyes. She didn't want to kill a kid. People thought she was heartless—she wasn't. She just hated disloyalty and stupidity. Carson Spade was disloyal; Angelo Zapelli was stupid.

Truth be told, this entire fiasco was Rogan's fault. Both of them, in fact—Kane and Sean. When they were six feet under, she'd consider the slate clean.

Unless of course any of their comrades attempted to retaliate; then she'd take the war to them.

Jasmine would not be made a fool.

CHAPTER ELEVEN

It was after two thirty by the time Ryan arrived back at FBI headquarters. Lucy told Ryan she was going to take a late lunch and check on her future sister-in-law. Eden had texted her multiple times with questions and had set off the alarm three times in the last two hours.

"You know what would help a lot," Lucy said to Siobhan as they slid into Lucy's car, "is if you can stay and keep Eden company. I was nervous leaving her alone in the house, especially since I can't reach Sean."

"Sure," Siobhan said.

Lucy waved at the guard as they exited the gated lot.

"Do you know her?"

"Never met either of them," Siobhan said.

"Was that Kane on the phone earlier? I was trying not to eavesdrop, but I heard his name."

She rolled her eyes. "He drives me up a wall."

Lucy smiled.

"What?"

"Nothing."

"Don't *nothing* me." She sighed. "He gets all macho protective but then treats me like I'm an idiot. Still . . . Zapelli threatened Mari. I don't know how, exactly—he had a note delivered to the group home. Kane thinks I should stay here for a few days."

"Kane was the anonymous tipster, wasn't he," Lucy said, more a statement than a question.

"He planned on telling you—"

"I know, he doesn't want me to feel guilty that I screwed up the investigation."

"You *didn't*. You had no choice."

"Noah and I both knew a judge could throw out our search as illegal."

"But you saved Mari's life. You saved all those women. I'd rather let one asshole go free than have nine more women dead."

Lucy concurred. She and Noah had discussed what they'd done and even were questioned by ASAC Durant as to the search that had been thrown out by a judge. In the end, she and Noah agreed that the search had been a gray area, but saving those women was a priority.

Next time, however, the result might not be what they wanted.

Truth be told, Lucy was surprised that Zapelli was still alive. When Kane learned that Zapelli had sold Mari and Ana as sex slaves two years ago, Lucy thought for certain Kane would assassinate him. Lucy had no feelings on the matter. She wouldn't have felt any guilt or remorse for Zapelli's death, though she wouldn't want Kane to risk himself for that weak-willed asshole.

"He cares about you," Lucy told Siobhan.

"Kane? I know. That's why he makes me so mad. I *know* he cares about me. I love him. He's arrogant and demanding and a borderline bully and completely selfless and honorable and brave. He thinks he's not good enough for me or some such nonsense."

"He spared Zapelli because you asked him to."

"Kane *told* you that?"

"Educated guess."

"He's angry that I asked him to. I didn't think Zapelli would have the guts to threaten Mari."

"It could be a hollow threat. Kane will straighten it out, you know that."

"I just wish he wouldn't push me away."

Lucy smiled as she pulled into her garage. In the year that she'd gotten to know Kane, she'd already seen a change in him—especially after losing a kidney. He was slowing down, like Jack had done after he got married a few years ago. Maybe Siobhan was just as big a reason for that as anything else. Kane had been a lone wolf for so long, he was getting tired of being alone. Lucy saw it, recognized it. Before Sean, she didn't think she'd ever be truly intimate with anyone—for different reasons than Kane's, but the result was the same: closing everyone out and protecting yourself.

It wasn't a fun life.

"Forget Kane. I'm just thrilled I get to finally meet Eden. I know next to nothing about her."

"You know that Kane and Eden and Liam had a big falling-out years ago."

"He's *Kane*," Siobhan said as if that were explanation enough. "Lucy, Kane has a solid moral code, but it's not like everyone else's. He doesn't forgive mistakes."

Lucy didn't see that, but she understood why Siobhan did. "Kane takes the world on his shoulders," she said. "Sometimes, it's a heavy burden."

"Exactly!" Siobhan grabbed her overnight bag and got out of the car. "You know, he adores you."

Lucy laughed. "I don't think Kane adores anyone."

"Okay, how about he's really happy—as happy as a man like Kane can be—that you're marrying Sean?"

"I'm glad." Sean and Kane had grown closer over the last year, and Lucy was pleased that their relationship was on solid ground. She had a feeling that Kane needed his family more than he would admit. The Rogans would never be the Kincaids, but they were finally coming together.

Maybe Eden extending the olive branch was exactly what the family needed to forgive whatever happened years ago. There had been a time in Lucy's family when Jack wasn't welcome in the Kincaid house. She never learned exactly why— Jack wouldn't discuss the details— but it revolved around a decision Jack made while in the military that their father had opposed. Two strong, stubborn men who wouldn't back down from their beliefs. Lucy loved them both and was relieved when they came to a truce.

She opened the door that led from the garage into a small room off the kitchen. She didn't hear the familiar *beep* of the alarm, and when she turned to check the security panel she noted that the alarm was turned off.

She wasn't surprised. She'd briefly spoken to Eden while driving back from Austin and she'd seemed frazzled.

Lucy reengaged the alarm out of habit. She didn't believe for a minute that Angelo Zapelli would come after her or Siobhan. But until Kane confirmed that the Flores cartel was decimated, she didn't want to take any chances.

"I *really* need to use the bathroom," Siobhan said. "I didn't want to ask Ryan to stop."

Lucy pointed to the short hall that led to the laundry room and a half bath. "Down there. I'll find Eden and then we'll have lunch. I'm starving."

Siobhan rushed down the hall.

Lucy put her purse on the kitchen counter and started down the wide, tiled hall that bisected the house. She was about to call out to Eden when she heard voices coming from Sean's office.

Sean's car wasn't in the garage; someone else was here

with Eden. That irritated Lucy—it wasn't being a good guest to invite people over without asking your host. The stray thought sounded so much like her mother in Lucy's head that she almost laughed.

The door was ajar and Lucy could see Eden sitting at Sean's desk talking on her cell phone.

"Inconvenience is part of life, Dante," Eden was saying. "Everything is in motion. We'll have the bonds shortly, and then we'll be there . . . Hardly. He's not here, which is a good thing . . . Yes, I know, but we have a backup plan, Liam is on it, we'll be in Tampico before you can say—"

Eden swiveled and saw Lucy. "I'll call you back." Eden closed her flip-phone.

"What's going on, Eden?" Lucy asked, her anger growing. Eden wasn't here to mend fences.

Eden shrugged.

"Just business."

Dante. Lucy knew of only one Dante—Dante Romero, who had helped Sean rescue Kane last month. And bonds . . . Sean told her he'd put bearer bonds that belonged to RCK in his safe. She hadn't thought twice about it.

Eden wasn't here for the wedding. She was here to rob her family. Lucy was furious that Eden had so blatantly used her. "I don't think it's a good idea for you to be here right now. When Sean returns, I'll have him contact you."

"Lucy, you don't understand."

"I understand that I should never have left you here alone."

Lucy didn't think Eden could hack Sean's computer, but perhaps she had some of Sean's skills.

She talked about the bonds . . .

Lucy glanced at the wall where a beach mural hid the safe. Easy enough to find.

"Sean doesn't like anyone using his office," Lucy said firmly. She motioned for Eden to leave.

Eden stood, frowning, obviously upset and angry. What did *she* have a right to be angry about? She brushed past Lucy. "I don't know what Noah has told you, but you can't believe anything that man says."

Noah?

"Noah *Armstrong*?"

Eden turned around, standing in the doorway of the office. Lucy could see her thinking, plotting, scheming. "Well. That changes things. I assumed he would have told you he came by to *chat* this morning."

Lucy hadn't spoken to Noah since he left this morning, before she and Ryan went to Austin.

She was missing something, but right now she didn't want to turn her back on Eden. She didn't trust this woman, Sean's sister notwithstanding. She pulled out her phone and brought up her contacts. Hit "*Noah.*"

Eden moved out of the doorway. Lucy followed.

"Hey, Lucy!" Siobhan called from the kitchen.

Movement to Lucy's left distracted her and she turned her head slightly. A man stood there and for a split second she thought it was Sean, then a cool mist hit her in the face. She put her hand up to wipe it away and the man sprayed her again. She dropped her phone and reached for her gun, but her hand felt numb and her vision blurred.

"Run, Siobhan!" she shouted as loud as she could. Her head was spinning.

He sprayed a third time and she fell to her knees, her hands up in defense, but her muscles felt thick and her eyes hurt. Different than pepper spray. She was completely disoriented.

She tried to warn Siobhan again, but all that came out was a gasp. She heard Siobhan's voice; it sounded far, far away . . .

"Catch her," she heard Eden say, and then all was black.

CHAPTER TWELVE

"Run, Siobhan!"

Siobhan was coming out of the kitchen when she heard Lucy shout. She looked down to the far end of the hall and saw a man and woman on either side of Lucy as Lucy fell to her knees.

The man hovered over her and Siobhan ran toward him.

"Leave her alone!" Not for the first time in her life, Siobhan wished she carried a gun.

The man caught Lucy before she fell to the ground, then turned and rushed toward Siobhan.

He looked familiar. Very familiar, though Siobhan had never met him.

"Liam?" she said. She started backing up.

"Did Lucy call you *Siobhan*? You're Siobhan Walsh?" He smiled warmly. "Wow, I love your work. You have an amazing eye."

She walked backward all the way into the kitchen, looked around for Lucy's gun—it wasn't with her purse.

"I'm sorry for this drama, but we're on a deadline, and I knew Lucy wouldn't cooperate."

He was closer, had something in his hand. *Gun?* No,

it was a small spray bottle. He sprayed it toward her, but she ran.

"Siobhan—please, this doesn't have to be difficult."

He caught up with her quickly, grabbed her arm, and turned her around. She spun, hitting him square in the jaw.

"Damn!" He was irritated but didn't sound angry.

Her phone was ringing. Where had she left it? The bathroom. She tried to run, but Liam grabbed her again, pushed her into the center island, and handcuffed her. He was so smooth and fast she didn't realize she was cuffed until she heard the click.

"Honey, I don't want to hurt you, so please calm down. Wrong place, wrong time."

Liam was shorter and leaner than both Sean and Kane, but he had hidden muscles. Siobhan was strong, but she couldn't break away from him.

Eden walked into the kitchen. "I cannot *believe* this."

"Sean is going to have your head if you hurt Lucy," Siobhan said. Why hadn't she made a run for the security panel?

Because you have no idea how it works.

But if she broke it, it would call the cops, right?

"We're not going to hurt Lucy," Liam said. He turned to Eden. "Lucy heard too much."

"I know, dammit!"

"But it's okay." Why did he sound so calm? This whole situation was a mess.

"None of this is okay. We were supposed to be in and out."

"Trust me. Just don't say anything else, Sis."

Eden was frazzled, but Liam was very calm. He ushered Siobhan back to Sean's office—right past Lucy's unconscious body in the hall—and sat her on the couch. Eden followed. "Stay, Siobhan," Liam said.

"Is she okay?" Siobhan asked.

"She'll be fine," Liam said.

Siobhan didn't like the look on his face. This wasn't a Rogan she knew.

She began, "If—"

"Don't talk. Okay, Siobhan? I don't have the time." Liam turned to Eden. "This is actually even better."

"I don't believe you. This is fucked."

"*Calm down.* You are never this jumpy on a job."

"Because this is *Sean.* Our baby brother."

"We're almost free." Liam walked back over to where Lucy lay and carefully dragged her body into Sean's office. Eden removed a large mural—a beach scene—from the wall and revealed a safe. Liam picked Lucy up, staggering under the deadweight, and Eden put Lucy's hand on the biometric pad.

At first nothing happened. Then the small red light turned green and Liam smiled.

He gently put Lucy down, making sure that she didn't hit her head, and opened the door.

"They're here," he said with both awe and relief.

"Let's go."

"First things first, Sis." He sat down at Sean's desk and started writing on a piece of stationery. "Might slow things down a bit. Might not. But we need time."

Noah couldn't drop everything because Eden Rogan wanted some damn bonds that Sean had in his safe. Where was the legitimate government business? He and Abigail Durant had been in and out of interviews all morning and afternoon. Ryan and Lucy were in Austin serving a warrant. Noah didn't work for RCK and he refused to take orders from Kane Rogan.

Kane made him as angry as Sean used to. But still,

Noah knew Eden, and she was up to something. As soon as he could break free, he would.

"Agent Armstrong, I don't think you heard anything that last candidate said." Abigail stacked the papers in front of her. "Fortunately, he was our last candidate for the day and I didn't particularly like him, so we don't need to discuss it. We do need to discuss why you're preoccupied."

This was why he didn't like the influence RCK had over Rick Stockton—if that's what he could call it. Noah liked and respected his boss, but where did Rick's loyalties truly lie? When the FBI and RCK were on opposite sides—as Noah was certain they had been in the past and would be in the future—what did Rick do?

"It's a personal matter. I apologize that it has affected my performance."

Durant shook her head. "Noah, if all my agents were like you, we wouldn't have had the problems we've had this year. I asked AD Stockton if there was a chance you would take a permanent post here."

"He told me, and I appreciate your confidence, but I don't think that would be the wisest decision. White Collar is still angry with me, and some of the other staff aren't pleased about how I handled the Elizabeth Cook situation."

"You called a spade a spade, Noah, and I needed to hear it. Still, you have my respect, as well as that of your squad and SAC Naygrew."

"Thank you. But this isn't my home. I'm going back to DC when Agent Kincaid returns from her honeymoon, as I already planned."

She flipped through a notebook. "Kincaid and Quiroz got a warrant today?"

"Yes. I worked with the AUSA this morning, a medical records warrant for a four-week-old male infant who fits the description and profile of one of the babies sold on the black market."

"And?"

"They served the warrant, received the files, and were following up with the parents. I haven't received a report from their interviews, though Ryan said he had a gut feeling they were on the run. He and Lucy planned to follow up with friends, neighbors, and employers."

"Let me know—your squad has done exemplary work in tracking as many of those missing children as you have." She paused. "May I speak freely?"

He was surprised. "Of course."

"I just don't want you to read anything into this comment. But Agent Kincaid—I know she's a friend of yours—she's been putting in far more hours than she should. What you and she went through in Laredo—the loss of life, the missing babies—not to mention the situation with the Spade family. I'm worried about Agent Kincaid's emotional state."

Noah had to choose his words carefully. "Yes, Lucy and I are friends, and I've worked with her many times. I'm not going to lie to you—this case has affected her. But not the quality of her work. And I haven't asked her to back off because she has a strong sense of duty. She's about to take two weeks off for her wedding and honeymoon, she wants to do as much as she can before she leaves. And to be perfectly honest, Lucy has one of those minds that see things that others don't. You know those agents."

"Like yourself."

"Thank you, but I was thinking Quiroz and Dunning in particular. And that agent on cyberterrorism . . . Devlin, I think." Durant nodded that she knew who Noah was talking about.

"I do know what you mean. They make connections

where no one else sees them, and then everyone looks and thinks, 'How did I miss that?' "

Noah nodded. "Lucy needs to do this, needs to find as many of these children as she can, for her own peace of mind."

"She hasn't seen a counselor. She was ordered to, Noah. I need it to happen."

"I'll talk to her."

Noah had already spoken to Lucy about the mandated psych eval after the shootings in Laredo. She was debriefed, but she hadn't gone through the evaluation, and he was wondering if she was going to try to avoid it.

"She missed an appointment last week."

Noah hadn't known.

"She has to go before her honeymoon, get that through to her, or she'll be on suspension when she returns. I don't want to do it, but I will."

"I'll talk to her when she gets back from Austin."

"What do you think of the candidates so far?"

Noah didn't think much—no one who wanted to move into Violent Crimes was suited for the high-stress, high-demand slot. He was trying to think of a diplomatic way to say that when Abigail nodded. "Me too."

"Excuse me?"

"None of them are going to work. I have a meeting with SAC Naygrew in the morning, I have some ideas. Go handle your personal business. You've been putting in twelve-hour days, you can leave early when needed."

"Thank you, ma'am."

Noah left the small conference room and looked at his phone. He had several text messages, and a missed call from Lucy. He immediately returned Lucy's call but her phone went to voice mail. "Lucy, it's Noah—I had a missed call from you. I'm in the office, call me if you need me."

He headed for his office but stopped when he saw Ryan talking to Zach Charles, the Violent Crimes analyst. "What happened in Austin?" Noah asked. He glanced around, didn't see Lucy.

"The doctor was cooperative. We have all the info on the kid, Joshua Morrison. It's him."

"You're certain?"

"Ninety-nine percent. The parents are gone. Bolted, I'm sure, after they saw the article in the *Times*. They recognized their son in the paper, just like the doc did. The neighbors haven't seen them since Saturday and, Morrison didn't go to work on Monday. He's a corporate lawyer. I got shit out of his employer, but we flagged their passports and the AUSA's office said they haven't traveled by plane out of the country—at least on their own passports."

Zach said, "I'm running credit and other reports, they're dead in the water, so I'm trying some other things."

"If they ran, they may have new identities," Noah said.

"That's what Lucy thinks, but Zach has some other tools at his disposal. We were just talking about it—Joshua is on very specific medication for his lung development. They're going to have to refill the prescription at some point—even if under another name. Zach can pull pharmacy records. If they're in the States, we'll find them."

"Good. Where's Lucy? I need to ask her about something."

"We didn't get back until after two thirty, missed lunch. She was going to take Siobhan to her house, grab a bite." Zach glanced at his watch. "She said she'd be back by three thirty."

Noah looked at his watch, too. Three thirty-five.

"You're not going to get on her for being five minutes late, just because she was late this morning?" Ryan shook his head. "She's exhausted, if you haven't noticed."

Noah had. He just tried not to care. Lucy was marry-

ing Sean Rogan, and Noah had never been in the running.
All the *if onlys* didn't matter because Noah would never
go after another man's girl. And Lucy loved Rogan, warts
and all.

But the differences between the woman he'd once loved,
Eden Rogan, and the woman he could have loved, Lucy
Kincaid, were as clear as day. And at that moment he realized that he deserved better than both—definitely
better than a thief and better than another man's woman.

Someday.

"Hold down the fort." He started to walk away. He'd
check on Lucy because he'd promised Kane he would sit
on Eden. And he was concerned that Lucy wasn't reachable. That was unlike her.

"What's going on?" Ryan asked. "Dammit, Armstrong,
something weird has been going on all day. You this morning, just bolting out of here, then Lucy getting a half-dozen
messages from her soon-to-be sister-in-law."

Noah stopped. "What? What messages?"

"Sean's sister, Eden. She set off the alarm, Lucy had
to walk her through the system, then she couldn't arm it
again, then she did something else—I don't know what,
but Lucy had to remotely reset the system. I mean, I know
Sean and Lucy have every reason to be paranoid, but Lucy
was preoccupied, and she's not like that."

CHAPTER THIRTEEN

Sean tried Lucy a second time; again no answer. He looked at his email messages. She hadn't responded to any of them. Where was she? He was waiting in Chicago for a flight to Baton Rouge, where he would take another plane to San Antonio. Damn marshals had insisted, in case someone was watching him. He was *hours* away and he was going crazy.

What the *hell* was Eden doing at his house? Today of all days? How could she have possibly known he would be out of town? Because there's no way he would have let her stay in his house. Just on general principles. But Lucy didn't know the history. Hell, even Sean didn't know the entire story. He trusted Kane when Kane said that Liam and Eden had worked for the wrong people. And that fit with what Sean knew of the twins.

But would they actually hurt Lucy? Why? They didn't even know her. And Sean had never done anything to them. The worst he'd done was refuse to help them with a project a few years ago. Duke had forbidden him, and Sean had almost grabbed the next flight to Paris because he really hated when Duke told him he *couldn't* do something. But Kane called him and told him the reasons, and Sean agreed.

And that had always been the crux of his problem with Duke. Duke gave Sean orders and rules without explanation, like a military leader expecting his soldier to follow orders without questions. Kane told Sean why. That's all Sean ever wanted from Duke. To be treated as an equal.

It had been better since Sean quit RCK last year. And now that he was coming back, he dealt directly with JT Caruso, which seemed to be working well. Sean wouldn't be fully engaged with RCK operations until after his honeymoon.

Honeymoon. Lucy.

Where was she? Why hadn't she called?

He walked over to the customer service counter for the airline. "I need to change my flight." He hated flying commercial. It drove him nuts, all the people, delays, and discomfort. More, he wasn't in control of the plane. "I leave for Baton Rouge in an hour; I'd like to fly direct to San Antonio. Do you have anything?"

"We don't have a direct flight to San Antonio tonight."

"Any other airlines?"

"Your ticket isn't transferable unless there is a problem with your flight."

"I'll buy another ticket."

She typed into the computer. Frowned. Typed. Frowned. "I can get you on standby with another airline for a plane that leaves in thirty minutes, but it's in another terminal and—"

"I'll take it." He slipped her his credit card and waited impatiently for her to print the ticket and boarding pass. He didn't blink at the nearly thousand-dollar charge.

"I'll notify the gate, but you need to hurry."

Sean was already running. While on the airport shuttle he sent Nate Dunning an urgent message.

I need you to find Lucy and stick to her like glue until I get back. I can't reach her. Call Kane, tell him Eden is at my house and I need him to drop everything.

He told himself that just because Lucy hadn't called him back didn't mean anything. It just meant that she was in the middle of something. It wasn't even four, she was probably still at the office.

He replied again to her message.

Do not trust Eden. Call Kane. If you can't reach Kane, call JT. He'll explain.

He waited to see if there was a read receipt. Nothing.

Dammit.

Right before he boarded the plane, he got a response from Nate.

On it.

He breathed marginally easier.

Marginally.

Because until he talked to Lucy, until he saw her, he feared she would be caught up in one of his sister's schemes.

Why are you in San Antonio, Eden? What are you up to?

And where the hell is Liam?

Noah tried calling Lucy while driving to her house; she didn't pick up. He parked in her driveway and peered in the garage window. Lucy's Nissan Altima wasn't there. Neither was Sean's Mustang.

Had he missed her? He tried her cell phone again. No answer. He called Zach, asked if Lucy had come in.

"No, sir, would you like me to call her?"

"No. If she comes in, have her call me, okay?"

"Is everything okay?"

"I don't know. Just—if you see her, I need to talk to her."

He went to the front door. If Lucy wasn't here, maybe Siobhan was. She might know if Lucy had changed her plans. He knocked.

No answer.

He rang the bell.

Silence.

"Shit," he muttered.

He tried Siobhan's cell phone.

It rang. And rang. And five rings later went to voice mail.

"Hello, this is Siobhan Walsh, please leave a message . . ."

Noah hung up. He was now officially worried and considered calling Kane Rogan again.

Dammit, why did Kane have to be right? Why hadn't Noah dropped everything and sat on Eden earlier?

He called the security company that Sean contracted with, but they gave him nothing—even though he'd identified himself as a federal agent with his badge number.

"We can send out a patrol, sir, but we cannot override the codes."

What good was a security company if they couldn't get into the damn house? Noah was getting ready to break a window when a Jeep Wrangler pulled up in front of the house. Noah was suspicious until he saw Nate Dunning jump out of the Jeep.

"What's going on?" Nate asked as he approached.

"I can't reach Lucy." Noah eyed him. "What are you doing here?"

"Sean asked me to hang with Lucy until he gets home. He's on his way."

"Her car isn't here, but she's not answering her cell

phone. I called the security company and apparently they can't let me in even though I'm a federal agent. *They* can't even get in."

Nate walked past him and typed in a code at the door. He already had his gun out.

Noah couldn't contemplate why Nate Dunning had the code to Sean's house. He pulled his own weapon and followed Nate. Nate motioned he was taking left, so Noah took right. Cleared the living room, dining room, kitchen, family room, garage. Looked out back; the pool house was dark. No one was in the pool. A small suitcase was sitting in the laundry room on top of the washing machine. Lucy's purse was on the kitchen counter.

Noah knew Lucy didn't put her gun in her purse—she wore it holstered—but he checked anyway; the gun wasn't there.

Nate met him back at the foyer and said, "Downstairs clear. Someone has been in the guest room and Sean's safe and computer have been tampered with. I don't know if they got in. I found Lucy's GLOCK on Sean's desk. With her badge."

Noah's heart skipped a beat. He pointed upstairs. Nate nodded and followed.

The upstairs was clear.

They went back downstairs and Noah pointed to the security panel next to the front door. "Do you know how to work that thing?"

"I only know the access code. Sean will have to walk me through it when he lands." He paused, then said, "Why are *you* here, Noah?"

"Eden Rogan," he said. His stomach fell. He wanted to believe that Lucy and Eden went out to dinner, *something,* but Lucy would never leave her service weapon out in the open. Or her badge. "You seem to know Sean and Lucy well. Does she normally leave her weapon in Sean's office?"

"No. She takes it whenever she leaves the house." Nate hesitated. "What do you know?"

"I know enough."

"I need to call Kane. Um, Sean asked me to. Unless this is a federal investigation . . ."

"Call him," Noah said. He couldn't consider right now where Nate Dunning's loyalties lay, with the FBI or with RCK. Later. When they knew that Lucy was okay. When they knew what the hell Eden Rogan was up to. "Tell him that we can't find Lucy or Eden. And Siobhan Walsh—she was here with Lucy."

"What's going on, Noah?" Nate asked.

"I have no idea. But I'll bet it has something to do with whatever Sean has been up to lately."

"Excuse me?"

"He's been out of town more often than here. Lucy has been preoccupied. *Something* is going on, and it's not just the wedding."

"Sean rejoined RCK," Nate said.

Noah hadn't known.

"And he's been using RCK resources to help locate the missing babies."

Shit! Nothing changed. Nothing.

"He should have told me."

"To be honest, I don't know that he trusts you anymore," Nate said bluntly.

That grated on Noah, not only that Sean didn't trust him—after everything they had done together, working undercover, Noah covering him on a whole host of things—but also that Nate seemed to know more about his own squad than he did.

Except he realized that wasn't it. Had Lucy said something about what happened between them on the human trafficking case? Except . . . *Nothing* happened between them. It had been a moment, on his part, and that was it. He knew Lucy loved Sean, and he would never do anything to hurt her.

Except . . . He'd had some choice words for Sean when he returned from Mexico. Sean wasn't an idiot. Sean heard what Noah hadn't said.

You're not good enough for Lucy.

Shit. Shit. Shit. Shit.

"Call Kane," Noah said, and stepped into another room. He looked at the special number Kane had given him and dialed. Rick answered immediately.

"Stockton."

"It's Noah Armstrong. Kane told me to call."

"What happened?"

"Eden Rogan is in San Antonio and I have good reason to believe she's taken Lucy."

"Where are the bonds?"

"What bonds?"

"They were in Sean's safe."

"Sean isn't here, he's on a plane doing god knows what. I'm in the dark, Rick, and I fucking don't like it."

"It's need to know. Now you need to know. Kane will fill you in, he's already on his way up there. Keep me in the loop."

"Why? I'm sure Kane Rogan can keep you in the fucking loop." Noah rubbed his eyes. Why was he yelling at his boss? This whole situation was fucked.

"I deserved that."

"I don't know who stands where anymore, sir," Noah said formally. "You. Me. I'm treading water and I don't like it."

"Noah, I trust you, and I told Kane as much. I understand your feelings on the matter, and all I can say is that I don't cross the line, but there's a lot of gray area. RCK plays in that gray area, and I trust Kane as much as I trust you. If Eden Rogan took Lucy, she has a reason. She's most likely going to leverage her for the bonds. We need to secure them and then track Lucy. Call me when you have more information." Rick hung up.

Noah almost threw his phone across the room, but that would do him no good.

CHAPTER FOURTEEN

"Why the *hell* can no one reach Sean?" Kane asked Dunning. He didn't raise his voice, but every cell in his body vibrated in anger. He had made good time driving from Laredo until he hit a wall of traffic outside San Antonio. He hated driving.

"A situation with Jesse. I don't want to say on the phone."

"Is the kid okay?"

"Yes. He's on his way back."

"ETA?"

"Lands in forty-five."

"I'm thirty minutes out." Kane hung up.

Eden and Liam had grabbed Lucy. Nate didn't know if they had the bonds because he couldn't get the safe open. But that's what they wanted, Kane was certain. They were holding Lucy either as ransom for the bonds or . . . why else would they take her? No reason *except* as ransom. Liam, for all his fucking-ass problems and disloyalties, wasn't a killer. At least, he hadn't been before Kane cut him out of RCK. He would lie, cheat, steal, and manipulate, but he wouldn't kill.

Kane was certain of it.

Almost.

But Liam would have been furious when he learned that Kane had stolen the bonds out from under him, and while he might not kill Lucy to make a point, he would want to hurt Kane. How did Lucy fit into that retribution? Because of Sean? Because Lucy was Jack's sister?

Nothing made sense, unless Liam and Eden hadn't been able to get into the safe. Kane had to count on that. He excelled in hostage rescue, and Lucy wasn't an ordinary hostage. She'd help her own cause.

Liam isn't an ordinary kidnapper.

Was Dante involved? He had to be. Dante and Liam had been best friends since they were kids. Dante's father had been Paul Rogan's closest friend. Why had Kane believed Dante and Liam had a falling-out?

Because Dante wanted you to believe it. Because you wanted to believe it.

Dante was the only one who could have told Liam about the bonds, and Liam's contact at RCK—whoever that bastard was—had given up Sean.

Kane *told* Sean not to invite Eden and Liam to the wedding, but he'd gotten all nostalgic and done it anyway. Because Sean didn't like anyone telling him what to do. Kane should have found another way to discourage his brother, but he was still bitter about what happened six years ago.

Sean didn't know the story behind the bonds. Kane never sugarcoated anything for his baby brother. But Sean had at one time been close to Eden and Liam. He could have too easily followed in their footsteps, and on more than one occasion Kane told Duke that if he continued to be so fucking hard on Sean he would rebel big-time. If someone with Sean's skill set went to work with Liam and Eden, no one would be able to stop them.

It was a fine line between the gray area and prison.

Or death.

Kane had wanted to preserve, at least to some degree, Sean's memories of Eden and Liam. Sean knew of course that they'd violated RCK rules and were cut off to pursue their own jobs. But Sean didn't know why Kane had been angry enough to essentially disown them. But now he would have to.

Under no scenario had Kane expected them to grab Lucy. It wasn't their MO. Lying to her? Yes. Tricking her? Sure, though she wouldn't be easy to trick. But . . . kidnapping her? That was low.

He called JT. This wasn't the kind of thing he could tell Jack on the phone, and no matter how secure the phone, he wasn't going to share details on a cell.

JT answered immediately. "What the hell is going on? Rick got a call from Armstrong. Did Eden kidnap Lucy?"

"I'm less than thirty minutes out. I'm still gathering intel."

"Is it true?"

"Dunning and Armstrong are on-site. Lucy's not there. Left her gun, badge, and purse."

"This is fucked, Kane."

"Someone needs to call Jack."

Silence.

"Dammit, JT, she's his sister."

"He's not reachable. Fort Bragg, deep cover, missing explosives. Jack's there with Duke."

"You have to reach him. If he finds out through anyone else, we're fucked."

"Where the hell's Sean?"

"Situation with Jesse. He's on his way back."

JT said, "Could Spade have set this up? I have a bad feeling . . ."

"No." Kane rarely relied on emotion or nostalgia, but this time no. "Liam and Eden are a problem, but they wouldn't turn Lucy over to be . . . an example." He couldn't say it. He loved Lucy as if she were his sister. More. She was the love of Sean's life, and if anything happened to her . . . "Look, I fucked up, okay? I didn't read Sean into the situation. And now Lucy is paying for it. I will contain this."

"This isn't all on you, Kane."

"They're my family."

"No. They're *our* family. I practically lived with you during high school. Your parents weren't perfect, but whose are? And whose parents would have let a kid like me with parents like mine move in, no questions asked? You're my brother, Kane, in every way that matters, which makes your family my family."

"Who is it?" Kane asked quietly.

"It's killing me that I don't know. I've handpicked every person who works for RCK. Who the fuck could have betrayed us like this?"

"Look beyond the obvious, J. Remember that Lucy's squad was infiltrated by the boyfriend of one of the squad members. Think outside of the damn fucking box. Think like Sean, because when he finds out that Lucy is gone I don't know that he's going to have his head on straight."

He hung up and realized that he needed to get his head on straight as well.

Lucy was missing.

So was Siobhan.

Kane swerved into a faster lane and sped up.

Gabriella quietly stepped outside to take a call from her brother.

"Yes," she said in French. Just in case anyone was listening.

"We're on our way."

"I can't leave."

"Gabriella, dear, this is our heritage. Everything we've been working toward for years."

"I'm trying to prevent war."

"That bad?"

"Worse than you can imagine. She's psychotic. And I do not use that word lightly." She looked around to make sure she was alone. "Dante, I'm serious here. It's bad and I'm going to call in the cavalry."

"Not who I think?"

"They created this problem, they need to clean it up."

"It's not a good idea."

"Why? You helped them!"

He didn't say anything. She knew her brother well enough to know that he was trying to find a way to lie to her.

"Goddammit, Dante, tell me the truth now."

"Lucy Kincaid overheard our plans and we had to bring her with us."

It took Gabriella ten seconds before she realized her worst fears had come to pass. "You . . . kidnapped . . . *Jack Kincaid*'s sister?" she hissed. "I don't fucking believe this."

"Language, darling."

"Don't fucking lecture me, Dante."

Jose stepped out of the house and put his hands around her waist from behind, kissed her neck.

"You're impossible." She hung up and prayed Jose hadn't heard anything else.

"What's wrong?" he asked, and kissed her again.

"Family."

"I have one of those. I understand."

He did, and he wouldn't ask questions. It's why her seduction of him last year had worked. He trusted her. She hadn't felt guilty about it until after she killed his evil brother Samuel. But she had to stick around; otherwise

Jose—who was trusting but not stupid—would know that she had used him.

The best con was when the mark didn't know they'd been conned.

She desperately wanted to call Jack Kincaid and tell him that Jasmine was on the warpath. But Jack would never trust her if he knew her brother had Lucy.

What have you done, Dante? Have you gone as crazy as Liam?

She loved her brother dearly, and Liam was his closest friend. She loved Liam as well, like a brother. But he had been obsessed for the last six years.

She knew something about obsession. While Liam was obsessed with finding the treasure his father had entrusted to him, Gabriella had been obsessed by revenge. Vengeance. Killing the man who had tortured and murdered the love of her life.

"You're still thinking, Gabriella." Jose kissed behind her ear. He was a kind lover, sweet and romantic. Sharing his bed hadn't been the worst con job she'd worked.

If anything happened to Lucy Kincaid, Sean Rogan would seek revenge. She knew exactly what it felt like. The anger. Rage. Soul-shattering grief.

Dante, you and Liam are fools.

"I love my brother, but sometimes I question his decisions."

"Can I help? We're spread thin, but I still have friends. Resources."

She turned to face him, took his face in her hands, and kissed him. "Jose, thank you for offering. But this time, Dante is going to have to solve his own problem."

And so would she. She couldn't very well ask Jack Kincaid for help when his sister was being used as a pawn.

CHAPTER FIFTEEN

Sean knew *nothing*.

Nothing, except that no one—*no one*—had spoken to Lucy since 2:35 that afternoon.

Six hours.

Sean felt nauseous. If anything happened to Lucy . . .

He drove faster.

Stop. Stop thinking that way. Eden won't hurt her.

But Sean didn't know his sister anymore. She'd manipulated her way into his house. Kane told him *nothing* on the phone except that Eden had taken Lucy and Siobhan and no one knew where they were.

"Get here, Sean—I can't make heads or tails out of your new security system."

And that was the point—that no one could get to them anymore, short of blowing up their house. He didn't want to worry about Lucy home alone when he wasn't around; he didn't want the sleepless nights to continue. He liked his house, but it was simply a place to protect those that he loved.

If the best home security that money could buy and Sean could enhance hadn't protected Lucy, he was right in telling Jesse to stay in witness protection. If he couldn't protect Lucy, a trained FBI agent, he certainly couldn't protect his twelve-year-old son.

He slammed on his brakes as soon as he pulled into his driveway, bypassed his security, and opened the front door.

Nate and Noah were sitting at the dining-room table, both of them on their phones; Kane jumped up as soon as Sean entered.

"What the fuck is going on?" Sean demanded.

"Calm down," Kane said.

"Don't." Sean's jaw was so tight he thought it would break.

"I need to know if they got the bonds."

"I don't give a *shit* about six million dollars. Lucy is *missing*."

"So is Siobhan. If they took Lucy and Siobhan in order to compel us to turn over the bonds, we need to know. You're early—we have time to plan. Check the damn safe."

Sean turned and walked down the hall to his office. Kane followed him; Noah and Nate wisely stayed back. Sean wanted to throttle his brother—it was Kane's idea that Sean keep the bonds here. Sean had thought, *Who cares? No big deal.* He had good security.

Obviously not. It was flawed. Security was only as strong as the weakest link . . .

He stared at his office. "Someone's gone through my desk," he said.

Kane looked at the uncluttered desk, the computer, the lack of garbage or disorder. But Sean knew. Lucy's picture had been moved.

Sean first sat at his computer. He booted it up, then ran through a security protocol. "Shit, she tried to hack into my computer. Why?" He ran through another log. "Disabled my warning system, but she wasn't able to get in. Still . . . I'm going to have to go through it with a fine-tooth comb." He typed in a security protocol that would run to ensure there were no viruses or trojans trying to attack his computer or extract information.

"The bonds, Sean."

"I know—but this is important, too. The home security system runs off this computer, if I want to see exactly what happened, I need to make sure I can see what *really* happened."

He stood and took the mural of the beach off the wall. It wasn't anchored properly. Eden had definitely found the safe.

He ran through a security protocol on the safe, to make sure that it wasn't rigged. He couldn't imagine that his own sister would try to kill him, but he also couldn't imagine that his own sister would kidnap Lucy. Yet Eden had been here and now Lucy was gone and unreachable.

"Someone definitely tried to hack their way into it . . . aw, shit."

Sean typed in his code, then put his hand on the security pad. Opened the safe. Inside was a phone and a folded piece of paper.

The folders with his most sensitive contracts and documents were still on the narrow top shelf behind a false wall—a double safe security measure—but the bag with the bonds that had been in the main compartment was gone.

He pulled out the phone and unfolded the paper.

> *Sean~*
> *Lucy and Siobhan are safe. Wait for my call. Don't trust Kane.*
>
> *~Liam*

Sean read and reread the note. "Why?" he said, his voice cracking. "Kane, what is happening?"

Kane took the note, read it, crumpled it in his fist. "You

never asked why I cut Liam and Eden out of Rogan-Caruso."

"Duke told me they took an off-book job for a small cartel."

"Yes. But there was more to it." Kane ran a hand over his face, then said, "Seven years ago, a small but powerful Russian criminal organization working out of the Yucatán was robbed by a local cartel. They lost millions in assets because they didn't know the territory or who to buy protection from. They hired Liam to retrieve two paintings that were worth a fortune. The Russians planned to sell the paintings to a wealthy Brazilian businessman who makes a habit of buying stolen art. I didn't know until after the fact. Liam was of course successful—he and Eden are damn good at what they do. But the money that the paintings brought was going specifically to human trafficking. There's a good reason why JT vets all our jobs—we don't always play with the good guys, but we don't contribute to the coffers of bastards who buy and sell human beings. I put Liam on notice: One more slip and I was cutting them out. Some things I can't turn my back on."

"And they slipped."

"They took another job from the same damn Russians the next year. This time, to retrieve bearer bonds that were being kept in the Russian embassy in Mexico City. I caught a whiff of the plan, and JT and I went in and extracted the bonds before Liam and Eden got there."

"And he knew you had them. But—"

"No, Liam didn't know I took them. Not until we brought the bonds to Guadalajara to use as leverage with the Flores cartel. I should never have asked you to keep them."

Sean was wholly confused. "You've had the bonds for six years and they didn't know?"

"It had to be Dante Romero."

"You said he and Liam had a falling-out."

"That's what they wanted me to believe. Liam's always been able to play the long game. Better than me."

"But how did they know *I* had the bonds here? This makes no sense!"

"There's a reason why no one else is here tonight," Kane said. "JT is investigating everyone at RCK. Someone on staff—someone inside or very close to someone inside—is the only way Liam could have known you had the bonds. Otherwise, Liam would have tried to get them out of RCK. He would have assumed I brought them back with me."

Sean sat heavily in his desk chair.

"Sean, you can trust me. Don't let Liam get into your head."

"He took Lucy. I sure as hell don't trust him!"

Sean's computer beeped, indicating the security scan was complete. Sean skimmed the logs. "Someone tried all morning to hack into my computer, failed. Except they disabled outgoing transmissions, so I wouldn't be informed that there was an on-site hack. Damn, I should have put in another fail-safe."

He typed again and brought up all security feeds. "I'm going to find out what happened today."

"I have something I need to explain."

Sean and Kane both turned and saw Noah in the doorway. He had lost his tie and jacket and his sleeves were rolled up. Sean didn't want him here. Noah had made it perfectly clear to him that he didn't think Sean was good enough for Lucy.

And sometimes Sean thought Noah might be right.

"Eden and I were involved more than six years ago. I found out she was a thief—she and Liam—when she lied to me. It's a long story, but I confronted her this morning. I'm sorry I didn't do something—put a car out front, sit on her, hell, I don't know, arrest her!"

"Did you know she was going to kidnap Lucy?" Sean demanded.

"Of course not! I thought—I don't know, that maybe she planned on stealing something in San Antonio."

"Armstrong called me," Kane said. "But I was too late."

Suddenly a whole bunch of things came clear to him. Eden and Noah. That's why Noah hated him when they first met two years ago. Probably still did. Sean didn't care anymore. He only cared about finding Lucy.

He logged in and ran through the security feeds. He didn't keep archives from inside the house—he didn't want cameras except on the doors, because it would creep Lucy out. He had hidden cameras, but only to watch live when they were activated. But he had all the entrances and exits recorded and archived.

Noah and Kane watched from over his shoulder. At seven fifty-five a.m. Eden approached the front door. Sean hadn't seen his sister in person in years. She'd aged, but she was still beautiful. Lucy let her in. Lucy left in her car forty minutes later.

The next person who arrived . . . *Noah.*

Sean whirled around and glared at the fed. "What happened?"

"I asked her why she was here. She didn't tell me anything. I threatened her, said I would call Kane. That seemed to get her attention, but she laughed it off. Like she always does. I should have—"

"Stop," Kane said. He turned to Sean. "I should have told you everything from the beginning. But it's a long story, and it goes back to before our parents died."

"Wait. I need to see this." Sean wanted to hear the truth, but he couldn't focus on the past when his entire future was missing.

He fast-forwarded the feed until Noah left twenty minutes later. Just after noon, Liam approached.

"Eden let Liam into the house," Sean said. "They disabled part of my security, but the external cameras are on a different system. Either they thought they disabled them or they didn't know."

The security system had gone on and off multiple times, and once around two Lucy had remotely disabled it. It was clear there was a pattern.

"Eden intentionally set off the alarm," Sean said.

"She wanted Lucy to come home," Kane said. "She didn't know if Noah followed through on his threat and called me, how much time they had. They wanted those bonds."

"Liam and Eden know about safes. But they couldn't have known Lucy's handprint would unlock it."

"Why not?" Noah asked. "She lives here, you're getting married."

"It was still a gamble."

"And it worked," Kane said. "Why does Lucy have full access?"

"Because we have no secrets," Sean said. He stared at his brother. "You wouldn't understand."

"I deserve that," Kane said. "But it could have backfired on them."

"They would have found another way," Sean said.

He fast-forwarded the security feeds and saw Lucy drive into the garage just before three. Siobhan was in the passenger seat.

Forty minutes later, Lucy's car left. Liam was driving. Eden was in the passenger seat. Neither Lucy nor Siobhan was visible. They could have been forced to lie down on the backseat, though it would have been cramped. Or in the trunk.

Lucy's car.

Sean started typing rapidly on the computer.

"You saw something," Kane said.

"Lucy's car has GPS. I disabled it so no one could track her, but I can reset it remotely with my own code. I can find her. Three minutes."

"They left at three-thirty," Noah said. "I got here just before four, Nate was right behind me. We barely missed them."

"You've been here for five hours and have no fucking leads on where they are?"

"I'm working my contacts, JT is working his angle, Rick is in the loop and has made all FBI resources available to us. But, Sean," Kane said, "we have to be careful who we inform of this situation. There are a lot of people out there who would love to get back at us right now, and that puts Lucy in danger."

"I cannot believe that someone at RCK betrayed us," Sean said.

"JT is—"

"Working on it!" Sean snapped. "I know! Everyone is working on it, but we still don't know where Lucy is."

The GPS program finished running and Sean zoomed in.

"Lucy's car is at Southfield. It's a private, unmanned airfield with no security to speak of. Dammit, where did they take her?"

Noah said, "I'll work on getting all flight records—"

"They're not going to file a fucking flight plan," Sean said.

"But they could have been picked up on radar, or by other planes. Don't forget I'm also a pilot and I still have friends in the Air Force."

Kane said, "Thanks, Armstrong."

Sean walked out. He didn't care if anyone followed him, but both Kane and Nate did. Sean pulled out of the driveway almost before Nate had his door closed.

"You've got to pull yourself together," Kane said. "They may not have taken her anywhere. It could be they left her car there to distract us—or that's where they had another car waiting."

Sean knew that. But he was so angry—with Kane, with Liam, with Eden, with everyone who had kept him in the dark.

"You should have told me the truth."

Kane didn't say anything for a long minute as Sean sped through the streets toward the airport on the outskirts of northern San Antonio.

"When JT and I started Rogan-Caruso, Liam and Eden were in college in England. I knew Liam wanted to be part of the business, but I told him no, we were only hiring former military. But after Mom and Dad were killed, I guess I thought we should make it a family business. JT was practically family. When I was hired for a hostage rescue in the former Soviet Union, I contacted them. They'd just graduated, and Eden is fluent in Russian. Liam had contacts. I used them for the job, discovered they had some admirable skill sets, and sent them for private security training. With Eden's grasp of languages coupled with Liam's planning ability, they were a huge benefit to Rogan-Caruso. But they both grew bored with what they called babysitting assignments. I knew but didn't care.

"A few years later—you were at MIT—they took an off-book job to retrieve a stolen painting. Stealing from thieves, Liam said. It paid extremely well, and JT opened the finances to me. My jobs—my causes, as JT calls them—don't pay as well, and Rogan-Caruso would have gone under if we didn't take some of these high-end corporate jobs. It worked well for a while. Liam and Eden kept Rogan-Caruso afloat, until Duke was able to grow the computer security end of the business. I don't think about the money—that's JT's job, and he's good at it. I didn't realize how dangerous some of Eden and Liam's assignments were, or who they were working for. They were in Europe—I worked mostly Mexico and Central America. But when they came into my territory . . . and I saw who they were working for . . . I had to put a stop to it."

"You should have told me," Sean said through clenched teeth.

"I was being nostalgic."

Sean shook his head. That was the last thing he expected Kane to say.

"Rogans have never done family well. Duke rode you hard, demanded perfection in all things. I disappeared for months at a time. Liam and Eden never wanted to come home, and when they did they treated you like a prince. You loved them . . . rightly or wrongly, and I didn't want to take away those memories."

"I can separate the past from the present."

"I didn't think they would ever do something like this."

"But you stole the bonds out from under their noses."

"If I didn't, the money would have gone to human traffickers."

"And you just let it sit."

"JT and I discussed it at great length, and we didn't know the origin of the bonds. We believe they were stolen from the Brazilian government by a cartel more than a decade ago—but they were never used. Why? Because it would alert authorities? We needed more information, and then out of sight, out of mind. We had other matters to attend to. The bonds became our emergency fund. Last month, we needed it."

Sean's head was spinning, but there was something

about these bonds that either Kane wasn't telling him . . . or Kane didn't know. Six million dollars was a lot of money . . . but Liam and Eden were thieves. If they needed $6 million they could get it in other ways. What was it about *these* bonds that was important?

If they were desperate for money, Sean could come up with it in a few days. He'd have to liquidate most of his stocks in the gaming company he'd helped start years ago, but he'd do it if his family was in trouble.

But they had taken Lucy. How could they be family if they stole from Sean the only thing he truly valued in the world?

"Sean—"

"I'm thinking."

"Liam wants you to doubt me. Divide and conquer."

"We'll talk about it later. After we find Lucy and Siobhan."

Three minutes later, they were at the airfield. Sean had considered housing his plane here when he first moved to San Antonio but didn't like the lack of security. The owner was absent and didn't seem to care much about who used his property—Sean had wondered if he let drug runners use the place. Sean wanted nothing to do with someone he couldn't trust.

The field was essentially a short runway that was marginally maintained, a small hangar that had seen better days, and an outbuilding. Lucy's car was parked between the hangar and the outbuilding. There didn't appear to be anyone here, and the sun had set thirty minutes ago. The light was fading fast.

Kane immediately took over, and though Sean was angry at him for keeping him in the dark for so long, he let him. Because this was Kane's world.

Kane motioned for Nate to stand guard, and then he and

Sean first approached the hangar. The door was unlocked. They went in cautiously, guns drawn.

Empty. There were no planes or people inside, no places to hide. But the smell told Sean that a plane had been here recently.

They next approached Lucy's vehicle. If Lucy had been locked inside all afternoon in the San Antonio heat, she'd be dehydrated and sick. Or dead.

Stop, Sean.

Sean had an extra set of keys and remotely popped Lucy's trunk. Kane shined a light inside.

All of Lucy's equipment that she was required to keep with her—her Kevlar vest, her extra ammunition, her riot gear—was shoved to the back of the trunk. Someone had been in the trunk, but they weren't here now.

"Hey! Is anyone out there?" Someone was pounding on the door of the outbuilding. "I'm locked in here! Let me out!"

Kane said, "Siobhan?"

"Kane? Oh, thank God you're here!"

There was a padlock on the door. Kane was going to shoot at it and Sean pushed him aside. He picked the lock in less than ten seconds and opened the door.

Siobhan stumbled out and into Kane's arms. Sean rushed inside, expecting to find Lucy.

The single room was empty. A gallon of water was in the corner, but nothing else.

He spun around. "Where's Lucy?" His voice vibrated with panic.

Siobhan had tears in her eyes. "They took her with them. In the plane."

Lucy was gone. Sean kicked the door and walked away.

Kane let him go. His brother needed to refocus, and

sometimes the only way to do that was a moment of solitude.

Besides, he needed to make sure Siobhan was really okay. He inspected her closely. "Are you hurt?"

She shook her head. "I'm fine. Really."

"Are you positive?" He looked in her eyes, searching for pain or lies.

"Yes." She hugged him, tightly. "I'm so sorry." She was shaking. Siobhan didn't scare easily. She wasn't a soldier or a cop, but she had always been brave. "I didn't know if anyone would find me. Liam said he'd call tomorrow and tell Sean where I was, but I didn't know if he was telling the truth."

"Did he hurt you?"

She shook her head against his chest.

Kane pushed her back, looked at her again closely. There was a bruise on her forehead. Her wrists were chafed. "He restrained you?"

"Handcuffs. He didn't hurt me."

Kane touched the bruise.

"I hit my head on the trunk of the car trying to get away."

Kane kissed the bruise, then kissed Siobhan's lips. He remembered the hospital, when she'd come to him, told him she loved him, kissed him. Kissed him with an intensity he still dreamed about.

He didn't want to stop with one kiss, but he did. Looked at her. The surprise in her eyes nearly undid him. "Kane," she whispered.

He pulled her back to him, kissed her again. Hard. Possessive. His head spun, but he knew for certain if he didn't figure it out he would explode. If figuring it out meant taking Siobhan to bed, he'd do it.

Once wouldn't be enough.

But the thought of never seeing her again—by his choice or someone else's—made him angry. She was the only good thing to come into his life in a long, long time. He wanted more.

"Later," he said.

She smiled, blinked back her tears. "Promise?"

He held her face and nodded. He kissed her again, then pulled himself away.

Kane's voice was rough around the edges when he spoke. "Lucy."

Her smile fell away. She looked around, worried. "Where's Sean? Is he okay?"

"He will be when we find her." He whistled. Sean and Nate approached from opposite directions.

"She's not here," Nate said.

"Where is she, Siobhan?" Sean was panicked, and that wasn't going to do any of them any good. That's why personal relationships rarely worked in their business. It's why Kane stayed away from women he could fall for.

He glanced at Siobhan.

Damn.

"Why are you here and not Lucy?" Sean continued. "Why'd they take her and not you?"

"I—"

"This makes no sense!"

"Sean!" Kane snapped. He turned to Siobhan. Calmly— because that's what this situation called for—he said, "Tell us exactly what happened. From the beginning."

She glanced at Sean, but Kane turned her to focus on him. Sean's fear and anger were just going to make Siobhan jumpy.

She said, "I was on the ride-along with Lucy, to Austin, with Agent Quiroz. Lucy felt guilty letting Eden stay at the house without Sean there, but she'd just shown up this morning. And then Eden kept setting off the alarm and calling Lucy to fix it. We hadn't had lunch, and Lucy wanted to check on Eden. It was late—after two thirty—and I told her I'd stay at the house with Eden so she could get back to work. She had a lead on the Morrisons—they have one of the babies we're looking for, Lucy and Ryan are pretty certain about it."

"The house, Siobhan," Kane redirected her attention to what was important.

"Sorry . . . I . . ." She cleared her throat. "It was nearly three I think by the time we got there. We went in through the garage, and I had to use the bathroom. I went down the back hall, to the guest room off the laundry—while Lucy went to find Eden. When I came out, I heard Lucy . . ." She hesitated.

"What?" Sean pushed.

Kane was close to benching Sean. If he could. He could, but it would hurt. Both of them.

"She said, 'Run!' I looked down the hall and saw a man. I didn't know who he was at first but then realized it was Liam. He, um, looks so much like you and Sean. Lucy collapsed. I think she was unconscious. He came down the hall, really fast—I tried to fight back. He apologized, promised he wasn't going to hurt me or Lucy."

"Why did he take her?" Sean demanded. "They have the fucking bonds!"

"They didn't talk much around me, but, um . . . from what I gathered, Lucy overheard something they don't want either of you to know. They promised they'd call tomorrow morning and tell you where we were."

"So you don't know anything? Any idea where they took her? Was she hurt?"

"Sean," Kane warned.

"Don't, Kane, just don't."

Tears rolled down Siobhan's cheeks and Kane wanted to

deck Sean for making her cry. "I'm so sorry, Sean. I don't think she's hurt, they—they had a, um, mist or something. Liam tried to spray it in my face, but I ducked. He said something . . . like 'she'll wake up in a couple of hours.'"

"I will kill him," Sean said through clenched teeth.

"We have to find him first," Kane said. "Sean, get in the car."

"This is your fault, Kane. You keep every fucking thing to yourself. You should have told me those bonds were dangerous. You should have warned me Liam might come after them. If anything—*anything*—happens to Lucy, I will never forgive you." He tossed Kane a set of keys. He caught them with one hand. Then Sean walked over to Lucy's car and got into the driver's seat. Nate glanced at Kane and he nodded. Nate ran over and jumped into the passenger seat before Sean peeled off the airfield.

"He doesn't mean that," Siobhan said.

Yes, Sean meant every word. Worse, Kane agreed with him.

"Don't do this to yourself, Kane. You couldn't have known."

"I should have." He hesitated. "Siobhan—"

"You kissed me this time."

He couldn't talk. She stepped closer to him.

He grabbed her wrist and pulled her against him. He kissed her hard. He was a hard man. He was violent and brutal with his enemies. He put everyone he cared about at risk, simply for being part of his world.

But he'd dreamed about Siobhan for years. And after he was injured in June, he couldn't stop thinking about her. He'd pushed her away, over and over, because of *this*. This lust, this almost desperate need for her. She was the light, the lightest of lights, a beacon shining for him. A reward he didn't deserve. A beauty he would destroy.

But still, he wanted.

Her breath caught in her throat. Her hands pressed against his chest and he still took her mouth with a firm intensity. His hands found her hair and he grabbed, held on, keeping her pressed against him.

He'd feared the worst. He didn't believe that Liam and Eden would hurt anyone, but he didn't know who they were working for or what the plan was or if they had changed. If the last six years of being out of RCK had turned them into something else.

And it would be his fault.

His fault, and still he wanted Siobhan. He didn't deserve her, or anyone.

But he was desperate for her light.

"Kane," she whispered. She turned her mouth from his, but he wanted more. He grabbed her mouth and turned it back to him, kissed her again. She was so soft. So strong. So . . . *everything*.

He walked her backward, toward the car, wanting to take her now, show her that he wasn't the man for her. Show this siren that he wasn't a good person. Her back hit the side of the car and she yelped.

He jumped back. He wasn't thinking. Hell, what the *fuck* was he doing?

"Kane—"

"Get in the car."

"Don't order me around."

"I'm not doing this."

"I know *exactly* what you're doing." She stepped toward him. It took all his willpower not to run away from her.

Or take her to the ground and make love to her.

He ran a hand over his face. "Please," he whispered.

"You're not going to scare me off, Kane Rogan. I know you. I've known you since I was a teenager. I've loved you half my life. You are impossible, you can be a bully, you are more stubborn than anyone I've met in my *life*—"

"That's the pot calling the kettle black," he muttered.

"—but you're a hero. You're loyal. Dedicated. You have more compassion than you would ever admit to anyone."

"I don't have compassion."

She laughed. She *laughed* at him. "Oh, Kane. Don't even start with me. I *know* you. You can try to scare me or intimidate me, but it's an act. Because I see the real you. I always have. And *that* is what truly terrifies you." She walked around to the passenger side of the car, opened the door, and looked at him over the top. "We'd better get back to Sean's house. I'm worried about him, and you need to talk to him."

"He doesn't want to hear anything right now."

"So make him listen."

CHAPTER SIXTEEN

Lucy had the odd sensation of floating, as if on a raft in water. A soft up and down, ripples in a lake, lightly splashing water on the sides of a metal boat.

Then she jolted into full consciousness, the memories of being restrained in the hull of a small boat flooding her. She reached out, almost expecting her hands to be bound, her mouth to be gagged.

They weren't. She opened her eyes. Everything was still blurry, unfocused. She saw light and dark, but that was it. Her arm hurt and she rubbed it. She blinked a few times, but her vision stayed cloudy. Did she have a concussion? Her head hurt, but she didn't feel any lumps or specific points of pain.

Her breathing was too fast, her heart still pounding, and she recognized the signs of panic. She hadn't had a panic attack in months—in nearly a year. But the fringes were there, and if she had been restrained she didn't know if she'd be able to control it. She breathed in and out, slowly, deeply, forcing her heart to slow down. Methodically. In. Out.

Focus, Lucy.

She put her head between her knees and squeezed her eyes closed. Every limb felt stiff, unused. How long had she been unconscious? She was on a couch, she thought, a soft and comfortable cushion, at any rate, that didn't feel like a bed. She thought back to what had happened earlier . . . she'd caught Eden at Sean's desk. She'd been talking to someone on the phone . . . Lucy couldn't remember exactly what Eden said, but it was about Sean. And bonds.

Tampico. What was Tampico? A person? A place? Lucy couldn't remember the conversation verbatim, but she knew it would come to her.

She'd told Eden to leave the office, but she hadn't wanted to turn her back on her. She didn't really know or understand what Eden was doing, and until she could talk to Sean she didn't want to leave her alone.

Dammit, Lucy, why did you let her into the house at all?

Sean had security, but looking back, this had a Trojan horse feel. Eden *wanted* to be left alone. Had she been able to break into his computer? Or was she looking for something? Why?

Why keep setting off the alarm and calling Lucy? Why had Eden wanted her to come home?

It had that feeling of a setup.

"No, Lucy, don't come home for me. I'll manage . . ."

Yes, definitely felt like a plot. Now, at any rate. Why couldn't she see it before?

You didn't want to.

What happened after Eden hung up the phone? She had tried to explain herself . . . Lucy sensed something was wrong, didn't want to turn her back to Eden. But Lucy had sensed something . . . someone. Reached for her gun. A cold mist hit her face. She heard Siobhan calling for her . . .

Run, Siobhan!

The spray again, then something in her arm. A prick. Nothing.

She didn't remember anything. No dreams, no sounds,

nothing. Not being transported, taken here—wherever *here* was. What had they done with Siobhan?

"Siobhan?"

No answer. Where had they taken her friend?

Lucy listened carefully. She didn't hear any breathing. Didn't sense anyone in the room, anyone watching her. Her vision was still clouded. Only light and dark. Whatever they'd drugged her with had taken away her sight. Was that even possible?

Of course it's possible because you can't see anything!

Panic clawed inside her. She didn't know where she was, why Eden and whoever she was working with had drugged her, what they wanted. It was quiet. The smells were unfamiliar. She wasn't home. She wasn't home and no one knew where she was.

Snap out of it!

Action. She needed to act. Her vision would return. It *had* to. *Right?* Already she thought she saw more. Not just light and dark but fuzzy images.

She willed herself to get up. Her entire body was shaking out of heightened fear. She patted down her body; her gun wasn't on her. She reached for her ankle; they'd removed her ankle holster and the gun that had been in it. No phone. No gun.

And no eyesight.

She put her hand on the couch to steady herself. She was still shaking. It took her several minutes before she could control her fear and move.

She closed her eyes, tried to sense something about the room. She was alone. Though with her heart pounding in her ears she might not be able to hear anyone else.

But you'd know. You know when people are watching you.

A curse, perhaps, after she'd been kidnapped and raped in front of an audience eight years ago. But her sixth sense, the overwhelming sensation of being *watched,* had saved her many times over the years. And she certainly didn't rely on her sight for that.

With her left hand on the edge of the couch, she reached out with her right hand. Moved it back and forth in front of her. Not being able to see her hand was unnerving. It was a blur in front of her. She could *sort of* make it out, but it was fuzzy, a blob. She saw a dark object in front of her, but she couldn't touch it.

Let go of the couch.

No. The couch was her anchor. She couldn't see where she was walking, how could she know that there wasn't something dangerous in front of her?

Let go. You have to let go.

Shaking, she pulled her left arm away from the couch and took one step forward, now both arms in front of her. She moved them back and forth and felt nothing. She had an overwhelming sensation of vertigo and stumbled forward, her knee crashing into a table before her hands landed on it. She fell forward, but the table—like a dining-room table—stopped her from hitting the floor. She stayed prone for a moment, catching her breath.

Okay. Good, Lucy. Now get up.

Using the table as a guide, she pulled herself up. She kept her right hand on the table and shuffled slowly forward, until she reached the corner. She turned the corner and walked, her left arm sweeping in front of her . . .

It hit something hard. Then next to her something heavy and breakable crashed to the floor. Shattered.

Good job, Kincaid. Now they know you're awake.

If they were going to hurt her, they would have done it already. Why would they? Eden was Sean's sister! They might have been estranged, but what reason would she and Liam have to kidnap Lucy?

Liam. Eden was talking to Liam. He was in her house.

*He'd been the one to drug her. Had Siobhan gotten away?
Was she hurt? Worse?*

Eden and Liam had kidnapped her from her own home.
Drugged her. Taken her eyesight . . .

It's temporary. It has to be temporary . . .

She was still fully dressed in the same clothes she'd
worn to work that day. Her shoes were still on her feet, so
she carefully walked over the broken glass, heard it crunch
beneath her low-heeled ankle boots.

*How far do you think you're going to get without being
able to see?*

Her hand skimmed a wall and she breathed a sigh of
relief. It was stucco, lumpy, but not sharp. Like the outside of a house. *Odd.* She was certainly not outside. She
walked forward and her knee connected with a low-lying
piece of furniture.

"Shit!"

She bit her lip. Well, what did she think, that her yelp
would attract attention more than the glass she'd broken?

She bent over, saw faintly that there was a waist-high
shelf of sorts. She reached down, walked around it, noticed
a darker blob against the white walls.

A door.

Three quick steps and she was there. Solid wood.
Carved. She scrambled for the knob. Turned it.

It didn't budge.

She fought with it, but the door wasn't moving.

She pounded on the wood. It was a solid, thick door,
but she pounded and shouted, "Eden Rogan! Damn you,
Eden, open this door."

Nothing. No response. Silence.

Silence.

Lucy had no idea how late or early it was. How long
she'd been out. She had an empty stomach and a full blad-
der. Hours? At least hours. She and Siobhan had arrived

at her house just before three. If she didn't get back to the office by three thirty, four at the latest, someone would have called her. If she didn't answer, someone would have come to the house, right? She'd left a message for Kane to call her . . . If she wasn't reachable, would he know something was wrong?

Too many what-ifs . . . But the last thing she wanted was for Sean to come home late and find her missing.

Focus on what you can control, Lucia.

You knew you were in a bad way when you called yourself by your full name. Only her mother called her Lucia, and it wasn't a name Lucy generally liked. It reminded her of getting into trouble—coming home late, being caught by her dad kissing her boyfriend on the front porch when she was sixteen. Reminded her of her youth, which seemed so long ago.

She listened. If she could figure out where she was, she might come up with an escape plan. There was no traffic. No sounds of cars, planes, trains. No voices. Either she was alone or the house she was in was huge. *House? Yes, a house.* A large house in the middle of nowhere. The lack of sound was fearsome—she didn't know why.

She pounded on the door again and screamed.

"Eden! Liam! I know you're here! Open this door, dammit!"

"She's awake," Dante said. He stared from Eden to Liam. "I cannot believe that you kidnapped a US federal agent— one who is a Rogan, no less."

"She's not a Rogan yet," Eden snapped.

She didn't know why she was still so upset about Sean marrying a Kincaid.

"A Kincaid is even worse. Jack helped Gabriella with her situation last month, she feels like she owes him something."

"So don't tell her," Eden snapped. "Lucy overheard my conversation with you. Didn't you specifically say that Kane can't know where we're going because he'll figure it out?"

"Point taken, but there were other options."

Liam said, "Dante, let's go now."

"We can't leave until dawn. You're not stupid, Liam. We're in dangerous territory. We leave here at six. We exchange the bonds for the other half of the map. That was the deal, and it will save all of our lives."

"Our lives wouldn't have been at risk if Kane hadn't betrayed us in the first place," Liam said.

Eden stared at the single bearer bond in front of her. They couldn't see the map now, but under the black light it showed the location of tens of millions of dollars in gold. Gold that, two centuries ago, was on its way to San Antonio before the Alamo fell. Gold that Dante's ancestors had believed was cursed.

She'd painstakingly copied the map when it had been under the black light, but this one note among the stack of six hundred ten-thousand-dollar bonds in front of her had ruined their lives. Maybe Dante's ancestors were right, the treasure was cursed. Because she had lost everything. She'd lost her parents, who were obsessed with this treasure. She'd lost Noah, the one man she truly believed she could love forever. And now she'd kidnapped the love of her brother's life. Sean would never forgive her.

"Sis?" Liam tugged her hair like he used to do when they were kids. "Don't go there."

"You don't know what I'm thinking."

He raised an eyebrow. "I'm your twin. I know everything about you."

She snorted.

"You're thinking, right now, that we're cursed. That we've lost too much pursuing this treasure. But this is more than the gold. It's history. What was hidden two hundred years ago is as much to do with wealth as it is to do with the history of our country, of Mexico, of our families. Dad was looking for this treasure for years . . . and we found it."

"And Mom and Dad are *dead*."

"Not because of the treasure. It was an accident."

"We don't know that, do we?"

"Eden, sweetheart, everything is going to work out."

She slammed her fist on the table. "You always say that! But this time . . . I don't know anymore."

"What do you suggest? Tell Kane why we really were after the bonds in the first place? Remember what he said after Mom and Dad were killed? When I wanted to continue their search?"

Eden nodded. She would never forget.

"Mom and Dad could never grow up and accept that the gold didn't exist. They wasted their lives pursuing a myth instead of focusing on what was important."

Kane would never understand.

Dante said, "Kane hasn't changed. Remember, I've seen him more recently than you—if anything, he's more driven and more volatile than ever."

"But this was between us and Kane," Eden said. "And now we've brought in Sean and his girlfriend. I don't want anyone to get hurt."

"Neither do I," Liam said.

Liam had always been a pacifist at heart, but he often turned his back on the truth. He liked to think that he was more noble than Kane because he'd never taken a human life, but how often had he done a job and turned his back on what most assuredly would be an assassination? Like when she and Liam traced insurance fraud in Russia after the fall of the Soviet Union back to the wife of one of the mid-level bureaucrats—they'd both been arrested and were either in prison or dead. Or when Liam seduced the wife of a duke—at the request of her husband—just to see if she would be faithful. She wasn't, and Eden hadn't heard from or seen her again.

Still, Liam was always hands-off. He wouldn't hurt anyone himself. Eden didn't believe that he would allow Lucy to be hurt, either.

"What do we do with Ms. Kincaid?" Dante asked. "And before you suggest it, we're not bringing her with us. She'll draw undue attention."

"Agreed," Liam said. "Eden?"

"How safe is this house?" she asked Dante.

"Safeish."

"Can Gabriella come? Keep an eye on her?"

Dante shook his head. "She can't leave right now."

"This is important!" Liam said.

"Brother," Dante said calmly, "to you and me, this is everything we have dreamed about our entire lives. But when Gabriella lost her fiancé, this quest just wasn't as important to her. It's just the three of us now. When we get the final piece of the map in the morning, we'll be hours away from doing what our parents were never able to do."

"I don't know that I feel comfortable leaving Lucy alone here," Eden said. "I can explain to Gabriella. Surely *this* is more important. We're family."

"It's complicated."

"I don't want to know," Liam said. "Sometimes, you're as bad as Kane."

"Let's put it this way," Dante said, sipping his Scotch. "I see the value of both Kane's approach and your approach. In this case, the man Gabriella killed deserved to be murdered ten times over. He was a filthy human being and I would have gladly pulled the trigger. Some people do not deserve to breathe air on our planet." He hesitated, thinking.

"What?" Eden asked. "What's wrong?"

"I'm not worried about Gabriella, but she does have a sense of loyalty to the Kincaids."

"This just gets better and better," she mumbled. She put her head in her hands and willed her growing headache to go away.

"Idea," Dante said.

"Anything," Liam said.

"How long does that mist last?"

"She'll have her eyesight back anytime." Liam looked at his watch. "It's been about seven hours. Maximum time I've seen is nine hours. I've only had to use it twice before."

"When we leave, we mist her again. That gives us at least eight hours' head start. She won't leave the house if she can't see, right? We'll convince her that she's safer here."

"I don't understand," Eden said.

"I get it," Liam said. "We'll tell her we're in the middle of nowhere and she'll get lost and die in the jungle if she leaves. But if she stays put, once we're in the clear I'll tell Sean where she is."

"Exactly. If the timing works, he'll be here before she can see again and take her away. We'll be deep into the ruins by then."

"I don't like it," Eden said. She sighed and rubbed her temples again. "But I don't have a better idea."

"Tomorrow I'll call Sean and explain to him what's going to happen. He follows my directives, he'll be with Lucy in twenty-four hours."

Dante laughed again.

"What?" Liam snapped, growing irritated. Eden had already grown past irritated with their old friend.

"You haven't seen Sean in a while, have you?"

"What does that mean?"

"You remember him as the handsome nerd genius kid who likes his toys."

"He does," Eden said. "All his electronics are state of the art, and most of his investments are in gaming companies. He's a little boy at heart."

"Not so much anymore," Dante said. "I saw him last month. He's more like Kane than you realize."

"Sean never went military. He hates authority, doesn't take orders from people," Liam said.

"That may be the case," Dante said, "but do not underestimate him or expect him to do what you want. You grabbed his fiancée. I saw what he did to save his son—a kid he didn't even know—I can only imagine what lengths he'll go to to find Lucy Kincaid, and how far he will go to punish those who took her."

"Son?" Eden could not have been more surprised.

"Well, I have a story for you, don't I?" Dante smiled. "I'll explain during our drive tomorrow." Dante drained his Scotch. Eden noticed then that he was tired, small wrinkles had formed around his eyes. They were all getting older, weary, and even though they were on the cusp of victory, there were too many variables they couldn't control.

Dante continued, "Liam, you are a smart man, but so are your brothers. They are going to realize that I am the only one who knew they had the bonds. I've burned that bridge for you, dear friend. I would do it again. But I will not take a bullet from either of them."

"Sean is a tech guy," Eden said. "Security. It's Kane we need to worry about."

"Do you even know your little brother? You said that to me before; I don't believe it. Baby Rogan is a younger Kane."

Liam laughed. "Sean is not Kane. It had to be Kane and JT who stole the bonds and then Kane left me to suffer the consequences."

"You should have told him—"

"I did! He knew what was at stake. He thinks he's noble, never-align-himself-with-a-drug-runner? Well, there are worse people in the world. We could have—"

"Preaching to the choir, friend," Dante said.

Lucy pounded on the door again.

"I'll explain the situation to her," Eden said.

Liam stopped her. "Let her stew a bit longer, then we'll go up. She's feisty." He grinned. "Maybe that's why Sean fell in love with her."

CHAPTER SEVENTEEN

As soon as Sean got back to his house, he went upstairs to grab his go-bag. He didn't particularly like that Noah Armstrong followed him.

"I have a lead on the plane."

"Call me when you know for certain."

"Where are you going?"

"None of your business."

"It *is* my business. Lucy is my agent, and my friend."

Friend. Right. Noah would love for Sean to fuck up.

"So are you," Noah added.

"Stop." Sean turned and pushed Noah against the wall. "I don't need you in my head, Armstrong."

"You're too smart for this shit, Sean. You have no idea where they've gone, you're grasping at straws, and when we need you here you won't be."

"I have a damn good idea where they went, and I'm not going to sit on my ass waiting for confirmation."

Sean brushed past Noah and ran down the stairs.

Noah pursued Sean to the foyer. "I'm coming with you."

"No!" Sean whirled around. "Just no."

"Don't be an idiot! You can't do this alone. Whatever plan you think you have, you need backup."

"You can't come. You're a federal agent."

Noah stared at him, confused, and Sean didn't have time to explain.

"Dante Romero," Sean said. "He knows what the fuck is going on and he will tell me exactly where Liam and Eden are."

Noah pulled out his phone, which was ringing. "Sean, take this call."

"Stop messing with me, Noah. I have to do something!" Sean would explode if he sat here doing *nothing*. He had to act, search, hunt . . . whatever it took to get answers and find Lucy.

Noah pressed SPEAKER. "Agent Donovan, you're on speaker with Sean and me."

"Kate?" Sean asked, surprised.

"Uh, yeah, I have something."

Sean stared at Noah, his turn to be confused. Noah said, "I called Kate when I first heard Eden was in town. Then, after you went to find Lucy's car, I had to tell her what's going on. We need all resources at our disposal, Sean."

"Where are they?" Sean asked Lucy's sister-in-law.

"I'm working on that, but I have some information. Don't know where it fits yet. Eden came to the US under another name—Sheila Benton. It's a very, very good identity—she's been using it for years."

Sean stared at the phone. "That's our mother's maiden name."

"She came into the US via JFK last night, flew first thing this morning to San Antonio, landed at six forty-five, and, based on time, distance, and traffic, likely took a taxi directly to your house, Sean. I have calls out to taxi services, see if she made any other stops. Doubtful. Noah said she arrived just before eight this morning.

"Liam Rogan," Kate continued, "flew under his own passport to General Mariano Escobedo International in Monterrey, direct from Heathrow."

"Monterrey?"

"I have friends in Mexico and with Interpol. He's on their non-terror watch list, but there's no travel restrictions on his passport."

"Are there restrictions on Eden's?"

"No restrictions on either, but if they fly into the US or any US territory the FBI is supposed to be notified."

"But if he flies into Mexico no one knows. Monterrey is only an hour from the border. When did he land?"

"Early this morning, before Eden landed."

"But it would still take him time to fly into San Antonio," Noah said. "According to Sean's security, he arrived here just after twelve noon. Used a small private airport twenty minutes outside of the city."

"I can run some scenarios, but—"

Sean interrupted. "He flew in using a small plane. Liam is a pilot, just like Kane and me. He flew in, under the radar—literally and figuratively. I'll bet Rick Stockton put that watch on his passport." Sean became angry again at Kane and Rick and JT. If he had known that Eden and Liam wanted those bonds, he could have warned Lucy. He would have done something else with them. But either way, she would have been safe.

Kate said, "I have something else. I don't know what it means, but it might help you figure out what they're up to. When Noah told me that Dante Romero might be involved with this, I called in a favor. Remember, Sean—I lived completely off the grid in Mexico for five years. I made some friends. Romero closed up his house in Guadalajara three days ago. No one knows where he is, he didn't take any of his staff except for a bodyguard he trusts named Philip Corsica. I've run Corsica, but he seems to be a ghost. He's an American citizen—I think. He may be an ex-patriot. I have some feelers out, but your brother probably knows who he is."

Sean had never heard of Corsica before.

"I'm running Romero as well. He was born in Spain on an American military base. I don't have his father's name, but his father was likely a soldier."

"Dante's father and my dad were friends, long before I was born. But none of this tells me where Lucy is."

"Not yet, but I'm running everything I have, Sean. Romero's property records. Corsica's property records. Banking information. When I find something, I'll tell you. Property records are going to be difficult, but for banking I can cut some corners."

"Kate—" Noah began.

"Lucy is my sister," Kate snapped. "Don't quote the law to me. If I couldn't do this, I would be on the next plane out there. But this *is* something I can do, and dammit, I'm going to do it. I'll call you as soon as I have something. Oh—and I asked Interpol to send me the files on both Liam and Eden. As soon as I get them, they're yours." She hung up.

Sean dropped his go-bag and stood there, uncertain what to do next. He had fully intended to go to Guadalajara and confront Dante Romero. But if Kate was right—and there was no reason she wouldn't be—he wasn't there. If he wasn't there, where was he? Where had they taken Lucy, and why?

Kane walked in with Siobhan. Sean said, "Who is Philip Corsica? How does Dante Romero know him?"

"Corsica is Romero's friend and bodyguard," Kane said. "I've only met him a couple of times. Keeps to himself."

"And Romero's parents? You told me last month Dante was an old family friend, through our fathers."

"Why?"

"Can you just answer the question? Kate might have found something, but if you don't come clean she won't be able to help us!"

Kane didn't say anything for a moment. "Carlo Romero was Dad's best friend. We called him Uncle Carlo."

Sean vaguely remembered a short, trim man with a mustache and good sense of humor. He had a hearty laugh, and when he came over Sean's father would stay up late at night talking and drinking Scotch.

"Carlo and Dad were in the service together. If I remember correctly, Philip was a teenager when his father was killed in action. He was a couple of years older than Dante, but Carlo took him in, gave him a home base. That's probably why Dante trusts him."

"Where is Carlo? Could Liam be there?"

"He lives in New Orleans."

"You can reach him."

"I can try—but that might not be the smart thing."

"I'm floundering here, Kane." Sean meant to sound forceful, but he sounded as desperate as he felt.

"I have an idea, but you need to give me some time."

"Lucy doesn't have time!"

"Listen to me, Sean. We don't know where they are. We assume they went to Mexico, but we don't know. Mexico is a big fucking country. They won't hurt Lucy, but"— Kane put his hand up when Sean was going to yell at him—"I know, just like you do, if they took her to Mexico she's in danger. I don't think they realize how much danger she could be in. I'm going to talk to Carlo. It'll take me two hours to get to New Orleans, but he *will* talk to me. Carlo and Dante used to be close—but I don't know anymore. I haven't spoken to Carlo in more than six years, and the first time I'd seen Dante in ages was last month."

"But you're going to try!"

"I said I would. Carlo may know something—he might not even know what he knows is important."

"I'm coming."

"You need to be here ready to go in case I get information." He glanced at Sean's go-bag that sat at his feet. "Follow the money, find the plane, find their destination. I'll get something out of Carlo, and between the two of us we'll find Lucy and bring her home."

"Then why are you still here?"

Siobhan had been standing behind Kane the entire time. Now she walked over to Sean and hugged him tightly. She didn't say anything, and Sean was grateful. Any false platitudes would have made him explode. But he accepted her hug.

She turned to Kane. "I'm going with you."

Kane caught Sean's eye. "Take her," Sean said. "Siobhan, if you remember anything, please—"

"Of course. I wish I'd heard more. I—"

Sean said, "I'm sorry I yelled at you."

She put her hand on his arm. "No apologies."

Noah cleared his throat and they all looked at him. "We have to tell the FBI."

"No," Sean and Kane said simultaneously.

Kane said, "Armstrong, I get it, you're stuck here. But if they took Lucy to Mexico, we cannot let anyone know she's down there."

"We have resources. She may not be there at all, and—"

"But *if* she is—and I think that's where Liam and Eden went—then if the FBI puts out a bulletin our enemies are going to hear about it. Right now, we can contain this, but if we're battling the rest of the Flores cartel trying to find her first it puts Lucy at greater risk."

"I can't keep this information from my boss."

"Your boss is Rick Stockton."

"Yes."

"He already knows. Call him."

"And what do I say tomorrow morning when Lucy doesn't show up for work? That she's home sick? Eden and Liam need to pay for what they've done. They need to be arrested for kidnapping and threatening a federal agent and whatever else they're doing. By taking Lucy out of the country against her will, they've broken more laws than I can count."

"Of course they need to be held accountable," Kane said, "but getting Lucy or them killed isn't an option. I can't stop you from talking, but call Rick first."

Noah walked out of the room and Kane turned to Sean. "What?"

"I'm calling Jack," Sean said.

"I told you, he's undercover at Fort Bragg. JT is trying to reach him."

"He knows these people—he knows Gabriella Romero."

"Gabriella is still in deep with the Flores cartel. She's the only reason we know that Jasmine Flores survived last month. She's the reason we have confirmed that three of the four Flores brothers are dead. If she steps out of line, her cover is blown and they will kill her."

"But she knows where her brother is. I'm certain of it."

Kane didn't say anything for a moment. "Maybe. But you can't go down there, Sean. It's suicide. Why do you think I've been living in Texas? We have to let this settle down, or they'll come after us."

"Lucy could be down there."

"They don't know her. They know your face, they know mine, they know Jack's. But Lucy is just a name to them. And she's smart enough to know that, if things go south." Kane hesitated, then said, "I've already asked JT to find a way to get to Jack. Jack's the only one who knows how to contact Gabriella."

There was nothing else to do. Sean didn't know how he was going to sit here and do *nothing*.

"Do what you do best, Sean. Dig into Liam's and Eden's lives. I know some of what they've been up to, but not enough. Feed me information, maybe you'll find the answers before I land in New Orleans." Kane clapped his hand on Sean's back. "We are going to find them. Lucy's smart and strong and resourceful and I love her. I will not let anything happen to her."

When Kane's voice cracked, Sean realized how much his brother kept inside. He was a warrior, a soldier, but he never shared much of anything about himself. Sean had never once heard Kane say *I love* to anyone or about anyone. He wasn't in this alone.

Sean couldn't speak. He didn't have to. Kane squeezed his shoulder, turned around, and left with Siobhan.

Sean stood there, in the middle of the foyer, and had no idea what he could do next. Kate was tracking the finances. Kane would meet with Dante's father. Noah was tracing the plane and figuring out what to tell the FBI. All Sean could do was think about Lucy, unconscious, not knowing what was going to happen to her . . . or why.

But she *was* smart, resourceful, strong.

Eden and Liam would absolutely pay for putting Sean and Lucy through this.

He dug into his pocket and pulled out the phone Liam had left him. He'd already checked for messages and numbers; it was a clean burner phone.

But he might be able to trace it—where it was bought, when, with what other phones.

He had to do *something,* because sitting around and waiting was never an option.

Noah went outside by the pool and called Rick Stockton. It was nearly two in the morning in DC, but he had Rick's personal number, the one he always answered. And he picked up after a lone ring.

"Stockton."

"It's Agent Armstrong. You've heard."

"Yes. JT Caruso and I have been in constant communication."

"The Rogans don't want me reporting this to the office."

"Correct."

"Lucy is in danger. I don't care that Kane doesn't *think* that his brother and sister are going to hurt her, they took her—and my gut tells me they took her out of the country."

"JT concurs."

"That puts her in danger not only because she's a Kincaid but also because she's a federal agent!"

"There is nothing the FBI can do to rescue Lucy south of the border. I'll call your SAC in the morning and fill him in on the situation. I also have a SEAL team getting ready. They'll be prepared to deploy by oh-nine-hundred tomorrow. JT told me that Liam left a note for Sean."

"He promised to call in the morning and tell him where Lucy is."

Noah wasn't surprised that Rick had a SEAL team at his disposal. Not only was he the assistant director of the FBI, but he also was a former SEAL himself. What bothered Noah was that this operation was off-book. Rick's alliance with RCK had pre-dated Noah's employment with the FBI, but he knew they were very close. Noah had had many run-ins with private military operations during his time in the Air Force. Some encounters were good, some were definitely hostile. And while Noah wouldn't flat-out say he opposed private military groups, he was cautious and suspicious. He didn't know, if push came to shove, where Rick would fall if RCK crossed the line.

If? They already have, multiple times. How far are you

*going to move the line, Noah? You used to believe in
order, in right and wrong, in the system.*

He still did. But he also believed in people like Rick
Stockton. Noah didn't like being put in this position.

But ultimately, if Lucy needed his help, even though
it was against procedure and protocols, he would go to
Mexico and help save her.

"Noah, I know this situation puts you in a difficult spot,"
Rick said.

"What do you think you know?"

"I knew that you were involved with Eden years ago."

"How the hell? Sean didn't know." Noah hadn't thought
Kane did, either, until he told him, but maybe Kane was
just keeping his mouth shut.

"I did a complete and thorough background check on
you before I recruited you into the FBI. More thorough and
more complete than the FBI normally does."

"What?"

"I didn't use RCK. When you filed your retirement
papers years before you should have retired, I wanted to
know why. Because I planned on bringing you into the FBI
before you even knew you were applying."

"Why do I suddenly feel that my life and decisions are
not my own?"

"There are very few people I can trust in the position
that I've put you in. I've had you work some of the most
sensitive cases in the Bureau—where any leak could mean
embarrassment or danger. The situation in San Antonio
after Agent Dunbar was killed? If the public got wind that
the FBI had a leak that resulted in the deaths of law enforcement officers in three different agencies, we would
have a huge problem. What I've had you do was not easy,
but it was necessary. Just like now. If it gets out that Lucy is
in Mexico, it would be dangerous for her—and potentially
damaging to the FBI. I have to look at both. We need to

locate and extract her as quietly as possible. I know Kate Donovan is working on it, and there are few people better than she is."

"I apologize for not asking you first about using Donovan."

"No apologies—she didn't tell me until I asked. As soon as I got off the phone with JT earlier I called to read her in and she told me she was already working on it." He paused. "Noah, don't you trust me?"

Noah didn't know what to say to that. Of course he trusted his boss . . . but he didn't understand what Rick meant.

"Sir, I should have called you this morning when I first saw Eden."

"Why?"

"I know she's a thief. I suspected she was up to something—when Sean and I were undercover together last year, he told me he hadn't seen Liam and Eden in years."

"But you had no proof that she had committed a crime or was about to commit a crime, there was nothing you could have done."

"I could have sat on her," Noah mumbled.

"No Monday morning quarterbacking. I need to know if we have a problem."

"No, sir."

"But."

"We'll discuss it when Lucy is safe."

"Fair enough."

What was he supposed to say? That he thought his boss violated the law every time he worked with RCK? That he didn't know if he could look the other way at times . . . but sometimes he had no problem? How did he define when and where? How could he be an effective agent if he bent the rules so often? What if he was forced to break them?

No one can force you to do anything you don't want to do, Armstrong. Remember that.

Maybe that was the problem. The rules and laws he believed in sometimes were wrong. But who was he to judge the right and wrong of the law? He was to enforce it, let the system correct itself when necessary.

Unfortunately, the system wasn't perfect.

And anarchy is?

"I gave JT your direct contact information," Rick continued. "You met him last month, correct?"

"Briefly."

"If he can't reach Kane, he's going to contact you."

"He should call Sean."

"Sean is too emotionally involved to make decisions. You need to be in charge on our end," Rick said. "RCK is going to extract Lucy when we find her. Kane Rogan is going to be in charge of the operation and Sean will be involved. But I need you, as Lucy's boss and a federal agent, to be completely in the loop. With JT in Sacramento trying to identify their mole, I need a diplomat to finesse what might come up. Call me, text me, anytime for anything."

"Yes, sir."

"I have to go—thank you, Noah."

Noah hung up. He wasn't quite sure what to make of that conversation with Rick, but right now knowing that so many people were working on finding Lucy gave him hope.

CHAPTER EIGHTEEN

Lucy heard voices downstairs, then nothing. Had they left? Gone to sleep? The quality of light didn't change, which told her there was a lightbulb on. She didn't know what time it was. Everything was still blurry, but she could see where she was going. She found a bathroom, used the toilet, then searched for a potential weapon.

There was nothing. There wasn't even a towel rack she could dislodge from the wall.

As her eyesight returned, she realized she was in a den of sorts. Two couches, a coffee table, a desk and chair. It was devoid of clutter, except for a few vases like the one she'd broken. She searched the debris for something she could use to stab or cut, but the ceramic had broken into pieces too small to weaponize. The bookshelves had only books and a few knickknacks. She picked up everything to judge the heft of each piece and determine if she could do any damage. The only thing that might work was a long, slender leaded-glass vase. It had some weight to it.

She carried it around with her as she continued searching the room. There were four tall, narrow windows. When she pulled aside the heavy drapes she found storm windows on the other side. *Great.* Through the narrow slats she saw it was black outside. Middle of the night? Early morning? She didn't know. But she'd come home at three in the afternoon, and now it was sometime between ten at night and dawn. She kept trying to read her watch face but couldn't make out the hands. She *thought* the small hand was between the one and two.

There were papers in the desk, but nothing she could read at this point. What if her eyesight never went back to normal? What if they'd hit her and that had affected her optical nerve?

Why are you worrying about it now? Getting away is your number one goal.

Finally, she sat back down and waited. Listened, but there was only silence. Eden and Liam hadn't even come to talk to her, to try to explain themselves. For all she knew, they'd left.

Why?

Her head ached and she closed her eyes.

Sean.

He would be home by now. He'd know she was missing. Or Siobhan was there, had called Kane or Noah. If she was okay. If they hadn't hurt her. Ryan would have worried about her when she hadn't come back to headquarters. Hours had passed and people would be looking for her.

Eight years ago she'd been kidnapped and her family had worked tirelessly to find her. If Dillon and Kate hadn't found her, she would have been killed. Patrick had been severely injured, and she still harbored deep-seated guilt over that. Knowing she wasn't to blame and believing it were two different things. She had come to terms with what had happened. Being raped and tortured had been soul shattering, but she'd battled and won. It had taken years, but she had survived and wasn't hiding in the shadows, fearful of the world. She was fighting to make it a safer place for everyone. She had found love and a peace she never thought she'd attain. Perfect? No, life would never be perfect. There would be times when her past would haunt her. And the life she'd chosen in the FBI forced her to face evil over and over. But the people she saved, the criminals she locked up, the crimes she solved—it all made the difficulties of her chosen profession tolerable.

But Sean was her anchor. Without him, she'd be sucked into the dark spiral of work as a vocation, as the goal of life, when Sean had taught her that the goal of life was to love and be loved.

She could too easily picture him at their house, controlling his panic and his rage, his fear for her life. He would do anything to find her, and while she wanted him to find her, she didn't want him hurt.

How could his own family do this to him? Why would they take Lucy? What had they done with Siobhan? Had they drugged her, too? Left her at the house? Was she someplace here?

Lucy might have dozed off, but a sound woke her up. She jumped up, listened. Definitely people moving around, slowly. She blinked and realized that her sight was back. Her eyes felt heavy and her head ached, but she could see clearly.

She glanced at her watch. Five forty. *In the morning?* She ran over to the windows. The narrow slats of the storm windows were gray—definitely dawn. She couldn't see anything else, had no idea where she was, but there were no sounds of traffic. No commuters, no planes, no commercial vehicles or tractors or people. Isolation. Her heart pounded.

Control. You have your eyesight back, you have your training, you need to maintain control.

She picked up the vase where she'd left it on the couch,

then stood next to the door. Listened. Someone was taking a shower downstairs. The house didn't sound big, but there were a few rooms beneath her.

The water turned off. Voices. The smell of coffee.

Her stomach growled.

She heard a female voice . . . *Eden*.

She listened intently but couldn't make out anything they were saying. There appeared to be two distinct male voices. Maybe three, but Lucy wasn't certain. She didn't recognize any voice except Eden's.

Then she heard a vehicle.

She ran to the windows. She still couldn't make out much of anything through the thin slats, though it was definitely getting lighter out. She craned her neck and saw dense brush, a few trees, no paved roads. The terrain was unfamiliar.

The vehicle—an old truck by the sound—became louder, then stopped near the house. The road was a simple flat dirt path that was called a road simply because it could be used as one. In the sudden silence the sound of the single door closing startled her.

She ran over to the door and listened. The group was talking downstairs. She strained, trying to hear what they were saying. She picked up on a few words, but nothing made sense to her. All she heard clearly was *mission*. What sort of mission were they on? It couldn't have been in their plans to take her. They wanted the bonds. What had Eden said during that conversation? She'd been talking to Dante.

Tampico.

She said they were meeting in Tampico. Lucy didn't know of a Tampico in Texas, though there could be. But there was a Tampico down the eastern coast of Mexico.

She didn't want to be in Mexico . . . it would be that much harder to escape and get home. She didn't have resources, people, money, her passport . . . Where was the

American embassy? Mexico City . . . There were probably facilities in all the major resort towns, but she wasn't at a resort. Where exactly *was* she? Had Eden and Liam really taken her to Mexico?

Someone was walking up the stairs. Lucy stood to the side, so they couldn't see her when they walked in. She only had one shot—if she could disarm whoever came for her, she might have an edge. Get to the truck and bolt. Find a phone, call Sean.

Someone knocked on the door. "Lucy, I know you're standing by the door." It was a male voice. Very familiar. "Probably planning to run, maybe fight your way out. You will fail. You are one person, probably very well trained, probably very smart otherwise Sean wouldn't be marrying you. Be smart now. Stand back from the door."

She hesitated, considering.

"I have no intention of hurting you, Lucy."

"Liam?"

"Very good. If Sean and Kane told you anything about me, you know that I don't kill people. It's not my style. And I don't want to hurt or restrain you if I can avoid it. In fact, we intentionally took off the restraints because I don't want you to feel like a prisoner."

"But I *am* a prisoner," she said through the door.

"Temporarily. I'd like to come in and talk to you, explain what's happening, and give you some good news."

What did she do? She could fight one unarmed person, maybe two. She had decent self-defense skills. But if Liam was even half as well-trained as Kane, she didn't think she would get out uninjured. And Liam wasn't alone.

"I'm coming in, Lucy. But if you attack, you will be taken down, understand? It's not just Eden and I. And while *I* don't have a gun—I abhor firearms—my friends like them."

"If you kill me, Sean and my brother will hunt you down to the ends of the earth."

"Jack, right? Haven't met him, but he has a reputation. I'm not going to kill you, Lucy. I promise. That doesn't mean you can't get hurt. Now back away from the door."

Reluctantly, she did it. Because she knew there were at least four people in the house—Liam, Eden, and two others—and she wasn't an idiot. She couldn't fight her way out of a house she didn't know and run through an unfamiliar and foreign land.

"Come in," she said through clenched teeth.

The lock turned, and in walked a man who looked so much like Kane and Sean that it was unnerving. He was shorter, less broad—but just as handsome. He had Sean's dimples and the same deep-blue eyes that every Rogan had. His hair was lighter, his features a bit more chiseled, but there was no mistaking the Rogan genes.

Eden stepped in behind him. She had a Taser in her hand. She smiled. "Just in case you thought to try something."

"Put it away, Eden," Liam said.

"Not yet." Eden looked at the long vase that Lucy held in her hand.

Lucy put the vase down and showed her hands. "Better?"

Liam smiled. "Thank you."

"You can't possibly think that this is a good idea," she said.

"It wasn't my first idea, true, but I couldn't have you telling Sean what you overheard. I'm really sorry we had to incapacitate you."

He reached out into the hall and brought in a bag. He put it on the desk. "Food and water. You're probably starving."

She didn't respond.

"Sit down," he said.

"I'll stand."

"Sit," he said more forcefully, and motioned toward the couch.

He crossed the room and sat at the desk chair. Lucy, keeping her eyes on both Liam and Eden, sat on the couch.

"I don't have time, so here's the situation. We're leaving, you're staying. In fact, if you leave this house you won't be safe. Not only are we in Mexico, the territory is rather hostile. You have no identification, and you wouldn't want to tell anyone that you're an American citizen *or* that you're a cop. Would not go over very well. But, as long as you stay here, you'll be safe."

"And you're leaving me here?"

"Temporarily. I left Sean a note saying that I would call him this morning. In a few hours, I'm going to do just that. It'll take him at least five hours to reach you, and that's if he's sitting in his plane when I call, flies as fast as his little Cessna can fly, has tailwinds, and lands in a nearby field. But I suspect it'll be six or seven hours before he makes it." He looked at his watch. "It's six a.m., I'll call him at noon, and he'll be here by dinner. One word of advice: If you don't get out before dark, don't leave until morning. Stay the night, the pantry is full, there's plenty of water."

"I don't understand why you're doing this."

"You overheard where we're going and who we're going with. If Kane gets that information, he'll know exactly what I'm doing, and that won't benefit us. I've been waiting six years for those bonds, but half my life for the treasure. Kane never had faith, he never believed, and I know he never told Sean the truth."

"Told Sean the truth about what?"

"Kane stole the bonds out from under my nose! That bastard betrayed me—betrayed our family. Our parents and their legacy!" As Liam spoke, Lucy saw his obsession. There was so much more going on than she understood, but the hatred in his voice spoke volumes.

As if he noticed his rage, he took a deep breath and waved his hand. "I don't care about the money. The bonds will buy Eden and me freedom from the people Kane forced us to go into business with when he took the bonds in the first place. But the information etched on one of the bonds is the final piece to the map that leads to tens of millions of dollars in gold, silver, and historical artifacts. My father was looking for this treasure for his entire life. He gave me everything before he died, told me I would find it. And together we did. Eden and Dante and I, we believed and worked hard, and now the treasure is only hours away." His eyes glowed, the anger and rage turning to lust—lust for treasure? He might not think it was about the money, but obviously that was part of it. The other part, Lucy was pretty certain, was winning. Liam had to prove to his brothers—and to the world—that he had accomplished something great. "Found something no one else could find. Six years ago, we were on the verge of finding the ruins, and Kane took the bonds. I didn't even suspect it was him . . . but what he did hurt us greatly."

"He hurt your feelings, so you kidnapped me?" she snapped.

"No!" He cleared his throat. "My feelings aside, Eden and I had to take jobs we didn't want to in order to get out of the debt Kane put on us when he took the bonds. Look, Lucy, I'm sorry we had to involve you—truly sorry."

He didn't sound sorry. Maybe sorry that he had to deal with her now, but he wasn't sorry he kidnapped her and took her to Mexico. He had to know that a US federal agent was in grave danger in certain parts of Mexico. And if anyone knew that she was almost related to Kane it would make it that much worse.

Jack made his fair share of enemies, Kincaid isn't a safer name than Rogan.

"What would you have done if Sean was at the house?"

"Tell him the truth. I would have loved for him to join me. I think he knows, somewhere in the back of his mind, that our parents were close to finding this treasure. They talked about it when we were very young, but after Molly died . . . they lost their drive. Years later my dad and Dante's dad started looking again. Between them, we had every piece of information we needed, except one, and my dad gave everything to me only weeks before he died. It took me *years* to find that last piece—that's why we etched the other maps into the bonds. To protect the information." He shook his head. "You don't understand."

"I do," Lucy said. "You're driven and selfish and have hurt people on this ridiculous quest."

He almost hit her. She could see that he wanted to, but he jumped up and controlled the urge. Who was this guy? He was nothing like Kane or Sean or Duke. He looked like a Rogan, but he didn't act like one.

"I don't hurt people," he said. "*Never* have I taken a human life. *Never,*" he repeated. "Kane can't say the same thing, can he? And from what I've been hearing, Sean can't, either. This treasure is more important than the money involved. It's our history. It's what my dad wanted *me* to find. *Me,* not Kane or Sean or Duke, but *me.* It's *my* legacy. It's the only thing I have left of my family. Kane never understood! *I'm* the visionary. I'm the one who not only dreams but makes them come true!"

Lucy glanced over at Eden—she was watching her brother. Lucy looked at the door. How many were downstairs?

If she got out of the house—and that was a big if—she had no idea where she was or how to get out. If they were truly going to leave her here, she could leave. All she had to do was find someone with a phone. She spoke fluent Spanish, she could understand any dialect; she could dirty up her clothes and pretend to be local or lost.

She relaxed, now that she had a plan. It would work. She just had to play along, listen to Liam—who she was beginning to think was borderline insane—vent about his brothers.

Liam stared out one of the narrow windows, and Eden turned her attention to Lucy. "Kane isn't one of the good guys," Eden said. "He disowned us. Who made him God? And Duke just lets him do whatever he wants. Duke went along with it, believed everything that Kane told him."

"Duke always conformed to the rules," Liam said. "But he had a lot of pressure on him. I don't blame him—he's lived in Kane's shadow his entire life. He rebelled by joining the Army instead of the Marines, but it was a small rebellion. He stepped up and raised Sean when our parents were killed, but he wouldn't let us be involved at all."

Eden said, "I wanted to come home. My baby brother needed me, but Duke had rules no one could live by."

Lucy didn't know whether she believed that or not, but she also knew that Sean had butted heads with Duke more than in just his teenage years. Duke was a solid guy—Lucy liked him—but he was rigid. Only recently had Sean and Duke made amends, and largely because Sean had left RCK for a year before coming back on his own terms.

Still, she could see the twins, nineteen and living abroad, wanting to come home after the deaths of their parents. They didn't like the same rules Duke did, so they stayed away. Or did Duke force them to stay away? Either way, it would hurt. Wounds festered. Family knew you better than anyone, which was why when they hurt you it stung worse. Because they knew what hurt, how to rub salt in the wounds.

Family was complicated. The Kincaids certainly weren't perfect. They'd faced horrific obstacles that would have torn other families apart. The murder of Lucy's nephew when he was seven was only one of many tragedies that tested the Kincaids. But through it all, they managed to persevere and overcome everything life threw at them. If Lucy had a problem, her family was there. Even when she pushed them away after her kidnapping and rape, they didn't abandon her. They were there when she returned, when she could start living again. They welcomed the prodigal daughter back into the fold, no guilt, no remorse, no questions asked. Anything was forgiven, because in the end family was all that mattered.

The Rogans were certainly not the Kincaids.

"When we lost the bonds six years ago, we thought we were done," Liam said quietly. "I had failed my father—the one thing he wanted from me, expected from me, and I couldn't deliver."

The dynamics were so clear to Lucy she could have written a chapter in a psychology book about Liam right then and there.

"You asked me what we would have done if Sean were at home? I think Sean would have given me what I wanted, after I explained everything. How he even had a part in decoding a map for our dad—he was part of this from the beginning, even though he didn't know it."

"Sean would never have given you the bonds," Lucy said. "You're deluding yourself into thinking he would be swayed by your arguments."

"He would be! I would have shown him the one bond that mattered, and he would have given me the rest when I explained that it was our heads on the line if I didn't deliver the money!"

Liam firmly believed what he said.

"Now you won't know," Lucy said. "Because Sean will never forgive you for this."

"I left him a note," Liam said, shaking his head as if

she'd failed an easy test. "You're missing the *point,* Lucy. After all this is over, I hope you'll convince Sean to forgive us. We haven't hurt you. You'll be fine."

"Fine? *Really?* You drug me, blind me, kidnap me from my own home, take me to *Mexico,* and hold me prisoner, and you think that either of us will forgive you? You're insane. This has nothing to do with your fight with Kane. This has everything to do with you taking me against my will."

He sighed, glanced at his sister. "I get it." He rose. "We're leaving now, and I'm serious, Lucy—don't leave the house. You're in the Tamaulipas region. Not too far from Ciudad Victoria, the closest major town. There is no safe passage." He took a couple steps toward Lucy, then squatted so they were eye to eye. She wanted to kick him in the face. She was angry and not a little bit scared—she didn't want to be trapped here, but she would find a way out. She was resourceful. Liam had no idea what she could do.

"I want to trust you, Lucy, but I also don't want you to get hurt." Before she realized what was happening, he sprayed a mist in her face. Her eyes burned. She tried to get away, felt nauseous. She teetered and he caught her. She pushed him away, stumbled, and fell back onto the couch.

"You won't pass out because I'm not going to inject you with the sedative this time. But"—he sprayed her eyes two more times—"you won't be able to see anything for a few more hours. I'm doing this to protect you, Lucy."

"You fucking bastard!" She rubbed her eyes, blinked, but that made the pain worse. Already everything was blurred again. He pushed her back on the couch and she tried to fight back, but she couldn't see anything.

"Eden," Liam said. Then Lucy felt her hands held over her head. She strained and tried to kick, but Liam sat on top of her. "You could make this easier on yourself, Lucy," he said.

Her entire face hurt and she barely felt him holding open her eyes, but the drops dribbled out the sides, and then she saw nothing. The headache she'd been fighting came back, pulsing, throbbing, and tears streamed from her eyes.

Liam got off her and her hands were free. She lashed out but didn't make contact with anyone. "It won't be too long, Lucy. Relax, have your breakfast. There's more food downstairs. Just be careful walking around until your sight comes back. I don't want you to hurt yourself."

She felt around for the vase on the couch next to her and threw it in the direction of his voice. It shattered against the wall.

She was blind, again.

The door slammed closed.

"Protection, my ass," she muttered, then put her head in her hands and willed the pain to go away.

CHAPTER NINETEEN

Sean jumped up from his desk, disoriented. He'd fallen asleep. How could he sleep when Lucy was in trouble? He shook his head to clear it, looked at the computer program he'd been running. The window was gone. Momentary panic disappeared when he realized his report was complete.

Six thirty in the morning. He'd dozed for an hour. He hadn't heard from Kane or JT or Jack. Liam hadn't called. Nate and Noah were doing god knows what.

And Lucy was still missing.

Sean had traced the serial number of the burner phone Liam had left him. Identified the chain that sold them, then hacked into their database to find out where it was purchased. Illegal, but he didn't the hell care.

Liam had bought the phone with cash from a electronics supply store outside San Antonio. Sean mapped it—it was halfway between the Southfield airstrip and Sean's house. He walked over to his printer—the printer coming to life was what had woken him up. The results of his search surprised him. He sat back down and ran another report from the results.

Liam had paid cash—no surprise there—but he'd

bought five phones, all with two hundred dollars of prepaid minutes and international access.

"He did take her to Mexico," Sean mumbled. Unless he left her somewhere in Texas, like he had Siobhan.

There was no way to trace the phones, but now Sean had the other numbers.

Even if Sean called Liam and he picked up, there was no way to trace the call quickly, and while Sean was capable of it, he didn't have the equipment to pinpoint the call's location. He might, however, get the general region.

And if he started with a general location, had the FBI bring in their equipment, they might very well be able to get a better location and faster.

His phone rang and Sean jumped. It wasn't the burner phone, it was his personal cell. An unknown number.

Lucy.

"Rogan," he said. He sounded desperate.

"It's Jack. I'm on my way."

"Jack." Sean didn't know why he felt relieved. He trusted Kane . . . but after the secrets with the bonds, the reasons Kane disowned Liam, Sean was beginning to question everything. Jack would do anything to find Lucy. He was her brother and wasn't blinded by Liam and Eden's shenanigans.

"JT told me what he knows. Any news?"

"Kane and Siobhan went to New Orleans to talk to an old friend of our parents. Carlo Romero, Gabriella and Dante Romero's father. I tried Duke earlier, but he wasn't answering."

"I pulled out of an undercover operation. I told Duke to stay, the situation is serious, and we need his tech skills on-site. He can't help us find Lucy."

"Dante Romero is involved."

"I know."

"Kane said you're the only one who can reach Gabriella Romero."

"I sent her a coded message. We have to be careful there. She is not with us or against us. She is and has always been on her own."

"She could be involved with kidnapping Lucy, Jack!"

"Remain calm, Sean."

Sean wanted to yell at someone, but he swallowed it. Noah stepped into the doorway.

"I'm trying," he said through clenched teeth. "Who's the traitor at RCK?"

"JT has it narrowed down to two people. I'm not telling you who, not until we are positive."

"It doesn't feel like I'm back, Jack," Sean snapped.

"Do you trust me?"

"Yes." He said it immediately and realized that he did. Jack might be the only person he completely trusted right now.

"Two things. First, get down to my house near Hidalgo ASAP. We'll be closer to the border, and you already know how to avoid border patrol from there. I am flying direct to Hidalgo, ETA four hours, ten minutes. I will meet you there. Second, do not go to Mexico alone. No matter what Liam says, you cannot travel south without a security team. After what happened in Guadalajara, you no longer have anonymity."

"Nor do you."

"I'm not Kane Rogan's brother. If you haven't noticed, I blend in in Mexico much easier than you do."

Jack definitely looked more like his darker-skinned Cuban mother than his fair-skinned Irish father.

So did Lucy. Lucy could pass for a native.

"Lucy will protect herself, right? She can blend in, too."

"Yes."

That made Sean feel marginally better.

"I'm not going to lie to you, Sean. The situation is fucked. Jasmine Flores is on the warpath, which is why RCK has pulled out of all operations south of the border. We're not taking any jobs outside the US right now, and it's going to have a ripple effect. When certain factions hear that we've pulled out—even temporarily—they'll get cocky." He paused. "Gabriella is not staying with the Floreses just because she's protecting her own cover. We need information, and she's helping."

"What do you need me to do?"

"Get to Hidalgo. Let me know when Liam calls and what he says. You and I are going in alone to extract Lucy. The fewer people the better, we'll slide in under the radar. But you have to promise to wait for me, Sean."

"I will." Sean hung up. He wished he felt more confident, but Jack had been honest with him. He wished that his own brother had told him everything from the beginning.

"I'm going to Hidalgo," Sean told Noah, after finding him in the kitchen.

"We'll go with you."

"No."

Noah raised an eyebrow. "Sean, you'll do Lucy no good if you can't get some sleep. I'll fly you down to Hidalgo while you sleep. I get it—you and Jack need to go in quietly and get her, but someone needs to stop Liam and Eden from doing whatever it is they're doing."

"Kane." Sean rubbed his eyes. He needed sleep. He needed to think. "Okay, fine. Fly. Just . . . please don't crash my plane this time."

Siobhan slept for nearly the entire flight. Kane was slowed down by some turbulence along the coast and ended up detouring north before heading back south into New

Orleans. He admired how Siobhan could sleep during less than ideal circumstances—he could do the same, if not for the fact that he was flying the plane.

And it gave him time to think.

Maybe thinking wasn't all that good of an idea, because all he could think about was the redhead sleeping in his co-pilot seat.

She wasn't much more than a little girl when Kane first met her through her older half sister, Andrea Walsh. Andie had been one of Kane's commanding officers when he was at the Quantico Marine base. The first and only female who had commanded Kane, and one of the best he'd served under. She was now number two ranked in the officer training program at Quantico, and Kane considered her a good friend.

Kane barely remembered Siobhan when he first met her—she was a teenager, had moved in with her father after spending most of her life living in Mexico with her missionary mother. The Walsh family were all career military—both Andie's father and older brother died in service to their country.

Over the years, Kane had seen Siobhan. Watched her grow up, in a way, but tried to ignore her. It was when Siobhan got into trouble in Mexico, when Andie asked for Kane's help, that he realized Siobhan was no longer a little girl. At first he was angry with Siobhan for worrying her sister. Siobhan was a photojournalist, not a soldier. She wasn't a fighter, didn't even carry a gun. She mostly worked freelance but spent a lot of time with the Sisters of Mercy, her mother's missionary group, helping them raise money. And sometimes Siobhan stuck her nose where it didn't belong. She stood out—she was a beautiful Irish redhead with a tall, athletic body and the fairest of skin. She had more compassion than most everyone he'd ever met . . . and yet was stubborn and, at times, reckless.

Especially when children were involved. He couldn't step foot in a particular region of Mexico because of her—he'd helped her rescue a twelve-year-old girl who was being married off to a forty-year-old man in order to merge two drug families. Someone in the household had contacted the Sisters of Mercy to smuggle the girl into the United States. The Sisters couldn't do anything . . . but Siobhan did.

And then Kane had had to rescue both her and the girl.

That was eight years ago, and that was when Kane started to think about Siobhan as a woman, not as a child. As a beautiful, impossible, reckless, compassionate woman.

He didn't want to. He didn't want to think about her at all. But when Andie called, Kane jumped . . . not just because Andie was his friend. He had been half in love with Siobhan Walsh when she risked her life for a little girl she didn't know and stood up to Kane. And dammit, he didn't want to be.

I love you.

She thought she loved him. He tried to explain it to her, that she really didn't know what she thought, but he couldn't get the words out.

And then she'd kissed him.

He wanted Siobhan in the worst way, but he knew that with his lifestyle nothing good would come of it. He wanted to take her anyway—she was willing, he was willing, they were consenting adults. But then he remembered that she wasn't like other women in his life. She was different. Special. Andie's baby sister.

A woman he could love, if he had a life that had room for love.

The problem was, he lived a dangerous life and his life had already put Siobhan in danger. She'd been used as bait for him by one of the violent cartels; she had just yesterday been grabbed by his own brother and locked in a car trunk.

He'd pound Liam just for that. She wasn't hurt—except for a bruise that Liam would also pay for. But didn't this whole thing just remind Kane that his life wasn't designed for a permanent woman? What would happen if someone hurt her because of him? Killed her? Used her against him? He couldn't be rational.

Of course you can be rational. You care about Lucy, she's practically your sister. And you're doing what needs to be done.

He wished his mind would shut the fuck up. He needed to convince himself that he had to keep Siobhan out of his life, not find excuses to bring her in.

Siobhan stretched and woke up on landing, which was rougher than Kane intended. "Sorry, sugar," he said.

She shivered and yawned. He handed her her sweater, then frowned. "That's not going to keep you warm."

"It's all I had with me. It hasn't been all that cold in Texas, I didn't think I'd need anything else."

"You should always be prepared." He pulled a sweatshirt out of his go-bag and tossed it to her. "Might not smell pretty."

"It's fine." She pulled it on. It was an old USMC sweatshirt that had seen better days. "Andie has one just like it."

He climbed out of the plane and held out his hand for her. She took it, and he held on as they walked over to the small office. Sure, it was six in the morning and lightly raining, but she was shivering as if they were in the middle of a blizzard. Her hands were like ice.

Gus McAvery ran this small airport mostly for charters and businessmen who didn't want to deal with the bigger airports. There was one well-maintained runway and it was one of the few spreads where they could land day and night. Gus had a small house on the edge of the property, and RCK had an account. They preferred using unmanned airports, but there were a few places around the country they used for fueling and maintenance.

"Rogan."

"Gus. Thanks."

"Fill her up?"

"Yes, I may have a long flight ahead of me."

"I'll check her for you."

"Appreciate it."

"When you need her by?"

"Three, four hours?"

Gus nodded. "Need a ride?"

"Yep."

Gus tossed him a set of car keys. "Just make sure you're back by eleven, the missus has her Tuesday afternoon book club over in Lake Charles and she'll need it."

"No problem."

Kane walked out with Siobhan. "He didn't even talk to me," Siobhan said.

"You didn't talk to him, either."

"I thought you'd introduce us."

"Not that kind of relationship."

"But you know him."

"Yep."

"You're impossible."

"So you've said, sugar." He opened the passenger door of an old pickup truck that had seen better days, then lifted her onto the seat.

"I can—" she began, then stared at him.

He kept his hands firmly on her waist, then he kissed her. Just a light kiss, though no less possessive than the kiss he'd laid on her when he found her earlier. He wanted to take her to the back of the pickup, but that would be for another day. "I know," he said, his voice rough. "You can do it yourself."

Then he smiled and slammed her door shut.

Maybe there was something about this relationship thing that he would enjoy after all.

CHAPTER TWENTY

"It's not even six in the goddamn morning," Carlo Romero said as he swung open the door.

Carlo had obviously been sleeping. Kane's dad would have been in his late sixties now; Carlo was a few years older than Paul Rogan would have been. His too-long gray hair stuck up every which way and he wore plaid pajama bottoms and a white T-shirt that was clean but could have used a bleaching.

"Hello, Carlo," Kane said.

Carlo stared. "Well, I'll be a motherfucker, Kane Rogan! Jesus H. Christ." He crossed himself as if that would forgive his swearing. "I would say I'm surprised to see you, but I'm not." He opened the door wider and motioned for them to come inside. He lived in a two-room flat in the French Quarter. Six a.m. might be the only time New Orleans actually slept.

Carlo grinned at Siobhan. "You brought me a looker."

"She's mine, and younger than your daughter," Kane said. "You need a damn haircut."

"Of course she is, and like hell I do."

"I'm nobody's," Siobhan said, irritated. She extended her hand. "Siobhan Walsh."

"Classy, too." Carlo took her hand, then kissed it. "Kane, make the coffee, I need to freshen up for your pretty lady."

"I don't have time."

"Make the damn coffee, because I'm sure as fuck not going to talk to anyone without a cup of joe."

He walked into the adjoining room and shut the door.

Kane turned into the kitchenette and easily found ingredients for coffee. Carlo might live in a dive apartment on the edge of the Quarter, but he was extremely tidy. You can take the man out of the military, but some things would remain the same. No clutter, no dirt, no dishes in the sink. Kane heard the shower go on. *Great.* Carlo had to pretty himself up.

Yeah, some things never change.

Ten minutes later the coffee was done and Carlo was dressed and coming out of his bedroom. He cleaned up well, his too-long gray hair brushed back into a stubby ponytail. A clean T-shirt, slacks, loafers. "I figure I won't be getting back to sleep this morning." He poured himself a cup of black coffee. "Help yourself," he said. "I ain't no fucking waiter."

Kane poured himself black coffee and one for Siobhan. He added a little sugar—he knew she drank it black but preferred it sweetened if she could get it.

They all sat in the living room. There were two couches that faced each other, and a large-screen television on the wall.

"I know why you're here."

"No, you don't."

"The boys found the gold."

The gold. The fucking treasure his parents had been obsessed with.

"Is that what this shit is all about?"

"What d'you think?"

"I don't give a damn about the gold. I'm here because

they stole six million in bearer bonds and my future sister-in-law."

Carlo raised his eyebrows. "Well, well. I see." He sipped his coffee. "You never had an imagination. I remember when you were little your mama—God rest her soul— would read these books to you and Molly. Duke was still a baby, but you and Molly were two peas in a pod. Irish twins, Sheila called you. She'd read these books with talking animals and elephants sitting on eggs and Molly would laugh, but you would stare at your mama and say, 'Penguins don't talk,' or, 'An elephant is too big to sit on an egg.' Always the realist."

Kane forgot that Carlo had been around forever. He was there when Kane was growing up. But even before his parents died, Carlo stopped coming around.

"What happened between you and my parents? You used to always be at the house."

"You know."

"I don't know."

Carlo shrugged. Then sighed. Then sipped his coffee. "The gold. It does things to people."

"My parents stopped looking for that damn treasure after Molly died."

"For a while. Grief does that to folks. But grief passes, it gets buried, it changes. And Paul started researching the treasure again. I did my share. It's my ancestors who were with Father Gregorio when they had the treasure in the first place. It's my heritage. Dante and Liam used to listen to Paul and me talk about the damn treasure for hours . . . for a while it was a real sore spot with your mama, but then she got sucked in, too. It does that to people, these things."

The treasure had been a fixture in Kane's and Molly's lives growing up—until she died. After, Kane rarely heard his parents talk about it. He'd already been in the military, he didn't spend much time at home. When he was home, he and his dad talked business. Practical needs of soldiers, because Kane's dad had military contracts. Never about some ridiculous shipment of gold and silver that had never made its way from Mexico to the Alamo before it fell. Kane doubted the treasure even existed. It was a fairy tale, like "Cinderella" and "The Golden Goose."

"Ya hear me?" Carlo said.

"I'm sorry," Kane muttered.

"I said after your parents died I lost the drive. I was close to your dad—and, well, Liam and Dante didn't lose the drive. It seems Paul gave Liam all his research, months before the plane crash. He'd planned on bringing the boys in, letting them find it." Carlo looked wistful, then shook his head. "We all were sucked in. But, as I said, it's cursed."

"What's cursed? The gold?"

"The treasure. Maybe just the search. Hell if I know, but nothing good has come from it. It was cursed from the moment it left its bedrock. Some say it was stolen from the Indians. Some say graves were robbed, the gold and jewels are haunted. Others say Stephen Austin cut a deal with the devil."

"If you believe in fairy tales."

"I believe, Kane." Carlo got up and brought the coffee-pot back to the table. He refilled everyone's cup and added a sugar cube into Siobhan's. The man might be old, but he had sharp eyes. He'd seen Kane doctor her coffee earlier.

"Thank you, Mr. Romero," Siobhan said.

He smiled, winked. "My pleasure, Ms. Walsh. Call me Carlo, Uncle Carlo, honeybuns. Whatever tickles your fancy."

Siobhan smiled and Kane tried not to rush Carlo into giving him information.

Carlo put the pot back and sat down across from Kane.

"Carlo, I have word that Philip Corsica is working closely with Liam and Dante. Have you seen him?"

"Not recently. Philip is like a son to me, like your pal JT Caruso was a son to Paul. They're friends, have been forever. You know that."

Kane wondered how much Carlo really knew. Paul had welcomed JT into the house—had never said anything when JT practically moved in when he and Kane were both fourteen. Everyone knew that JT's father was bad news. But by the time Kane was in high school his parents were traveling more often than not or spending time in their research lab. They weren't engaged with what was going on at home. Sometimes he wondered if they even remembered JT lived there.

"Dante led me to believe he and Liam had a falling-out."

"They did, but they made up. Unlike you and Liam."

"Because Liam was working for a drug lord. There are lines that cannot be crossed. He knew it."

"Liam is more a free spirit."

"Liam is a criminal. Look, I'm not here to debate the pros and cons of my brother's decisions. I'm here because they fucked up. They kidnapped Sean's fiancée and took her to Mexico against her will. Lucy is an FBI agent—I shouldn't have to explain to you why it's dangerous for her in certain areas."

"I'm certain the boys will protect her. They're not violent. You know that." He didn't sound worried at all.

"Dammit, Carlo! I don't have a lot of faith in my brother and sister right now. Dante damn well knows who Lucy is and why going to Mexico right now is extremely dangerous. I don't have time to go into every detail, you have to fucking trust me!"

Carlo frowned and sipped more coffee. "Kane, your temper."

"My temper is not your concern!"

Siobhan put her hand on Kane's arm. He wanted to hit it away but was surprised that it had a calming effect. He took a deep breath, was about to continue, when Siobhan said, "Carlo, I'm a photojournalist. I've been working with Lucy while she's been investigating a black-market baby network. Yesterday, I went home with Lucy for lunch. When we arrived, Eden and Liam drugged Lucy, handcuffed me, and left me in a shed at an airfield. They took Lucy with them. I don't think they'll intentionally hurt Lucy, but we have to find them. These people she's been investigating, they know who she is. I've worked with the Sisters of Mercy most of my life—I've faced people like those in the Flores cartel. Lucy isn't safe. And she's one of the best people I've ever met. I can't bear the thought of her suffering at their hands."

Carlo stared at Siobhan for a long moment, and Kane wondered what he was thinking. Sometimes his father's old friend was difficult to read, especially now, when Kane hadn't seen him in years.

Carlo then turned to Kane. "I am truly sorry that I didn't stay in touch after your mom and dad died. I moved here because I was so angry."

"At my parents'?"

"Paul was a visionary. He was so smart—brilliant. Little Sean, he was so much like Paul, so smart. I would love to have seen him grow up. But Duke—you know your brother cut a lot of ties."

Kane had known, but not the extent. "You should have called me."

"Duke is a good man. He knew what your parents were up to—that they were looking for the treasure. He didn't approve, he's practical, like you."

"You cannot be saying that their accident was because of some damn treasure hunt."

"No—not directly. Maybe not indirectly. But many people believe the treasure is cursed, that anyone seeking it will perish. Your parents were meeting with a military contractor in Colorado, I believe, right?"

"Yes. To demonstrate their latest invention. They took Sean with them, because he had helped make the thing work. I don't even remember what it was now."

"It was a small-weapons laser guidance system—I don't remember the details. Sean was only fourteen then, yet figured out what Paul had been doing wrong in the programming. He expanded the range of the weapon."

"Whatever it was, it helped pay for Sean's education. Duke sold it after our parents died, but all the money went to Sean's college fund." Kane hesitated a moment. "I don't think Duke ever told Sean. Sean had a hard time after Mom and Dad died."

"Survivors usually do."

"He was with them?" Siobhan asked.

Kane nodded. "He doesn't talk about it."

"Poor Sean," Siobhan murmured, and crossed herself. Kane wasn't religious, but for some reason Siobhan's quiet, steadfast faith calmed him.

Kane looked from Siobhan to Carlo. "You're off-topic, Carlo."

"The treasure is cursed, to those who believe it is cursed. Your parents planned on selling that technology and funding the expedition. Paul and I knew the treasure was somewhere along the eastern Mexico coast, but we needed many things to prove it. One of them was a code in the Romero family Bible. I never could figure it out. Paul gave the code to Sean but didn't tell him why. Sean solved it—it's the way that mind of his works—and Paul then created a map based on Sean's key.

"Then they died. I used the code and couldn't find the treasure. Spent most of my savings, all of my inheritance, then gave it up. Per Paul's request, I handed everything down to Liam and Dante. They included Philip, because Philip was like a brother, but Philip wasn't obsessed." He paused. "This last year, Philip has been spending a lot of time with Dante. I suspected they were searching again."

"This doesn't explain what the bonds have to do with the gold."

"They have nothing to do with the gold. Except, Eden etched the map in a special ink visible under a black light onto one of the bonds. Put that bond with the others for safekeeping. I don't know exactly how they figured it out, but at one point they determined they had the wrong starting point, so nothing matched old maps. They went back to the originals, realized the mistakes Paul and I had made and were basing all our conclusions on. But the bond that Eden had etched the map on had been stolen. They planned to steal it back, but when they got there the bonds were gone. To them, that was everything. The bonds were the treasure because the bonds protected the map."

Carlo sighed, rubbed his eyes. "I told them to forget about it. It's not meant to be found. I can survive on my pension. I work part-time at a bar, I don't need much.

"Then Dante called me last month. Long ago, they knew where the last puzzle was to the map, but without the bonds it was worthless. Now Dante said they knew where the bonds were, that they were going to retrieve them, pay off Liam and Eden's debt, and find the gold."

Carlo stared at Kane. "I didn't know that Sean had the bonds. Fitting, I suppose, since without him Paul could never have broken the code in the first place."

Siobhan asked, "What is this treasure?"

"Some say it's the San Saba treasure. Others, the Alamo treasure. If it exists, it's gold and silver and jewels that were on their way to the Alamo, to Bowie and Crockett, to fight General Santa Anna. But before the battle of the Alamo, Santa Anna took over the main port on the gulf to cut off supplies and reinforcements and Stephen Austin was imprisoned in Mexico. When the water route was cut off, a Franciscan priest—a cousin of my ancestors—became part of the expedition to Texas. They were attacked by rebels, slaughtered—except for the priest and his nephew, who was my great-great-great–I lost track how far back. But a direct paternal line. The thing was, the rebels had no idea that they were transporting gold and silver. They didn't want anyone to pass through their land—angered, perhaps, by some battles in the area that had burned crops. It's conjecture at this point. But Father Gregorio believed the gold was cursed. He and his young nephew hid the treasure and vowed never to disclose it. The priest died shortly thereafter from wounds sustained in the attack, and the boy wrote everything down in a journal. He spread the map around to places that were important to the family. That was the code Sean was able to break. But the starting point . . . Paul and I always assumed the starting point was the place they were attacked. The starting point was, in fact, where the priest was buried."

"And they needed the map to retrace the steps."

"Exactly—we looked for it before, but without the correct starting point none of the markers were accurate."

"So where is this treasure?"

"The remains of Father Gregorio's church, which was lost to history more than a hundred years ago."

"He wasn't buried there?"

"No—he was buried in an unmarked grave that only Dante's ancestor knew about. His dying wish was that he not be buried with the treasure; he felt God would punish him by not letting him into Heaven, or some such thing."

"Where is it." It was a demand, not a question.

"I understand your concern, but you have to promise me something."

"They kidnapped Sean's fiancée. She's practically my sister."

Carlo raised an eyebrow.

Kane was losing his temper. "Liam and Eden violated Rogan-Caruso rules multiple times and I looked the other way. I shouldn't have, because they became reckless and I had to cut them lose."

"Why did Sean have the bonds?"

Kane leaned forward. "I stole them before Liam got to them, because I knew the bonds were destined for a drug lord."

Carlo shook his head. "Liam . . . he always felt inferior to you, to Duke, even to little Sean. Always something to prove. The bonds were never intended for a drug lord, God no. I don't know why he told you that."

"He didn't—but he took a job for a drug lord, then started planning the heist."

"Damn him," Carlo said, but not with real anger.

"Excuse me?"

"He was playing a game, a dangerous game. He got in with some shady people, but the bonds would have freed him—they still will. He was going to buy his and Eden's way out of working for those same people you abhor."

"He should have told me from the beginning!"

"But you don't believe elephants can talk."

Kane squeezed his eyes shut. "I don't know what the hell you're talking about, Carlo."

"You don't see the possibilities. The dreams. You would never have let Liam steal those bonds for the real reason he wanted them—to get the map. So he had to do things he wouldn't otherwise do."

Kane was beginning to understand . . . but Carlo was wrong about one thing. "Liam is a master manipulator.

He may have wanted just the one bond that had the map, but the others would be used to finance his plan. He's not liquid, never has been. He juggles with the best of them, lives life to the fullest, and Rogan-Caruso funded him for a long, long time. When I cut him off—before the bonds—I knew he was going to screw up. He can't play both sides, not for me."

"But the dream was bigger than all of us. He did it for your parents, and for me. For all of us who believe in fairy tales, that dreams can come true."

"I don't."

"Which is why he never told you."

"Don't make him sound noble, Carlo. He kidnapped a federal agent in the process of stealing the bonds out of Sean's safe, and I have to find her."

"I'll tell you where they are on one condition."

"You know? You know where the treasure is?"

"Dante called me last night. He wanted me to join them, because it had once been my dream. I told him it was their dream now. I don't need a treasure."

Kane was livid. "You've known for this entire conversation and only now tell me?"

"You're angry, Kane. Your anger is going to get people killed."

He was ready to explode. He prided himself on controlling his emotions, but right now he was about to lose it. "You're playing a game, Carlo, and time is running out."

"Promise me you won't hurt them. Maybe your mother was right—the treasure was cursed, it affected all of us. The closer we got . . . things happened. Your parents died. I lost all my money pursuing the dream. And now the boys are doing awful things like kidnapping a woman. But don't hurt them. Try to understand."

Kane let out a deep breath. "I will do my damnedest to protect them, Carlo—that I can promise—but there are consequences to their actions, and RCK cannot let them kidnap one of our people in order to make a fucking point. Now do *you* understand?"

Carlo got up, found a notepad on his small, uncluttered desk, and wrote down some numbers. "The longitude and the latitude. The church was buried in an earthquake more than a hundred years ago, but the key artifact is a broken cross wedged into the mountainside, which will be in front of the cavern. The cavern is guarded by Saint Michael the Archangel. I don't know if it was literal, or perhaps a plaque or statue or prayer. Locals stay away out of fear and superstition—they think the place is haunted, that the earthquake was a sign from God, punishment. But under the foundation of the old church rests not only the souls of the departed but also tens of millions of dollars of gold and silver Stephen Austin intended for Davy Crockett and Jim Bowie. That's not only a treasure, Kane, but history."

CHAPTER TWENTY-ONE

Noah didn't know if Sean was sleeping. Nate was in the back of the plane passed out completely like most soldiers learned to do in training. Take ten minutes whenever and wherever they could. Noah was lost in his thoughts, about his conversation with Rick, his meeting with Eden, what he should have done, and what he would need to do.

His phone rang and he answered it, surprised that he had service up here.

"I have a cell booster," Sean said from the co-pilot seat without opening his eyes.

Noah answered, "Armstrong."

"It's Ryan Quiroz. I've been trying to reach Lucy, we have intel on the Morrisons."

"The couple suspected of adopting Baby John?" Noah had to completely change gears. He had put all that aside yesterday.

"Yes—she didn't come back after lunch yesterday, but I didn't think much about it. But now I can't reach her."

"There's a situation I can't go into. I'm out of the office today, take over for me."

"Sir?"

Noah realized he should have gone through proper

channels. He hadn't told anyone he wasn't coming in. "I'll call Durant and clear it. Dunning is with me. I can't explain right now."

"It has to do with Sean's sister, doesn't it? She was calling and texting Lucy all day yesterday."

"I'll explain when I return. What do you have on the Morrisons? If you need a warrant, contact the AUSA directly, she knows you're working with me on this."

"Yes, sir, but they're out of the country. They left Sunday night, direct flight to Cancún."

"Talk to Durant. She'll start extradition procedures and contact our Legal Attaché down there. Have them detained as soon as possible. There's a consulate near Cancún—Mérida, I think. Remember there is an infant involved, we want to make this as quick and easy as possible to prevent anyone from getting hurt."

"I'll make sure the office knows." Ryan paused. "Anything else?"

"Is Lucy okay? I know something's going on."

"She'll be okay. Keep me in the loop." ·

"Will you do the same?"

The tone was borderline insubordination, but Noah couldn't blame him. The situation was unusual.

"I'll do my best, Ryan."

He disconnected. Ryan would do the job he was supposed to do, but this whole situation was a mess.

Noah hadn't flown much recently—only once or twice since he'd flown Sean's plane in the Adirondacks and was shot down by pot growers last year. He reflected that since he'd met Lucy and Sean, since Rick Stockton had brought him in to investigate the murder of Lucy's rapist nearly two years ago, he'd been involved in far more dangerous—and admittedly exciting—situations than during his first three years in the FBI. Even in the Air Force, being a Raven—part of the Air Force security force—had its moments, most of the time the work was monotonous, broken up on rare occasions by intense, high-stress situations.

But he didn't know if he could do this all the time, not when people he cared about were in jeopardy.

He glanced at Sean. His eyes were closed, but Noah knew he wasn't sleeping. He had to admit, he thought Sean was going to snap last night. Yet he'd kept it together. Noah was hard on Sean, and he knew why—Lucy's career. Sean broke laws Lucy needed to enforce. And while he might be keeping his nose more or less clean, he was still a wild card and Lucy could end up paying for his sins.

Noah often asked himself why he cared—Lucy was a good agent, but she was a grown woman who could make her own decisions about what was right and wrong. If she crossed the line, she would accept the consequences.

Yet he'd half fallen in love with her. Being attracted to her wasn't the problem—he'd been attracted to many women over the years, both before and after he fell in love with Eden. Not all of them had been available. But when he started working with Lucy, watching her work, seeing how she processed her cases, how she thought, and then the few times she'd exposed a hidden vulnerability . . . yeah, he would have fallen for her hard if Sean weren't in the picture.

Sean knew it. It was one of those things that guys knew about other guys, and maybe Noah hadn't kept his feelings completely to himself. But Sean had grown up a lot in the last two years, and Noah wanted their marriage to work. For Lucy, if no one else.

Sean's cell phone rang and he grabbed it. "Kane," he said, sorely disappointed. "What do you know?"

Sean listened for several minutes, asked a few questions, then said, "We're thirty minutes out of Hidalgo. Jack's on his way. Where the fuck is she, Kane? Did they take her on their fucking treasure hunt?" He listened, then hung up without saying anything more.

When Sean didn't volunteer anything, Noah pushed. "Tell me."

"The bonds have some sort of treasure map hidden in them. Hell if I know what Kane meant, he wasn't all that clear. Or I'm too tired to make sense of it. Something to do with a treasure my parents were looking for before they died. Gold and silver buried somewhere in eastern Mexico. The bonds are part of a treasure map—at least that's what I think Kane said."

"So he knows where they are."

"He's sending me the coordinates, which will be close to their location, but we're going to need supplies and cash—it's not a friendly area. Someplace in the middle of nowhere between Tampico and San Luis Potosí in the mountains. Kane's reading maps, and there's no place to land a plane nearby, so we'll need a jeep or two."

Sean rubbed his eyes. Everything Kane told him was spinning around, and he didn't know how to make heads or tails of it. He still couldn't believe that Liam took Lucy. Was this a vendetta because Liam and Kane hated each other? Was there more to the falling-out than Kane had told him? Or were they simply keeping Lucy from talking about what she heard, like Siobhan had said?

"What are they doing, Noah?" His voice cracked. This last month had been hell. Finding out he had a son. Saving Jesse's life, then losing him to witness protection. Telling him yesterday that if they were lucky they could see each other once a year—and making Jesse believe that was a good thing. Sean wanted more, dammit, and he couldn't have it.

And now Lucy, missing. He hadn't been able to keep Jesse, and now he was about to lose Lucy.

You're not going to lose her!

He'd almost lost Lucy last month because he'd lied to her. He hadn't deserved her forgiveness, but she stood by him and he would never let her down again. They were getting married, and everything was more or less coming together until fucking Liam came in and took her. Took the one good thing in Sean's life. *Why, dammit? Why?*

Panic wasn't going to get her back, only being smart. And ruthless.

"Are we meeting Kane?" Noah asked.

"*You're* not," Sean said automatically. "Neither you nor Nate can go down there. I'll wait for Jack in Hidalgo and then Jack and I are meeting Kane at an airfield outside of Tampico. The good news—if there is any good news—is that this region isn't controlled by the Flores cartel or their allies."

"I am going," Noah said.

"You're a federal agent, the risks are too great, and you know damn well the FBI will disavow any knowledge of your activities. They're not going to get you out if things go sideways."

"Stop, Sean. You forget, I was a Raven. I understand the dangers. I've been to the region, I know the area, and however bad-ass Kane and Jack are, they need backup. I'm not going in as a fed."

Sean wanted to say no, that he didn't want or need Noah, but he didn't. Because they needed all the help they could get and Noah was good under fire.

"How many people are we dealing with in Liam's group?"

"Three or four—Liam, Eden, Dante Romero, and possibly Philip Corsica. Philip is Dante's friend and bodyguard."

"Gabriella Romero isn't with them?"

"Jack says she's not." Sean didn't go into the details of why. "I don't think they would have anyone else with them, if they're truly looking for buried treasure. Maybe hired locals to help carry supplies, but that's just a guess. They may not trust anyone. I wouldn't. I just—" Sean shook his head.

"Spill it."

"Why take Lucy? She would be a hindrance for them. How would they force her to go along with it? Threaten her? Me? But even if she went along with it, they wouldn't give her anything that could be used as a weapon. They knocked her out. They took her to a foreign country with no backup, where they damn well *knew* she'd be in danger." He paused. "Maybe that's it—that's how they're keeping her in line. If she could, she'd call me. Just to let me know she was safe."

"They could have put her in a locked room, like they did with Siobhan. Liam said he was going to call you."

"It's the friggin' morning and he hasn't called," Sean said, then stopped and looked at Noah. "So what did Eden do to you? Everything makes sense now. But she must have really done a number on you for you to hate me so much."

"It's a long story."

"Condensed version."

Noah hesitated, then said, "I met Eden nearly seven years ago. I was stationed in Germany and she and Liam were still affiliated with Rogan-Caruso. Before Kincaid. She lied to me from the beginning. I learned the hard way that they were both thieves."

"She and Liam did a variety of jobs when they were with the old Rogan-Caruso. Including sanctioned thefts."

"If Rogan-Caruso sanctioned the crime I witnessed, I doubt Rick Stockton would be singing your praises."

"That's when Kane cut them off."

"Eden used me and our relationship. I suspected she was up to something, but she lied so smoothly, so sweetly, I didn't even think she was lying. She and Liam stole a painting from a private collection at an embassy in Germany—an invitation I had from my commanding officer. She made a point of telling me how much she wanted to go, and I took her. I saw the painting later, when she was packaging it up. She thought I'd left, but there was something strange about her behavior so I went back to her loft and saw her and Liam with the painting. I should have turned them in, but I couldn't."

"What was her excuse?"

"She offered no excuse. Just begged that I not report it. I wanted to—and that I didn't haunts me. She used me. *I* was the one with the invitation. I was in my dress uniform. I was representing my country. That means something to me, more than you can know." He paused. "Kane would understand. When you put on the uniform, you are no longer an individual. You stand for your country and every other man and woman who wore the uniform. She could have caused an international incident. But I think what was worse, she laughed it off. Tried to distract me with sex, and suddenly I saw through every one of her games for the six months we'd been together. I don't think it was the first time she used me, which made me wonder if our meeting was chance like I'd thought or part of her overall plan."

"I'm sorry," Sean said, and he meant it. "I guess that's why you've hated me from the beginning."

"I don't hate you."

Sean grunted. He was too exhausted to argue with Noah, too upset and worried to prove over and over that he was good for Lucy. Because how could he prove it when his own brother had kidnapped her?

Noah said, "I never hated you. I didn't like you very much, and sometimes I thought you deliberately baited me."

"I did."

Noah let out a brief laugh. "Good to know my instincts

weren't all shot to crap. But in truth, you also had a big black mark against you because Eden and Liam used me and I wasn't going to let another Rogan do the same."

"Fair enough."

"We're almost to Hidalgo." Noah adjusted the altitude and skirted the town toward Jack's ranch southwest of the city limits.

Sean let Noah handle the plane. He was a good pilot— he should be, trained by the US Air Force. As soon as they landed and slowed to a stop, Sean said, "Do you still love Eden?"

"No."

"You answered quickly."

Noah pulled into the hangar that Jack's caretaker had opened for them. He shut down the engine. "For the last six and a half years, I wondered if I really had loved her, or it if was an illusion. When I saw her yesterday, everything I'd ever felt came back. Once, I had loved her. I knew it yesterday—there had been a time when I thought the sun revolved around her. But she lied to me, used me, and when I saw her again I knew there was nothing left. Whatever had been there is gone. But that doesn't mean I don't have feelings for her. I think Liam manipulates her in much the same way she manipulates others. He controls her damn *life,* and she can't do shit without his okay. It's certainly not healthy. But there is nothing she can say or do that will make this right. I will arrest her and Liam and bring them back to the States to stand trial for drugging and kidnapping a federal agent and a civilian."

"Okay."

"Okay?"

"They're my blood, Noah, but they're not my family. Not anymore."

CHAPTER TWENTY-TWO

As soon as Lucy was certain that Liam and the others had left, she considered her options.

They hadn't locked her in, but her head still hurt and she could see nothing except light and dark. This time she knew what to expect. She wasn't sure what she should do, but staying in this room wasn't an option. She took the water bottle from the lunch Liam had given her and drank half of it, then rinsed her eyes out with the remainder. It didn't restore her sight, but the water took some of the sting away.

Her eyesight had returned about eight to nine hours after she'd been drugged the first time. That meant she'd be blind or mostly blind until the middle of the afternoon. She didn't want to stay here, but Liam was right: She couldn't leave if she couldn't see. She was in the middle of Mexico—she couldn't very well tell anyone she was a US federal agent. Some of the locals might be willing to help her with a phone or finding the embassy or consulate if she lied and said she was a lost student or something, but she needed her vision to assess her surroundings and anyone she encountered.

Last spring, when she, Kane, and Sean had crossed the border to rescue DEA Agent Brad Donnelly, Kane had specifically told her if she was captured not to speak English or tell anyone she was a US citizen or in law enforcement and never to give her real name. She could be used for ransom—or worse.

"Be smart, Lucy. Read the people around you. Know what to say and when to say it. Buy time for us to find you."

As loath as she was to obey Liam, staying in this house seemed to be the safest thing to do. She needed to find a weapon and more bottled water, get a sense of the layout, and find a hiding space if necessary.

On alert, she left the room and felt along the wall, moving slowly so she didn't tumble down any stairs. Based on how she'd heard Liam approach this morning, the stairs were to the left of the door; first, she explored the right. There wasn't much to explore. There were three doors. The first was to a closet—she bumped into shelves, felt towels and linens. She inspected every shelf by touch, searching for something she could use as a weapon, but there was nothing.

The second door was to a small room that didn't appear to be furnished or have a purpose. The final door opened to a bedroom. By the subtle perfume, Eden had slept here.

Lucy searched the room as best she could without her eyes. It was simple, functional. Double bed, dresser, desk, chair. She tripped over the chair but caught herself.

Desk.

She searched the desk, feeling around for a letter opener, but only found minimal office supplies, including several pens. She took what felt to be the sturdiest metal pen— the closest thing to a weapon—and put it in her pocket.

She opened the bottom drawer; it slid on a metal rod. *That* would be far more useful than a pen. She got down on her knees and spent far too much time getting the drawer out, then another twenty minutes trying to pry the rod out, until her fingers were sore and she cut one nail to the quick.

"Dammit," she muttered. *What a waste of time.*

Time is all you have, Lucy.

She sat up against the desk. She realized how much she relied on her vision for everything—she felt helpless. Her sight wasn't just to see where she was going but also to investigate. To look at a room and find clues. To read people, their physical reactions to questions, if they averted their eyes, had a tell, were planning an attack. She wasn't locked in a room, but she was still a prisoner.

In the past, being a prisoner would have caused full-out panic. But after the minor panic attack last night when she first regained consciousness, she was more angry than scared.

Finally, she got up and made her way back to her room, then carefully stepped past her door, searching for the stairs. She kept one hand on the wall. Even though she was expecting it, her foot stumbled at the first stair and she nearly fell. She sat down heavily and used her hands to judge the length and width of the landing. She was about to stand up when she realized that was foolish—there was no railing to hold on to.

She scooted down the stairs on her butt, one at a time, like a crab. She would have laughed at herself if she weren't so angry at Liam and Eden for putting her in this position. When she reached the bottom, she used the wall as leverage and stood up.

The downstairs definitely felt bigger, airy. There wasn't a lot of light, though—the windows may have been shuttered, blinds closed, or obscured by trees. Maybe that was for the best, so the house would appear empty.

Her second step forward, she tripped over a single stair and fell down to the tile floor.

"Shit!" she exclaimed.

Don't make assumptions, Lucy.

She heard a vehicle and froze. It wasn't close, and in a few second the sound faded. But that meant there was a road nearby. The sound was faint, the road could be far off, but it was close enough that when her sight returned she could reach it. It gave her some hope.

She focused on what she could hear. For the longest time, it was only silence; now she made out the sounds of the house. One of the toilets ran intermittently. A refrigerator hummed. Outside it was still, quiet, but she heard birds periodically. A dog barked twice, then nothing. No voices. Another car passed on the far-off road, disappeared.

Lucy breathed easier and moved toward the sound of the refrigerator.

She didn't trust the food that Liam brought. He'd drugged her once, why wouldn't he drug her again? She was hungry and thirsty but didn't want to eat anything that wasn't in a wrapper or closed bottle.

The kitchen might also hold potential weapons. She found the counter and quickly determined that there was nothing on the counter—no butcher block for knives, no glasses, no scissors. She searched the drawers. They were all empty. Did anyone actually live here? Had they hidden all the utensils suspecting she'd search the house?

She opened the refrigerator and felt around. There were water bottles in here; she took one out, listened carefully as she opened it . . . the plastic ring broke.

She drank the entire bottle in two long gulps.

Lucy inspected the kitchen with her hands. It was very small. A table and two chairs had been pushed against a short wall. There was another door. It opened, to a pantry. Very small with shallow shelves. Carefully, she felt around. Canned food. A unopened bag. She squished it—chips? Cereal? She opened it, smelled. Salty corn. Tortilla chips. She tried one. Not bad. She sat at the table, ate, and considered her options.

They weren't many.

Find a better weapon.

Search for a phone.

Locate a hiding place . . . just in case.

Wait for Liam to return.

Believe Liam will call Sean and tell him where I am.

She had no control over the last two, but she could definitely inspect the house. The longer she used her other senses, the more valuable they became. She heard voices—very distant, possibly carrying in the still air, words here or there. Sounded like a work crew, possibly on the road. She heard more cars . . . not a freeway, but maybe every five to ten minutes another car drove by. Somehow, that was comforting. She wasn't in the middle of nowhere. She should be easy enough for Sean to find if Liam had told her the truth.

She finished the bag of chips, drank a second bottle of water, and continued her search.

The three of them were standing inside a ten-foot-by-ten-foot tent they'd set up at a clearing near the narrow path that would take them into the canyon. Dante's bodyguard, Philip, had procured basic equipment, but if they found what they were looking for they might have to bring in heavy machinery.

Philip and Dante had also handled the trade last night—the rest of the bonds for the final piece of the puzzle, as well as buying Liam's and Eden's freedom from a nasty Russian organized-crime gang. Everything had gone exactly as they planned. Except for bringing Lucy Kincaid along for the ride, Eden thought, but she agreed with her brother—they hadn't had much of a choice.

Philip was staying behind at the airstrip. There were still other problems he had to take care of, and besides, this hunt for the San Saba treasure was for the Romeros and the Rogans.

"Gabriella should be here," Eden said to Dante.

Eden missed her old friend. Gabriella was a year older than them, but there had been a time—before Gabriella fell in love, before her fiancé was murdered—when the four of them had been inseparable. Eden missed that friendship. Gabriella had been one of the few real friends she'd had because Liam didn't trust most people. Who could blame him?

Dante glanced at her. "You know she can't."

"I still don't understand. She got her revenge, she should be with us."

"I told you it's complicated. She's fine, just has to lay low."

Dante looked worried, and that meant something was up and he wasn't sharing the details. His speech last night about Kane and Sean and what Eden did and didn't know about her baby brother bothered her.

"I wish Mom and Dad were here," Liam said. "And Uncle Carlo."

"I talked to him last night," Dante said. "He gave us his blessing."

"We'll give him part of the treasure," Liam said. "It's only right—he's the only one who had faith in us."

Dante said, "It's going to take us over an hour to get to the site—we need to get going. We have to leave by seven p.m.—I don't want to walk this path late at night."

They were in the mountains northwest of Tampico. The church was located on a plateau in the valley between two steep mountains. At one time it had been easily accessible, but an earthquake and landslides had destroyed the dirt road from the east. Now the only way to reach the area was through a treacherous path on the western slope.

Everyone had their own water and rations and tools. Liam carried the maps. They left the tent up—they were miles from civilization. They'd had to park nearly a mile down the mountainside because the road was too narrow.

There hadn't just been a church in the valley—there'd been an entire village of nearly one hundred people who had perished in the earthquake. Those who'd survived moved away.

They walked in silence. Though much of Mexico was a desert, so much of it was beautiful—hidden pockets of paradise that most people never saw. They'd driven up here from dry, scorched earth, but the mountain was covered in green. It was cooler here; plants, including trees, grew at this elevation that were not seen thousands of feet below. They were south of one of the least-populated protected reserves in Mexico, which was more jungle-like terrain—here there were more pines and oaks—but because of the moisture, they had ferns and extensive plants and birds. It was stunning.

It would be beautiful, Eden thought, if she weren't so worried about poisonous snakes and bugs and spiders. She wasn't a fan of camping, and she definitely wasn't a fan of wild animals. There were jaguars in these mountains. Liam had promised her he'd researched the area and the jaguars were to the north, but she didn't buy it. He often lied to her to put her at ease.

So she focused on the flowers, the fresh air, the narrow path. Liam led the way; she and Dante walked several feet behind.

"Is Gabriella really going to be okay?" she asked quietly.

Dante didn't say anything for a long moment. They heard water but couldn't see where it was falling. The forest was noisy—quite different from the house where they'd left Sean's fiancée fifty miles southwest.

"She will be," Dante said after a few moments. "Greg was the love of her life. He was a good man. He didn't deserve what happened."

"What did happen? She never told me, just that he'd been murdered."

"You don't want to hear this, Eden."

"I do."

Dante sighed. He took out his water bottle and sipped, put the lid on tight, and put the bottle back on his belt. He was definitely comfortable out here. While Dante enjoyed luxuries, good food and drink, he was far more comfortable walking in the middle of the jungle than she and Liam.

"Greg was a US soldier turned mercenary. He and his team had been hired to track a fugitive in Mexico—a mid-level drug runner who'd killed a US federal agent. The US government was working through diplomatic channels, but you know how these things are."

"Not really. It's why Liam and I always avoided taking jobs down here. It's far more violent."

"Perhaps, but I love much about this place. It's not all violent. The people are wholesome. Real. It's not how you see it on television or in the movies. Yes, there is violence. Yes, there are gangs and drug cartels who control certain territories, and there are corrupt police and politicians. But Mexico is a big country. There is far more harmony than not. You just have to know where to look for it." He smiled wistfully, shook his head. "Anyway, Greg and his team were ambushed. He was shot and his men tried to retrieve him, but he was taken. Tortured by Samuel Flores."

"That's horrific."

Dante didn't speak for several minutes as they walked up a steep part of the trail; then as they started back down the path, sheltered by overhanging trees and tall ferns, he said, "Do you know much about Ms. Kincaid?"

"I don't want to know anything." She glanced at him, eyes narrowed. "What?" She didn't want to have this conversation, but it seemed Dante was going to push in his own subtle way.

"I'm no saint. Neither is my sister. But there's a certain . . . diplomacy, for lack of a better word, that I've preserved since we've made Mexico our home. I've had a lot of autonomy to work down here. I earn a good living. Not completely on the side of the law, but I pick and choose my associates carefully. One of the reasons is because of Greg—Gabriella has many friends through him. Including Jack Kincaid."

Eden stumbled and Dante caught her elbow. "Oh, God, this is just getting better and better."

"All I'm saying is that I wish you'd called me before you made the decision to transport Jack's little sister into hostile territory. When I tried to talk to Liam about it yesterday, he wouldn't even listen to me. Does he have another reason for taking Lucy?"

"No," Eden said. But she really didn't know what Liam had been thinking. Liam had been so angry, so volatile, since he found out that Kane had been the one to betray him. And he'd always disliked the Kincaids, who had usurped his and Eden's positions at Rogan-Caruso. Yet he couldn't possibly be using Lucy for anything else. She hoped.

But, Eden acknowledged only to herself, she could be blind when it came to her twin brother.

"She's safe where she is," Eden said.

The path turned sharply right and had walked for several hundred meters when suddenly they broke into a clearing. A waterfall fell to the right, and they could see the valley on the left. It was stunning.

She realized then that Liam hadn't called Sean.

"Liam, hold up."

He stopped, irritated. "What?"

"You didn't call Sean."

"So?"

"You promised you'd call him and tell him where Lucy was."

"She's fine where she is. I'll call him tonight."

"You told her he'd be coming for her—really, Liam, you have to call."

"I'm sure there's no cell coverage here."

Dante cleared his throat. "Liam—buddy, what's your plan here?"

"You know the plan!" He ran a hand through his hair. "Look, I've been thinking—what if Lucy tells him about Tampico? And then he and Kane track us down here? I know Kane has resources, he might figure out where we went. I don't want to deal with them until we have the treasure in our hands."

"That wasn't the plan," Dante said.

"So? Little Miss Federal Agent is just fine in your house, Dante. If she wanders, whatever happens is her own damn fault."

Eden grabbed Liam by the arm. "Dammit, you promised you would call!"

"Lucy will get over it."

"You promised *Sean*. Or did you forget leaving that note and phone in his safe? He's probably sitting there waiting for your call. It's nearly noon. Don't do this to him—he's still our brother."

It was clear that Liam didn't want to call him. "Fine," he finally said, "but if they fuck with us, my moratorium on violence is over. This is *our* heritage, Eden, it's everything we have wanted since Mom and Dad died, and I'm not going to let Kane screw it up again."

Eden watched as Liam took his phone out. She had to make sure he called Sean—what if he tried to trick her?

Liam was acting more obsessed than usual. She didn't lie to herself—Liam was no saint. Neither was she. They were exactly what Noah Armstrong had called her six and a half years ago: thieves.

But Liam was her brother, and she would stand by him. He showed her the phone, then walked to the edge of the path for better reception.

"Everyone who has searched for this treasure has died or lost something valuable," Dante said quietly. "I don't want to lose you, Liam, or my sister."

"You can turn around now," Eden said. "I have never seen Liam happier or more excited. He's been on this journey since our parents died. This is important to him—to all of us."

"I'm not going back." His eyes sparkled. "I may have doubts that the gold is there, but I know in my heart the ruins are. The history alone is worth the risk."

"That is one thing we can agree on."

Dante followed her gaze to her brother. What was he thinking? That Liam was willing to risk Lucy Kincaid's life over this?

Or was that the plan all along?

CHAPTER TWENTY-THREE

Noah helped Jack's caretaker, Ezra, fuel Sean's plane and check the systems while Sean talked to Jack. Noah meant what he said—he was joining them. Not just because of Eden, but because Lucy and Sean were *his* friends.

Noah might not like many of Sean's methods, but the one thing he'd always admired about him—Sean's saving grace—was his honor. Something neither Liam nor Eden had in their wheelhouse.

Sean walked over. "Jack is less than thirty minutes out."

Ezra, who couldn't be a day under eighty, nodded and said, "Eat."

Sean shook his head.

"Sean," Noah said.

Nate came over with a paper bag. "Ezra made sandwiches." He handed them out. "Now or in the air, Rogan. We need fuel just like the plane."

Noah stared at him. "Dunning, you're not going. This is a personal decision for me, but I'm not letting another federal agent cross the border."

"I got my orders from higher up."

"I know you're close to Kane, but you don't work for him."

"No, sir, I work for the FBI. To my knowledge, Rick Stockton outranks you. He told me that no matter what you did or where you went, I was to protect you."

"I don't need your protection, Dunning."

"Take it up with Stockton. Sir." Nate took a bite of his sandwich, then smiled at Ezra. "Good stuff, thanks much."

"I'll load the ice chest," Ezra said, and went back to the plane. But instead of food, he packed the ice chest with guns.

"Nate, you're at just as great a risk as I am," Noah said. "The fewer federal agents south of the border, the better."

"I'm not going as a federal agent, and neither are you." Nate took out his wallet and badge and put them on the worktable. He then removed his service weapon and put it with his badge. "I suggest you do the same."

Nate was right—now the guns Ezra was loading into the plane made sense.

Sean paced. He didn't want to eat. He didn't want to do anything but get in his plane and find Lucy—then hunt down his brother and beat him to a pulp. But he took a bite of the sandwich because both Noah and Nate were watching him. He didn't need either of them on his case or telling Jack he was messed up.

He *was* messed up, but he would have it together. He had to.

The phone in his left pocket rang.

Liam.

He pulled it out and answered before it rang a second time. "It took you long enough! If Lucy so much as breaks a nail, I will kill you."

Sean's heart was racing, but he forced himself to remain calm. Took a deep breath. Let it out. Turned away from Noah and Nate. He didn't care if they heard the conversation, but Sean needed to remember every word.

"Sean," Liam said, "you know I would never hurt your little girlfriend."

"You've made a huge mistake, Liam. Where is she?"

"Sean, you're being an ass, and I don't know that I want to tell you anything. She's safe where she is, maybe I should just let you sit and fume and realize that this isn't me, this is Kane."

"What the hell are you talking about? Kane didn't kidnap Lucy. You're insane, Liam. Tell me where she is or I will break you."

"Testy, aren't we?"

Sean's stomach twisted and turned into a knotted mess. "What do you want from me? I will do anything, Liam—just . . . Please. Tell me where Lucy is."

"*Please.* That's a nice touch. Kane would never say *please* for anything. Just so you know, this is *all* Kane's fault. He lied to me, disowned me, replaced me with an outsider, and kept those bonds hidden from me. I'm not done with him. But if you promise to retrieve your sweet little girlfriend and stay out of my business, I'll tell you where she is."

"I want nothing to do with your business, Liam."

"Do you have a pen?"

Sean did.

Liam gave him a longitude and latitude. "That's a small airstrip—you're flying, right? You should, anyway. The house she's staying at is only three miles from the airstrip. I left a jeep at the end of the runway. In the glove compartment is a map. There are no street names, so you'll have to follow my directions."

"This isn't over. You've made an enemy."

"So your word means nothing? You promised me you'd stay out of my way."

"I don't care about your business, but you fucked with me."

"Don't be that way. Sean, I did this as much for you as for me."

Sean lost it. "You kidnapped the woman I love *for me?* You bastard! You are a selfish prick, and I will hunt you down to the ends of the earth—"

The phone was dead.

Sean threw the burner phone against the wall. It shattered.

"Lucy isn't with them," Sean managed to say. "She's in the middle of nowhere."

He pulled out his tablet and launched his navigational mapping system. He plugged in the coordinates that Liam had given him. If Liam was telling the truth, Lucy was nearly seventy miles southwest from where Kane was heading. Sean slammed his fist against the worktable.

Ezra was talking on his radio. Sean didn't hear what he said until Ezra came over to him. "Sergeant Kincaid is landing. I'll have his plane fueled and ready in ten minutes."

Noah came over to him. "Sean, it makes sense that Liam wouldn't bring Lucy on this excursion. She would only slow him down. There's no reason he would lie about where she is."

"I don't know anymore—he was so angry. He almost didn't tell me. I mean, I don't think he even wanted to tell me where Lucy was." Sean paced. "He hates Kane. I don't care what Kane did, I trust he did it for the right reasons. And Liam is . . . He sounded crazy."

Sean didn't understand what Liam and Eden were doing, but he was going to find Lucy, take her home.

Then he'd hunt down his brother and sister to the ends of the earth and make them pay for everything they'd done.

CHAPTER TWENTY-FOUR

Gabriella Romero almost left the Flores compound in the middle of the night. *Almost.*

Three things stopped her.

First, she wasn't positive Jasmine Flores didn't have someone assigned to follow her if she left the estate. She had had a few odd encounters with some of Dominick's people, people who now answered to Jasmine. Gabriella had thought she'd made alliances with some of them; now she wasn't certain.

Second, Jasmine was up to something. She'd been secretive last night, spending a lot of time in her office and sending a team out of the compound on God knew what errands.

And third, Gabriella's need for revenge.

She'd thought that killing Samuel, the man who had tortured and killed her fiancée, would have been enough. But Jasmine was just as evil as he was, and the more she learned about the witch, the more Gabriella knew she needed intelligence to either stop Jasmine herself or give to Jack Kincaid so he and his people could take her out.

Maybe, Gabriella thought, vengeance had driven her for

so long that she didn't know what to do without it in her heart.

But the *how* was the crux of the problem. She was still working through it.

Gabriella walked in from her early morning swim, the one time in the day when she was mostly alone and could think without distractions. She wrapped her robe around her lithe body and sauntered over to Jose, who was drinking coffee in the large atrium. Though RCK had damaged much of the exterior of the Flores compound, the interior was mostly preserved. Nothing a bit of paint and a few plaster repair jobs couldn't fix. Jasmine had hired local crews to rebuild the exterior walls, plus they were in the process of building a tower in each corner to prevent future attacks—from RCK or any of their other enemies.

She leaned over and kissed Jose, but he was distracted. She sat down, sipped his coffee. "What's wrong, handsome?" she said.

"Something's going on, and Jasmine isn't talking to me."

Gabriella leaned forward. "Honey, she wants to be in charge. She's already taken over."

"That's fine, I don't want to be in charge, but Dom always talked to me."

"Because you are a reasoned planner. If Dom had listened to you, he would still be alive."

"You don't know that."

"I do. Because you cared about your brothers and you understood the value of negotiation over revenge."

Jose leaned forward and said quietly, "Jasmine is bringing in a new lawyer. She wouldn't tell me who, but someone who's supposedly as good as Carson Spade."

"That would be a feat," she said. "Spade was the best money could buy."

"That's what I told her and she got all defensive. Talked

about leverage and how she wasn't going to make the same mistakes."

"Rewriting history, I'd think."

"Shh. She's very angry with you."

Gabriella took his hand. "Let's go away. Anywhere. A real vacation." She smiled and kissed his palm. "Let Jasmine get her affairs in order, do what she needs to do, we don't have to be part of it."

He brought her hand to his lips, kissed it. "There's nothing I would rather do than take a week . . . a month even . . . and relax with you. But right now it's too dangerous."

Jose was right about that—he was the last Flores male still alive. There was Alberto's infant son, who was back in the States, but the word Gabriella had was that his identity was a carefully guarded secret, in case someone wanted to grab him.

Jasmine was an American, distrusted even though she was Don Flores's illegitimate daughter. That she was just as ruthless as her father and three older brothers wasn't a factor to most of the Flores enemies.

"We can go to Spain," she whispered. "My family has a villa there, you would be safe."

She feared she had too much affection for Jose. She didn't love him—she would never love another man after Greg—but she cared for him, as much as a woman like her could care for anyone. Spain would be safe for both of them, until things settled down here.

"You tempt me," he said with a sigh. "I can't. Not now."

She pouted but considered that this was a possible out from this situation without Jose suspecting she'd been with him for reasons other than sexual attraction.

"We'd both be safe there," she whispered.

He squeezed her hands. "I know this last month has been especially hard on you."

"I'm worried. I'm not a shrinking violet, but this whole thing has the potential for war. One reason Dante and I have survived in our business for so long is that we've avoided these kind of conflicts."

"I want to fix this. If you need to go, I understand."

"I don't want to." But she said it in such a way that Jose would be thinking that she might leave out of fear.

Jose tensed. "Someone's here."

Gabriella turned toward the door at the opposite end of the atrium. She hadn't heard the car approach, but she heard doors slam shut. Jasmine stepped out of her office flanked by two men. They walked immediately to the front doors.

A moment later the doors opened and a man and woman stepped in flanked by two bodyguards whom Gabriella recognized as Jasmine's most trusted men. The woman carried an infant. The couple looked exhausted, but the man was angry. Or possibly annoyed. He glanced around, suspicious and not a little worried.

"Thank you for coming so quickly," Jasmine said.

"You didn't give me a choice."

"There's always a choice," Jasmine said coolly. She turned to one of her men. "Please show Mrs. Morrison to her suite. I'm sure you'll like the accommodations—two bedrooms, a private kitchen, a spacious living room. We've been remodeling this past month, but I had my men working overtime to get the suite finished." She stepped close to Mrs. Morrison. "He's so beautiful."

"Thank you," Mrs. Morrison said, holding the baby close to her.

"What's going on?" Gabriella whispered.

Jose hesitated, then said, "The lawyer I told you about."

Her stomach fell. *The man brought his wife and newborn to Mexico?*

You didn't give me a choice.

Sounded like a Flores family plot. Morrison had taken the job, but with it came his complete loyalty because he'd been forced to put his wife and child under Jasmine's protection.

Mrs. Morrison looked at her husband. He kissed her lightly, then said, "Go ahead, you need to sleep."

"Christopher can watch Joshua for you if you'd like to rest," Jasmine said.

"No, thank you," Mrs. Morrison said sharply. But she followed Christopher across the atrium and up the stairs. She didn't give Jose and Gabriella more than a passing glance.

"Danielle understands the situation, correct?" Jasmine asked. When Mr. Morrison didn't answer immediately, she pushed. "Thomas, you explained the situation to your wife."

"As much as I could," he said. He was definitely more focused on Gabriella and Jose than his wife.

Jasmine led him across the atrium. "Thomas, my half brother, Jose, and his girlfriend, Gabriella. They live here, at least for now." She stared at Gabriella.

"I need to make sure my wife is settled."

"Of course. Upstairs, down the hall, turn left. The only set of double doors leads to your suite. But don't take long, we have work to do. Meet me in my office in thirty minutes."

Thomas nodded to the group, then went upstairs.

"He's not on board," Jose said when Thomas Morrison was out of earshot.

"He is."

"He doesn't seem happy about whatever arrangement you have with him," Gabriella said.

"This is not your affair."

"I've been here longer than you." Gabriella had learned early on that she had to maintain the upper hand with bullies like Jasmine. If Jasmine thought she was scared, Gabriella was in trouble.

"Where's your brother?"

She wasn't expecting that question, but she shrugged. "Dante does what Dante does."

"He closed down his house and didn't tell you?"

"I'm not my brother's keeper."

"Maybe you should be. I don't trust him—and I don't trust you."

"Jasmine, please don't do this," Jose said.

"Isn't it just convenient that she was here when those bastards from Rogan-Caruso swooped in?"

"What are you talking about?"

"Don't play ignorant, Jose," Jasmine snapped. "She was here, and they had inside information."

"Gabriella saved my life. She tried to save Alberto, but he panicked. I was there, I saw her risk herself for my brother."

That was partly true. Gabriella had gone to make sure Alberto's girlfriend and kid were safe and out of harm's way. Alberto was there and she tried to make him listen to her, but Alberto was a pig. He wouldn't listen to any woman, actually called her Jose's whore. It was Alberto's own fault he got himself killed. Gabriella didn't like him, but her goal was to kill Samuel—a goal she achieved without a moment of regret.

Samuel had killed the man she loved. The man she would have married. And eight years later she had her revenge.

She could sit here and gloat while also protecting her own ass. But Jasmine was becoming a bigger problem than Dominick. Dom had been violent and ruthless, but he always had a plan . . . he rarely acted out of anger, and he was never stupid.

Jasmine wasn't stupid, but her ideas were dangerous.

She had a need for people to worship her—she wanted to be adored, feared, loved. Sometimes her decisions—like to bring in a new lawyer, with a family—bordered on insane. They should be laying low, taking care of local business to ensure no one went after it, then rebuilding. Inside out. It's what Dom would have done—it's what Dante would have recommended if he'd been consulted, as he often was about these sorts of things.

Gabriella was going to have to leave. She'd set it up with Jose—she would have to leave sooner rather than later. Jasmine was a wild card, and one she didn't care to test.

But could she leave Danielle Morrison and an innocent infant under this roof?

Not your problem, Gabriella.

She'd get out, then alert Jack Kincaid. Let him deal with the situation. Or not. She didn't owe anyone anything.

Jose cleared his throat. That was when Gabriella realized that she and Jasmine were in a staring match.

Gabriella stood. She didn't take her eyes off Jasmine. The woman would shoot her in the back if she thought she could get away with it. And someday she might be able to. But she needed Jose to solidify her power; if Jose put the word out he wasn't supporting Jasmine, she'd be dead in a week. Gabriella wanted to make that happen. She thought she might have an opportunity, if she could stick it out.

"I'm going to our room," she said to Jose. "I'll meet you for lunch?"

Jose rose, kissed her cheek. "I'll be down here."

She smiled at him, then went upstairs without looking back at Jasmine.

"You can't trust her," Jasmine said in a low voice. Not low enough.

Jose said, "Leave her alone."

Then Gabriella couldn't hear them anymore.

Something was up.

She ran to her room and pulled out her cell phone. She had the microphone set on Jose's phone so she could listen to his conversations if necessary. She put her earbuds in and turned up the volume.

Jose was speaking. "—it's done."

"You are a fool."

"Don't start with me. Gabriella has been loyal to me. I won't have you threatening her."

"I'm sure Gabriella is exactly what you think she is." By Jasmine's tone, she didn't believe it. "But her brother is the one who brokered the deal with Dom for Kane Rogan, and that deal lost us our lawyer and half our money. Dom deserves to be dead for his stupidity, but Dante Romero set us up. If he didn't do it on purpose, he's an idiot and should still be punished. Maybe Gabriella wasn't party to his deception, but I will find out."

"What are you going to do?"

"It's already done. Dante Romero skipped town, but I know where he is. I've sent my men to collect him, and he will answer my questions."

"Don't do this. The Romeros have always been neutral in Dom's business. Dominick respected Dante."

"Dominick this, Dominick that. He's dead because he was stupid."

"Jasmine—"

"It's already done, so leave it alone."

"You'll be sorry."

"Is that a threat? Whose side are you on, Jose?"

"How dare you, Jasmine. You come in and take over and start making threats? I don't want the business. I liked how it was before, so I didn't challenge you. But you're reckless. You should have known that the feds would come down on you eventually! You think you're on par with Dom? He was brilliant. He was far from perfect, but he was smart, and he told you not to deal in the US sex trade. But you did it anyway. And then he told you not to sell that girl's baby. You did it anyway. Then created a fucking *business?* You think that was smart?"

"It was fucking *brilliant* and even Dom admitted it was a solid plan."

"Because he didn't know how you'd screwed it up."

Jasmine laughed. "Wait. Just wait. I have resources that Dom never had."

"Leave the Romeros alone."

"I'll leave your little whore to you, but Dante will answer for what he did. We'll see what he has to say, and he will prove to me that he didn't set up the RCK raid. Because *my* sources tell me that Dante Romero might be playing both sides."

There was some static then Jose said, "Show Gabriella more respect, or I'll leave."

"Go ahead."

"If I leave, you will have nothing. You think you're all-powerful, but you've been in the States most of your life. Everyone thinks you're an outsider. There's only so much loyalty you can buy."

"You're my only family, Jose. We're going to make this work—together. But you have to trust me."

There was silence for a long minute. Then Jose said, "Earn it."

Maybe Jose was more seasoned than Gabriella gave him credit for.

CHAPTER TWENTY-FIVE

Lucy didn't know how much time had passed, but it was warm. Not unbearable, but hotter than San Antonio had been lately. Was it noon? Later? Her eyesight hadn't returned and bright light hurt her eyes, so she stayed in the kitchen, which was the darkest and coolest room in the house.

If Liam was true to his word, he would have called Sean by now. She didn't know where she was, but Liam said it would take Sean six to seven hours to get here. He should be here before dark.

Liam, you better not have lied.

Like she was in a position to punish anyone.

She *would* get out of this.

She'd grown more angry and frustrated than scared while she sat waiting. She walked around multiple times, then tested herself to see if she could remember where everything was. She wasn't half-bad, she realized, as she navigated the furniture through each room, after a half-dozen attempts. She drank water, but there were no more bags of chips to eat. If her sight returned before Sean arrived, she could check out the canned food and make herself something.

She heard another car on the road. At first she thought it would pass by like all the others, but almost immediately she realized it was coming closer. Not one, but two vehicles.

Sean?

She stood quickly and almost ran to the door, but she hesitated. Listened carefully. She couldn't be sure this was Sean.

"Stay here," a male said in Spanish. His voice was deep and commanding. She didn't recognize it. "No one goes in or out. We wait."

She left the kitchen and walked as fast as she could to the back room. During her hours of exploration, she'd checked every door, touched everything within her reach. There was a half closet under the staircase that cut the back room in half. She had no idea who these people were, if they were coming into the house or waiting outside, but fighting in her condition was not an option.

Before she even closed the door to the small closet she heard pounding on the door.

"Romero!"

There were shouts, someone telling his partner to go around to the back. Lucy sat in the closet, frozen.

The front door was kicked in and several people stormed into the house. They swarmed the place, upstairs and down, heavy boots on tile floors. With each thud she jumped, and she willed herself to stay calm. A few minutes later one of the men said in rapid Spanish, "Hide the vehicles, I don't want Romero to get spooked. There's food and water here, he'll be back. We'll be here waiting."

"Want us to talk to folks?"

"Yeah," the first guy said. "Shake down the neighbors, find out what the fuck he's doing. We can't go back to Flores empty-handed."

Flores? But the Flores cartel had been wiped out.

Almost. Jasmine, the head of the black-market baby

ring, and Jose, the youngest, were still alive. Jasmine had fled the country and there was a warrant for her arrest. Jose had never set foot in the United States and there was no active warrant for him. What had Kane said? He was the sane brother? Or was that the oldest? She didn't remember, she'd had a lot going on when Kane and Sean returned from Guadalajara last month. She knew Kane was being cautious, but she thought the problem had been handled.

We started this war, Lucy. RCK doesn't start wars, but we didn't have a choice. Now we have to lay low and see what happens.

What would Jasmine or Jose Flores want with Dante Romero? Was this about the bonds? The treasure they were hunting? The Flores cartel had taken a major hit when their accountant turned state's evidence. They'd need cash to continue operations. Maybe that was what this was all about—Flores knew about the bonds, heard that Dante had them, was going after him for the money.

Or did they suspect that Dante Romero had helped Kane and Sean last month? *Had* he helped? Hardly— he'd simply arranged the trade, according to Sean. Lucy wished she had paid more attention to what had happened, but this last month had been hell for both her and Sean and she wanted to put it all behind her. Lately, she'd been so focused on finding the missing babies, she hadn't kept up with what was going on with the Flores family.

Whatever they wanted with Dante Romero couldn't be good. Lucy had seen the results of Jasmine's criminal enterprise—she was violent and brutal. But she'd always been hands off, leaving the kidnappings and murders to her employees. Lucy had no proof that Jasmine Flores herself killed anyone but she had evidence she'd orchestrated the selling of newborns. Carson Spade, the Flores cartel's lawyer and accountant, was turning state's evidence against her. She would be extradited as soon as the indictment was handed down—if they could find her.

Did Jasmine Flores know who Lucy was? She thought not. Though Lucy was a federal agent, most people wouldn't recognize her. Her name was another story, so Lucy needed to come up with a story in case she was found.

Lucy made herself as small as possible and remained in the crawl space under the staircase, praying to God that she wouldn't be found. Even if they believed whatever story she told them, she was playing a dangerous game.

CHAPTER TWENTY-SIX

Kane Rogan landed northwest of Tampico, Mexico, just before one p.m. Tuesday.

He turned to Siobhan. "You do exactly what I say."

She didn't argue with him. That was a first. She'd been surprisingly quiet on the long flight south. Maybe he'd really scared her off with the way he'd kissed her. Kissed her? He'd devoured her. Maybe she didn't want him anymore. He couldn't blame her.

But his stomach tightened. He couldn't do this forever. He would have to cut her loose as soon as possible, to save them both.

He glanced at her again. He didn't want to cut her loose. Maybe it was nerves. Definite possibility. The flight had been bumpy, he'd gone too far out in the gulf, but it had been the fastest route to Tampico. He had access to a small unused runway, but the landing had been hairy. Could have taken its toll on her. But Kane didn't want to use any facility that might employ someone who'd recognize him and spread the word to the wrong people that he was back. His main problem was he didn't have enough fuel to get back to the States. He could do a short jump somewhere, but he might have to temporarily dump the plane and fly back with Sean.

He was stunned to find another small plane at the end of the runway. He almost aborted his landing, but then he'd really be in fuel trouble. He pulled out his gun and drove the plane toward the unknown craft. "Get down," he ordered Siobhan.

She immediately complied.

As soon as he saw the call numbers, he recognized it was Sean's. He taxied to a stop. Noah Armstrong and Nate Dunning came out of the bushes, but he didn't see his brother.

"We're good," he told Siobhan, and she slowly sat back up. She was pale. Okay, she was always pale, but this time she looked downright ghostly. "Sorry, sugar," he said.

"I'm okay."

She didn't sound okay.

"Bumpy ride."

She took a deep breath and drank half a bottle of water. "I'm okay," she repeated.

He smiled, then positioned the plane off the runway but in a place where he could easily take off in an emergency.

"What are you doing here?" Kane asked Armstrong as he jumped out of the plane. "Are you insane? Where's Sean?"

Noah said, "Sean tried to call you."

"I was over the Gulf. No signal."

"Liam gave Sean a location on Lucy seventy miles from here. Jack and Sean went after Lucy. You needed backup here."

"Not from a fucking fed," Kane said. "Shit, Armstong, do you understand the danger you put yourself in just by stepping across the border?"

"About as much as you."

"The cartels might kill me on sight, but they'll *enjoy* torturing a US federal agent."

Noah tensed. "I get it, Rogan. But you're one person against four—maybe more. Dunning and I are trained, and I damn well know that Stockton hired RCK to vet the entire San Antonio FBI office after the leak this summer, so you know that Dunning and I are capable."

"There's only one commander, and that's me. You have a problem, fly away now, and take her with you." He nodded toward Siobhan.

"Don't talk about me like I'm not here," Siobhan said. "I get it, I don't have training, but I have something none of you have."

"Excuse me?" He almost smiled at whatever it was she thought she could do.

She tilted her chin up. "You came without ground transportation. Fortunately, the Sisters of Mercy have a small clinic in Tampico. I contacted Sister Bernadette before we left New Orleans, and she said there would be a truck waiting for me a mile from here."

"How did you know where I was landing?"

"I can read a map, just like you, *sugar*."

Kane had planned on stealing the first vehicle he found. The runway was twenty miles from where Liam was supposed to be, but it was the closest private landing strip he knew about in the area.

Kane grinned and winked at Siobhan. He turned to Noah. "You good, Flyboy?"

"Yes, Commander," Noah said.

Armstrong was beginning to grow on him.

The weight of his responsibilities grew as they walked through dense foliage in the midday heat. While Noah and Nate may have come down here *thinking* they knew what they would face, they hadn't been in the field in years. They were federal agents. Nate didn't look like anything but a soldier, but Noah was too . . . *clean*. Kane didn't care that neither had family; he didn't want to have to go to Rick Stockton, a man he considered as close as or closer than his brothers, and tell him he got his agents captured or killed. Not to mention the fact that Siobhan was with them. He had wanted to leave her in New Orleans—it would have been safer all around—but Siobhan had some use. She knew the people of Mexico better than Kane. Kane knew the bad guys—the cartels, the gangs, the violence. Siobhan knew the good guys—the regular people, the shop owners, the religious folk. She spoke their language, and he wasn't talking just talking Spanish. She understood how to put them at ease. Kane didn't know what to expect at the ruins of the old church, but Siobhan's knowledge of the area could come in handy.

Maybe it was an excuse to keep her with him to protect her and keep her out of trouble; maybe it was because he had a moment of fear that Liam had changed, that he could have hurt Siobhan and Lucy when he kidnapped them. Kane was used to feeling a cold rage deep inside, not pain. Not the deep sorrow that had swept through him in the moment he thought he might never see Siobhan again.

That Siobhan was unharmed gave him hope that Lucy was also okay. It also gave him hope for his own humanity. He didn't feel emotions like he used to . . . except with Siobhan. He didn't necessarily like it, but he didn't *not* like it, either.

Kane couldn't let Liam walk away from his actions. He may have truly wanted those bonds for one special bond that included the treasure map, but what did he plan on doing with the nearly $6 million? He had to have funded this project in some way, and Kane's fear was that Liam had traded the bonds for cash to someone who could do far more damage. And what did Carlo mean about Liam buying his freedom? Freedom from whom? Who had the bonds now?

And maybe . . . *maybe* Kane could have let it go if it were just about the money. He would have taken care of the situation quietly, after the fact. He was good at that—like when he stole the bonds before Liam could get to them six years ago. But Eden and Liam had manipulated Lucy, broken into Sean's safe, lied, and put both Siobhan and Lucy at risk. Lucy was still in danger, and she was under Kane's umbrella. If Kane didn't go after Liam, Jack would—and Jack wouldn't pull any punches. When it came to his family, he was stalwart. No one touched them, or they would pay.

Liam was going to have to face the music this time. Kane would bring him back to the States and turn him over to Noah and the FBI. Him *and* Eden. Maybe a few years in prison would finally get through to them. Actions had consequences, and some actions had serious consequences.

Kane hadn't been much of a brother to his siblings, especially after his parents died. Duke—who had sacrificed so much to raise Sean—had a completely different style. Kane was hands-off; Duke micromanaged. The twins shut them both out after a while, so it was no wonder that they started down a dangerous path without guidance. But didn't they have a conscience? Didn't they understand some lines couldn't be crossed?

He should have done things differently, but he was a soldier, not a father. Not a very good brother. He saw things as black-and-white, right and wrong. His idea of *wrong* might be subjective based on the situation, but he lived comfortably with situational ethics.

He'd thought more about the past in the last two days than he had in the last ten years. He never second-guessed himself; why was he starting now? Because this was family? Or because he had misstepped?

The truck that Siobhan procured was exactly where she'd said it would be. The keys were in the glove box—not smart, but helpful.

Kane told Noah to drive with Siobhan in the cab, and he and Nate sat in the truck bed. They kept their weapons out of sight but within easy reach.

Twenty minutes later and Kane could count the cars they'd passed on one hand. They were heading deep into the mountain range, about equidistant between Tampico, San Luis, and Ciudad Victoria.

Kane had felt the turbulence coming over the gulf in his little Cessna, but now the clouds slowly moved in. There wasn't much wind, but by tonight there would be rain. Weather reports had called for brief but violent thunderstorms in the gulf region up into eastern Texas as well as Mexico, moving up to a hundred miles inland, which was where they were. If the predictions were right, the storm would blow over by morning, but they'd definitely be grounded until then. Kane didn't want to stay any longer than necessary, but flying in a thunderstorm was foolish.

Noah had flown Sean's plane, which, out of the three aircraft down here, would be the best equipped to handle the weather. It was newer, larger, and Sean was a better pilot than Kane. Noah, too, could handle it. But none of the planes were big enough to carry all of them. Sean's could take eight, maybe nine people. Kane's maxed out at four, plus he didn't have enough fuel. Jack's plane sat six.

As Kane mentally ran through how to safely get out of Mexico, he realized he was avoiding thinking about what to do with Liam and Eden.

Because he'd already decided.

He closed his eyes. He was not looking forward to this confrontation.

The truck slowed as Noah turned onto a rougher, steeper

road. Kane scanned the eastern horizon and valley below them. It was peaceful here. Few people, cooler up here in the hills, greener. He'd been in areas of Mexico that made him want to believe in God. Vast, gorgeous, endless land without people, without violence. There were some places he thought he could stay forever, disappear, forget the rage that burned inside him, a rage he didn't always understand.

And sometimes, when he looked at Siobhan, he thought the same thing. He could disappear with her, bury the pain, forget the violence man did to man. The violence Kane understood, even participated in.

Sometimes.

The road grew steeper, and Noah pulled over to the side and shut off the truck.

Kane jumped out. Noah didn't have to tell him the rest of the road was impassable. They needed transportation and if they continued going they'd be stuck. "How far?" he asked.

"Approximately a kilometer."

Kane was torn between leaving Siobhan in the truck and having her join them. He didn't want to believe that Liam was willing to kill for this gold, but he could be . . . or he could be working for someone willing to kill.

"You remember Andie's lessons." It was a statement, not a question. But he had to make sure.

Siobhan stared at him. "Just give it to me."

He slipped her a small but well-maintained 9mm that he used as backup to his backup. He knew Siobhan didn't like guns, but her sister had made sure she knew how to handle one, and other than a revolver—which didn't have more than six rounds—it didn't get much easier than a 9mm.

They walked the kilometer—Kane leading, Nate taking the rear. In the distance, Kane saw a tent partly hidden in the trees. He held up his hand to stop the others, motioned for Noah to stay with Siobhan and Nate to join him to inspect the tent.

They approached silently. Kane recognized the standard military-style ten-by-ten pop-up. It had been staked down, so they'd planned on staying awhile. The front flap was zipped but not locked. There were vents at the top, but he couldn't see in.

Kane listened. He didn't hear anyone inside. He motioned for Nate to unzip on three. It was a difficult move, using the tip of his rifle, but one every soldier had trained for.

Nate got into position.

Three. Two. One.

Nate unzipped rapidly, and Kane stepped inside, gun out, looking for movement.

The tent was empty.

He whistled for Noah and motioned for Nate to guard the area.

Inside there were three sleeping bags, an ice chest, two large satchels. Kane searched the tent for weapons; there were none. The ice chest was locked. He picked the lock; inside was food and water. It wasn't cool, but the ice chest protected the food from predators.

Noah searched the two bags. Inside were two extra cell phones; he tossed them to Kane. Some cash—two hundred US dollars and maybe eight hundred in Mexican currency. "No bonds," Noah said. He pulled out a file folder. "Kane."

Kane opened the folder and they both looked at the contents. The handwriting seemed feminine, most likely Eden's. Information about Sean and Lucy, their address, Sean's security system, notes about Lucy and her family, mostly Jack. Another page was information about the region they were in, roads and paths, and a supply list.

There were many doodles, but Kane didn't know if they meant anything. Noah took the sheet outside to Siobhan.

"You know this area—these marks look like a map of sorts."

Siobhan stared, turned the paper. "This looks like it could be the floor plan for a church—this is a vestibule, an altar, these crosses a cemetery. Don't know if it means anything."

Kane stuffed everything back into the pack and zipped up the tent. "Three bags, three people. Liam, Eden, and Dante. They'll be back, probably by dark." Did he wait for them or track them?

Nate whistled from a hundred yards away. Kane couldn't see him, motioned for Noah to stay with Siobhan, and followed the sound. He approached and saw Nate standing at an opening to an overgrown path.

"They went this way." Nate motioned to recently broken branches, footprints.

Pursue or wait. How far had they gone? Where did the path lead? Kane saw thick foliage ahead, but according to the topographical maps he had studied earlier, the other side of this mountain was a series of valleys and plateaus. There were hidden dangers—human and animal—and Kane didn't like going into any situation blind.

"They plan to return," Kane said. "Otherwise they would have taken their packs. Which means the journey is less than half a day. They'd want to return before dark, so my guess is their destination is no more than four hours, otherwise they would have brought their supplies down to the ruins."

"They could have two camps."

"Possible, not likely. They left food and water here. They have three people—no one to carry extra rations and equipment. Guess? They wanted to start the excavation or simply confirm the old church is where they think it is. Once they do that, they'll return here, head out again first thing in the morning, probably with all their equipment. Or hire some locals to go with them."

"You want to wait."

Kane considered his options. "I don't trust Liam, but confronting them in the middle of this jungle wouldn't be smart. They know the terrain better—they've been studying these maps for years. They have equipment. Dante will have a gun. And if we get the upper hand, how do we get them back here? I don't like going into the unknown. I want to get a handle on the area."

He and Nate walked back to the tent. "Siobhan, how well do you know this place?"

"We're about twenty kilometers south of the botanical reserve. The greatest threats are poisonous snakes and jaguars. And spiders." She shivered. "I have a fairly good topographical map for this region, but most locals don't come up here. It's considered haunted—there was a village in these mountains that completely disappeared after an earthquake more than a hundred years ago."

"Do you know where it is?"

"Not specifically. Do you think that's where Liam and Eden are going?"

"Yes. If there was a church there, that's where they're going."

"Could have been—I haven't heard of one, but there were many missionaries and priests converting the Mexican Indians to Christianity back then. Some kindly, some violently. If they had converted an entire village—which may have only been a few hundred people—they most likely would have built a church."

"You now want to follow them?" Noah asked.

"No. I want to recon the area. We're going to wait here—they'll be back before dark. They won't be expecting us."

"Unless your friend in New Orleans called them."

"He won't." Kane was 90 percent certain Carlo wouldn't call his son. He was counting on it, but if Carlo talked, there were still only a few ways to escape. Kane would find them. "Dunning, you and Armstrong search everything within two hundred yards. Siobhan and I are going to follow their trail. I'm not going to engage—I need an idea of what's going on, confirm there are only three of them, determine if they have additional weapons." He pulled out his radio, turned it on. "Test your equipment. If you hear or see anything, alert me. We won't be more than fifteen minutes away." He looked at Siobhan. "This time, sugar, you get to lead."

Eden watched her brother and saw the joy in his eyes.

Everything they had done, everything they had suffered, was going to be rewarded.

Eden had never told Liam that she had doubts about the treasure. He had been obsessed since they were nineteen, before they returned to college, when his dad first told him how close he was to finding the ruins. After he'd passed the baton to Liam, anointed him in a way, Liam had never lost sight of the goal. There had been times when he and Eden were stumped, when they had no direction, and then six years ago when they thought everything was lost.

Now Eden knew everything they'd done had been leading up to this moment. The gold was within their grasp. Their father had given them this mission, this legacy, and they would not disappoint him.

Eden loved history—Liam loved adventure. Together, they used their skills and their knowledge to uncover treasures all over the world, to right wrongs, to return to museums what belonged to the world, and sometimes they had to break a few laws to do what was right. Or take jobs they didn't want to pay for the hunt.

Liam believed. And Eden loved her brother for that.

Reaching the ruins had taken nearly an hour longer than they'd planned. The trail was impassable in places and they'd had to find an alternate route twice. They were forced to cut through thick vines and underbrush. They were all tired, sore, and nicked from the plants and branches.

But they were here.

A waterfall dribbled from high in the mountains into the valley below. A stream cut through the middle. It wasn't technically a valley, Eden thought—it wasn't bigger than two odd-shaped baseball stadiums joined together, separated by the narrow river. Had this stream been here two hundred years ago?

The mountains on the east were much higher than the hills on the west, which was why originally the access was from the west. But the earthquake had crumbled the mountainside, making it impassable, and no one had tried to clear it. Because of the dead, the ghosts, the memories.

The curse.

Eden shivered, tried to put the idea of a curse out of her head. She didn't believe in that nonsense. She did believe in history, however, and that human behavior could be shaped by events far more readily than a supernatural *curse*. Such circumstances might lead the more primitive of people to believe in an ethereal curse. Better to blame something intangible and fearsome than one's own ineptitude.

They saw nothing but a velvety growth over the ground, save for a lone stone on the far southern side of the valley. "It's the cross," Liam said.

He handed her his binoculars. She looked, refocused. Two stones, broken, collapsed. Yes, they could have once made a cross. But from here it was nearly impossible to tell.

"This is it, Eden!"

Dante, more practical than the Rogans, was silenced by what they were seeing. The green was greener than she had pictured; the flowers, brightly colored and vibrant. Overhanging tree branches, heavy with vines and leaves, fell eerily, beckoning them at the same time they seemed to say, *Stay back*. The hues were so vivid Eden almost wanted to avoid touching anything, for fear of contaminating something that had not hosted human beings in so many years. Eden was glad they weren't staying here overnight— the predators would come out, if they weren't here already. There were so many places for them to hide. They could be anywhere, using the beauty of the valley to draw in their prey. Watching, waiting for a big meal.

She shivered.

Stop scaring yourself.

Eden was definitely a city girl.

"Let's go," Liam said.

"We have three hours," Dante reminded him. "Then we have to head back. We'll start earlier tomorrow."

Liam didn't say anything, and Eden hoped he wasn't planning on staying longer. Or staying through the night. Even though the valley looked like paradise, Eden was scared, and she couldn't explain why. Maybe because they were the only three people in a fifty-mile radius. Maybe because there were long-dead villagers buried in the ruins. Maybe because there was no one to call for help if they were stuck.

She took a deep breath. "Three hours," she repeated, hoping that Liam would listen to her, if he didn't listen to Dante. "We cleared the path, we'll get back here much faster tomorrow."

They followed Liam across the valley floor toward the broken stone cross.

Gold or not, they would find history in these ruins.

CHAPTER TWENTY-SEVEN

Jack clicked off the satellite phone without saying much.

"Who was that?" Sean asked.

"Gabriella. She couldn't reach Dante."

"And?" Sean pushed when Jack didn't continue.

Jack had circled the point that Liam had given them to land at, wanting to make sure he didn't see anything unexpected. He banked the aircraft, adjusted the controls, leveled off, and headed straight for the short runway.

"Gabriella learned last night that Liam left Lucy at Dante's safe house—the same location that Liam gave you. She couldn't call sooner."

Sean breathed marginally easier. If Gabriella had the same information, that meant chances were good that Lucy was here and safe.

Jack landed the plane smoothly. He taxied and stopped. "But we might have a situation. Gabriella risked her life to call me—I want you to know that, Sean."

"Tell me."

"Jasmine Flores sent people to grab Dante. She thinks Dante is the one who set up the attack last month—or that he helped you and Kane."

"Dante knew the risk."

"She may know the location of his safe house."

"May know?"

Jack didn't respond. He didn't have to. Jack maneuvered the plane into a spot that would be hard to see at first glance. That's when Sean spotted the truck Liam had promised him, parked between two short trees.

"Gear up," Jack said.

Sean strapped a Kevlar vest over his T-shirt. He checked his guns and ammo, dropped extra cartridges into his cargo pants. Sunglasses, hat, his emergency pack. Jack did the same. He tossed Sean a radio.

"Look at me," Jack said.

Sean strapped on his knife and turned to Jack.

"I have not stopped thinking about Lucy. I've been where you are. I know you won't be stupid. But this is my op. Understood?"

Sean nodded.

"Let's get my sister."

"Tom! I found someone!"

The foul-smelling, wiry man dragged Lucy out from under the stairs.

"Look at you, pretty young thing."

He first spoke in broken English, then said in Spanish, "What's your name, little girl?"

She was shaking. Partly out of very real fear, but she exaggerated it. She kept her eyes averted and played the part of a terrified, timid girl.

"What the hell, Jorge?" a voice said.

All Lucy could see was light and dark. She sensed more than saw movement. But she'd walked through every inch of the small two-story house. The owner of the voice stood in the doorway.

"I found her under the staircase. She must have been there for quite a while."

"What's your name?" Tom barked out in Spanish.

Lucy spoke in a common Spanish dialect. "Rosa Lucia, señor," she said. "I'm just a servant girl, helping Mr. Dante, he take pity on me."

"What? Speak up, girl! I can't hear you." Tom spoke rapid but clear Spanish. He didn't have as thick an accent as Jorge.

She cringed. "I—I just help Mr. Dante. He had to leave, I clean, I hear men come in, I was scared. I hid."

"What's wrong with your eyes? Look at me!"

She looked up. She couldn't see any details.

"She can't see, Tom," Jorge said.

"Are you blind?"

"Sí, señor, I don't see well," Lucy said.

He snorted. "How can you clean if you can't see?"

"Mr. Dante, he pities me, I need money to eat, it's just me and my *abuela*. We live down the road."

"What do you think?" a third man said. "I think she's lying."

No one said anything for a moment. Then the voice she recognized as that of Tom said, "She ain't lying. No one can stand still with a gun in their face and not react."

Lucy realized she was in deep trouble. She had to buy time. Someone would be here for her, right? Either Liam or Sean . . . someone!

"When is Romero coming back? Girl, answer me!"

"I don't know! I don't know!"

"Search her," Tom said.

Hands roughly patted her down. They didn't take the pen. Hands squeezed her breasts. "Nice tits."

Now she was really shaking; this fear wasn't exaggerated.

"Please, please don't hurt me," she cried. She aimed to stay in character, not fight back, but she wanted to lash out. Instead, she took her crucifix from under her shirt and started to pray out loud.

Stay in character, Lucy. Your life depends on it.

"No one is going to hurt you. What did you say your name was?"

"Rosa Lucia."

"Rosa Lucia. That's kind of pretty. Where do you live?"

"Up the road, too far to walk. Mr. Dante takes me home when I work."

"We'll just wait here for Mr. Dante, all right? Then maybe I'll take you home, talk to your *abuela*."

Tom's breath on her cheek startled her. He was right in her face. Too close.

"Please, sir, please, I don't want no trouble, sir."

"Then sit down."

From her earlier exploration she remembered a large chair in the corner of the small room. She made her way toward it, feeling around, and tripped over something right in her path. She cried out and fell to the floor.

The men laughed. "Just checking, Rosa," Tom said. "Help the girl up and keep your hands off her tits. I'm not going to condone that shit."

"You're no fun."

"I'll tell Marguerite that you had your hands all over her, see what happens then."

"You wouldn't dare."

"Just put her down in the chair and keep your eyes on her, Jorge. Eyes, not hands, got it?"

Jorge grabbed Lucy and pushed her into a soft chair. She breathed heavily, working to control her anger and fear.

She felt eyes watching her. They weren't going to leave her alone.

"What can you see?" Jorge asked. Everyone else seemed to have left the room. Lucy's instincts of being watched had saved her many times in the past, and now without sight she was even more acutely aware of what was going on around her.

"J-ju-just shadows and light," she said. "Daytime and nighttime. Things moving."

"So you can't see how many fingers I'm holding up?"

She shook her head.

"You're too pretty to clean up after people. Tell me the truth. Do you give Romero a little something extra between the sheets?" He touched her face and she flinched.

"No-no, sir, no."

He laughed.

She heard him pace the room, muttering to himself.

She took several deep breaths to calm herself, then mumbled a prayer. It was one her mother always recited when she was stressed, and it made Lucy feel a bit better. It was a Cuban prayer, there was nothing close to it in English.

Sean will be here. He will be here—

Commotion at the front of the house made Lucy jump.

"Stay," Jorge said. She heard him stomp out. She considered making a run for it, but where would she go?

Get out of this first, then worry about your sight. Better to be alive.

She was *not* going to be blind forever. Just a few hours more. If she could find a place to hide until her vision returned, she could run.

The commotion was louder, men were shouting, then Jorge came back into the room. "You're coming with us."

"No, no! Please, don't hurt me."

He pulled her out of the chair and held her in front of him. "Got the girl, Tom!" Jorge pushed her through the doorway. She stumbled and he held her up.

"Leave her—I can't deal with a blind *chica* slowing us down. We're leaving Daniel's team here to take care of whoever is approaching, but I got a line on Romero."

Another voice said, "What blind girl?"

"Romero's girlfriend or servant or just some little whore from the village, hell if I know."

Silence fell in the house.

"Well, I don't fucking believe it."

She recognized that voice. Why did she recognize that voice?

"You know her?"

"Yeah, I know her."

No. This could not *be happening.* Who knew her? No one! No one knew who she was, right?

Rough hands grabbed her by the hair and pulled her head roughly back. "I never forget a cop."

He slapped her and she hit the wall, flailing around trying to catch herself, then fell to the floor.

"A blind cop?"

"She's not blind."

Angelo Zapelli. The man who sold Marisol and Ana into the sex trade when Marisol was pregnant with his child.

The fear exploded inside and she whimpered involuntarily.

Angelo hauled her up. "You will regret the day you were born."

A man ran into the house. "Two paramilitary types are coming parallel to the road."

"I'm taking her to Flores. Turning over FBI Agent Lucy Kincaid will solve all my problems. Tom, grab two men and come with me. Daniel, keep the rest of the team here and kill anyone who approaches who isn't named Dante Romero. When Romero comes, grab him and bring him to

Flores. I don't care if he's bleeding, as long as he's breathing."

Tom said, "I have word that he's—"

"Who's fucking in charge here?" Angelo said. "Just do as I say, got it? Romero will be back, he's obviously working with the fucking US government. You know what that means? His sister is probably in on it. Let's go, Senorita Flores is going to be very happy tonight."

CHAPTER TWENTY-EIGHT

Jack put his hand up and Sean stopped in his tracks.

Movement in the bushes to the east. Jack put up two fingers, then motioned for Sean to go northeast and Jack turned around to the south.

Kane had spent more time training Sean in covert operations since he'd been living in Texas, but Sean still felt out of his element. Jack and Kane had decades of training. They'd both been in elite Special Forces, they'd both been mercenaries, they'd been members of long-standing teams of soldiers both in and out of the military and had a keen sixth sense about how the enemy would behave.

Sean had instincts and skills, even if he didn't have the experience and training. He trekked as quietly as possible through the dry brush, staying low because the trees were scrawny, barely large enough to hide behind. It was mid-afternoon and a thick, high cloud cover had turned the air stagnant and damp. A storm would be coming in that night, but right now it was hot, humid, and miserable. Fortunately, the sunlight wasn't beating down on them, it was already late in the afternoon.

Sean realized what Jack's plan was—there were three men in the bush, and Jack wanted to surround them. Sean didn't have time to think about why the men were here, so close to where Lucy was. Liam had told Sean she was alone. Had he lied? Or had Flores's men already arrived?

Sean saw a lone man looking away from him, standing guard next to a jeep. Beyond the jeep was a small two-story adobe house, hidden in part by trees and overgrown bushes. A thump to the south—near where Jack had gone—had drawn the man's attention. Sean had circled around him to get behind when he heard a shout.

"Daniel! Behind you!"

The man Sean was stalking whirled around and aimed his gun at Sean. Sean fired twice and the man went down without firing a shot.

A bullet whizzed past Sean. A man stood on the roof. Sean shot at him and missed, then took cover against the side of the house.

There was more gunfire to the south, and then Sean saw Jack coming through the trees.

"Roof!" Sean shouted. Jack sidestepped and hid behind a tree.

Over the radio that had fallen next to the dead man by the Jeep, Sean overheard the man on the roof asking for a status report. No one responded.

In Sean's earpiece, he heard Jack.

"We need him alive."

Jack already believed Lucy wasn't here.

Jack continued speaking in a low, calm voice. "Stay. I'm going to circle around to your location, then we'll clear the house and detain the shooter on the roof."

"Roger," Sean said. He itched to go inside. What if Lucy was injured? Restrained? Dead?

Lucy is not dead.

Sean waited in silence, listening for signs of an ambush. Nothing. No footfalls, no voices. He heard birds and intermittent static on the radio twenty feet in front of him. Footsteps above on the roof, the lone survivor pacing, nervous.

He should damn well be nervous.

Sean heard a whistle to his right. It sounded exactly like Kane, but Sean knew it was Jack. Sean stayed close to the house, rounded the corner, and saw Jack at the door. He was inspecting it for a booby trap. When he was satisfied, he held up his fingers.

Three.

Two.

One.

Jack went in high, Sean low. They cleared the ground floor quickly—there was only a small room in the back, a living area, and a kitchen. Jack led the way upstairs. There was a bedroom and a small den with an adjoining bath.

Sean held up a jacket. It was Lucy's. She had been here. He glanced around. Broken glass. Untouched food on the desk. A toppled chair.

Jack nodded, then whispered, "The only roof access is from the balcony off the bedroom. I need him alive. There's a tree that appears sturdy at the northeast corner of the roof. I'm going to climb it and get him in my sights. I'll give you the signal, you—" He stopped, listening. Sean didn't hear anything. "Scratch that, he's coming in."

Jack glanced around the doorjamb, holding up his hand for Sean to stay where he was.

Jack then shouted an order in Spanish. Sean knew a little but wasn't fluent. He thought Jack said, "Stop or die."

The man fired on Jack. Jack waited a split second, then fired back. Jack was the better shot. The man went down, writhing in pain.

"Cover me," Jack ordered, and ran into the hall. He disarmed the man of two guns and a knife, searched him, then pulled a rag from his back pocket and tied it around the shooter's arm. Blood seeped through.

Jack spoke rapidly in Spanish. The shooter spit in his face. Jack hit his wound and the man screamed. Jack spoke again. Fast and calm. Whatever the guy said wasn't the right answer; Jack punched him in the chest, then spoke again. The shooter swore. Even Sean could understand the vivid expletives.

Jack hauled the shooter up and said to Sean, "Guard the main door."

"Do you—"

"Now."

Sean hadn't seen this side of Jack before. He knew it was there—he'd seen hints of it over the years—but this was the Jack who'd been an Army Ranger, who had been a mercenary, who had saved Lucy eight years ago from a psychopath. Cold. Dark. Hard as a rock.

Sean went downstairs and stood sentry. He didn't hear anything for several long minutes. As the silence continued, he worried about Jack . . . he almost went upstairs to make sure he was okay.

But he waited. An earsplitting scream broke through the silence, then nothing.

Two minutes later, Jack came downstairs. Sean couldn't read his expression.

"When Flores learned Dante Romero left Gundalajara, she sent men to find him. My guess is as long as he was within her domain she felt she could control him. Or, she thought his disappearance was a sign of guilt. This morning his team leader got a call from Flores with the location of Dante's safe house. They didn't find Dante. Instead, they found a blind woman."

"A blind woman? Who?"

"They kept her here waiting for Romero to show, believing she was his mistress and they could leverage her to force him to cooperate. Then Angelo Zapelli came in."

Bile rose in the back of Sean's throat. He couldn't speak.

"The man said Zapelli recognized her, that she was someone of interest, but he didn't hear her name or why the interest. He is just a low-level thug. Zapelli took Lucy to Jasmine Flores. The compound is a four-plus-hour drive. He has no plane, and none of the men who went with them can fly. That gives us the edge. Four hours puts him arriving well after sunset. We'll ambush him before then."

"Jack—"

"Don't think about it. You fly, I plan. You can hot-wire the jeep?"

Sean nodded. Zapelli had many reasons to hate Lucy, not the least of which was because she was a federal agent. She'd interrogated him, she'd manipulated him during questioning, she and Noah had forced him to cooperate and had ultimately stopped the Flores black-market baby operation based in part on information they'd obtained from Zapelli. But Zapelli would also know that Lucy was a Kincaid.

A federal agent *and* Jack's sister. She was a prize to them. A big, juicy prize they could do anything with because she was now their prisoner.

"Sean!" Jack exclaimed. Sean jumped. "Do it. I'm going to search for maps and information, I'll be out in two minutes. Get the jeep working."

As soon as Sean stepped out of the house, Jack closed the door and called Kane.

"We have a big fucking problem. If anything happens to Lucy, there is no place on earth that Liam can hide from me. And when I find him, he will wish he'd never been born."

CHAPTER TWENTY-NINE

Gabriella slipped into the room next to Jasmine's office and quietly closed the door. It was dark and cool in here. Months ago, Gabriella had discovered that the corner of this sitting room provided perfect sound whenever Dominick—and then Jasmine—was at the desk. It helped that Gabriella had created a makeshift amplifier. She put the earpiece in her ear and listened. If anyone questioned her, it was hooked up to her iPod. She could simply be listening to music . . . not eavesdropping.

Jasmine was on the phone with one of her henchmen. "Are you certain?" she said. She sounded cautiously excited about something. "And Romero?" A long silence. "Have them wait. I don't care how long it takes, I want him . . . Yes, even though you have someone better. I didn't get to be in this position because I let my enemies go free. Come straight here, I want to meet this woman."

Jasmine hung up. Typed on her computer. A knock on her door, then, "Sit, Thomas. We have more work to do."

"I do not think you understand how complicated this process is."

"I don't want to hear excuses, I want it done. With your expertise comes money and protection."

"Ms. Flores, I need to establish brand-new accounts, new corporations, it takes time."

"Then why are you talking when you can be working?"

"The banks are closed in the Western Hemisphere until morning. I have the paperwork drawn up for the corporations, but we first need to establish the accounts. Then I need—"

"I don't need the details, I just need it done. What else?"

"You asked me to verify your family assets. I'm not an accountant—"

"Then find an accountant! Why is it that no one can think for themselves anymore?"

Gabriella recognized that tone. Dominick had the same level of frustration before he had someone killed—only it usually took him much longer to reach that boiling point. Jasmine was definitely more volatile than the former head of the family.

Thomas Morrison would need to tread very carefully.

"I have a rough estimate. I'll bring in someone tomorrow."

"Have Herman vet whoever it is."

"Yes, ma'am."

"Well? Don't keep me waiting. What is your rough estimate?"

"Two point six million."

There was silence. Gabriella half expected to hear a gunshot. This Thomas Morrison was an idiot. Never give Jasmine Flores bad news. Always send someone else to do it.

"You're right," Jasmine said after a long minute. "You're not an accountant. I'll have one brought in. Get everything ready for him. You're off by tens of millions of dollars."

"Yes, ma'am. It's just that—you, um, there have been many expenses incurred over the last month. And, um, the US government seized every US bank account and shut down several companies, plus several foreign accounts have holds on them."

"Get the holds off."

"It's not possible."

The pounding of Jasmine's fist on her desk made Gabriella jump. "I"—*pound*—"don't"—*pound*—"care! Make it"—*pound*—"happen!"

"I'll see what I can do."

"Just do it! Idiot!"

The door opened, and closed quickly.

"Where the *fuck* is the money? That prick Spade didn't control it all." Jasmine started muttering. Talking about Dominick, about lies and hidden accounts.

Dominick had tens of millions of dollars. While not all of it was liquid, he definitely had money he could access. Was Carson Spade smart enough to put it all under his control? Maybe. Gabriella didn't like the jerk, but he was brilliant when it came to dollars and cents and managing people.

Still, Gabriella knew Dominick, and he would never entrust one person with *all* his money. Two point six million? Peanuts compared to the Floreses' true wealth.

What had Dom done with his money? This was an area that Dante knew far more about than she did. And while Dante didn't like working with the cartels, he sometimes did favors to keep the trains running on time, so to speak. Safety was a premium, and Dante might have given Dom advice on how to manage his resources in the event of a coup. Dom hadn't been worried about Jasmine—he'd always thought Samuel would be the one to betray him.

Dom wouldn't give Dante control over his funds, but information was almost as important.

She heard Jasmine's voice again. It took Gabriella a moment to realize she was talking on the phone.

". . . ten million."

Gabriella leaned forward.

"It's not a lot of money for you, darling," Jasmine said. "She's not just *any* federal agent. Her last name is Kincaid."

Her? Kincaid? Gabriella's hand drifted to her mouth. How had Jasmine found Lucy Kincaid? Jack's little sister? What had Dante done? Had he really left her in the safe house? Left her to fend for herself?

"I have proof. I'll shoot you a photo. Will that do? . . . I need to talk to her first. She has information I need . . . Yes, I know for a fact that she's Jack Kincaid's sister . . . I have no idea . . . No . . . Not my problem . . . Good. As soon as I receive confirmation that the payment went through, I'll send my people over with her . . . No, the picture will be proof of life, Raymond . . . Good." She hung up. More typing.

Gabriella slipped out of the room. She had to get out of here. Find a way to tell Jack—but Jack must know by now. She'd sent him the information about Dante's house, but he must have been too late.

Why do you care? You don't know the girl.

Jack was Greg's friend. Jack saved your life, helped avenge Greg's death.

Gabriella hated owing anyone for anything. She made a point of wiping the slate clean. Jack would come for Lucy—he was smart. He'd figure out where she was.

But could she count on it? Before Jasmine sold Lucy to the highest bidder?

She bit her lip. Never was she torn about anything. When she'd fallen in love with Greg, she'd fallen hard. When she'd lost Greg, she mourned hard. When she decided to seek revenge, she'd done so patiently, quietly, systematically, ruthlessly.

She and Dante wouldn't be able to return to this area, but they'd already known that after they'd helped Kane and Sean Rogan last month. She could hide in New Orleans—living with her father wouldn't be fun, but it would be safe. Until she figured out what to do.

Could she just walk away from Jack's sister? It wasn't her problem, but it wasn't Lucy's fault that Liam was an idiot. What had he been thinking?

He wasn't thinking.

Or this was his way to get revenge on his family. It was just so twisted . . . you never hurt an innocent when you sought vengence. That was a sure path to a living hell.

But Liam hadn't been in his right mind since he lost the bonds six years ago.

Lost in her thoughts, Gabriella almost walked into Danielle Morrison carrying her baby.

It's not her baby. She bought it.

Jose had told Gabriella the truth over lunch. He had been unnerved by the information, upset even. But he still wouldn't leave with her.

Now Gabriella didn't have a choice. She wasn't safe here. Jasmine was behaving erratically and she was already suspicious. But could Gabriella leave when an innocent infant was at risk?

Not your problem, Gabriella. You didn't buy or sell the baby.

"Have you seen Thomas?" Danielle asked.

Gabriella shook her head. "Sorry," she mumbled.

"Joshua has a fever. I want to take him to a doctor. All this travel . . . it's not good for him."

Gabriella wanted to slap some sense into the woman. "I thought I heard his voice down the hall." She pointed toward Jasmine's wing.

"Thank you."

Gabriella ran upstairs to her suite. "Jose?"

No answer.

She opened her lingerie drawer and pulled out her secure

tablet. Wrote Jack a message, then encrypted it. He was the only one who had the key.

Jasmine is selling Lucy tonight—ten mil to Raymond Reynoso. I'm going into hiding.

She hid her tablet and started packing an overnight bag.

Slow down. You're acting like a fool.

She took a deep breath, then went about her business as if she were going on a weekend getaway.

"Where are you going?"

She jumped. She hadn't heard Jose walk in.

"I called for you, you didn't answer." She walked over and kissed him.

"Where are you going, Gabriella?" he asked again.

"Remember our talk this morning? I just have a bad feeling—I need to get away. Jasmine hasn't made any secret that she doesn't like or trust me. I get it—she's a paranoid bitch." She waved away the comment. "I'm sorry. I don't scare easily, Jose, but she's beginning to scare me."

She walked over to him, took his hands. "Come with me, just for the week. You're tense, you need to relax, too."

"I told you I can't go anywhere." He walked over to her lingerie drawer and opened it.

"What are you doing?"

He held up her tablet. "What's this?"

"Mine."

She didn't make a move for the tablet. She couldn't let him see that she was terrified.

"Jasmine said you were a spy for Jack Kincaid. I didn't believe her."

"I am not anything! We've been together for a year, Jose."

"I didn't want to believe it, but it's all been a lie."

He sat down on the edge of her bed and looked dejected.

"I have never lied to you," she said. And really, she

hadn't. She hadn't told him everything, but she'd never outright *lied* to him.

"You never told me you had once been engaged."

Her blood ran cold. "What?"

"Jasmine told me everything. That you were engaged to some US Army soldier and he was killed down here. That you seduced me out of revenge."

"I didn't seduce you, Jose."

"And then I thought, How did we meet? It was by chance . . . or so I thought. Dom was doing business with your brother. You came. I saw you . . . you smiled at me. I fell in love with you, Gabriella. I *loved* you, and you had my entire family killed!"

"That is not true." *I only cared about killing Samuel, the others died because they messed with the Rogans.*

"Don't lie to me anymore!"

"Jasmine is twisting your head. She's good at that."

"I didn't trust her. But . . . I found this. Why are you sending encrypted emails?"

"To my father. He lives in New Orleans. You know that."

"Encrypted emails. To your daddy."

Jose didn't believe her. He *always* believed her.

"I saw you leave the office next to Jasmine's. You came right here, sent a message, and started packing. You heard."

"Heard *what?*"

"That Jasmine has a US federal agent in her custody. She told me exactly what you would do if you found out— that you would send a message to whoever you're working with, and then leave."

She shook her head. "You're wrong."

"I wish I were."

"I'm going." She opened the bedroom door. Two thugs stood there. Jasmine was behind them.

"Your lover lasted six days before he died. Six days of constant pain." Jasmine stepped forward. "You won't last six hours."

Gabriella saw red. She tried to grab Jasmine, but the thugs pulled her off and held her down.

"My brothers may all have been fooled by your pretty face, but not me. Not only do I have FBI Agent Lucy Kincaid, I have you. And I'm pretty certain you've been in contact with Jack Kincaid, because your poor dead lover was under his command. Boohoo. When I find your brother, he'll either run away—leaving you to die—or try and rescue you. Honestly? I'll bet you that Jack Kincaid and Dante Romero will both be here before midnight.

"And then I'll kill them. You can watch. It'll be fun."

CHAPTER THIRTY

"Liam, we need to head back to camp *now*." Dante looked pointedly at Eden.

Eden hadn't wanted to push Liam, but she no longer had a choice.

"You promised," Eden told her brother. "It's getting dark. We have to get out of here before we can't see. The trails are too dangerous to navigate at night. And the animals—it's not safe."

"I *know* it's here."

They'd been at the valley floor for three and a half hours. It had taken them hours to clear away the vines and shrubs that had grown around the area. They knew they were at the right place—they'd uncovered part of the stone foundation of the church. Just as described in the journal.

But they hadn't found the cavern. They had inspected every inch of the hillside behind the church for a cave or inlet or something that indicated there was a path into the mountainside, but rock blocked them.

This wasn't a one-day job. They could be here a week. Longer. They needed more supplies and equipment. The three of them couldn't do it all themselves.

"Ten more minutes," Liam said.

Her brother sounded desperate, and desperation bred mistakes. She knew how important this was to him—proving, once and for all, that the treasure their parents had been searching for was here, that their hunt was almost over. It had become an obsession, and Eden fed it—because she wanted to look Kane in the face and say, *I told you so.*

"Liam—" Eden stopped, looked at Dante. She didn't know what to say. When they first arrived, she had never seen her brother so happy—so in awe. A child again. As if their parents hadn't suddenly died, as if their brothers hadn't disowned them. As if everything were right again in the world.

They *knew* they were in the right place, but time had worked against them. Storms. Earthquakes. Mother Nature. Time shifted, changed what had been.

"Oh my God, Eden!"

Liam's voice sounded odd, and she walked over to where he was kneeling at the corner of the foundation, directly behind the broken stone cross. He had used a pickaxe to break up the stone. It was grueling, tiresome work, but Liam hadn't stopped. A full three-foot-by-three-foot stone wall had been reduced to manageable pieces, which Liam had pushed aside one by one.

Liam fell to his hands and began digging into the hard dirt. The rocks slipped, and that's when Eden saw. The rocks and dirt were falling into an underground cavern. Liam began to slip as the foundation sagged. Eden screamed and grabbed on to him, but the slide stopped.

Dante rushed over, stood behind Liam. They all stared into the dark hole, shining their flashlights.

"I have to go in," Liam said.

"It's too late," Dante said. "We don't know what's down there, we don't have enough lights. We need to get back to camp. The sun officially sets in forty minutes, and the woods are already getting dark. We have to go back now."

"No!"

Eden saw a glint of something in the earth below. She shined her light down. Shallow stone steps led into darkness. On a shelf built into the earth next to the steps was something that caught her light.

"It's a statue," Liam whispered. "I have to get it."

"No," Dante said. "If you fall down there, we don't have the equipment to get you out."

"Lower me," Eden said. "I'm the lightest. If you hold my feet, I can reach it."

Liam turned to Dante. "I have to know. If that's Saint Michael the Archangel, this is it. *This is it!*"

The journal had told the story that the head of the heavenly host, the warrior of God's Army, Saint Michael himself, guarded Paradise. It was a biblical story, but one Father Gregorio had believed would protect the treasure from the enemies of God, those who had slaughtered members at Father Gregorio's expedition.

Liam begged. "Please."

Dante relented. Eden lay on the ground. Even though the earth had shifted when Liam had found the opening, the ground around them appeared solid. She shimmied over to the opening, took a deep breath and tasted dirt and clay. Then she said, "Grab my feet."

Her brother and Dante held on to her as she hung upside down into the cavern. Her fingers brushed the statue. "A couple more inches!" she called. Pebbles fell around her, but she was going to get the statue for Liam. It might be the only way to convince him to go back to camp tonight.

She slipped and gasped. She grabbed hold of the statue with her right hand and shouted, "Get me out!"

Dante and Liam pulled her out. The statue was

extremely heavy—heavier than it looked. As soon as she was back up she scrambled away from the opening, breathing heavily.

"Eden—please—" Liam held his hands out.

She handed him the statue.

Liam took the statue from Eden as if it were an infant. He poured water over it, rinsing away generations of dirt and dust.

Faint color came to life. Chipped paint over the dull gleam of gold. A sword that should have been in Saint Michael's hand had broken off—when Eden couldn't tell, but the breakage was as dirty as the statue, telling her it had happened long ago. One of his wings was missing, but the body was all there. The detail in the statue told them this was in fact Saint Michael the Archangel. The statue that guarded the treasure. As it was written in the journal, as they'd always believed.

Liam and Eden had spent their life studying art and artifacts. There was no doubt that this statue was solid gold. It stood approximately eighteen inches high and weighed at least twenty-five pounds. If it was pure gold, they held nearly half a million dollars in their hands. Even if it wasn't pure gold, its value was historically immeasurable.

"It's here," Liam said, caressing the statue. "It's really here."

"We'll come back tomorrow with lights, rope, equipment, whatever it takes." Dante was equally excited but far more pragmatic. "But now we need to leave before it gets any darker."

"Liam," Eden said, "I'm not leaving you here. But I don't want to be stuck down here all night. There's a storm coming in, we have no shelter. We don't know if the stream will flood. We need to be smart about this."

She held her breath. For a split second she thought Liam was going to argue with them. Fight them. Refuse to leave.

She and Dante couldn't force him, and she wouldn't leave him alone. He walked over to his backpack, took out his extra shirt, carefully wrapped the statue, and packed it up. "We did it. Eden, Dante, we did what our parents could never do."

"I wish Gabriella was here," Dante said.

Eden took his hand. "Me too. Call her when we get back to camp. She'll come tomorrow, I know it."

They left the site of their dig, packed their tools, and started up the trail that would take them around the edge of the valley and back up the mountainside.

It wouldn't take as long to get back to camp as it had to reach the valley—they had marked their path, cut away shrubs and trees, so while they were mostly going up, it had been cleared. They stopped once to drink water and silently watch the sunset.

Eden wondered what her parents would have thought. If they had really believed or had just given Liam the quest so that he would feel special. Either way, good or bad, they had done something that no one in two hundred years had been able to do. They had found the Alamo Treasure. They had uncovered history. And that, alone, would sustain Eden for a long, long time.

"Fifteen more minutes," Dante said, "give or take. I'm starving. We eat, sleep, then pack up before dawn. It took us three hours to get to the site this morning—it'll only take us half the time now that we've cleared the way."

"We can't tell anyone," Liam said. "There'll be people all over this place, destroying the church, looting, taking what's ours."

"You mean, what's going back to the people," Dante said. "We agreed—take a finder's fee, then the rest goes on the museum circuit. First to the Smithsonian to authenticate, then to Mexico. This is world history. It belongs to everyone."

"That's all in the plan, but we can enjoy it alone for a while." He cuddled the statue. Eden hadn't seen him take it out of his pack.

Eden wasn't certain Liam would give any of it up.

Kane walked over to where Noah was monitoring emergency transmissions. Already the winds had picked up accompanied by light, intermittent rain, though the tent Liam's team had pitched was shielded on two sides by the terrain and would provide decent shelter. "Weather report?"

"Upgraded to a tropical storm, but right now doesn't look like hurricane-force winds. We'll get wet here. The coastal area will get hit hard, forty-five-to-fifty-mile-per-hour winds with surges up to seventy. Storm hits land by midnight. Small craft west of McAllen are grounded at ten p.m., advisories west of Laredo, through six a.m. If we leave tonight, we would have to fly west of these mountains, then northwest around Monterrey, then a northeast route into the States through Rio Grande City, then backtrack to Hidalgo, though getting there might be problematic because of the winds. We'll be eating up the fuel. It's about an additional one hundred fifty miles."

"I won't have enough fuel even if it was a straight shot."

"Where were you going to refuel?"

"I have a few places I can go, but nothing in that direction. How's Sean's plane?"

"In this weather? I can make it at least to Rio Grande, but then it'll be hit or miss. I can use the winds getting there, but as soon as I turn east I'll be blasted. If we get out sooner, I might be able to make a straight shot up to McAllen before the advisory goes into effect." Noah looked at him oddly. "You're not planning on leaving tonight, are you?"

"I have to get to Guadalajara. Jack's gone dark. I need you to take everyone to the States as soon as they get out of that goddamn jungle."

Kane was worried. About Lucy, about Sean, about Jack. He'd been sitting here for hours waiting for his brother and sister to show themselves. They were playing treasure hunters while Lucy was being held captive by a drug cartel.

"Did you call Stockton?"

"Yes. His SEAL team won't be ready to deploy until twenty-one hundred, and they can't do a damn thing without intel. They'll be within fifty miles of the Flores compound by twenty-three hundred awaiting orders."

Kane heard a whistle from the head of the trail. Nate had taken the last hour of standing guard. The whistle indicated that the subjects were approaching and would be visible within five minutes. Kane and Noah both turned off their flashlights. It had gotten dark rapidly over the last thirty minutes, and for the last ten Kane had thought he was wrong about the camp, that Liam and the others had decided to stay in the valley below after all.

Siobhan was in the tent—the safest place for her at this point. He leaned inside and whispered, "Stay put."

She nodded, and Kane partially zipped the tent.

He and Noah positioned themselves on either side of the path, far enough into the trees that they wouldn't be spotted. Nate would be taking up the rear, waiting until the targets passed him, then trailing them and cutting off their escape route.

Kane wanted to take care of business quick and without injuries. He saw movement in the brush, then heard Liam's voice. Kane couldn't quite make out what Liam was saying.

Dante stepped into sight first. He saw Kane a fraction of a second after he stepped toward Dante. Kane immediately brought Dante to his knees and pulled the weapon from his back holster. Kane then pulled Dante up and pushed him away from the entrance of the path.

"What the hell?" Dante said.

"Quiet."

Liam and Eden came into view. They were twenty feet from Kane. Noah was closer, but Liam was carrying something in his arms. "Hold it, Armstrong. Liam, put down the rock," Kane ordered.

"Kane? What are you doing here?" Liam glanced around, spotted Noah. "Well, I'm be—"

"Put the damn rock down, *now*."

"Rock? This is a gold statue! We found the treasure Mom and Dad looked for their entire lives! This is a solid gold statue of Saint Michael the Archangel. The journal said that Saint Michael would guard the treasure."

"Down."

"No!"

Liam took a step toward him and Kane adjusted his gun.

"You wouldn't," Liam said. He had no fear. He never had.

"Stop it, both of you," Eden said. She looked from Kane to Noah and back at Kane. "What on earth is going on?"

"I don't want to hurt any of you. Put your tools down, keep your hands up. This ends now, Eden," Kane said.

"Didn't you hear us? We found the treasure! The gold that was intended for the Alamo—it's real! We found it and made history."

"You kidnapped a federal agent. Your sister-in-law."

Eden blinked. "Sean's girlfriend?"

"You have no idea what you've done. But this farce is over. Put down the pickax, Eden!"

She hesitated, glanced at Liam. He pressed the statue against his chest. "How did you find us? Who betrayed us?" He looked at Dante. "Was it Gabriella? I knew you both had softened!"

"Gabriella wouldn't betray us," Dante said.

"But she's all tight with Jack Kincaid. Isn't that what you said? That Gabriella might be upset that we brought Jack's sister with us?"

"If you'd asked me first, I would have told you hands-off, but you haven't been thinking lately, Liam! Just— Let's go back to the safe house. We'll talk about this."

"Your days of diplomacy are over," Kane told Dante. "You crossed a line there is no returning from."

Liam was shaking. "You are a fool, Kane! This . . . this is so much bigger than any of us!" He held up the statue. "This is history. We're going down in history. I succeeded where so many have failed. *I* did."

"You worked for some nasty people in order to get this treasure. Was it worth it? Worth selling your soul?"

"That's all on you, big brother," Liam spit out. "You took those bonds six years ago—you put me in a bind. I couldn't imagine that you, of all people, would cost me my freedom."

"You're wrong, Liam. You made your own decisions."

"You took the bonds! I owed people, and I couldn't deliver—I've been in debt to them ever since, because of *you*! I never thought you'd do something like that—"

"I didn't know what you'd gotten yourself into, Liam. If you had come to me, told me the truth from the beginning—"

"Right, the *truth*. You are a self-righteous prick, Kane. Thinking you're better than me. You took everything from me. The family business—replaced me with an outsider! You took the bonds, forced me and Eden to work for assholes. That's on you, Kane, you!"

Kane could scarcely understand the rage and venom in Liam's voice. This wasn't his brother. Maybe he had never known Liam. He certainly didn't know the man he had become.

"Eden, tell him to stand down," Kane said.

"Don't talk to her!" Liam shouted. "You never listened. And you aren't any better than me. I haven't killed anyone, Kane. How many people have you killed?"

"This isn't about blood. This is about honor. You think our parents would be proud of you because you sold your soul for gold?"

"Don't twist this around. Everything I did was for the greater good!"

"You are delusional."

"Stop saying that!"

Noah spoke for the first time. "Put the statue down, Liam."

Liam was breathing heavily. Kane glanced down at Dante—he was trying to get up. Kane put a foot on his back. "Don't, Romero."

"It was my dad," Dante said quietly. He sighed. "I shouldn't have confided in him."

"Uncle Carlo understood the ramifications of you kidnapping a federal agent and bringing her to Mexico."

"Is that what this is about?" Liam laughed. "Your precious little Lucy is just fine. I called Sean hours ago and told him where to get her."

Kane wanted to hit him.

"The Flores cartel kidnapped Lucy from Dante's house," Kane said through clenched teeth. "The same cartel that held Sean's son hostage. The same cartel that killed Gabriella's fiancé. Lucy and Noah stopped their human-trafficking organization in Texas—do you think the cartel is going to give her a medal? They're going to torture and kill her if Sean and Jack can't find her in time." Kane kicked Dante. "And you, I expected better from you, Romero. You left Gabriella unprotected to chase after some gold?"

"Gabriella is fine—she stayed behind to protect herself."

"Jasmine Flores is on the warpath. She sent her people to get you, Romero—do you think when she finds out that Lucy was at *your fucking house* she's *not* going to think Gabriella is a spy?"

"If Gabriella is in danger, I have to go." Dante tried to get up.

Kane kicked him back down. "You are all going back to the States. Rick Stockton is on his way to Texas, and he's handling the paperwork. You're not getting out of this."

"Goddammit, Kane!" Dante exclaimed. "I can help."

"What are you all talking about?" Liam said. "You're going to go and fight the damn drug cartel? You'll all get *yourselves* killed. This is insane—you're insane."

"Liam—" Eden said.

Liam shook his head. "Kane, you never understood! I wasn't the soldier like you or the good son like Duke or the genius like Sean, but I have something none of you ever had. Faith. Dreams. I found the treasure. I found it!"

Kane glanced at his sister. She looked frozen in place. The wind whipped her long hair around her face. Fat raindrops began to fall.

"Liam, it'll be here," she said. "No one knows where it is except us. Dad would understand." She turned to Kane. "This is all your fault. None of this would have happened if you hadn't taken the bonds six years ago."

"You think Dad would have wanted you to kidnap Sean's fiancée and leave her as bait for a drug cartel?" Kane couldn't have this conversation. Time was against him, and Liam was flat out crazy or obsessed. Both. "Sean and Jack are in danger. Lucy is being held by a ruthless bitch who will not stop until every Kincaid and Rogan is dead. If you think you're getting out of this with a slap on the wrist, you're insane. Dammit, Eden! What the hell were you thinking?"

Kane prided himself on controlling his inner rage. It was with him always, but locked deep inside. It's why he was a good soldier, a good leader, why he had solid instincts and had been able to get out of many dangerous situations. But for the first time, he felt himself losing his control. His family—his brother and sister—stood here in front of him and tried to justify their bad behavior. They tried to explain away kidnapping Lucy, putting her in danger. Where was their compassion? Their guilt? Why couldn't they see that this treasure hunt had corrupted them?

"Liam—we'll come back for it," Eden said. "Kane has no legal authority over us. Neither does Noah. He's a US agent with no authority to bring us back to the States."

"I'm not here as a federal agent," Noah said.

Kane noticed that Noah was inching closer to Liam. Against his training and instincts, Kane holstered his own gun. He had to talk his brother out of this insanity. Kane didn't recognize this man. When had he lost it? When Kane disowned him? During the decades of searching for this treasure?

Liam said, "Eden and I are going back to the valley. Do not follow us."

Kane rushed him. He hit Liam full force in the chest and he went down. He hit him once in the jaw to keep him down. The statue Liam had been clutching with such intensity fell to the ground and hit a rock. Its head broke off.

Kane jumped up before he seriously hurt his brother. "This is over, Liam."

Liam stared at the statue. "For two hundred years that statue was preserved, and after ten minutes in your presence it's damaged. Like everything in your life!"

Liam slowly stood up.

"Stay down," Kane ordered.

Liam shook his head, and that's when Kane noticed the gun in his hand. The sight of Liam standing in the rain with a gun surprised Kane. If it were any other person in any other time Kane would have shot him in the head. Kane was only feet from him. But this was his brother.

You could draw and fire before Liam knew what hit him.

Kane didn't want to kill his brother. Even after everything that had happened, Kane didn't want to kill Liam.

"No, Liam, don't!" Eden cried. "Don't hurt him, Kane!"

"Rogan!" Noah ordered. "Put the gun down."

Liam stared at Kane. "I hate you!"

Kane saw the hate. He'd helped create it. He'd created Liam by bringing him into the business, training him, and then destroying him by disowning him. He had no idea the bonds were part of this damn treasure hunt. All Kane saw was Liam working for the Russian mob, the bad guys. Kane never saw this obsession. Liam justified everything he'd done as a necessity for a greater cause, a cause given to him by his father months before he died. Kane couldn't explain it, he couldn't tell Liam that he was wrong. He wouldn't see it.

"Liam, let's go," Eden said.

"You're not going anywhere," Noah said. "Stand down, Liam."

"Stay out of this, Noah!" Eden screamed.

"I'm sorry," Kane said, his eyes on Liam's eyes. Kane wasn't a talker. He was a man of action. But right now he had to find the words. "If you had told me the truth from the beginning, we could have discussed it."

"Bullshit! You don't discuss anything. You give orders. You expect them to be followed. I'm not a soldier, Kane."

"I *am* sorry. You are right—I am a soldier. I give orders.

I expect them to be followed. It's all I know. But I'm just one person in this family. Do you think Duke and I see eye to eye on everything? Or JT?"

"JT," Liam spit out. "Mom and Dad took him into the house and you treated him more like your flesh and blood than me."

"You've twisted everything, Liam!" Kane raised his voice to be heard. The winds had increased as the rain fell harder.

"Eden and I are leaving." He looked at Dante. "Are you coming?"

From where he sat on the ground, Dante shook his head. "Gabriella is my family. If you were thinking straight, you'd help save her and Lucy."

"It's not my battle." He stepped backward. Eden started walking toward Liam.

Kane had to make a judgment call. He couldn't let them go. But would Liam shoot him? Yesterday Kane would have said no.

Today he wasn't certain.

Going back into those mountains during a storm was dangerous. And they had to answer for their crimes.

Kane rushed Liam.

Liam pressed the trigger, once, twice.

A burning pain in Kane's chest had him on his knees. Another pain in his arm hurt worse.

Then he heard a third gunshot but didn't feel the corresponding pain.

Eden screamed. Her anguish echoed in the wet night.

Kane sat up. His chest hurt, but he had on a Kevlar vest. Liam's 9mm couldn't penetrate it, just hurt enough to send him to the ground. His arm burned, but it was a glancing wound.

Liam lay in the dirt.

Noah rushed over and kicked away his gun. Eden

punched Noah in the chest, but in two strides Nate had her restrained.

"Let me go!" Eden screamed. Nate held her tight.

Kane and Noah knelt by Liam. "I'm sorry," Noah whispered.

"You did what you had to do," Kane said. He tore open Liam's shirt. He'd been shot in the upper right shoulder and was losing a lot of blood. Kane immediately put pressure on the wound. Liam breathed erratically.

"Hang on, Liam," Kane said. "Dammit, this isn't ending like this."

"No, you bastards!" Eden cried.

"We need to get him to a hospital," Noah said. "I can fly him to the border. Three hours in this weather, if I punch it."

"It'll take twenty minutes to get him back to the truck."

"We don't have a choice."

Liam groaned, "Eden."

Noah glanced at Nate and nodded. Nate let Eden go. She ran to her brother's side, took his hand. "Liam, fight. Don't leave me."

"Statue."

Kane wanted to scream. All his brother could think about was the statue?

"I'll get it. I'll get all of it."

"Thank you for believing in me when no one else did." He coughed.

"Stop talking that way. Stop it! You're not dying. Noah! Do something!"

"We're going to get him to a hospital as fast as we can," Noah said.

"It's all your fault, Kane, it's all you!" Eden sobbed.

Siobhan rushed out of the tent with towels. "Use these. Stop the bleeding as best you can." She put her hand on Kane's arm. "You're bleeding."

"It's fine," Kane said. "Dante, get the table from the tent, collapse the legs, we'll make a stretcher."

Dante complied.

"Eden," Noah said, "how far to your vehicle?"

"I can't believe you shot my brother."

"Eden, I have a plane, we'll get him to a hospital. Where is your car?"

"Ten minutes."

"That's closer than ours," Kane said.

"You never understood anything," Eden said. "Never. All Liam wants is for you to appreciate him."

"Eden, you don't believe that. Not after tonight." Kane rubbed his eyes. He felt sick. He had failed his family. Eden and Liam. Both. He hadn't been a good mentor, a good teacher. He hadn't paid attention. He'd missed the signs. He'd cut them off when they stepped repeatedly out of line because that's what he did . . . but they were family. He should have done something else.

"He did it for the family. He had to. He had to . . . for Dad—"

"Don't. Just stop." Kane couldn't defend his father, he had no idea what Paul Rogan had said to Liam, but Kane knew it wasn't to find the treasure at all costs. But Liam always heard and believed what he wanted to.

Still, Kane didn't want him to die.

Siobhan and Dante put a sleeping bag on the table, then the men lifted Liam onto it. They strapped him down with duct tape and tied another sleeping bag over him.

Kane stared at Eden. "Search her, Dunning."

Nate complied. Eden stared at him as if he were crazy. As if she hated him.

She probably did. As much as Liam hated him.

"Liam had a gun, you could, too."

"I don't have a gun."

"She's clean," Dunning said, then handed Kane a knife and a Taser.

Eden bent down and picked up the statue.

"Eden," Liam said from the makeshift stretcher. "Eden."

She went to his side. "What?"

"Can I?"

She put the head of Saint Michael into Liam's hand. "I'll carry the body," she said.

Noah took it out of her hands, put it in a backpack, and handed the pack to Nate.

"Bastard," she said.

To Noah's credit, he didn't respond. "Ready, go," he said.

The four men picked up the table with Liam and walked down the path, Siobhan and Eden silently leading the way with flashlights.

CHAPTER THIRTY-ONE

Jack aborted the rescue as soon as he spotted the convoy.

In addition to the truck with three men in the cab, there was a jeep in the rear carrying two men. Jack couldn't see into the covered rear of the truck to determine how many more there were.

Worse, he couldn't see Lucy. She *might* be there, but they didn't know—and they couldn't risk her being killed during the attack.

"No, Jack!" Sean jumped up from their hiding place and almost exposed himself.

Jack pulled him down and held him, pressing his hand over Sean's mouth. He was taking his own life into his hands by restraining Sean, who was armed with a knife and gun and fear. He was lashing out at the one person who could turn this fucked situation around.

Sean fought, connected squarely with the side of Jack's head, but then stopped almost as suddenly as he started. He went limp. Jack continued to restrain him until the trucks had passed.

Then Jack sat down next to Sean, breathing heavily.

"She was there," Sean whispered.

"Did you see her?"

Sean shook his head.

"It would have been a suicide mission." Jack closed his eyes. Letting those trucks pass by had been one of the hardest things Jack had ever done. "Five men minimum, likely another in the back with Lucy. We couldn't risk her life, not with so many unknowns. We need to be smart about this."

"Jasmine Flores will kill her."

"Jasmine is shrewd. Lucy is a high-value asset. Gabriella thinks Jasmine is hurting financially because the government seized most of her accounts. Carson Spade was laundering money for the entire cartel, not just Jasmine's end of it. Money makes the world go round down here. If the other cartels think she's weak, they have a tactical advantage, and she knows it. She'll have other uses for Lucy—which buys us time."

"Unless she's a psycho and wants to kill her on general principles. Lucy took down her operation, Jack. Sent her into hiding. Vengeance is a powerful motivator."

"So is greed. But it doesn't matter at this point—they didn't kill her at the house, they're not going to kill her now. We need a tactical plan. The weather is turning quickly. We need to get to our shelter and contact JT. He might have information."

"I can't do this, Jack."

"You *can*. You can and will."

Sean was falling apart, and if Jack couldn't get him back into top form he'd be a liability. But Jack couldn't bench him. He needed a second man, especially one with Sean's unique skills. And Sean would never forgive Jack—or himself—if he lost it. Jack had to push him.

"Sean, if you fail me, you fail Lucy. This is an operation. Put your emotions aside. If you can't, you're no good to me—or to Lucy. Understood?"

Sean took a deep breath, then nodded. "I'm okay."

Jack stood and helped Sean up.

"Camp, JT, plan. Let's go."

Kane asked Siobhan to go with Noah and Nate and try to save Liam's life.

"This is not your fault," Siobhan said. They stood in the warm rain as Noah and Nate strapped Liam into the small plane. "You know that."

He stared at her. "I failed him."

"Liam chose his own path," Siobhan said firmly. "He alone is responsible for his choices."

Kane knew she was right, but Liam was his brother. They had never been close, but he was family. That had to mean something. It meant something to Jack Kincaid, who would step up anytime one of his family was threatened, even if they had disagreements.

Kane was at a loss—he couldn't see how he could have done anything differently. It was a character flaw, on his part, that he had never been able to understand Liam. More important, Kane hadn't taken him seriously. That was the crux of the problem. Kane had dismissed Liam as if he were a mere employee, not a brother. And Liam had rebelled in the most destructive way. Kane didn't know if Liam really believed everything he said or if it had all been twisted up, but it was clear that Liam hated Kane, that he blamed Kane for everything bad that had happened to him, and there was no coming back from that.

"Kane." Siobhan stepped forward and touched his face. "I love you."

He kissed her. This time, it wasn't possessive and demanding. It truly was a kiss of affection. Of love.

"I don't deserve you," he said, his voice cracking.

"Stop. Just . . . stop." She kissed him again.

Nate cleared his throat. "We're ready," he said.

Kane walked Siobhan over to the plane and helped her

up. He turned to Eden. His sister. He'd failed Liam, and he'd failed her.

"I'm sorry about all of this," he said. Now wasn't the time to tell her she also had choices. That she too could have stopped this insanity.

"You should be. If he dies"—tears rolled down her face—"it's on you, Kane."

"No. I made mistakes, but this is not on me, and you know it. Go. Save him. Sean and Lucy need my help. You have no idea what you have all done, the danger you put her in."

Eden slapped him, then climbed into the plane herself, pushing away Nate's offered assistance.

Liam probably wasn't going to survive. They all knew it, except maybe Eden. But there was a slim chance—and the only way they might be able to save Liam was to get him back to the States as soon as possible. Kane turned to Noah. "Get them back safe," he said.

"I will."

Kane and Dante walked over to the edge of the runway and watched as the plane took off. The flight would be treacherous if the storm moved in any faster, but Noah was a competent pilot. He would get them to the hospital as fast as humanly possible.

It was all Kane could hope for at this point.

As soon as they were off, Kane said, "I need to find a place to fuel."

"I have a plane," Dante said. "Philip procured fuel, supplies. He'll fly us."

"I'll fly us. Where's the plane?"

"A small commercial airfield ten minutes from here." Dante walked over to the jeep, took one look at Kane, and tossed him the keys. Kane got behind the wheel and they sped off as fast as he dared on the rough, wet road.

"I'm not going to let anything happen to my sister,"

Dante said. "I got sucked into Liam's dreams. I love your brother, as if he were my own." Dante took a deep breath. "He's not going to make it, is he?"

Kane didn't want to discuss Liam. Not now, especially when he was so damn confused about everything that had happened over the last two days. Days? Try years. He was never confused about anything. He always knew what was right, what was wrong, how to get out of any situation. He didn't live in a world of what-ifs or regrets. Those thoughts led to insanity, especially in his line of work.

"You can trust Philip," Dante said.

"He's not coming."

"Kane, I'm truly sorry about what happened. I didn't know that Liam planned to grab Lucy. I didn't know until he called me when he was already on his way to the safe house. I honestly believed she would be safe there. I never would have left her unprotected if I thought Flores's people were looking for me. Kincaid saved my sister. I owe him. I'm not letting Gabriella or Lucy die."

Kane hadn't wanted to bring Dante with him, but what choice did he have? Not only was Gabriella his sister, but Dante knew the compound and the area, he had resources and people. He knew things. Information was critical.

But so was trust, and Kane was having a hard time trusting anyone right now.

"You don't get a pass, Romero."

Dante didn't say anything. Kane drove where he'd directed, to a small commercial airfield. As soon as Philip saw Dante with Kane, his face fell.

"What happened?" Philip asked.

"Long story. Eden and Liam are on their way to the States. Liam was shot."

"How bad?"

"Bad."

"Oh, God. Did you find it?"

"The treasure?" Kane exploded. "You can only think about the damn treasure? Your father was right, Dante. It's cursed. I don't even believe in fucking curses, but I believe in this one."

Dante said to Philip, "Jasmine Flores was looking for me, found Agent Kincaid at the safe house."

"Oh, shit," Philip mumbled. "I'm sorry, Rogan."

"You both should have known better. I turned my back on a lot of your shit because no one I cared about got hurt. You'd never been a fool, Dante. This time—" Kane needed to get his head clear. His brother was dying, and Kane's emotions were too close to the surface. "Is the plane ready?"

"Yes. They're not letting anyone take off, but I'll make it happen. Give me five minutes." Philip walked away.

"Kane—" Dante began.

Kane glared at him, then walked away. He couldn't listen to any more excuses.

The Beechcraft was a good plane, built for both speed and comfort. The controls were state of the art. He had never flown this particular model, but it wasn't all that different from most twin-props in the same class.

Kane tried calling Jack. There was no answer. Kane sent a coded message telling Jack he'd be in Guadalajara in ninety minutes or less.

He hoped. The storm raged, but he trusted the weather report Noah had given him. As they moved inland, it should level off. And right now they would have tailwinds.

Dante climbed into the plane. "Is there a way to reach Gabriella?" Kane asked him.

Dante pulled out his phone and handed it to Kane. "Gabriella will pick up this number. Last number called."

Kane put the phone on speaker and pressed resend. A moment later a female voice came on the phone.

"Finally, you call."

Kane didn't say anything. He watched Dante closely.

"Jasmine." Dante's face was white as a sheet.

"You are a fucking traitor. You betray my brothers, betray me, and then run like a little girl. You think I couldn't figure out that Jack Kincaid and Kane Rogan inserted Gabriella into my brother's operation? That little whore was good at her job, she was probably screwing Dom as well as Jose."

Dante said through clenched teeth, "No one controls my sister."

"Your pathetic excuses will determine whether your dear sister dies slowly or quickly. But I'm willing to have the conversation, face to face."

"I'm in Tampico."

"If you're anywhere near that little so-called safe house you can get here in less than two hours."

In the background, they heard, "Don't do it, Dante! She'll kill you!"

Then Gabriella cried out.

"Don't touch her!" Dante said.

"My men will be waiting for you at my airfield. If you don't land in the next two hours—alone—I will cut off Gabriella's fingers one by one and shove them down her throat!"

Jasmine hung up.

Dante hit Kane in his sore arm. He winced but didn't cry out. "Bastard! I knew this would happen. Gabriella helped you, and you left her to die."

Kane never left any man—or woman—behind.

"Gabriella was in it for the long game," Kane said quietly. "You know that. She could have left with us, she chose to stay and ensure that the Flores operation was destroyed."

"And you let her!"

"Like you said, no one controls your sister. I have a plan, let's just get this bird in the air and get to Guadalajara as fast as possible. I'm not going to let anyone else die tonight."

Gabriella stood in front of Jose. She was handcuffed and her face burned from where Jasmine had slapped her when she tried to warn Dante. But now it was just her and Jose.

"Your sister is insane," Gabriella said. She didn't have any hope of saving herself, not anymore. If Dante came, he would be dead. She would be alone again, without her love Greg, without her brother. Death would be a viable alternative.

She didn't have much of a choice at this point.

"You lied to me."

"I never lied. There were things I didn't say."

"Same thing!" Jose ran a hand through his hair. "I loved you."

Jose didn't want excuses. She had none to give.

"Look at me," she said.

It took him a long minute before he could look her in the eye.

"I have no excuses. Deep down, you know the truth. You know who I am."

He waved his hand dismissively, but his eyes watered.

"I fear for you. Jasmine is not Dominick. Dom was a precision weapon—a bullet, aiming at his target and only destroying his target. Jasmine is a nuclear bomb. She'll decimate everything around her. There will be fallout for not only your business, the last of your family, you—but your country. There will be war. Blood will run in the streets. She doesn't value family or human life. But worse, she's volatile."

Jose was staring at Gabriella as if he didn't know her. And maybe he didn't.

But Gabriella suspected Jose was much smarter than he acted.

"I've accepted that Jasmine will kill me. I don't want to die, but I've accepted my fate. Jose—you need to leave. Disappear. Before Jasmine gets you killed."

"You don't care about me," he said. He tried for forceful, it came out hurt.

"Outside of my family, you are the only one who knows the real location of my villa in Spain. Go there."

He stepped back. "I can't believe anything you say."

"You don't have to. Actions, Jose, speak louder. When you get there, you'll know."

He turned his back on her but didn't walk away.

Gabriella said, "We have no choice who we are born, but we choose who we are when we die. Don't die for Jasmine."

He walked away and left her. Did he really mean to leave her alone? Was there hope that she could simply walk out?

A moment later two guards came in and took her to the basement.

No, there was no hope. Not anymore.

Eden held Liam's hand. He was so pale. Where was her vibrant brother?

Siobhan checked the bandages. "The bleeding has slowed," she said. "That's a good sign."

"Go away," Eden said. "Just leave us!"

"If you need me, I'm right here." Siobhan sat in the seat behind Noah.

"Of course you are, there's no place to go in this damn plane! My brother is dying!" Eden bit back a sob and put her forehead on Liam's chest. No matter how many blankets they had piled on him, he was still cold to the touch. "Please don't leave me," she whispered.

Eden felt sick, but she didn't know if it was from the turbulence or the fact that her brother was dying.

Liam reached for her with shaking hands. The head of Saint Michael fell out from under the blanket. She picked it up and stared.

Don't let Liam die, God. Please don't let him die.

"Remember when we decided to go to college in England?" Liam whispered.

"It was our dream."

"It was *my* dream," Liam said. "I wanted to go."

"So did I."

"Not at first. You wanted to study art history in New York and paint."

"Art history in England was even better. And then we went to Rome—that was the best year of college."

He smiled. "It was."

Liam started coughing. Blood dribbled out of the side of his mouth and she wiped it up. Her tears fell on his chest; she wiped them away.

"You searched for this treasure for me, Eden. I wanted to find it."

"I did, too!"

"Because I did. I see everything now, so clearly."

"Don't talk like that."

"You always believed in me. My dreams. My ideas. Never once did you tell me I was a fool."

"You are the furthest thing from a fool. You found the treasure. It was there, right there, and you put the clues together. Only you."

"I couldn't have done it without you. Everything is going to be okay now."

She started crying harder. She couldn't stop. The only true thing in her life was her twin brother. For thirty-six years they had each other, had depended on each other. They had their own lives, Liam had a few women, she had a few men, but in the end everyone let them down in one way or the other.

It wasn't normal, she knew that, but what was normal? They hadn't had a normal upbringing. Their parents had loved them in their own way but were never around. Eden and Liam had practically raised themselves. They raised each other.

"Don't leave me, Liam."

"Paint," Liam said. "For you, not to make forgeries or trick a mark, but paint what you want."

She put her head on his uninjured shoulder. "Please, fight, Liam. I need you."

"I love you, Sis. And I'm sorry."

"There's nothing for you to be sorry about."

He didn't say anything. His chest went up, then down. She waited.

Waited.

Waited.

It didn't rise again.

CHAPTER THIRTY-TWO

Lucy had lost hope for a rescue. Her eyesight had started to return during the long drive to the Flores compound—she could see, but everything was still blurry. She had the worst headache she'd ever had in her life and felt perpetually nauseous. She didn't let on that she could see better than before, but she surreptitiously inspected her captors.

She'd thought about escaping and looked for every possible angle, but she didn't have an opportunity—not even a small one. Not only had they kept her bound the entire trip, but two armed guards also watched her. Worse, she wasn't 100 percent. She wasn't even 50 percent. But the first opportunity to escape she would. Sean had no way of knowing what happened at Dante's house, why she wasn't there, where she could have gone. He might have thought she'd walked out on her own or Liam lied.

Maybe Liam hadn't called Sean at all.

The caravan stopped hours after it started. She didn't move. She heard doors open and close, men talking mostly in Spanish, but she couldn't make out any distinct words.

"Up," one of her guards said.

She tried to stand, but her legs had fallen asleep and she stumbled forward. She couldn't catch herself because her hands were tied behind her back. The men laughed, grabbed her under her arms, dragged her out of the back of the covered truck, and dropped her to the gravel road.

They're going to execute you here, in the middle of nowhere.

It was dark out, but she saw lights shining from a large structure—a mansion, it appeared, though to her it looked like a big squarish blob with yellow windows. She wasn't in the middle of nowhere, she was at the Flores compound.

She would be executed, but it probably wouldn't happen fast.

You have to escape.

A man approached. From her position in the dirt, she saw him only from the waist down—he wore expensive shoes dirty from the day and slacks that were unlike the jeans and camos the other men wore.

Zapelli.

"Your plight is my good fortune," he said to Lucy in English. He leaned over her so she could almost make out his face. "You will pay for what Rogan did to me," he whispered. "I will record every cry, every scream, I will have you begging for mercy, you will curse your family, and they will hear it all and know you are dead but never find your body."

Lucy couldn't control her shaking body. Every nightmare came back. Her greatest fears realized. Eight years ago she'd been a teenager, fearing her family would watch her die.

Zapelli was cruel enough to do everything he said.

To his men, he said in Spanish, "Haul her to the basement. Lock her up—I don't trust her."

Two men roughly pulled Lucy to her feet. She half walked and was half dragged past the large house and around the corner. Two men guarded a staircase that went down to doors leading into a basement. The men pulled Lucy down the stairs and through the opening.

A lone, bare bulb burned in the center of the dank basement. Hard-packed dirt served as the floor; the walls were made of both dirt and stone. The low ceiling prevented anyone over six feet from walking upright, but the men who dragged Lucy in were short.

She smelled blood and death, both new and old.

They pushed Lucy down. She could see little in the dimly lit room, but her hand scraped over a metal ring. The clank of chains make Lucy cry out even more than the pain in her body from the men twisting her around. One of them attached a manacle to her ankle, then pulled the chain hard to ensure it was secure.

They left. A bolt slid into place and Lucy jumped. They talked about sports as they walked up the stairs and disappeared into the night.

She let out a long sob. Then she froze. She wasn't alone.

"Who's there?"

She listened carefully. Someone else was in the basement. Her eyes still weren't focused completely and the dim bulb didn't help, but she looked around her surroundings. Behind her, against the wall and restrained by the same type of manacle as Lucy, was a woman with long dark hair half covering her face.

The woman stared at her. "You must be Lucy."

The woman spoke in English with an exotic accent, but Lucy couldn't quite pinpoint the origin. It could be the woman traveled extensively, adopted different nuances from different countries. Her voice was rough from exhaustion and possible dehydration.

"I don't know you."

"Gabriella."

"Oh—oh, God, Gabriella . . . what happened?"

She of course knew who Gabriella Romero was—she'd helped Kane and Sean rescue Jesse last month. Dante Romero's sister. *Jack had told her Gabriella stayed to protect her cover and ensure that the Flores cartel was broken.*

"I underestimated Jasmine." She laughed, then coughed. "I never underestimate people, but when you're dealing with crazy everything you think you know is skewed."

"We'll find a way out. We have to."

Gabriella didn't say anything for a moment. "I like your faith, dear Lucy, and I'm willing to do anything to survive. But time is not on our side."

"You know the compound, how it's laid out—"

"We have to escape from here first, the pit of hell," she said, and spit on the ground. "This is where they tortured my love. This is where they bled him dry. I die in peace because this is where I took my revenge."

"I'm not going to die. Neither are you. What do you know? Information is important—"

She laughed again. "Yes, information. It's my brother's business. I am sincerely sorry you were dragged into this nasty affair. Had I known, I would never have allowed it. And I like to think that Dante wouldn't have allowed it, either."

"What? You mean what Liam and Eden did?"

"Bringing you here. Jasmine learned of Dante's safe house at the same time she convinced Jose that I was a traitor. My own fault, I suppose, being cocky, that I didn't continually check for listening devices and cameras in my own bedroom. She caught me sending a message to Jack. Or she thinks she did—she couldn't break my encryption."

"Jack? My brother?"

"We've been friends—well, not friends. More . . . oh, reluctant associates, I suppose . . . for years. Greg was in Jack's unit, and Jack risked his life to retrieve his body for a proper burial. I craved revenge, but I should have done it Jack's way at the beginning. Instead, I convinced myself that cold-boiled revenge was more satisfying."

Lucy wondered if she had her idioms mixed up. "You sent Jack a message? Does he know you're in trouble?"

"He knows you're in trouble—I told him Jasmine knew about the safe house. I told him I was going to disappear. I didn't disappear fast enough."

"Then he's coming."

"Jasmine knows he'll come for you."

Lucy's stomach fell. Jack would come and walk into a trap.

"She's in trouble. Financially in deep trouble after you took down her operation and Spade turned state's evidence. She needs an influx of cash, and you're worth a lot of money."

"Wh-why?"

But she knew. She knew exactly why she was worth money. As bait.

"It's a trap." Lucy answered her own question. "Someone wants to kill my brother."

"Many people want to kill Jack, some more than others."

"We have to warn him."

"He knows."

"What? How?"

"Because it's logical. You have to think like these people, and Jack does." Gabriella let out a long sob, then stopped.

"Gabriella—what's wrong?"

"Other than I too am bait? Jasmine spoke to my brother. He's walking into a trap. I told him no, I told him it was a trap, but Dante—he's a hard man, he can be vicious, and he can be an opportunist. But like your brother, with Dante family always comes first. Now we all die."

"We are *not* going to die."

"If you have a plan, I'm listening."

She didn't have a plan, not yet. But she wasn't going to be bait for Jack, and she wasn't going to let the woman who saved Sean and Jesse die.

"Lucy?"

"I'm thinking."

"Think faster."

A moment later the door was unbolted and swung open. "It's your lucky day, Agent Kincaid," Angelo Zapelli said. "Ms. Flores is ready to see you now."

CHAPTER THIRTY-THREE

"You're an idiot, Rogan," Dante muttered. They didn't have much time. Kane had seen the flash of lights as Dante landed the plane. The rain had slacked off as they traveled west, but it was damp outside and the rain would follow.

"Just lock it."

"You know how to get out, right?"

"Yes." Kane lay in the small, cramped secret compartment in the belly of the plane. For the plan to work, the compartment needed to be locked and sealed. That meant Dante needed to slide the seats back into place—over the door.

Good thing Dante was a criminal, Kane thought. Though Sean had the same type of secret compartment in his own plane.

Less than two minutes after Dante sealed the container there was a pounding on the plane's door.

"Romero, out. No tricks. We can and will shoot you."

"I'm coming," he said.

Kane closed his eyes and listened. Four to six men. Someone hit Dante—he fell against the plane with a grunt.

Someone climbed into the plane and searched it. "Weapons!" he called out. "Some clothes, nothing more."

Idiot. Maybe Kane didn't need to be locked in a bin; though the plane was small, the search had been minimal. So what if he lost a few guns—it didn't sound like they'd opened the side panel where Kane had stored the explosives.

He heard two jeeps drive off a few minutes later, but still he waited. Listened. The wind started to pick up and the plane rocked slightly. The rain pounded harder.

No vehicles, no aircraft, no voices.

Just like in the movies, there was a release hatch for the smuggling compartment to dump cargo in the event of trouble. The problem was, the release was in the cockpit, so Kane had to manually release the hatch. Not as easy when crammed in with minimal maneuverability.

But ten minutes later the bottom fell open and Kane hit the hard ground three feet below the plane. He lay there for a minute, making sure he saw nothing unusual, that there wasn't a guard left with the plane.

Nothing.

He crawled out and went back inside the plane. Grabbed his go-bag—damn, they'd taken his favorite SIG—and the guns and explosives hidden in the side compartments.

Then he called Jack.

"Where are you?"

Sean knew that Jack sent him to check the perimeter because Sean was unable to sit still, frantic about Lucy but trying to keep those emotions in check. By the time he returned fifteen minutes later, he was calmer and focused.

Jack proved to be a good commander.

"JT and Kane are both on their way," Jack said. He had been studying a map of the area under the lean-to he and Sean had put up to protect them from both the elements and detection.

"JT?"

Jack folded the map and stared at Sean. "He found the mole."

"Someone in RCK *did* betray us." Sean didn't want to believe it, but JT wouldn't reveal the information if he wasn't certain. "I had hoped—I don't know, some sort of hack."

"You told JT to look outside of the box, and he did. He made several logical assumptions. First, Liam didn't know that RCK had the bonds until we revealed that information to Dante. That makes sense because only Kane and JT knew about the bonds—at least, they knew the history and origin of the bonds. Only them, you, Duke, and myself have access to the main vault at RCK. JT maintains the storage logs and Duke maintains the security system."

"You're not telling me anything I don't know."

As if he hadn't spoken, Jack continued, "It would be logical for Dante to believe that the Flores cartel had possession of the bonds or that we had retrieved them and returned them to the RCK safe—but he knew you had them. So JT made a list of everyone who knew that you had the bonds—and the list is short. Only the few of us, plus Lucy and Matt Elliott. However, there's one person who would know whether the bonds came back to RCK and who may have been able to logically assume that you had them."

"You lost me."

"Jayne."

Sean blinked. "Jayne Morgan. No way in hell did she betray us."

"JT announced what happened with Liam to a small group of staff—including Jayne. She told him what happened. On her own."

"I know Jayne. She's brilliant and loyal and we're friends. We've been friends for years."

Jayne was as good with computers as Sean. She handled

all the back end of RCK, she handled security, she knew the ins and outs of background checks, could get anything on anyone.

"Jayne didn't know that Liam was going to steal the bonds, and she didn't know he would take Lucy. He used her, like he uses everyone. She's one of the few people who was with RCK before Liam and Eden left. And while JT made it clear that they were persona non grata, Jayne occasionally did jobs for them because as far as she was concerned they were family. Nothing she did for them was terribly illegal—mostly background checks, helping move money, helping clean some IDs. Last month— three days after you took possession of the bonds, but after everyone else had returned to RCK—Liam contacted her at home, on her personal phone, and asked if everyone was okay, saying that he was worried specifically about you, wanted to find a way to mend fences. He'd played on her sympathies and her affection for your family. He told her that he heard that RCK had paid off a drug cartel to save a young hostage, that he couldn't contact Kane because of their falling-out, but anything he could do to retrieve the ransom he would do. In the end, she told him not to worry, everyone was safe, and the ransom was safe with you."

Sean let it all sink in. *Jayne.* Jayne had been working for RCK for ten years—maybe longer. She'd always supported him, she'd always defended him to Duke. And yet she was communicating with Liam regularly? Behind their backs?

"She resigned. There's nothing more that we can do now until we get back to Sacramento, but at least we know what happened."

"That bastard," Sean said. "He used her."

"Now we focus on rescuing Lucy and Gabriella."

Sean agreed, but he was shredded inside. What had he

been thinking? That Liam had obtained the information because security was bad? Or guessed that the bonds were with Sean? He hadn't wanted to believe that someone he trusted—someone he liked and respected—had given up the information. Not out of hatred or anger but out of . . . ignorance.

"Sean."

"I'm with you," he said.

"JT and Kane are here."

"How do you know?"

A second later a faint whistle cut through the air. Jack waited, heard a second whistle, then responded in kind.

Two minutes later JT and Kane stepped under the lean-to and shook off their topcoats. They were wet and soggy, but they didn't dare start a fire for fear of being seen.

"You know?" JT asked Sean.

"Yes."

"It's fucked, but we deal with it later."

Kane said, "Dante turned himself over to Jasmine. Jasmine has Gabriella and Lucy at the compound."

"You confirmed?" Jack asked.

"Yes. I put a tracker on Dante, and his bodyguard Philip is working their contacts. Jasmine has nothing outside of the compound, it's the only place she can protect."

"What happened?" Sean asked. He knew planning this operation was crucial, but Liam and Eden had put them in this position and Sean couldn't fathom that Kane had let them go. "Did they get away? Disappear? They're not getting away with this—I will hunt them down to the ends of the earth."

Kane put up his hand. "Sean, I'll tell you everything when we're done. But Liam was shot and probably won't survive. Armstrong took Eden into custody and flew both of them back to the States. Stockton is on his way to Texas if he's not already there."

"No, dammit! He'd better not die. He let this happen—He—" Sean pounded the tree. Waves of emotions he didn't understand flooded him. "All this for what? What, Kane? What was worth Lucy's life? A stupid *treasure*?"

"It's more complicated, but yes."

Unbelievable. Sean couldn't even confront Liam about what he'd done. He didn't even know his brother. As far as Sean was concerned, the twins didn't exist. They weren't family. They weren't Rogans.

JT cleared his throat. "I just now got confirmation that Rick is in McAllen. He has word from Armstrong that their ETA is fifteen minutes. An ambulance is en route to the airport. Rick also has a SEAL team on standby. They're waiting at the border but can deploy immediately for an extraction. Once we establish the timeline, they'll be on the clock."

"Then let's get this going," Jack said. "I have a plan."

The two guards brought Lucy around to the main house and sat her in a chair in an elaborate office. They flanked her and didn't move. Her head ached and her eyes were raw and dry, but she could see, for better or worse. She could also hear the rain blowing against the shutters.

She sat there in silence for what seemed like an hour, but the clock on the mantle told her only thirteen minutes passed before the door behind her opened.

"Agent Kincaid."

The woman stood in front of Lucy. Jasmine Flores was not as crisp and put together as she'd been last month when Siobhan Walsh photographed her outside the house where she'd held captive nearly a dozen pregnant women. In all of Lucy's research, Jasmine kept control over her enterprise with a firm hand and follow-through on threats. But no one in law enforcement knew who she was because she'd stayed under the radar and had never been caught on film.

Until Siobhan. Until Lucy.

Now Jasmine seemed primitive. Her dark-blond hair was still swept up into a chignon, but it was messy, frizzy. Her makeup was less than perfect. Bags under her eyes told Lucy she hadn't been sleeping well or had been drinking too much. Probably both.

Jasmine stared at her. "Do you understand why you're here?" she asked.

"Yes."

"Really. You probably think I'm going to negotiate for your release, have your big important family pay a nice ransom. They couldn't possibly afford you."

"No."

"No, what?"

"No, that's not what I think."

"Enlighten me."

"I'm here because you want to kill me."

"I do want to kill you, but that doesn't benefit me. Other people will pay to kill you. Win-win."

Lucy involuntarily shivered. She had to control her fear or Jasmine would use it against her. As it was, Jasmine was sneering. "Yes, Agent Kincaid, you're worth a lot to the right people."

"You need the money because I destroyed your sick business of buying and selling infants. My death will not be in vain. I've already found half the babies; my team will find the rest whether I live or die. Your lawyer is giving everything to the government and you'll never find him. You have no resources, no people, no loyalty—"

Jasmine's hand shot out so fast Lucy couldn't brace for the violent slap across her face. The chair rocked and nearly fell over. Lucy swallowed the blood that pooled in her mouth as tears clouded her eyes.

"Arrogant, self-righteous cop," Jasmine said. "You think I care about you? About your little world? I will rebuild stronger and better than before. I *am* the Flores cartel. I *am* the one in power. Everyone will bow down to me. Your efforts were a temporary setback. Do you think that I will run away and hide? I will be more powerful now that I control it all."

Jasmine paced. Lucy realized that Gabriella was right—Jasmine was not wholly sane. She was a narcissist, but not tempered by self-preservation.

"Reynosa will pay top dollar for you. I'm sure he'll have a very special spot for you in his harem. Or, perhaps, you'll serve as the bait he needs to finally destroy the gnats who call themselves RCK. Your brother. Your fiancé. That arrogant asshole Kane Rogan. I will have his head—but I am not an idiot. They are worth more alive than my own satisfaction in killing them. They are worth millions to the right people, and one by one they will all walk into my web and I will have my money back. Do you understand? Do you understand that you're nothing but rat bait?"

As she spoke, her voice rose. Lucy had faced psychopaths more than once, and Jasmine certainly fit the mold. But Lucy suspected she'd had some sort of mental break after her operation was shut down by the FBI. This was lunacy.

"Do you think that Carson Spade can hide from me forever? Or that I don't know that his brat belongs to your fiancé? I know everything, Agent Kincaid. *Everything.* You will be long dead, but know, before your last breath, that everyone you love, everyone you know, will die. You should thank me that you'll be the first."

"Is that why you brought me up from your basement? To tell me I'm going to die? Like I didn't already figure it out?"

"You could beg for mercy. That would be fun."

Lucy stared at the woman. Jasmine tilted her head, leaned over, and said, "You should be more scared." Then she pushed the chair over and Lucy fell backward, hitting her head on the stone floor. She was stunned and for a moment feared she'd lose consciousness.

"Take her back to the basement until Reynosa gives me my money. Oh, wait. Get her up."

The two guards pulled Lucy to her feet. She staggered as they held her.

"Say cheese!" Jasmine held up her cell phone and took Lucy's photo. "Proof of life. Like they don't take me at my word."

She walked out, whistling an unfamiliar tune.

CHAPTER THIRTY-FOUR

Rick Stockton was at the hospital when Noah followed the ambulance there. There was no rush. Liam had died before the trip was halfway over. Siobhan had tried artificial respiration, but he was gone.

Eden had remained quiet the rest of the flight. Good or bad Noah didn't know, but he was relieved he didn't have to worry about anything except flying in the rough weather.

Rick turned to Nate. "The administration gave me an office down the hall," he said. "Let's go down there where it's private. Noah—I'll be back in a few minutes. Take a breather. You earned it."

"What happened in Guadalajara?" Noah asked.

"No word. I'll be back. Wait for me."

Rick and Nate flanked Eden as they walked down the hall. She was still in shock. She hadn't looked at Noah since Liam died. Noah didn't blame her. He'd shot and killed her brother.

Nate hadn't handcuffed Eden, though he—not Noah—had read her her rights as soon as they landed on US soil. Nate Dunning had been solid from beginning to end, and Noah never had to tell him what to do. He always did the right thing.

Men like Nate Dunning were rare.

It was three in the morning and no word from Kane or Sean? Noah didn't know if his friends—if Lucy—were dead or alive. Siobhan had been steady the entire trip—she'd taken care of the body, she'd cared for Eden, she never once raised her voice. What was it about the Rogan men that inspired such amazing women to fall in love with them? Because truly, if Kane Rogan couldn't tell that Siobhan was in love with him the man was a fool.

Noah walked down the hall to the restroom. He splashed cold water on his face and stared at the mirror. Liam hadn't been the first person he'd killed. He'd killed twice as a soldier. He'd killed in the line of duty. But this . . . this was different.

It wasn't the line of duty, not officially.

Noah knew Liam. He knew him well and hadn't liked him.

He'd shot him in front of his family. In front of Eden. But he didn't have a choice.

All those cop shows gave people the illusion that cops could just shoot a man's hand and he'd drop the weapon. That bad cops shoot to kill and good cops shoot to injure. The truth was, cops were taught to stop the threat. If you aim at a small target you have a greater chance of missing and hitting an innocent bystander or the criminal being able to continue to enact violence. You never go for the small target. Always aim center mass. Always aim to stop the threat.

Noah couldn't let Liam kill Kane. When Kane holstered his gun and tried to talk sense into Liam, Noah realized Kane didn't want to shoot his brother. He might have been able to, but when Liam fired the gun Noah knew he would continue shooting at Kane until someone stopped him.

Noah had to do it.

Noah would survive. But would Kane have survived—emotionally—if he'd been the one to kill Liam? Noah was glad they never had to find out.

Noah turned off the running water. He didn't know how long he'd been staring at it spiraling down the drain. His hands gripped the edges of the sink. The last of the adrenaline from flying through the storm drained away. He'd wanted to say *something* to Eden, but what could he say? *I'm sorry* wasn't going to cut it.

Nate came in. "Stockton is looking for you."

Noah nodded. "One sec."

"You had no choice."

"I know."

Nate was a good cop, but he wasn't going to last in the FBI. He was too much a soldier. Too much like Kane Rogan.

"Why'd you join the FBI?" Noah asked him.

Nate hadn't been expecting the question. "My dad was a cop. What else was I going to do when I got out of the Army?"

"Why didn't you reenlist?"

"I gave the Army ten years of my life. I wanted another life." He paused. "I know what you're thinking."

"No, you don't."

"Why the FBI. Why not a private agency, like RCK."

Maybe Nate did know what he was thinking.

Nate continued, "Some choices we make to prove to ourselves that we can be better. Better people. Better men. Some choices we make to prove to those who love us that we are the person they see. My dad died in the line of duty. He should have retired, but it was all he knew. He was a beat cop in Chicago, didn't want to be anything else or anyone else. At his funeral, I realized I didn't want to be a soldier for the rest of my life. I'm good at it and I love serving my country. Some things are worth dying for. Some things aren't. There were fewer and fewer assignments I was willing to die for.

"I honestly can't say if I'm cut out for the FBI, but right now . . . this is where I'm supposed to be. If OPR ever comes down on me, I can walk knowing I will always have done what needed to be done to protect the most people. And being here, I understand my dad a lot more than I ever did growing up. There's satisfaction in putting bad guys in prison, not in the ground. There's satisfaction and honor in standing up for the law that, as a soldier, I fought to protect." He paused again. "Have you heard from them?"

Noah shook his head.

"Neither has Stockton."

Nate left. A moment later Rick came in. Noah felt as if he were in the middle of an interrogation room, not a men's bathroom.

"What's going to happen?" Noah said.

"I had the doctors admit Eden to the hospital. She's under a twelve-hour suicide watch."

"She's not going to kill herself."

"She's in shock, and I need to keep her under close watch. I have two agents coming in to guard her door. Tomorrow I'll get Eden to plead."

"Good luck."

"I don't need her to, but damn if I'm going to let this shit go to trial. She'll plead."

"I killed her brother."

"Dunning gave me a verbal report. I'll need a report from you as well, along with the weapon you used. But the reports aren't going into the official record. "

Noah didn't know how Rick Stockton could do what he did and sleep at night. Except now . . . maybe he was beginning to. And he didn't like it.

Noah turned over the sidearm he'd used. He didn't know where it had come from, it had been in the plane when he left Hidalgo for Tampico. His service weapon was still at Jack's place in Hidalgo.

"I'm not going to tell you this will be easy, but—"

"Stop," Noah said. "I can't discuss this now. Have you talked to anyone about Lucy?"

Rick sighed, rubbed his face. "I don't know anything except JT left Sacramento at eight p.m. Pacific time and I haven't heard from him since."

"What about the SEAL team? You said—"

"I know what I said, Noah," Rick snapped. That's when Noah saw the fatigue and worry in his eyes. "I can't send them to a location I don't know. As soon as I know something—anything—I'll send them in. They're waiting for actionable information. Just like we are."

Rick pulled out his cell phone. "Stockton." He listened. "Send the coordinates and the pickup time." He hung up.

"Well?"

"They have a plan. I need to get the team ready."

CHAPTER THIRTY-FIVE

Gabriella thought Dante was dying. He hadn't moved since Jasmine's men brought him into the locked basement and dumped him unceremoniously on the dirt floor. She crawled over to him. Her foot was still chained, but she managed to sit cross-legged and put Dante's head in her lap.

They'd taken Lucy hours ago and she hadn't returned. Was she already dead?

Gabriella checked Dante's pulse often. He was breathing, his heart was pumping, but he had been beaten until he lost consciousness. He hadn't even stirred since they brought him in. There were no windows, she didn't know what time it was, and she didn't know what Jasmine was going to do. She'd assumed Jasmine would kill Dante on sight. Dominick Flores would have, at the first sign of betrayal. So why keep them alive? Why not kill them? No one would buy them, they didn't have value like Lucy Kincaid did.

Except . . . Dante had information about every major, minor, up-and-coming, going-out player in central and eastern Mexico. He had contacts, he knew who had loyalties to whom, who was on the outs, who could be bribed, who was screwing whom. Which businessmen and politicians had odd fetishes, who could be blackmailed, and how much they could be taken for. He knew which cops and politicians could be bought, whose payroll they were on, and if they could be approached. Dante didn't deal in drugs or humans; he dealt in information.

Jose knew that. Jasmine? Probably not, unless Jose had told her. Gabriella deserved this fate—she had hurt Jose, used him to seek her revenge on the man who had murdered the love of her life. She was willing to pay the price.

Not Dante . . . not her baby brother. He did this all for her. He had never wanted her to infiltrate the Flores cartel, but when she couldn't be deterred from this path he had freely helped. He had always been there for her, from when they were children.

She didn't know how long she sat holding Dante in her lap, thinking about growing up the good and bad. How Dante and her father had been so obsessed with the treasure. How Liam and Eden were convinced the four of them were meant to find it. She should have been there with them . . . if she were, there would have been no reason for Dante to risk his life to come to her.

But her need for vengeance outweighed everything else, and she'd believed—convinced herself—that if she stayed she could walk away later.

She'd wanted to take down everyone, including Jasmine. And if Jose got in her way? She would have taken him out, too.

She was no better than the animals she battled in this pathetic war.

Dante shifted and moaned.

She lightly tapped his face. "Dante . . . It's me, Gabriella. Thank God. You're okay."

He grunted and shifted. "Gab—"

His voice was rough.

"I don't have any water, I'm sorry. I'm so sorry."

" 'kay."

"Why'd you come? You knew it was a trap."

He nodded, then winced and clutched his side. "Not a trap for me."

"What are you talking about?"

"Kane."

She froze. "What?"

"Leave no man behind."

"You're talking nonsense."

"They'll come."

He drifted off. "Stay awake, dammit! You have a concussion. You're sick. Dante."

He groaned when she lightly slapped him.

"I'm awake. What time is it?"

"I don't know."

"Be ready. And— I might need some help. Help me up—I need to be able to walk."

She didn't want to, but she did it anyway. Dante winced. "I don't think they're broken, but they hurt like hell."

"What happened?"

"We found the treasure."

She hadn't even been thinking about the treasure. "The treasure. It exists." She didn't know whether to shake her brother or jump for joy.

"Yes. Exactly where we thought. The valley is beautiful, Gabby. Glorious. Then Kane found us, as we headed back to camp. Liam would have killed him . . . Liam's in serious condition. I don't think he's going to make it."

"No, no, that can't be."

"We found the statue of Saint Michael. Liam carried that statue out and he was obsessed, worse than ever before. It's like the longer he had the statue, the more delusional he became. Kane was there, at our camp, told us about Jack's sister, and still Liam wouldn't listen to reason."

"I knew that treasure was cursed."

"He had a gun."

"Liam? He never carries a weapon."

"He shot Kane. Then the man Kane was with shot him."

"Kane's . . . dead?"

"No. He's fine, but Liam would have killed him."

"Dear Lord, Eden must be insane with grief."

"It was awful, Gabby. But at that moment, I didn't care about the treasure. I knew if Jasmine had tracked me to the safe house she suspected you weren't loyal. I feared for your life. No treasure, no amount of money, is worth losing my sister."

He lowered his voice. "Kane was with me when Jasmine picked up your phone. They're putting together a team. We just have to be ready."

"It might be too late. Jasmine sold Lucy to Reynosa. Reynosa wants to use her to kill Jack and anyone else who comes for her. I thought she'd be back hours ago, but they must have already exchanged her for the money."

"Do you remember when you told me you and Greg were getting married?"

Tears welled in her eyes. She nodded. "You were kind of a jerk."

"I knew what it meant—I would have to ease out of certain entanglements. That was me being selfish. But you were so happy. And you deserve to be happy. I liked Greg. But do you remember what I said?"

"You said a lot of things."

"Specifically, I said, 'You marry a man, you gain his platoon.' That platoon was Jack Kincaid and everyone on his team. RCK never condoned my work, but I respect them. And this is why they have my respect—Jack isn't going to let you die, not like this. I saw the same thing in Kane, and I didn't expect to, not after everything I heard about him from Liam. I wanted to see the same in Liam—I wanted him to drop the treasure hunt and help us save you and Jack's sister. And he couldn't. Kane would be dead if he weren't wearing a bulletproof vest."

"Dad always said the treasure was cursed, that bad things happened to anyone who looked for it."

"Maybe it is cursed . . . maybe finding it, disturbing the spirits, hell, I don't know, I don't believe in that shit, but none of it's worth losing our lives over. And if it is cursed, and that's why you're locked away down here, I don't want it." Dante smiled. "I'm smart enough to make money the old-fashioned way."

"Hard work?"

He laughed, then winced and clutched his side. "Of course not. Blackmail."

"That why Jasmine wanted you. What's in here." She tapped his head.

"No. She wants what's in my safe. I didn't even think of it, but Kane did. That man is superscary, but he understands the criminal mind even better than I do."

It was nearly nine in the morning when Jasmine had confirmation that Raymond Reynosa's $10 million was in her account. She'd sent the proof of life photo last night when she first met the feisty federal agent.

Jasmine ordered Morrison to transfer the money into a secure account immediately. All her accounts had been seized by the US government, save for one under a shell corporation that Carson Spade had never known about. She had learned much from her traitorous accountant and had created her own separate but parallel enterprise. Smaller, for emergencies. Now that Morrison knew about it, she would either have to kill him—not really an option at this point because she didn't have anyone to replace him—or create another parallel account Morrison didn't know about.

Once that was complete, she called Raymond. "Darling, I'll have my men bring Agent Kincaid to wherever you want. She's all packaged up and ready to go. I'll even put a bow on her if you'd like."

Raymond laughed. "You've always had style, Jasmine, but style isn't going to win points. Agent Kincaid is a consolation prize. I want her brother."

"As I told you last night, I have word that he is, in fact, in the area. I would not be surprised if he made an appearance in an attempt to rescue his beloved sister."

"I'm counting on it. No federal agent is worth ten million, not even a Kincaid."

"What about a Kincaid who is marrying a Rogan?"

Raymond was silent.

"Agent Kincaid is supposed to be married in a week to the youngest Rogan."

"Is Kane Rogan here?"

She hesitated. She could lie . . . but that wouldn't help her in the long run. She decided at this point honesty would be the best. "The only word I heard was from my men who captured Agent Kincaid in the first place. Two mercenary types stormed the house after my men left. One was confirmed to be Jack Kincaid. The other was too young to be Kane Rogan. I suspect it was the betrothed."

"Hmm. What about the rest of their people?"

"I'm still rebuilding Dom's network." Meaning, she had no way of knowing, but she wasn't about to admit that to her competition. The only reason she knew about Jack Kincaid was because one of her idiots had escaped without engaging him. He'd recognized Kincaid, described Sean Rogan. Could have been Kane, but she doubted it.

"One thing you should know about these people," Raymond said in a condescending tone, "they don't operate in a vacuum. I suggest you spend more time building your intelligence network."

"And I suggest you don't insult your colleagues."

"We'll see, Jasmine, we'll see. Thirty minutes, my office." He hung up.

Office? Where the hell is that?

"Get Zapelli in here," she told her bodyguard.

Reynosa might think she wasn't worthy of taking over her family organization, but he didn't know her. He didn't realize that she'd kept business flowing for decades. She was better than her brothers in so many ways . . . but she needed to learn *this* end of the business, and fast.

As soon as Reynosa thought he had her cowed, she'd show him she wasn't weak. If she had to kill him to do so? So be it.

Thomas Morrison walked into her office, not Zapelli. "Jasmine," he said, "I need to take Joshua to the hospital. He's had a fever for twenty-four hours. It could be serious."

"No."

"He has serious medical issues. He needs care."

"No one leaves the house today. It's not open for discussion."

"You promised that my wife and son would be protected. That includes their health."

"You work for me. You walk out, you'll be dead. I don't think you've grasped the precarious situation we're in right now. If you want your wife and son to each have a bullet in the back of their weak skulls, leave. Take them. Watch them die."

Thomas visibly paled. *Good.* He needed to understand that while he may have been the partner of his law firm, he had no power here. He was only as good as what he could do for her.

Zapelli walked in, glanced at Morrison. "You wanted me, Ms. Flores?"

"Leave, Thomas."

"Tomorrow?" Morrison said. "Can I take them tomorrow?" He cleared his throat. "Please, Jasmine."

She needed him to comply, and he didn't push the issue now. *Good.*

"If it's safe, I'll have a doctor brought in this afternoon. Fair?"

"Yes."

"And?"

He stared at her, as if not understanding what she wanted. Then it dawned on him.

"Thank you," he said slowly.

She smiled. "You are so very welcome."

When Thomas left, she turned her attention to Angelo Zapelli. His face had met with a brick wall, it seemed, dark bruises on his jaw and cheek only just starting to heal. He had proven to be useful over the years, but he was a wild card. Mostly because he was a wimp. He would bend with the wind, and break when pushed. How he handled that little whore breeder Marisol de la Rosa proved he couldn't be trusted. But he had given Jasmine valuable information of late, and he had brought her the Kincaid girl. He knew more of the local players than she did.

She could have asked Jose, but even though he'd stood with her when they confronted Gabriella, she wasn't positive he was truly *with* her. She had her own people—people who didn't have loyalties to Dom or Jose—watching him. Last she heard, he was sulking in his room.

"How many armed men do we have on-site?"

"Eleven. Not including you and your brother."

She didn't like those odds. She also didn't like Jose having a weapon, but she couldn't very well take it from him without making him suspicious—and half of those eleven men were loyal to Jose.

"Kincaid took out three at Romero's safe house," Zapelli said. She didn't need to be reminded of that failure.

"Where's that fool who ran?"

"In hiding."

"When he gets out of hiding, kill him."

Zapelli frowned. "He called it in as soon as he could."

"And now we have the girl, which is good, *and* two mercenaries on our trail, which is bad. Dom had twenty men here and Kincaid and Rogan took out half of them and killed three of my brothers before they escaped."

"I can bring in more men, but it takes money."

"Like everything," she muttered.

"I have a flight back to Monterrey this afternoon," he said.

"Like hell you do. I need you here."

"I did my job."

How dare he argue with her! "You will stay as long as I tell you to stay."

He opened his mouth. Then closed it. *Good.* He understood who was in charge.

"Where's Reynosa's office?"

"Office?"

"Yes, dammit! He told me to bring Kincaid to his office. What the hell does he mean by that?"

"I suspect he means a barn he converted into a jail."

"He has his own jail?" *Very cool.* She wanted her own jail, too.

Zapelli nodded and shrugged at the same time.

"You're in charge of the handoff. Take Kincaid and three men with you. No tricks. Leave her and walk away. I need you back here ASAP. Reynosa is expecting you in"—she looked at her watch—"twenty-two minutes. Don't be late."

It was clear to her that Zapelli didn't want to do this, but he wasn't in a position to argue. "Yes, ma'am," he said, and walked out.

No way in hell was Jasmine leaving the safety of her

compound. Not now, not when Jack Kincaid could be on his way. The fences and walls had been reinforced, this was the safest place for her right now. When Zapelli returned, she would work on bringing in more people. She needed money to do that. Lots of it. She had the money from Reynosa, but that would only go so far.

She hated Carson Spade with all her heart and soul. That *bastard* had stolen everything from her and turned it over to the government to save his own ass. If she could get to him, she would put a bullet in his head. Torture? Hell no, she wanted him *dead, dead, dead*!

"Is something wrong, Ms. Flores?" her bodyguard asked.

"I'm fine," she snapped. "Secure the grounds once Zapelli leaves—no one gets in or out before he returns. *No one*."

The bodyguard had opened the door to leave when Danielle Morrison ran into Jasmine's office.

"I don't have time for this," Jasmine said.

"Joshua needs a doctor. He has a fever. He's only a baby."

"Give him two aspirin and call me in the morning," Jasmine said.

"You don't understand!"

"You don't understand, Danielle. You think that some teenager who didn't use birth control got knocked up and let you adopt her kid? No. Your precious Joshua was born to a prostitute. She was dying and my on-call doc cut little Joshua out of her stomach just for you. Because you so desperately wanted a little-bitty baby."

Jasmine stood up behind her desk, leaned over, put both hands flat on the surface. "But get this—when your husband came to me about finding a baby for you, I gave him pick of the litter. And I'm not talking about the babies." She laughed as Danielle realized exactly what Jasmine meant. "If you doubt it, do a paternity test. Joshua wasn't any test-tube baby. Your dear, darling husband screwed the whore multiple times to ensure she got knocked up. Paid extra to make sure she didn't fuck another man because he wanted to make sure it was his sperm that did the job. I mean, nights are money. And when she was pregnant? He came back. Maybe you are as cold and rigid as you look and he needed some hot Latina spice."

"Shut up. Shut up!"

Jasmine laughed. "I obviously know your husband a lot better than you do. And you know, he didn't use a condom . . . because he was trying to get her pregnant. But she was a whore. Are you sure he didn't catch something? Give it to you? Maybe you should get it checked out." She crossed the room. "I don't like you, you needy, weak bitch, so let me make this perfectly clear: Your husband works for me. As long as he does his job—which is not only to make me money but also to keep you in line— then you, Thomas, and little Joshua get to live. But if you push me, I will kill you myself. I'm sure Thomas will find another whore to keep his bed warm at night."

It was perfectly clear that Danielle Morrison hadn't known anything. She hadn't known about Joshua's conception, his mother, his birth, or Thomas's arrangement with Jasmine. *Stupid, naïve idiot.*

"Get out of my office," Jasmine said. "Now!"

Danielle could barely walk. She staggered out of the room as if she'd suffered a physical blow.

"Have someone watch her," Jasmine told her bodyguard.

"Yes, ma'am." He walked out. She liked her new bodyguard. Not quite as much as Lance, but at least this one didn't talk as much. She was tired of being second-guessed and questioned by every damn person.

Jasmine was going to clean house. If her men weren't

100 percent with her, they were against her, and they would die.

She sat down at her desk again and looked at the numbers Thomas Morrison had run. She was in deep trouble.

Jose walked in with two cups of coffee. He handed one to her.

"I hope you didn't poison it," she snapped.

He stared at her. "Why would you even say that?"

"Are you with me?"

He sat down across from her. "Jasmine, I need to give you some advice. You are family. My only family now. I would be lying to you if I said I didn't miss Dom. He was a good brother—he was more a father to me than our father was to either of us. But he's not here. You are. I don't want to run the business. Dom knew my strengths. I like people. I'm a good negotiator. Dom's associates trust me. You have to earn that."

"Dom kept control with fear."

"No, he kept control because people respected him. He did what he said. He could be ruthless, but only when he had to be to make a point."

"And he had money," she said. She was only half-listening to Jose. She was focused more on her cash flow problem. "We have a fraction of the resources that we had before the Rogans came in here and killed Dom."

Jose's face clouded. Jasmine used that. "Still have feelings for that little whore?"

"I gave her to you, didn't I?"

"No one will buy them. I asked around. Oh, a few thousand here and there, but I remembered something Dom said a long time ago. The Romeros were people with information."

Jose nodded. "Dante Romero is primarily an information broker. If it's worth knowing, he knows it."

"He blackmails people."

"Mostly, he sells information to people who want it. But he knows everyone and he brokered the truce between Dom and Reynosa years ago, and the truce between Dom and the Hernandez people. The truces have been good for business."

"I need that information. I can't trust what he says, but he must have the information somewhere."

"His house."

"You know this for a fact?"

"I can get it for you. I've been to his house, I know where his safe is."

This was too easy. Much too easy.

"Why would you do that?"

He shook his head. "We're family, Jasmine. I hope that you'll listen to me about how to handle the business without Dom, but in the end, if we don't have family, what do we have?"

She considered that. Her family had never trusted her. She was the bastard daughter, the bitch in the States. She and Dom had an alliance, but he didn't trust her and she never trusted him. They talked about family, but that meant nothing to them because she was the illegitimate daughter.

Was Jose going to obtain the information and then ice her out? Would he make a deal with Reynosa or another player to have her assassinated? She couldn't trust Jose with information, she couldn't trust him with anything, until he proved his loyalty. And there was only one way to do that.

"You will give me all the information about the safe and I will go to Dante's house and retrieve it."

"I don't think that's smart—"

She threw her coffee mug at Jose. He ducked and it fell on the floor behind him, spilling black coffee on the Persian rug. "Do not tell me that I am stupid! You want to prove to me that you are with me? I expect to see Gabriella and Dante Romero's dead corpses hanging from the gate when I come back. They will hang there until they rot and then everyone will know I am in charge!"

CHAPTER THIRTY-SIX

As soon as Jack signaled to Kane that the truck had exited the compound they waited. Kane was positive that Jasmine would leave alone or with one other person to retrieve the files at Dante's house. Dante's Guadalajara property was twenty minutes away. That gave Jack and JT forty minutes to neutralize any threat, find Gabriella and Dante, and get to the rendezvous. Jack had to make it on time—the SEAL chopper wouldn't land until they were all there. The risk was too great, and they couldn't wait or return.

But Jasmine wasn't leaving. Gabriella had said nothing about a second exit, but the idea nagged at Jack.

"We need to go in," he told JT, "I have a bad feeling we've already missed her."

Just as he said it he spotted Jasmine Flores on the wide veranda. She did indeed have only one man with her, and he led her to a Hummer. A moment later they drove off through the gates.

"Now we go," JT said. "I know you're worried, Kincaid—but this was your plan and it's damn brilliant."

Based on previous intel from Gabriella, they knew Jasmine had eight to twelve men at the compound. Four had left with Lucy; they could see one with Jasmine—that left three to seven on-site.

JT disabled one camera and they went in over the back wall. Gabriella's intel over the last month had been solid. Everything Jasmine Flores had done to security, people, the grounds, Gabriella had sent over, even if she didn't think it was important. That's how they knew the cameras were all on a dedicated system shown on one large computer screen in the security room. If they took out all of the cameras, someone might notice. But one camera might not be noticed at all—at least that was the theory.

The only secure place to hold anyone, especially after the breeches last month, was the basement. One entrance, from the outside, no windows. It was easy to see—an armed guard stood outside the door. Kane told Jack that Jasmine wouldn't kill Dante until after she verified the information she wanted was in Dante's safe. Then she would make the call and have him and Gabriella executed. In theory. Of course, she could have already killed them.

Jack wished it were night. Operations like this always worked better under the cover of darkness. But it was 0900 hours. The steady rain helped, but it was still daylight.

Jack easily took out the guard and JT ran down the stairs to the basement. A minute later he came out. "They're gone."

"Fuck!"

JT pulled out his phone. Dante had a tracker on him, and JT brought up his signal.

"He's in the house. About a hundred feet inside."

"There's a windowless panic room that Dominick used for interrogations," Jack said.

In silence they ran along the side of the house and went in through the closest door. It was locked, but Jack broke it, walked in, swept the hall. He had memorized the floor plans before the first assault on the house last month to rescue Sean's kid, and he had refreshed his memory while walking through the plan with JT.

Jack had given up international fieldwork after he got married six years ago. But some skills you never lost; some instincts were so finely tuned that you could sense a silent footstep in your sleep. When he'd come back to Mexico last month, it was like he'd never left. He'd told Sean he wasn't at his best, that he had lost his edge, and part of that was true. But he hadn't lost the important stuff.

He walked up behind a guard and slit his throat. Killing never came easy, but Jack was on autopilot. These people were part of a violent cartel. They'd been party to kidnapping his sister. They would have killed her. They planned to give her to Jack's enemies to lure him out. Six years was nothing to men like Raymond Reynosa.

Jack motioned for JT to go down the hall to the kitchen. The panic room was underground, and not much bigger than a root cellar. But if Gabriella and Dante weren't in the main basement, they would have to be here. Unless they were already dead.

Jack took the rear. He didn't hear anyone else in the house, but there had to be at least one more armed man. A maximum of five more.

Just before they approached the dining hall JT put up his hand and Jack froze. He put up two fingers and gestured directly to his right, then forward and to the left. Two men. JT would take the first one, Jack would rush and take the second. JT put down his hand and they both rushed.

JT's target went down silently, but in his fall a vase crashed to the floor.

A voice came from the hall. "Robbie, what's going on?"

Jack's target stepped into the room from the opposite hall and raised his weapon to fire. Jack shot first, twice in the chest, and he went down. Dammit, he'd now alerted everyone they were here.

Jack rushed through the kitchen, cleared it, and reached the basement door. It was locked from the outside. He slammed the butt of his rifle on the lock twice and it broke open.

There were shouts from two corners of the house, but Jack was surprised there weren't more people.

Jack went down the stairs while JT guarded the door. It was dark down here, and he would be a sitting duck.

"Romero!" Jack called out in a loud whisper.

"Jack?"

Gabriella. She wasn't dead. *Thank God.*

Jack shined his flashlight around. Gabriella was in the corner trying to help Dante up. "He's hurt," she said.

"Can he walk?"

"Yes," Dante said.

"We have to go."

Gabriella wrapped her arm around Dante's waist. They went up the stairs first, Jack behind them.

Gunfire rang out and JT stepped onto the landing of the basement and fired twice. "Now," he called.

They went back the way they came, JT leading and Jack again taking the rear. JT held up his hand.

Just then Jack saw a woman holding a bundle of blankets that looked like it was a baby—a *baby*?

Gabriella said, "Danielle!"

"Take him." Danielle showed JT the infant's face. "Take Joshua, please Gabriella. He's not mine. I didn't know—I didn't know any of it."

"Come with us. We can get you to safety," JT said. It was an order, not an offer.

"I'm not leaving." She pushed the baby into Gabriella's arms. "Save Joshua."

"Gun!" Jack called.

Danielle turned and ran away from them. She had a gun in her hand.

"We have to get her—" Gabriella said. "She's going to get herself killed."

"This is one of the babies Lucy is looking for, isn't it?" Jack said.

"Yes, but—"

"We don't have time."

"Jack—"

"Get her moving, Kincaid," JT said.

"Gabriella, we have to go," Dante said.

Suddenly a single gunshot rang out from down the hall. Then silence.

Jack wrapped one arm around Dante's waist and pushed him forward. "Now, G. We have to go."

They left as fast as they could with an injured man and a newborn.

Jack spoke into his mike. "Leaving extraction point B now. Over."

There was no response.

CHAPTER THIRTY-SEVEN

It had taken all of Sean's willpower to remain in hiding as the truck that held Lucy slowed to a stop.

Jack's entire plan was subject to Lucy being taken to a barn on Reynosa property. If Jack was wrong, they would lose her.

"I'm not wrong."

But until Sean saw the truck in the distance, through his binoculars, his stomach had been tied in knots. If they were wrong . . . if they were at the wrong place . . . if Lucy was already dead . . .

Then he saw her.

She was restrained in the back of a pickup truck. Two men in the cab, two men in the rear. Her eyes were closed. She wasn't gagged or blindfolded, but he adjusted his binoculars and saw her hands tied in front of her. Her clothing was torn, bloodied. She was shaking, soaking wet, as the rain continued to fall. Red rage filled his vision and Sean had to bite his own finger to keep from rushing into the road and getting both him and Lucy killed.

The truck slowed, then stopped at the fallen tree. He and Kane had pulled it across the road when Jack gave the signal that the truck had left the Flores compound.

Sean saw Angelo Zapelli in the passenger seat. Zapelli ordered the driver to go out and clear the log. It wasn't a one-man job. The driver called out to Zapelli. Of course Zapelli didn't get out and get wet, he ordered one of the two men in the rear to assist. But he was suspicious—Sean could tell by his expression.

Sean waited . . . each second feeling like an hour. The men were moving the tree over to where Sean hovered. He was waiting for Kane's signal.

In his earpiece he heard: "Now."

Sean fired two bullets each at the two men by the side of the road. They both collapsed. One dead, the other in pain. Sean shot him again as he jumped up and ran past him.

The report of a rifle sounded and Sean looked just in time to see the armed guard sitting next to Lucy fall over and slump against the truck.

Zapelli slid over to the driver's seat and started moving, trying to drive around the fallen tree, which had been partially moved aside. His wheels spun in the mud, then jerked forward. Three more rifle rounds echoed and the truck stopped.

Zapelli slumped over the steering wheel, blood spatter sprayed all over the side window. The bastard was finally dead.

"Clear!" Kane said in Sean's earpiece.

Sean ran from the side of the road and to the back of the truck. "Lucy! Lucy!"

"Sean?"

Her voice was weak.

"Are you shot? Are you hurt?"

"No." She ended on a sob. "It's a trap. For Jack."

"We know. Jack is fine." He hoped. They had to run the two rescues simultaneously or they would all have been in jeopardy. "It's just Kane and me right now. I'll explain everything as soon as we get out of here, but we don't have a lot of time."

He took out his knife and cut through the rope. It took far longer than he wanted. Her wrists were raw and she winced but didn't cry out.

"Can you climb out of the truck?"

She nodded. Sean jumped out, then put his hand out to help her. Her legs were unsteady and she reached for his hand and missed. He grabbed hold of her wrist to keep her from falling and she cried out.

A blind woman.

"What's wrong? Lucy, what's wrong?"

"Everything is blurry. I—"

Kane rushed over to them and helped Sean maneuver Lucy out of the back of the truck.

"Reynosa's people heard the shots," Kane said. "He has a fucking army surrounding the barn. Let's go."

Sean wrapped his arm around Lucy's waist and helped pull her along, but she stumbled and fell in the mud. He pulled her up and she winced. "Where are you hurt?" he asked, trying to keep his voice calm.

"I'm okay. Just dizzy. Let's go."

"She has a concussion," Kane said.

"Something else is wrong," Sean said.

"We'll check her out as soon as we get to the jeep," Kane said. "Move it!"

Both Sean and Kane supported Lucy as they ran over the damp earth. They had a jeep waiting on a parallel road, but it was a quarter mile away.

As if Kane had eyes in the back of his head, he said, "Down down down!"

Sean dropped to the muddy ground with Lucy. He covered her body with his, expecting to hear gunfire. Kane was down next to him. They were hidden only by low-lying shrubs and the gray, wet morning. Reynosa's men stopped at the truck. Sean heard intermittent voices but couldn't make out what they said.

"Stay," Kane said in a low voice.

It sounded like someone was giving orders. Kane pulled out his phone and hit a preprogrammed number.

"Brace yourself," Sean whispered in Lucy's ear.

The explosives Kane had set under the truck went off. The ground shook. Screams from the men behind them echoed in Sean's ears.

"Go go go!" Kane helped Sean pull Lucy up and they ran across the field to the jeep. Sean and Lucy got into the back and Kane jumped into the driver's seat and sped away. Kane got on the radio. "I have the birdie. Over."

Sean didn't hear any response. He sat in the back with Lucy. She had her eyes closed and for a minute he thought she had passed out. "Kane—what happened?" Sean asked.

"He clicked his mic, he's good, can't talk." Kane glanced back. "How is she?"

"Luce?" Sean asked.

"I'm here."

"Where are you hurt? And don't tell me you're not."

"My head. Liam put something in my eyes that blinded me. It was temporary, about twelve hours, but nothing is clear, and I'm so dizzy." She reached for his hand. He grabbed hers, squeezed it.

"I am so sorry." Sean's voice cracked.

"Not your fault."

Lucy didn't sound right.

"Anything else? Who hurt you? There's blood." Sean didn't want to think about anyone striking her.

"Just pushed me around. The blood was from my nose. And I might have a bruised rib."

Sean pulled up her torn shirt. Her rib cage was bruised

and swollen. Likely cracked. If it were broken, she would probably be in more pain. Unless she was going into shock. "We'll get X-rays. No wonder you couldn't climb out of the truck."

"I'll be fine."

"Don't let her sleep," Kane said.

"Where's Jack? Reynosa expected him to come after me. He paid ten million dollars—"

"Well, hell," Kane said, "you're worth more than me, Sis."

Lucy cracked a smile, then winced.

"It was for Jack, he thought Jack was coming for me."

"Jack's with JT rescuing Gabriella and Dante from the compound."

"I didn't see Dante there."

"It's a long story."

"I'm supposed to stay awake, right?" She paused, opened her eyes, and looked at Sean. Her vision was still blurry, but close up she could focus. "I love you."

"Love you, princess. God." He touched his head to hers. "Too close, Lucy. That was too damn close."

"We have a fifteen-minute drive, keep her awake. The SEALs will have a medic," Kane said.

"SEALs?" Lucy asked.

"I said it's a long story," Sean said. "And parts of it are kind of cool." Or would have been if he hadn't been frantic about Lucy. "Kane played the part of Han Solo and hid in a secret compartment on Dante's plane . . ."

"Where is he?" Lucy asked Kane not for the first time. Kane was probably getting tired of her worries. "You said Jack would be here in fifteen minutes. It's been twenty."

Sean said, "We still have five minutes before the SEALs get here."

"He'll be here," Kane said. "Sean, anything?"

Sean had been fixated on his tablet ever since they reached the field where the rescue Hawk would touch down.

"What is going on?" Lucy asked.

"You don't need to worry about this," Kane said.

"Tell me. It's Jack, isn't it? Is he in trouble? Is he hurt? Tell me!"

"Jack is fine," Kane said. He turned to Sean. "You can tell her."

Sean turned the tablet so Lucy could watch. She saw a live video feed of a wall in a relatively nice-looking library. "What is that?"

"Dante's office," Kane said. "I didn't want you to have to take on another burden."

"No secrets, Kane."

Sean said, "Remember when I told you that Jasmine most likely wanted Dante Romero because of his files? She probably made a big play of wanting revenge and accusing him of setting up her family, but Dante is an information broker and he has valuable information that protects him from harm."

"And you think Jasmine is going to steal it."

"She'll try," Kane said. "But I have everything." He glanced at a duffel bag that looked nondescript. "It Dante makes it out of this alive, he's relocating and will have no use for the intel."

The unspoken word was that RCK would benefit—or would Kane give it to the FBI? Lucy didn't think so. The FBI couldn't be involved in operations on foreign soil, except under very specific circumstances.

As Kane spoke, two people came into view of the camera. Lucy shivered, and Sean wrapped a hand around her waist. "She'll never hurt you—or anyone—again."

The man with Jasmine, her bodyguard—Lucy couldn't remember his name, if Jasmine had ever said it—removed a large painting from the wall. Behind it was a safe. Jasmine took out a paper, handed it to the man, and he opened the safe.

There was no sound, but it was clear when Jasmine looked inside that she was furious. She reached in and picked up a small object.

That's when Lucy saw Kane with two phones in his hand. He used one, autodialed a number. On the tablet, Jasmine stared at the phone. She answered it.

Kane said, "You fucked with the wrong people."

Then he pressed an autodial number on the second phone.

The screen went blank. There was a faint, deep *BOOM* in the distance. On the horizon, they saw a ball of flames shoot into the air.

Lucy blinked. "You set explosives."

"They will not stop going after the people I care about. *Ever.* Do not feel guilt."

She didn't. She'd just watched two people die and she didn't feel anything about it. She'd watched Angelo Zapelli shot and killed and she hadn't felt a thing. Maybe sadness. A deep sadness that the world had become such a terrible, awful place.

For the first time in her life since she had learned she couldn't have children herself she thought that maybe that was a blessing in disguise. How could she bring children into such a violent, corrupt, horrible world? The thought made her eyes water.

Lucy turned to Kane. "No guilt."

The heard the rescue Hawk approach. "Jack's not here," Lucy said. "Kane—where is he?"

"He's coming."

"You keep saying that, but how do you know?"

Kane took out his earpiece. He put it in Lucy's ear. "Hear for yourself."

She listened. She heard a vehicle moving. Then Jack's voice: "Alpha One, I see the bird. ETA one minute."

Tears streamed from her eyes. "He really is okay."

"I told you."

Then she heard the cry of a baby.

CHAPTER THIRTY-EIGHT

Twelve Hours Later

Sean stepped out of Lucy's hospital room and leaned against the wall.

So much had happened in less than seventy-two hours, he could hardly process it all. Seeing Jesse Monday morning and convincing him to stay in witness protection. Coming home to learn that his brother and sister had kidnapped the woman he loved. Traveling to Guadalajara to rescue Lucy. Seeing her so beat up, so broken . . .

He'd been so close, too close, to never seeing her again.

"How is she?"

Sean looked up. Jack stood in the hall, unshaven but clean. Sean realized then that he'd been sitting outside Lucy's door, on the linoleum floor, unable to focus on anything specific. But he didn't want to leave her. The nurse had gone in to check her injuries and vitals and Sean had stepped out. The nurse had left, but Sean remained outside. Because he was feeling so lost.

He wanted to hit someone. He wanted to take out his anger on Liam, who had started this entire ordeal. But Liam was dead. Sean hadn't seen him in years, he'd barely talked to him, and yet Liam had nearly destroyed his life.

Now he was dead. And Sean had no one to punish.

Jack squatted. "Sean. Lucy."

"Sleeping. They want to keep her a couple of days, but I'm going to take her home in the morning. A cracked rib. Concussion. Bruises. Her vision is better now, but she needs to see a specialist. Her wrists . . . God, Jack." His voice cracked. "They tied her up."

Jack sat down next to him. "Don't think about it. You can't or it will tear you apart. We got her back. That's all that matters."

"I know." *But*. There was so much more going on. Kane had tried to explain what Liam and Eden had done and why. Well, he *had* explained, but none of it made sense to Sean. They had endangered Lucy's life because of money. The crassest, most basic of all greed. And some odd sense that Kane owed them? Sean didn't know. He didn't want to understand anymore.

As far as he was concerned, whatever mistakes Kane made with Liam and Eden six years ago were justified. When Sean really needed Kane, he was there. He risked his life to save Jesse last month and he risked his life to save Lucy yesterday. He was the most selfless person Sean knew. As Jesse said, he was a hero.

"I'm not leaving," Sean said. "Rick said I should go back to your place, but I'm not leaving Lucy. I just needed to . . . She's sleeping. I needed to get out of there. Looking at her . . . what if . . ."

"Don't. That's never good. By the way, it isn't my place anymore. Kane's moving in."

"He's been staying there a lot anyway."

"He wants to be closer to you and Lucy, but he's not one for the city."

"I'm glad. He probably wants to be closer to Siobhan."

"He didn't say."

They sat there in silence for several minutes. Sean had

been thinking of a way to ask Jack to participate in the wedding, but it had been awkward. But after this week, there was nothing awkward about their relationship.

"Jack, I'd like you to do something for me."

"Anything."

"I know your dad is giving Lucy away when she walks down the aisle, but I want you there, too. Lucy loves you so much, but I have two brothers—" Two brothers. Liam was no longer his brother. He hadn't acted like a brother when he was alive, he didn't deserve brotherhood in death.

Jack almost smiled. "I'm not hurt that you didn't ask me to be an usher."

"It's not that—but your approval means everything to Lucy. And, honestly, to me."

"Sean, you've always had my approval. From the very beginning."

"You're the only one," Sean said. It was true. From the beginning, Jack had shown a quiet respect for Sean, and he didn't always understand why. Not back then. Now? It was because Jack loved Lucy and he wanted her to be happy. Sean had always done whatever he needed to make Lucy happy, to keep a smile on her face.

Sean continued, "I've heard the ring bearer is supposed to be a little kid or something, but I think—I know—Lucy will consider it special if you hand us the rings. It would mean something to me, too."

"Of course." Jack cleared his throat. "Can I sit with Lucy for a while? I'll stay until you get back. There's a shower in the doctors' lounge."

"Is that a hint?"

"You stink, Sean."

Sean laughed, otherwise he might have cried.

Jack stepped into the hospital room and stared at his baby sister. Her wrists were bandaged and all he could picture was Lucy eight years ago, battered and bruised, with her wrists bandaged in just the same way. But for different reasons.

He blinked back tears. He didn't cry. But damn, he was close.

He sat in the chair next to her bed. Lucy opened her eyes.

"I didn't mean to wake you."

"You didn't. I pretended to sleep so Sean would go get some rest."

"You did good, kid."

"I did nothing. I had to be rescued."

"That wasn't your fault." He didn't mean to sound so stern, but if Lucy took any of the blame for this he would throttle her.

"I know—I know. I just . . ." She took a deep breath. "I don't think you'll understand."

"I do."

"How?"

"Because I know you, Lucy. Better than you think. I don't care where you are, what happens, whose fault it is— if you're in trouble, I'll be anywhere in the world for you. So will Sean, which is why he's probably the only guy I'd ever be happy seeing you with."

"I was so scared, Jack."

"So was I."

"If you died trying to save me I couldn't—"

"What did I just say? Do you think I could have lived with myself if I didn't find you? This entire situation was out of our control."

"Kane blames himself."

"I've talked to him. He'll work through it. I just told Sean that Kane is permanently moving to Texas. He's moving into my place after the wedding."

"I'm glad. Kane needs to find peace."

"He is. He's not as broken as you might think he is. I've known Kane for a long time, and there's no one I would rather partner with." Jack changed the subject. "Where are you going for your honeymoon?"

"I don't know."

"You don't?"

"Sean planned everything." She yawned. "I let him."

Jack leaned over and kissed her forehead, then took her hand. "I'm sure it'll be exactly what you need. Sleep, okay? It's nearly midnight. I'm going to sit right here until Sean comes back."

"Aren't visiting hours over? Sean should get some rest."

"Haven't you heard? You're a Very Important Person." Jack smiled. "Rick has a lot of sway, but if you want me to keep people out I will."

"No—well, everyone but Sean. At least until I can think straight."

"Sleep."

"I will—but first tell me that the baby is okay."

"The baby is okay."

"You're not just saying that."

"Joshua is fine. He has a minor infection and is on antibiotics but is otherwise healthy."

"Do you believe Danielle Morrison? That she didn't know?"

"I think she didn't want to know. But when she learned the truth, she couldn't live with it."

Jack didn't know what happened to her or her husband. He had a theory—that she had killed her husband and left or killed her husband, then herself. But he couldn't verify it. The only Flores who had survived was Jose. Jack hadn't seen him in the house and feared he'd retaliate, but Gabriella assured Jack that there would be no retaliation.

"Jose was the best out of them. That doesn't mean he

was a good guy, just not a bad guy. He has a lot of friends. But revenge isn't in him. If it weren't for Jose, Dante and I would have been dead."

Jack wanted to know how Gabriella could be so confident. She had pulled a note out of her pocket and shown it to Jack. It was written in Spanish, but he quickly translated.

> *G~*
> *I love you enough to let you go. I know you didn't love me in the same way, but you liked me. That can't be faked.*
>
> *~J*
>
> *P.S. I didn't tell Jasmine everything.*

Jack assured Lucy that the Flores family was no longer a threat.

"Does that mean that Jesse can come out of witness protection?" Lucy asked.

Jack hesitated. "I, uh, that's really not my expertise. From my understanding, Carson Spade is wanted by more than the Flores cartel. But . . . since they are all dead, and the government doesn't have much of a case against Jose Flores, I don't know what they're going to do."

"Sean wants to raise his son."

"And?"

"And what?"

"What about you?"

"I can't have children. For years that bothered me so much, but after the last two months, seeing all the despair and violence, I didn't even want to bring a child into the world. I didn't even think I wanted to adopt anymore." She took a deep breath. "And then you handed me Joshua on the Black Hawk and I realized that children are the only hope in this world."

"What's going to happen to Joshua?" Jack asked. "Noah gave me a bunch of legal shit I didn't care to understand."

"He'll be a ward of the court until someone adopts him is the simple answer. But there's a lot that needs to happen."

"What about you? You would make an amazing mother. And Sean—" Jack smiled.

Lucy didn't. "I want to, Jack." She paused and seemed to look beyond him. She was still troubled. His beautiful, brave little sister was so deeply troubled and it pained Jack that he couldn't take away her anguish. "I delivered one of the babies last month. The mother had been used as a shield, shot in the neck, was dying—the baby nearly died. A girl." Her voice cracked. "And I thought, 'She's mine.' But she's not mine. I desperately wanted her. But I'm not in a place where I can devote my time and energy to a child. I can love a child—I could love baby Lucia and Joshua and I hope someday . . ." She shook her head. "But I'm not ready to be a mother. I'll know when I am."

"You are the wisest woman I know."

She squeezed his hand, then closed her eyes.

She was asleep two minutes later.

Sean had put on scrubs a nurse found for him, because his clothing was only fit for the incinerator. The shower worked wonders for him, and he could finally think clearly after being in a fog all day waiting for answers about Lucy.

He stepped out and ran into Rick Stockton. "Do you have a minute?"

"A minute or two. Jack is sitting with Lucy."

Rick motioned for Sean to follow him down the hall. "The doctors say she's better, she'll be released tomorrow."

"I'm taking her home at the crack of dawn." He looked

at his watch. That was only eight hours from now. "We both hate hospitals."

"Noah and I are transporting Eden to DC, where she'll face charges. We're trying to do this quietly, but she's already said she won't plead. She fucking asked for a lawyer."

"Noah didn't do anything wrong."

"We know that. It's complicated."

"Fuck," Sean muttered. "She thinks she can walk because no one wants on record what happened in Mexico."

"That—and the fact that you had in your possession bearer bonds stolen from a Russian consulate six years ago. I don't have to tell you that Eden is a compelling liar."

"I can withstand the questioning."

"So can Kane. And so can Jack and JT and everyone else at RCK. And so can Lucy. But I want Eden to plead because any public testimony is going to create untold problems for me, the FBI, and RCK."

Then it clicked. Sean was definitely tired, because it took so long for him to catch on to what Rick wanted him to do.

"You want me to convince her."

"You're the only one who can. She wants to talk to you, I believe to apologize for what happened to Lucy and to explain why she did what she did."

Sean didn't want to see Eden, let alone talk to her.

But he didn't want Noah to face scrutiny for being a federal agent in Mexico involved in a shooting death. It would cause international problems, not to mention problems for Rick and Noah. Lucy would be forced to testify about what happened to her . . . and what happened in the rescue. Now Sean understood why Kane had suggested she not be involved with the explosion Kane had rigged at Dante's house. If anyone had questioned her on it, she would have to lie or admit to being an accessory after the fact. Jasmine Flores was an American citizen—yes, she was a wanted fugitive, a killer, a kidnapper, but she still deserved due process under the law.

And none of that even delved into the bonds in the first place—their origin, what Eden might say as to why she was stealing them, why they were in the RCK safe for six years. How they landed in Sean's safe.

Everyone had banded together to bring Lucy home safely. Everyone *except* Liam and Eden.

She didn't deserve a pass, and Sean would move heaven and earth to make sure she didn't drag everyone through the mud.

"I'm working with the AUSA to offer Eden ten years on the single charge of kidnapping a federal agent, with the chance of parole after five."

"No."

"Sean, I can't cut out any more time. The AUSA wanted twenty to life."

"I'm with the AUSA on this one."

"I'm weighing my options here. Eden will never give up twenty years. Five? Yes. I think you can convince her." He paused. "And I'll do everything in my power to keep her in for the full ten."

Sean didn't want to talk to Eden, but he didn't see that he had a choice.

"Do you want to discuss this with Lucy?"

"Yes."

"I'll meet you downstairs in fifteen minutes."

Sean went back down the hall to Lucy's room. Jack was sitting on the chair, eyes closed. Sean was certain he was asleep, but he opened his eyes when the door swung shut.

"You look and smell much better, Rogan."

"Rick wants me to convince Eden to take a plea deal. Five to ten."

Jack didn't say anything.

"You can't think this is a good idea."

"You know it's the only option."

Sean sat on the edge of Lucy's bed. "Eight years ago, the powers that be made a plea deal with one of Lucy's rapists behind her back. I'm not going to do it, not without her knowledge."

"Do what you think is best, Sean." Lucy opened her eyes.

"I woke you up."

"I don't think I'll sleep well until we go home."

"I'd take you there right now if I could."

She smiled. "I know." She looked so exhausted. "What is the deal?"

"Five to ten. Sealed plea."

"It's a good idea."

"You could have been killed." *Worse.*

"I wasn't." She took Sean's hand. "I listened to them. Liam was driven solely to find this treasure, and resented Kane for . . . well, everything, it seems. For stealing the bonds, for kicking them out of RCK, for being himself. Liam hated Jack because he thought Jack replaced him at RCK. Liam felt inferior to Kane on one hand and superior on another. If I had more time, I could make a better assessment."

"You seem to understand already."

"Eden just wanted to make her brother happy, and she felt isolated from the family. She said something—I don't remember the exact words, but she wanted to come home and help raise you after your parents died but didn't want to live by Duke's rules."

"That was her choice." But Sean hadn't known Eden even had considered coming home.

"She has this sense that if she were there you wouldn't

be siding with Kane, you'd be with them. For her, it was like a . . . competition for your loyalty. And then Kane cheated and you picked his side."

"People died, Lucy. Because of her."

"Liam died, and she's not going to get over that anytime soon. Sean—I'm not going to tell you to talk to her if you don't want to. But I'm okay. I'm here no matter what you do."

"Okay." He looked at Jack. "Can you—"

Jack put up his hand. "This chair is a hell of a lot more comfortable than sleeping in that damn jeep under a dripping tree last night. I'll be here when you get back."

"You're a hard man to find, Kane Rogan."

Kane turned from the window and faced Siobhan. What a sight for sore eyes.

She walked over to him. "I told you that you needed stitches."

He looked at his bandaged arm. "This wasn't because of the bullet in the mountains. This was a stray during the rescue. Stubborn slug needed to be surgically removed."

She leaned up and kissed him. He wanted to kiss her back, but his thoughts were a mess.

"Hey," she said. "What happened? Is this about Liam?" She took his hand and sat him down on the hospital bed. He was getting ready to leave—head over to Jack's place— but he needed to make sure everything was square with him and Sean.

"He shouldn't be dead, but Armstrong didn't have a choice. I get that. The whole situation was fucked from the beginning."

"Liam worked himself up into a frenzy, Kane. You can't be responsible for the insane conclusions he came to."

"I don't feel responsible—except that I didn't tell Sean everything to begin with."

"Sean forgives you."

"Rick's taking Sean over to the local FBI office to talk to Eden, convince her to plea."

"Sean is a smart guy. He's going to see past any lies."

"But Liam and Eden believed it all. I saw that when Liam was talking up on the mountain—I saw that he believed every word he said. And I thought of all my failures."

"Of course you did."

He glanced at her, surprised. He'd heard Siobhan angry and frustrated, but this tone was pure venom. She saw his failures, too.

"Kane," she said sharply, "you always take the world on your shoulders. *Always.* You have to recognize that Liam and Eden made their own decisions. They were based on truths that only Liam and Eden believed. They worked up this fantasy in their minds, based on some truths, some fictions, some partial truths, and twisted it all up. To make you into the bad guy. Dammit, Kane, you are not the bad guy!"

"I *can* be."

"You are *never* the bad guy, Kane. Yeah—sometimes you do things that could be considered *bad* when taken out of context, but you are a hero. To everyone who matters, including me."

He wasn't. But damn, he loved hearing Siobhan say it. A ray of hope that she actually believed it had him begin to forgive himself.

"Rick told me earlier that the information you got out of Zapelli, about Marisol's son, led to his identification. The New York FBI office has put the boy into protective custody, and as soon as the DNA tests come back and prove he's Marisol's son they'll be reunited."

Kane hadn't known. He still wished he hadn't let Zapelli walk away from the barn and wasn't sorry he was dead now. But at least that bastard had given him one solid piece of information that led to Marisol's son.

"You did that, Kane. Without you, Marisol may never have found her son."

"I am glad about that."

"Look at me."

He did. He touched her face. She didn't flinch. Instead, she moved closer.

"I don't think you've truly processed all of this—I saw that when we were talking to Carlo in New Orleans. You looked . . . lost. I've never seen you look that way before."

"Why do you love me, Siobhan?" he whispered.

"Because I would be a fool not to—and you would never love a fool." She smiled and kissed him.

He pushed her down to the hospital bed and returned the kiss. Hard. He was a possessive man and he wanted to possess Siobhan. Having her in his life, every day, would be worth giving up his solitude. Only her.

She moaned into his lips. "Kane . . . we can't—"

He touched her breast, through her blouse, and she gasped.

"Come home with me." His voice was low.

"Home? What home?"

"Jack's place. I'm moving to Hidalgo."

"You are?"

"I need to put down roots." He pushed himself off of her—reluctantly, but the last thing he wanted was for someone to walk in and see them in bed together. Even if they were clothed now, that wouldn't last. Not for long.

He wanted to make love to Siobhan in private.

"You're really doing it? A *house?*"

"With a private airstrip and easy access to jobs in Mexico when needed. Away from people—remote. The house belongs to RCK, but it's mine. I would be more inclined to make the arrangement permanent if I had a gorgeous, stubborn, smart, impossible, sexy redhead in my bed every night."

"Every night? You want me to move in with you?"

He liked that she looked a little scared and a lot excited at the same time.

"You don't have a house. I know this because you own the house with Andie in Virginia, but you only visit twice a year."

"You and Andie talk too much."

"I want you, Siobhan."

"You just want me?"

"Just?"

She kissed him. It was a long, slow, deep kiss. "I. Love. *You*."

He was a smart guy, but it took him a long minute to realize he'd never told her the truth. "I fell in love with you when I saved your gorgeous ass in Tamaulipas ten years ago. When you told me you weren't leaving without Hestia and I could go to hell if I didn't help rescue her."

He kissed Siobhan. "That was ten years ago and I have loved you ever since. I didn't want to. My life—it's not a life I wanted for you. But now . . . I don't want to say goodbye. I don't want you to leave me. If I have roots here, you're part of that."

She touched his face. He kissed her fingers. "I'm never leaving you, Kane. Let's go to your new house."

"*Our* house, Siobhan. Home is only where you are."

Eden was being detained in the local FBI office. Two armed guards were on the door, and Eden was handcuffed to the table. There was a cot in the room, and she'd evidently be sleeping there tonight.

She looked like hell. But when she saw Sean, she smiled. "You came."

"I heard you wanted to talk to me."

An odd mix of emotions flooded Sean and he had to sit down. He tried to make it casual, pulling the chair out, sitting down, adjusting the seat. But he was conflicted. About everything.

When they were young, Eden and Liam had taken Sean everywhere. Eden had to—she was tasked with babysitting him until he was eleven. Sometimes she treated him like the annoying younger brother, other times she was fun. They played games. They rode bikes. He helped her with her math homework, even though she was five years older than him. He'd always understood numbers.

Eden and Liam both loved movies—in fact, they'd instilled in Sean a deep love of movie theaters. Sean had always been partial to action adventure, but Eden loved the classics—and Sean would watch them with her. She would talk about history and the art of the time period and gossip about the actors and why she loved Eva Marie Saint or Cary Grant or Humphrey Bogart. She loved everything Bogart was in.

"I'm sorry," she said.

Sean didn't say anything, and Eden took his silence as permission to keep talking.

"We made a mistake. A big mistake, but you've got to understand, Sean. Mom and Dad searched for years for the treasure. Four months before Dad died, he gave Liam everything. All the notes, the journal, the clues, the codes. You're the one who cracked the code! If it wasn't for you, we'd never have found anything."

Kane had said something about that, and Sean remembered a project his dad had him work on. All his dad said was that it was an old book dug up and preserved from a dig in Mexico, but he couldn't figure out the code, it seemed sophisticated for the era. It wasn't sophisticated, but because of its age it seemed foreign to anyone living in the modern era. Once Sean realized that, it was easy.

"We wanted to include you in the search. It's a family journey. It started with Mom and Dad and Uncle Carlo, and you should have been just as involved as any of us."

"Why didn't you wait until I came home?"

Her eyes shifted, just a fraction, and Sean knew she had an excuse. Or thought she did. "We didn't have time."

"Bullshit."

"Kane took the bonds out from under us and put us in a serious situation with some bad people. We were under their thumb for six years—we had to get them the bonds. They knew we'd found them; if we didn't bring them, they would have gone after them."

"You're lying."

"I'm not! The only reason we had to take Lucy with us was because she overheard me talking on the phone to Dante and if she told Kane what she'd heard we'd be screwed."

Eden leaned forward. "You're my brother, Sean. I hate that Duke and Kane got between us."

"They didn't."

"They did! They were the main reason Liam and I preferred to live in Europe."

"You lived in Europe because you went to college there, and you worked for Rogan-Caruso overseas."

"You should have been with us, Sean. On our side."

"There are no sides, or there shouldn't be, in family."

"You're right! But they made you take sides."

She was borderline delusional. "I'm thirty-one, Eden. I've been a legal adult for thirteen years. You could have contacted me. Called. Emailed. Visited. The last time I saw you was what . . . four years ago? I was in France with an old girlfriend and we all had dinner. And before that . . .

seven years ago. Before that?" He shook his head. "When I was expelled from Stanford, I was at the lowest point in my life. You knew what Duke had done, but you didn't reach out, didn't call, didn't say, 'Hey, move to Europe and live with Liam and me.' You know what? I would have. That's how angry I was at Duke for micromanaging my life, and at Kane for staying out of my life.

"But you didn't. Because I wasn't of use to you and whatever con you had going on at the time."

"That's not true."

"Let me explain something to you, Eden. I don't know or care what Kane did six years ago. I—"

"How can you say that? He replaced us with the Kincaids!"

Sean stared at her. *What the hell?* He had no idea what she was talking about.

Eden continued, "He got rid of Liam and me, brought on Jack and Patrick Kincaid."

"There was no connection."

"If you believe that, you're an idiot."

"No, Eden." Sean stood up and leaned over the table. "I've reached out a dozen times over the years. I sent you an invitation to my wedding. You used it against me. You took the woman I love more than life itself to a country where there was a fucking *bounty on her head*." He pounded his fist on the table to avoid punching his sister. Eden was sitting here trying to justify her actions? And yet she claimed she was *sorry*? "Lucy was kidnapped and blinded by you, then taken by brutes and bound, and almost sold to a drug cartel as bait for Jack. This damn treasure is a pathetic excuse to justify your indifference to Lucy's pain and suffering."

Sean took a deep breath and lowered his voice. "You do not know me. You do not know Jack Kincaid. But I know you. You're selfish and conniving. Liam is dead, and you're trying to cast blame on everyone but yourself and your twin."

Her bottom lip quivered.

"I'm truly sorry Liam died. If he hadn't, he would have paid for his crimes just like you will pay. And I wish I could make him pay, locked up in prison, sitting and realizing that he was solely responsible for what happened to him."

"No—"

"You will take whatever plea agreement Rick Stockton offers you, because if you don't, I will fight tooth and nail to have you locked up for the rest of your life."

Tears dripped onto the table. "You don't mean that."

"I *do* mean it. And if you think I can't make it happen, you don't know me." He leaned closer to her and spoke quietly. In case the FBI was recording this conversation, there were some things better left off the tape. "I gave up hacking years ago, but I am still the best in the business. You prolong this, you will face my wrath, and I guarantee you will beg for the plea deal when I'm through with you."

Sean walked out, ignoring Eden crying behind him.

CHAPTER THIRTY-NINE

Nine Days Later

St. Catherine's was an old, traditional Catholic church, and with tradition came reverence—including organ music. Sean supposed the music was nice, but it wasn't his style. All he wanted was to kiss the bride and disappear. He and Lucy hadn't been alone—just the two of them—in nearly two weeks. Sean was a people person, but he had had it up to his eyeballs with people.

Federal agents. Cops. Doctors. Friends. Family.

Family.

It was enough to have him run from the chapel, grab Lucy as she was walking down the aisle, and whisk her away to Las Vegas for a quickie wedding and a long, long honeymoon.

Of course he wouldn't do it. In one hour Lucy would be his wife, they would be joined forever in front of the God Lucy believed in and Sean was beginning to believe in. In front of their friends and family. But mostly, most important, it was him and Lucy. What they had done, what they had endured, to get to this point.

The organ music stopped, then an acoustic guitar picked up. Sean didn't recognize the tune, but it was a million times better than the mournful organ. He smiled—then froze when the door opened. He'd wanted just one minute alone and sought out Father Mateo's office to have that minute, and now he was reaching for a gun that was no longer in his holster. It was his wedding day, and he'd be damned if he was going to stand at the altar armed.

He was pretty sure his brother and soon-to-be brother-in-law would both be packing.

He relaxed when he saw Kane enter. He was in his dress blues. The last time Sean had seen Kane decked out like this—with a chest full of medals—was for their parents' funeral.

"I asked Siobhan to do something about the music, I hope you don't mind. Father Mateo said you hadn't gotten back to him about what to play, so he picked something."

"Thank you, it was on my to-do list, and then, well . . ." He listened. "Is Siobhan playing?"

Kane nodded. "She agreed to stay with me at your house while you're gone, then we're moving to Jack's place."

"You mean your place."

"Right. My place. Siobhan and me." Kane smiled. He rarely smiled, and when he did Sean was relieved. His brother deserved to find the same love and happiness that Sean had found.

Sean liked Siobhan, and Kane needed to slow down. Siobhan might be the only woman on the planet who could entice him to take it easy. "I told you, Kane—my house is your house, too."

"It's a big place. In the suburbs."

"It's one of the oldest established neighborhoods in San Antonio."

"Too many people. I'm not a city person. Hidalgo suits me."

"Don't be a stranger."

"I'm proud of you, kid. You're better than all of us."

Sean shook his head, but Kane kept talking.

"I should have told you about Liam. I should have told you the truth from the beginning, let you come to your own conclusion. I manipulated you—told you what I wanted you to know—maybe because I was worried you would join them on their fool crusade, or some such thing."

Sean put up his hand. "It's done. I wish I'd known the truth—but the Rogans have always been a dysfunctional family. We never had a normal life. I loved Mom and Dad, but they kept a lot of secrets as well. They didn't seem to know what to do with any of us."

"It is what it is."

"You are my brother, in every sense of the word, and I love you. I'm trying to forgive Liam and Eden. It's hard—" Sean shook his head. He would not go back into that dark place when he had realized that Lucy had been captured by the Flores cartel. "And now he's gone. Eden is going to spend at least five years in prison."

"Would you have it any other way?"

Sean shook his head. "But she's our sister. I told her she wasn't my sister anymore, but she's still a Rogan."

"Rick is going to have someone look out for her. She's in federal prison. She'll be protected."

Sean knew that, though it didn't make knowing his sister was in prison for kidnapping Lucy any easier. Eden had agreed to the plea deal—five to ten years. When she was released, she'd have a clean slate—all her other crimes would be erased.

Sean clapped his hand on Kane's shoulder. "It's done. This is my wedding day, and Lucy is—" What could he say? She was beautiful. Amazing. The most important thing in his life.

Kane hugged him. The affection was rare—had Kane ever hugged him? Sean couldn't remember.

The door opened again. Patrick, Jack, and Duke walked

in. His other brother and his two soon-to-be brothers-in-law.

Duke crossed over to him and shook his hand, then pulled him into a tight hug. "Sean. I'm so proud of you."

Duke's voice cracked. Sean couldn't handle all these emotions from his brothers, two men who never showed emotion.

"I'm sorry," Duke said. He stood back. His eyes were moist.

"We should both be sorry. But not about what you think." Sean glanced around, straightened his spine. "You did the best you could. I didn't make it easy. And . . . I've never said thank you."

A lot had happened between Sean and Duke over the years—and maybe Sean would still butt heads with him over the job. Duke might never understand Sean, but that was okay. Sean could handle whatever was thrown at him. He was far more comfortable with his own decisions, with his mind, with his goals.

And his first goal was to get married.

"Look—the love of my life is waiting to come down that aisle," Sean said. "I don't want her to wait another minute."

"Good," Patrick said, "because Father Mateo wants you out now. Guys, we have some escorting to do."

Sean exchanged glances with Jack. They didn't need words. In some ways, having Jack's respect was more important than having that of any other Kincaid. The colonel was walking Lucy down the aisle, but it was Jack's approval that mattered the most. Jack nodded, then followed the others out. Sean had asked Jack to carry the rings. Odd, perhaps, for a forty-something-year-old man, but it meant something to him to have Jack part of the wedding. He too was in his dress blues. Army, a different uniform than Kane's, but with just as many medals and commendations.

Sean was proud of both of them.

Sean took a deep breath, adjusted his tie, and walked out to the altar. Father Mateo smiled and winked. Sean tried to relax. He rolled his shoulders, looked out at the crowd that was waiting—none of them were even half as excited as he was.

The Rogans didn't have much family—a few cousins whom Sean didn't feel the need to invite. He and Lucy wanted to keep the wedding small, intimate, though there was nothing intimate about the Kincaids.

Nora, Duke's wife, was on the groom's side, along with Molly, who was now six months old, dressed in pink. Siobhan was playing the guitar, and Sean realized then that everything happened for a reason. Siobhan had walked back into Kane's life—against her will—in June and hadn't left. She was as stubborn as he was.

Also on the groom's side were the boys Sean and Lucy had rescued from a violent cartel last March. They lived in the house across from St. Catherine's, and Sean had somehow adopted them. The boys had no one then, having been used as drug mules, and now they had the church, their guardian Father Mateo, and Sean. He'd built them a pool, he came over to help them with math homework, and he listened.

Sometimes all kids needed was someone to listen.

If Jesse could have been here, the day would have been perfect. It *was* perfect, Sean reminded himself. And he'd see his son soon—the marshals were already working on a visit before the end of the year. Sean had hoped after Jasmine Flores was killed that Jesse wouldn't need witness protection, but Carson Spade had a lot of information on a lot of cartels and criminals, and until the US Attorney's Office finished with their work and handed down indictments there would be no way Jesse could leave.

But maybe it wouldn't be forever. It might not even be

the full six years before Jesse was eighteen. There was a new light at the end of the tunnel, and Sean would persevere. He would find a way to get through this. Having Lucy at his side made it so much easier.

He glanced at the crew from Rogan-Caruso-Kincaid. He had returned to the fold, but on his terms. He'd only invited those closest to him. JT, of course—he was practically a brother. Mitch and Claire Bianchi, who were now working with Patrick in DC since Sean had moved to Texas; the DA of Sacramento, Matt Elliott, who'd served in the Navy SEALs with JT; and Rick Stockton. Sean wasn't surprised that the assistant director of the FBI had chosen to sit with his old friends. Matt's girlfriend—wife? Sean couldn't remember if they'd gotten married—used to be a cop, now worked for RCK. And then Dean Hooper and his wife, Sonia. Sean and Duke had once been hired to protect Sonia's adopted parents from her criminal father; Dean was a fed—specialized in white-collar crimes—and the last person Sean would ever expect to have as a friend. Yet here they were.

His friend pool was a lot bigger than he'd thought.

Lucy's entire family was there—brothers and sisters and their spouses. Dillon sat with his mother; Jack's wife, Megan, next to Dillon; Carina's husband, Nick, had the baby John Patrick in a car seat in the pew. Connor and his wife, Julia, were there with their niece Emily. Elle Santana, Patrick's plus-one, sat with Connor's family. Lucy's mother had wanted to invite extended family and many other friends, but Lucy put her foot down. She gave in to almost everything else her mother wanted, except for the guest list. The only extended family in attendance were Lucy's aunt, the only sister of the colonel, and her immediate family.

Nelia, Lucy's oldest sister, hadn't come, but Lucy told Sean she was relieved. Nelia had sent Lucy a long letter, and that had given Lucy a peace she hadn't known for a long time. At the end, Nelia had written: *I'm truly sorry for how I treated you after Justin was killed. You did not deserve my grief, my pain, my rage. You were a little girl who was forced to grow up too fast. You have grown into an amazing woman, and the empathy and compassion you show crime victims is the greatest tribute Justin could have had. Forgive me.*

There were numerous FBI agents and cops in the room. Maybe more of them than family—and there was a lot of crossover. Most of Lucy's Violent Crimes Squad were there—Nate, Ryan, Emilio, even Kenzie, who had distanced herself from Lucy after a whole bunch of shit happened on the job, but they'd seemed to be getting along better. DEA Agent Brad Donnelly, whom Sean grudgingly respected; Agent Suzanne Madeaux's boyfriend Joe DeLucca—Sean and Lucy had met him a few times in New York when they'd worked cases with Suzanne and last summer when they'd spent a long weekend in the city. Assistant Director Hans Vigo had flown in from DC with Rick and sat in the back, next to Noah.

Noah looked like he hadn't slept in a week—and maybe he hadn't. He'd been through hell and back, and Lucy had confided in Sean that Noah was thinking of resigning. Sean hoped Noah didn't—and had tried to explain that he didn't harbor any ill feelings toward him for anything. Not for half loving Lucy, not for shooting Liam, not for arresting Eden. Noah was a rare man, and Sean knew the FBI would be worse off without him.

Sean took a deep breath as the guitar stopped playing and the organ started another song. Siobhan walked over and sat next to Nora.

The room turned to face the doors in the back.

Duke escorted Suzanne Madeaux up the aisle. Suzanne wore a pale-lavender dress, simple, flowing, classic. She had been a good friend to Lucy over the last couple of years and was a sharp FBI agent.

Then came Kate Donovan, Dillon's wife, wearing an amethyst dress in the same style as Suzanne's, a few shades darker than the lavender. Kate walked with Kane, both of them looking a bit nervous. She didn't come from a large family, and the Kincaids had overwhelmed her. But she had become Lucy's best friend and closest confidante. Kate didn't like crowds, but she loved Lucy and so she had sucked it up and walked down the aisle.

Patrick, Sean's best man and Lucy's brother, escorted their sister Carina, the matron of honor. Carina was stunning in deep purple. No one would guess she'd given birth four months ago. Carina had taken over the planning of the wedding for Lucy, knowing Lucy wouldn't have been able to do it and her job. Sean and Carina had butted heads the first time they met, but after they had planned the wedding together Sean had grown to respect her and had a bit more insight into how the Kincaids had grown up. He and Carina might not ever be close, but Sean would do anything to keep Lucy happy, including getting along with all her brothers and sisters.

Jack walked up alone, and the doors closed behind him. Sean swallowed; his mouth was dry. This was it.

Jack stood to the side of the altar. The music switched. The doors opened again in the back of the church and everyone stood.

Sean saw nothing and no one, except for Lucy.

She glided down the aisle, the train of her long strapless dress flowing behind her. Her hair cascaded down her back in curls pinned back with diamonds. Her light-brown skin practically glowed and her lips curved when Sean locked eyes with her.

This was it. His wedding. His and Lucy's.

Patrick hit Sean in the arm. Sean realized Lucy's dad
was waiting to hand Lucy off to him. Sean walked down
the three steps, shook the Colonel's hand, then took Lucy's
arm. Led her to the altar. They'd rehearsed the wedding
ceremony the night before, what they were supposed to
say and do, but all that disappeared from Sean's head.
He leaned down and kissed Lucy.

Father Mateo cleared his throat. "You're supposed to
wait until after I pronounce you husband and wife."

Light laughter from the crowd. Sean whispered, "I
rarely do what I'm supposed to do."

Lucy's eyes moistened, but she smiled brightly. She
leaned forward and kissed him back. "I love you, Sean
Rogan. Now let's get married."

Noah approached Rick Stockton at the reception. Everyone from the wedding was at Sean and Lucy's house—
though Noah suspected the bride and groom would be
disappearing in short order. After what happened last
week, he didn't blame them.

Rick was talking to Kane. Noah didn't know Kane well
but doubted he had ever been as relaxed as he was right
now. Maybe it had something to do with Siobhan, whom
Kane couldn't keep his eyes off of. She was across the
room, laughing at something one of Lucy's brothers said—
Connor, Noah thought his name was. The PI. Or was that
her brother-in-law Nick? Noah couldn't keep them all
straight. He was an only child.

Noah had known Lucy came from a large family. But
seeing them all together at the wedding, and now at the
reception, reminded him that he had no family. His parents
had been older when they had him. His dad had died years
ago, and his mom had moved to Florida, where she was
very much enjoying retirement. Noah saw her twice a year,
it was pleasant, but he had never felt particularly close to

either of his parents. They were good people who loved
him but hadn't expected him and didn't really know what
to do with a child when his mom found herself pregnant
at the age of forty.

"Do you have a minute?" Noah asked Rick. Rick had a
flight out early in the morning—that he could break away
from headquarters for a couple of days had been a feat unto
itself. But Rick had a lot of secrets, Noah had begun to
realize.

Kane said, "Glad that you came, Noah," and shook his
hand.

"I wouldn't have missed Lucy's wedding."

Kane nodded. It wasn't that, and Noah knew it. Everything that had happened this last week had a dampening
effect on his relationships with—well, everyone. It wasn't
that the Rogans didn't want Eden in prison. But they'd lost
their brother, and Noah didn't think that had sunk in yet.
Or was that Noah's own guilt clouding his perception?

Maybe Kane had always believed that Liam was dead,
at least in spirit. Yet . . . Noah had been there. He'd seen
the pain Kane tried to hide.

Noah understood the need to keep emotions locked
up tight. Still, he'd never forget what had happened. Or
his part in it.

Most of the guests were either in the large living room,
where every door was opened onto the back patio, or outside, where there was a full bar and beautifully catered
buffet. Rick motioned for Noah to follow him to Sean's
office. He closed the door. "I expected this."

"What?"

"You want to leave."

"No, I—" He stopped. Rick was right.

Rick continued, "I don't want you to go."

"I'm having some difficulty reconciling your role in the
FBI and your role with RCK."

Rick nodded, then sat down on the couch. He waited until Noah sat down in the chair across from Sean's desk, then said, "It's complicated, but Kane, JT, Matt Elliott, and I are brothers in every sense of the word except parentage."

"You think I don't understand?" Noah shook his head. "It's the gray area I'm having a hard time with. You sent Nate Dunning to Mexico, knowing I was going to go. I went on my own, expecting a reprimand. Expecting I might die. Or that I might create an international situation. Or that I would be fired. It was *my* choice. Dunning didn't have a choice."

"Everyone has a choice."

"Dammit, Rick, you know that's not true."

"I asked Dunning to protect you, because I knew you had an emotional reason for following Eden Rogan."

"I can separate my feelings from my job."

"But if it was just the job, you wouldn't have gone."

Noah shook his head. Rick was right—and Noah didn't like that his boss might understand his actions better than he did. "I don't know anymore, Rick. I have always prided myself for being a good soldier, a good leader, a good agent. I believed in the system, and now . . . I don't know if the system works. I've broken more rules than I care to admit. I've violated the law. I've done things I'm not proud of, but the alternative would have been worse. I don't know who I am anymore. I need to leave, figure out what lines I can live with crossing, which lines I can't cross. Everything is blurry right now."

Rick leaned forward. "I don't want you to go. It's because you believe in the system that I have groomed you for the cases I've sent you on. The cases *are* complex, and a less ethical—less noble—agent could have made very bad choices. I trust you."

"I don't know that I can trust you, Rick." Noah almost

couldn't believe he'd said that, to the assistant director of the FBI, but it was the truth.

A flash of pain and surprise crossed his face, then Rick nodded. "I understand."

"I don't think you do."

"I do. But I'm not accepting your resignation."

"You don't have a choice."

"Take a sabbatical, Noah. Will two months give you enough time to wallow in self-pity?"

"That's not what I'm doing."

"Isn't it?" Rick stared at him. The man was one of the most tactically brilliant men Noah had known. For all his loyalties to others outside of the FBI, he also believed in the system, in justice. What was right and wrong? Who made that determination? It was these gray areas that bothered Noah, but for the longest time he had been comfortable with Rick Stockton making the final call.

Now, not so much.

"You arrested a woman you once loved. You can lie to yourself and say you no longer had feelings for Eden Rogan, but you did. You still do. Now she's in prison and she's not getting out for a long time. You killed Sean's brother. You had no choice—Kane could be dead right now if you didn't take the shot. But Sean is your friend, and you're having a difficult time accepting that this was a clean kill. The important thing is you saved Kane from killing his own brother. I know that is hard on you, and I have never once seen or heard Kane hesitating or being indecisive. Until now. He hesitated and Liam was able to get two shots off. Kane would have been dead if he weren't wearing a vest—or was hit in the head. Kane would have come out on top, he would have drawn and killed Liam, but you took that awful decision out of his hands."

Noah hadn't thought about the situation exactly like

that. Kane and Liam were brothers, but they were so different that Noah almost forgot.

"We can play Monday morning quarterback for the next year and never know if what each of you did in Tampico was the right thing to do," Rick said. "But in those circumstances, at that moment in time, it was the only thing that could have been done." He paused. "If Liam had killed Kane and you didn't stop the threat, you wouldn't be here now. Because you wouldn't be able to look Sean in the eye and tell him you did everything you could. But you're here, and I know that you did everything that could have been done. You went above and beyond. You instinctively know that, even if you haven't run through all those thoughts.

"It's Sean you're really thinking about, because none of what happened last week was his doing. He and Lucy were caught up in a family feud that neither of them knew anything about. I can tell you with a clear conscience that Liam Rogan would have killed Kane out of anger, spite, I don't know, but he hated his brother. I'm sorry it happened and I'm not saying that one life is more valuable than another, but Liam Rogan put Lucy in extreme danger because of his own selfish reasons. She could be dead right now solely because of Liam's choices.

"You have to deal with what happened. That's why I'm giving you the time. But I know who you are and there is no one I trust more. I want you back on my team, but if you come back in January and say you can't work for me, I'll send you anywhere you want."

Noah was full of conflicting thoughts and emotions. He had planned on resigning, facing denial from Rick, walking out, and never returning.

But maybe he just needed time.

Rick walked to the door, put his hand on the knob.

"You're one of the best men I have ever worked with, Noah."

Then he left.

Noah stared at the beach scene on the wall. Behind that beach was the safe that had housed the bonds that started this whole mess to begin with. If not for the bonds, Noah would have gone back to his old life, working for Rick, taking interesting but sensitive cases, constantly wondering if there was an ulterior motive to what he was doing.

Now he had options. And for the first time in a long, long time . . . maybe his entire life . . . he could make a decision about his future solely based on what *he* wanted to do. Take time to think, to figure out if he could work under Rick's ethics, or run his own squad, or teach at Quantico.

Or leave the FBI and seek a third career. Doing what? He didn't know, but he had two months to make the decision.

Noah sat down, pulled a piece of paper from the printer, and wrote Sean and Lucy a letter. Truly, they had become his closest friends, and the two people he trusted the most.

He couldn't leave without saying good-bye.

He sealed the letter, slipped it into Sean's laptop case knowing that even on his honeymoon Sean wouldn't leave without his computer, and walked out of the den, and out of the house.

He had some soul-searching to do. Two months to make a decision that would affect his future and maybe how he saw himself in the world.

Sean whisked Lucy away to his office, closed the door, and kissed her.

"Mrs. Rogan."

She laughed, kissed him back. "What if I want to keep my maiden name?"

"You can call yourself anything you want, but you'll always be mine."

She kissed him again, this time without laughter but with a deep longing. "I love you so much."

"Lucy." He held her close. His life had fallen apart around him over the last six weeks, except for Lucy.

"We're going to be okay."

"I know." He didn't know, but he wasn't going to lose one moment of the time they had together. "I could hold you like this forever."

They stood there, arms entwined, Lucy's head on Sean's shoulder. The noise of the party seemed to disappear. All that Lucy heard was Sean's heartbeat.

"Let's leave," Lucy said.

"We can't leave. Your parents. Family."

"We can leave. Jack told me everything is packed, keys in the ignition, and he'll cover for us."

"Jack?" Sean smiled. "I really love your brother. All of them, but there's no one like Jack."

Lucy touched his face. "Sean—we're here. We're married. I love you. Let's go. We have ten days . . . *where*?"

He smiled. She saw some of the weight he'd been carrying disappear, and she almost sighed in relief. "I kept that surprise well, didn't I?"

"You did."

"I'm not telling you. Not yet."

"But you have to—we're leaving."

"I'll give you a hint. We're driving, not flying. Because I'm really sick of flying right now."

"Okay. Where are we going?"

"Not Texas."

"That leaves forty-nine other states."

"Hmm, it would be hard to drive to Hawaii and too long to drive to Alaska."

"You're impossible."

"Okay, I'll tell you, because I can't keep it to myself any longer." He kissed her. "I bought a house—I would say 'cabin,' but I had it remodeled and it's a damn nice two-thousand-square-foot cabin. It's in Vail, Colorado. Remote, but not too remote. I'd thought about taking you to Hawaii, but really, I just want you to myself. We have everything we need. Food, water, a hot tub. If we want to go into the town, there's a big art festival this week, or we can go out to dinner. Lots of great restaurants. Or not. I can cook for you every night. We have no plans. No schedule. No time we have to get up or go to bed. We can do anything we want, or nothing at all. But I will be making love to you a lot. I will be kissing you a lot." To prove it, he leaned down and kissed her. He stepped back and frowned. "Don't cry. Why are you crying?"

"It's perfect. I could not have imagined a better honeymoon than you and me, together and alone."

"Okay." He blinked. His own eyes were damp. "Then let's go, Mrs. Kincaid-Rogan. Our wedding night at the hotel, then an early morning drive to Vail."

She wrinkled her nose. "That's *Mrs. Rogan* to you—and to everyone else." She kissed him. "And let's not make it *too* early. I might want breakfast in bed." She grinned.

"Which I will be more than happy to accommodate."

EPILOGUE

Outside Tampico, Mexico

Gabriella wasn't one for camping, but she agreed with Dante that if they wanted to do this right they needed to stay for the duration. At least until the weather turned.

The sun was setting over the hidden valley, and Dante had already made the fire. There were four-legged predators out here, but somehow, Gabriella felt safer here than she had in a long, long time.

She stirred the pot of stew as it warmed. They had made three trips down here with gear and equipment, and their old friend Philip Corsica would return for them in ten days.

She and Dante had a lot of soul-searching to do in the next ten days.

And a lot of digging.

Dante came up from the cavern. "Nothing has been disturbed," he said. "I didn't go far inside, but . . ." He tossed her what she at first thought was a stone.

She caught it. It wasn't a stone. It was a rough uncut emerald.

"Oh, my."

Dante sat down across from her on the log. He pulled out a bottle of Scotch—a pricey bottle she'd told him not to bring because they shouldn't be drinking while alone in the lost valley, handling dangerous tools and needing to watch for predators. But he had anyway. He poured two fingers in each of two plastic cups, handed one to Gabriella.

"Along the way, Liam lost sight of what was important," Dante said. "And I didn't keep him in check."

"That's not your fault. Liam had some serious problems. He was obsessed. We knew it, we just didn't know how bad he was. And truly, Eden enabled him. She did anything Liam wanted her to do—even kidnapping Jack Kincaid's sister."

"And she's paying for it. We got a pass this time, Gabriella."

"Because of Jack."

"Because of us. We chose to help, and that earned us some brownie points. But our luck is going to run out."

"Because the treasure is cursed?"

"Liam cursed himself," Dante said. "But he was still a friend, and I'm going to miss him." He held up his cup. "This is for you, Liam. Without you, we'd never have made it this far." He sipped.

Gabriella drank, put the cup down, and stirred the stew. Tasted it. *Blah*. She took the Scotch bottle and poured a liberal amount into the stew.

"That's a two-hundred-dollar bottle!"

"And our dinner will taste much better because of it." She let the stew simmer. "So when is our so-called luck going to run out?"

"I don't know, Gabriella, but I do know one thing—I want to enjoy the ride. After Greg's death, your revenge, Liam's obsession—my former business—I'm tired of the violence. I just want to have some fun, with whatever time we have left on this earth. I want to fall in love. I want you to find someone else. I want to live."

She leaned over and squeezed her brother's hand. "So

do I. And unearthing this treasure will go a long way in paying for our lives." She handed him back the emerald. "Do you know how much that little stone is worth?"

"No."

"A minimum of twenty thousand dollars."

Dante remained silent.

"I'd better get up to speed on gems."

"Yeah," he said, "because there were six more just like it in the bag."

"Bag?"

"I didn't open the chests.

"Chests?"

"I think this is a far bigger find than even Liam knew," Dante said.

"Do we tell Kane?"

Dante smiled. "Not unless he asks."

Read on for an excerpt from

SHATTERED

Allison Brennan's next Maxine Revere thriller, which
finds Max teaming up with Lucy Kincaid

Available August 2017 from Minotaur Books

"Andrew? I'm going to put you on speaker. Sean's here."

Rookie FBI Agent Lucy Kincaid Rogan put her cell phone down on the island in the kitchen where she and Sean had been eating a late dinner.

"Stanton?" Sean mouthed. Lucy nodded. Her former brother-in-law had never directly called her before, and she'd known him her entire life. She was both suspicious and curious. Why would the DA of San Diego reach out to her? Family or work? She'd last seen him over a year ago during the Christmas holidays, and that hadn't been under the best of circumstances.

"Hello, Sean," Andrew said.

"Andrew."

"I'm sorry to call so late."

"Nine isn't late for us," Lucy said. "Just tell me that everything's okay."

"Yes—in a manner of speaking. Your family's fine, as far as I know. They don't really talk to me anymore."

Lucy knew why—her sister Nelia was Andrew's ex, and Andrew had cheated on Nelia. There was more—a lot more—but Lucy had been so young when they split up she didn't truly understand the situation. Andrew had always been kind to her, and when she needed his help last Christmas to get information, he'd come through. She respected that.

Andrew continued. "I don't know exactly how to broach this subject, so I'll get to the point. An investigative reporter is looking into Justin's murder. She claims that she has compelling evidence that Justin's death is connected to two or more homicides in the southwest. She'll be in San Diego tomorrow."

That was the last thing Lucy expected Andrew to say. She didn't know how to respond—her nephew Justin's murder had haunted her for nearly twenty years, but she'd put it behind her. She'd been seven. So had Justin. They'd been best friends and had grown up together until Justin was kidnapped and murdered. It had torn the family apart.

"A reporter?" Sean said, his voice edged with anger. "Why are you calling Lucy?"

"I think there might be something to this woman's theory. Lucy, I don't have a right to ask for your help, but the last time I wanted to revisit Justin's murder, I ran up against a brick wall known as the Kincaid family."

That didn't surprise Lucy. Her family never wanted to discuss Justin or his murder. It had been a dark time in the Kincaid family history. Twenty years was a long time to sit unsolved, and most crimes this old were never solved.

"I didn't know you had wanted to reopen Justin's case."

"As an unsolved homicide, it's never been closed. Eight years ago—you'd just left for Georgetown." He paused. "I never told you this, and I don't want to bring up bad memories."

"I'm a big girl, Andrew."

Sean took her hand, lightly kissed it, and held it. She could feel the tension within him—this was nearly as difficult for him as it was for her. The past. *Her* past.

"After your kidnapping—when you came home—I

wanted to be there for you, for your family. Even after everything that has happened, and all the mistakes I've made, I care about you and all the Kincaids. Your parents have always been cordial, but your brothers and sister never forgave me. Especially Connor and Carina, maybe because they still live here and I work with them. They didn't want me around, and I walked away. But I thought maybe—if I could put Justin to rest—they could find peace. Not knowing why someone killed my son . . ." His voice faded away, then he cleared his throat and said, "I approached your father. He was adamant that I stand down. Carina found out I had pulled the case files, and confronted me—it wasn't pretty. At the time, Patrick was still in a coma, I knew your family was suffering, you'd moved cross-country, Dillon—who has always been the diplomat of the family, and the only one who I know forgave me— was living in DC. I didn't have a buffer, so I shelved it."

"I didn't know any of that." It stunned her, truly. She caught Sean's eye. He was listening closely to Andrew.

Sean said, "Why? If you had something new, why would you shelve it?"

"I didn't have anything new—I just wanted to look at the case with fresh eyes, time, new technology. But I couldn't put your family through a new investigation when they had nearly lost you, Lucy, and Patrick's future was so uncertain."

"I understand," Lucy said, and she did. "And the reporter changed your mind."

"Yes. She has. But your family isn't going to want to go through this, and I don't want to hurt them."

"Then why do it at all?" Sean asked.

"Because Maxine Revere is going to investigate whether I want her to or not. And honestly, Sean? I want answers. God, I want to know what happened. For years I deferred my pain to your family—Nelia's family. When every lead dried up, they put it behind them. Not completely—I know Justin haunts them as much as he haunts me. But Nelia moved to Idaho, and that was it. They wanted no part of me, no part of my ideas or talking about what happened. But I'm a prosecutor—having any crime unsolved bothers me, but my own son? It's fingernails on the chalkboard, every waking minute. I've looked into this Revere woman. She has a solid track record solving cold cases."

"But what is she going to do after?" Sean asked. He caught Lucy's eye. She knew exactly what he was thinking. "Lucy and I steer clear of reporters."

"She wants my help, and I plan on laying down ground rules. Protecting you is my number-one priority, Lucy."

"I don't need your protection, Andrew." Lucy saw the darkness cross Sean's face. She took his hand. "What do you want from me? Do you want me to talk to my family? Convince them to cooperate? Talk to this reporter?"

"Actually, I want you to listen to what Revere has to say. You're an FBI agent. You have the training and experience to weed through the bullshit and get to the meat. I know you've had a rocky start to your career—but I have friends in high places, Lucy. You have closed some extremely difficult cases."

True, though she wasn't the only agent involved in those complex cases.

Andrew continued. "In hindsight, I don't think anyone understood the pain you went through when Justin died. He was as close as a brother to you, we all knew that, but in his death everyone seemed to forget that you were grieving. They shielded you from the investigation, from the truth of what happened that night because you were only seven years old. You're probably the only Kincaid who doesn't have a preconceived notion as to anything that happened. I think you're the only one who can look at the evidence with an unbiased eye. Who doesn't blame me."

"No one blames you, Andrew."

He laughed, but it was filled with anguish and sorrow. "I wish that were true. Connor said it when the truth came out—when your family found out I was having an affair. He said if I'd been there, at home that night and not in bed with my mistress, Justin would have been alive. A bit more crudely, but that was his message. There's not been a day that has passed that I haven't thought about that, whether it was true. If I am ultimately, even indirectly, to blame." He took a deep breath. "Nell and I have made peace with each other. I talk to her, once a year, on Justin's birthday. We made a lot of mistakes, but Justin wasn't one of them. She's content now. She has Tom, he's been good for her, and while I don't know if she's happy, I know she's at peace. I don't want to hurt her. I will keep her out of this as best I can, but in the end, she may have information that she doesn't know she has. I know that no one, not even Dillon, will discuss it with her. Except you. I think you would do it."

What did that make Lucy? Cruel? Was that what Andrew thought of her, because she had a reputation for being cold?

"Andrew—"

"I don't know that it'll come to that," he said, interrupting her. "I'd just like you to hear what this woman has to say. If you tell me there's nothing, that going down this path will result in no answers and only heartache for your family, I'll do everything in my power to stop her. But if you see what I see, that we might finally get answers as to why Justin died, that we might find out who killed him . . . I don't have anyone else, Lucy."

"A moment, Andrew," Sean said. He put the phone on mute. "It's your choice, Lucy. Whatever you decide, I'm with you."

The grief Lucy experienced when Justin was killed nearly twenty years ago had been young and immature, but no less painful. She didn't know what had happened to him, not right away. She didn't know why her mother cried all the time, why her sister Nelia wouldn't talk to her, why there were policemen in her house, why Carina needed a lawyer, why no one would let Andrew come over for dinner anymore. All she knew was that Justin, her best friend since they were born, was gone. One day he was there, playing catch with her in the backyard, swimming with her at the community pool, teasing her when she lisped after her two front teeth fell out. Her mother watched Justin during the week because Nelia and Andrew both worked—Lucy spent more waking hours with Justin than any other person her age. They'd even been in the same first-grade class together. And that summer was supposed to be the most fun ever. They were going to go to a sleep-over camp for the first time for two whole weeks. It was all Justin could talk about, he was so excited.

But that never happened because he was killed two weeks before they were going to leave.

He was gone. One day there, the next not. She'd been gutted, but she didn't talk to anyone about it because everyone was so sad and talking about Justin seemed to make them sadder.

Maybe that was why she'd always kept her emotions deep inside. Partly because of her own kidnapping and rape when she was eighteen . . . but it had started a long time before then. It had started when she grieved for her best friend and couldn't talk to anyone about it.

Now, while she understood death, she had faced evil, she knew that bad people did horrific things to innocent people—she didn't always know *why*.

Maybe finding out who killed Justin wasn't as important as finding out *why* he was killed.

And if there were other victims of the same killer, did

that mean the killer was still out there? After twenty years? Would he kill again? Destroy another family?

"I have to," Lucy whispered to Sean.

He kissed her hand. "I know."

She would have smiled if she wasn't so melancholy. "I love you."

He winked. "I know."

Now she did smile, because if she didn't, she might cry. And tears weren't productive.

She un-muted the phone. "When is this reporter coming?"

"Tomorrow afternoon. I don't have the exact time."

"Text me the details. I'll be there."

Danielle Sullivan didn't like going out with people from work, but it was expected. For every time she declined an invitation, she had to accept one—otherwise people would look at her too closely. She just wanted to do her job and go home, drink a bottle of wine, and try to sleep.

Try being the operative word. Sleep was a rarity for her. When she felt herself being dragged under from exhaustion, she would take a sleeping pill or three. Her body needed the rest, even if her mind couldn't.

There had been a time . . . more than once . . . when she considered taking the entire bottle of prescription sleeping pills, a large glass of wine, and reclining in her bathtub. Just fall asleep. Slip under. Disappear forever.

But would the nightmare end in death? Or would earth's cruel God force her to relive the worst day of her life? Over and over and over . . .

Nina Fieldstone poked her head into the bathroom. "Danielle, are you coming?"

"Just touching up my make-up. Two minutes?"

Nina smiled. She was a pretty woman, and smart. One

of the few in the office Danielle felt a rapport with. Nina was technically her supervisor, but had never made Danielle feel stupid or unvalued. Because Nina had been the one to ask her to join the group for their "Wine Wednesday," Danielle had agreed.

"Alright, but remember, happy hour is over at seven, so don't be long."

Danielle turned to the mirror and pretended to put on more mascara. She didn't wear a lot of make-up, but too many sleepless nights required it. She pulled out a tube of concealer and hid the dark circles. Added a little color. Better.

She still felt like a ghost beneath the gloss and glitter.

The bar—called The Gavel because of the proximity to the courthouse—where the legal secretaries hung out every Wednesday night was two blocks from their law office in Glendale. It was a large firm, and anywhere from four to ten women met once a week to let off steam and enjoy company and gossip.

It was the gossip Danielle hated, almost as much as the small talk.

Tonight six of them sat at one of the booths and drank wine. Danielle had to regulate herself. Alone, she would drink an entire bottle. With people, one was all she could handle.

Nina put her hand over Danielle's. "I'm so glad you decided to join us tonight, especially after the victory you helped secure."

"I didn't do anything," Danielle said. "Just my job."

"You caught two huge mistakes that saved our client tens of thousands of dollars, and a major embarrassment for our firm. Your drink's on me tonight."

Danielle didn't want the accolades. Yes, she was good at her job. It was all she had. Work, or dying slowly. Those were her options.

The women all chatted amongst each other. Danielle responded to questions because it was expected. She asked a few of her own—she could play the small-talk game when she had to. Half the women at the table were married—Grace had no kids, Natalie had a teenage daughter, and Nina had a son.

An eight-year-old boy named Kevin.

Danielle didn't want to ask, but she couldn't help herself. As the conversation turned to relationships and children, she said, "Is your husband home with Kevin? Does he watch him every Wednesday?"

It was casual, and fit with the conversation, but one that had been on Danielle's mind a lot lately.

Ever since she saw Tony Fieldstone watching his law partner, Lana Devereaux, at the Christmas party six weeks ago. The way he looked at her. The way he watched her walk. Danielle knew the look.

She knew it well.

Too well.

Nina rolled her eyes. "Sometimes he does—he loves spending time with Kevin, don't get me wrong, but Tony is all work, work, work. And tonight he had a poker game with Judge Carlson and the gang. Third Wednesday of the month. I say, why not Fridays when you don't have to be in court the next morning? But *men*."

Men. Right.

Danielle had worked for Taggert, Fieldstone, Finch and Devereaux for three years. She knew of the poker game, it was common knowledge just like Wine Wednesdays and the monthly Bunco game Grace pushed that she had, thankfully, avoided almost every month. But she wondered how long the game really went. If maybe Tony Fieldstone had someplace else he wanted to be.

A place he wasn't supposed to be.

With a woman he wasn't supposed to be with.

"You okay, Danielle?" Nina asked.

"Sorry—long day. Little headache."

"Another glass of wine? You can Uber home and I'll pick you up in the morning. You don't live too far from me."

"No, I'm fine." She smiled, such a fake smile, but no one knew. "Do you have a regular babysitter for Kevin? He's such a good kid." Nina had brought him into the office a couple of times when there were minimum days in school and she didn't have a sitter. Danielle tried not to pay attention to him, but she couldn't help it. He was a perfect child.

Perfect.

Tony didn't deserve a perfect son like Kevin when he was off screwing another woman.

You don't know that he is having an affair. You only suspect.

She knew. She damn well *knew* and she would prove it. She always did.

"Tony's mom watches him after school—she lives only a couple blocks from his school, walks over and gets him every day. It's nice, Kevin being able to spend some time with his grandmother."

"It is," Danielle agreed.

But you should be picking him up at school. You should be spending the time with him. Instead you're sitting here laughing and drinking wine with a bunch of selfish, arrogant women.

"We have a regular babysitter when we have to work late—Maggie Crutcher."

There was a lawyer named Wayne Crutcher. Maggie was his daughter. A teenager. Probably brought her boyfriend over to fuck when Kevin went to bed. They all did. They couldn't be trusted.

The talk turned back to the office, and Danielle was

relieved. She still needed to get out of here. Forty-five minutes . . . that was long enough, wasn't it? She showed her face, made the small talk, did the dance, she needed to go because she was already on edge.

"You know, I'm really tired after today," Danielle said. She finished her wine and smiled. "I think I'm going to call it a night."

"Do you want to join us Friday for Bunco? It's at Shelly's house in Burbank," Grace said. "You had so much fun last time you came."

Danielle barely remembered the last time—it was six months ago. She had had too much wine, that she was certain.

"I don't know—my mom is having a hard time getting around and I help her on the weekends. Shopping, fixing things around the house, you know."

"You're so good to you mom," Nina said. Danielle had told her all about her mother years ago, mostly to get out of socializing. "To drive all the way up there."

"Where does she live?" Natalie asked.

"Sacramento," Danielle lied. But it was a lie she told often, so it was one that came out smoothly. "It's only five, six hours depending on traffic. I don't mind, put on a book-on-tape or listen to music. But if she doesn't need me, I'll consider Bunco. You know me, I'm not really an extrovert. Too many people makes me antsy." That was the truth.

Nina smiled and patted her hand. "No pressure, but I would love you to come. It's one night a month, a great way to get out and just relax, no work the next day."

"Thanks." She got up, said good-byes—why did it take so long to just tell people *good-bye*? Why more questions, more small talk, more *nothingness*?

Finally, she was free. She walked back to the parking garage and retrieved her car. She intended to drive home where she could open a bottle of wine and maybe eat something, but she found herself outside Judge Carlson's house.

The judge had a private address, but she'd followed Tony Fieldstone here last month, after she suspected he was screwing Lana Devereaux. She saw Tony's car in the driveway of the opulent house in the Glendale hills.

And Lana's car. Did Nina know that Lana played poker with "the boys"? The only female partner . . . was that how it started? The one night a month . . . turn into something more?

For two hours Danielle watched the house from down the street. Then a car left.

Lana.

Five minutes later a second car left.

Tony.

She followed him.

Tony didn't go home. She knew where he lived, because she'd once gone to Bunco at Nina's house when she first started the job with this law firm. Instead, Tony went to Lana Devereaux's condo in Los Feliz.

Heart racing, she drove past his car as he got out. He didn't pay any attention to her. And her black Honda Accord was common. It didn't stand out. Just like she didn't stand out.

Danielle went straight home. When she pulled into her garage, she turned off the ignition and sat there. Her knuckles were white. Slowly, she peeled her hands off the steering wheel. They were sore from gripping so hard.

She went inside and poured a glass of wine. Drank it quickly, then poured another and picked up her phone.

"Hello," the familiar voice said. A voice that belonged to a man she had once loved with all her heart and soul . . . and now hated.

"Have you cheated on your wife yet? Because you know you will. You're all the same. All of you. Disgusting."

"Danielle."

"Why did you do it? Why?"

She asked the same question every time she called him. He never had a good answer. Because there wasn't a good answer.

"I was a fool."

"I hate you."

"I know. Is that why you called? To tell me how much you hate me?"

"No." She closed her eyes. "I loved you so much. I loved you so much it hurts. And . . ." Her voice cracked. The pain was real. Still so very real. Time didn't heal all wounds. Whoever said that hadn't lost their entire world.

"I'm sorry, Danielle. I truly am sorry."

"It should have been you. I wish you had died instead."

"So do I, Danielle. But you can't—"

She ended the call, unable to listen to her ex-husband anymore. She threw her half-filled wine glass across the room and screamed as it shattered against the wall. She watched the red liquid run down the plaster for several minutes, her mind blank.

Then she walked back to the kitchen, retrieved another wine glass, and poured more wine. She sat at the table and stared straight ahead as she drank.

Thinking.

Planning.

Hating.

It was so much easier to hate than it was to forgive.